THORN TREE

ALSO BY MAX LUDINGTON

Tiger in a Trance

THORN TREE

MAX LUDINGTON

ST. MARTIN'S PRESS
NEW YORK

First published in the United States by St. Martin's Press, an imprint of St. Martin's Publishing Group

THORN TREE. Copyright © 2024 by Max Ludington. All rights reserved. Printed in the United States of America. For information, address St. Martin's Publishing Group, 120 Broadway, New York, NY 10271.

www.stmartins.com

Library of Congress Cataloging-in-Publication Data

Names: Ludington, Max, author.
Title: Thorn tree / Max Ludington.
Description: First edition. | New York : St. Martin's Press, 2024.
Identifiers: LCCN 2023027334 | ISBN 9781250288714 (hardcover) |
    ISBN 9781250288721 (ebook)
Subjects: LCGFT: Novels.
Classification: LCC PS3612.U27 T46 2024 | DDC 813/.6—dc23/eng/20230616
LC record available at https://lccn.loc.gov/2023027334

Our books may be purchased in bulk for promotional, educational, or business use. Please contact your local bookseller or the Macmillan Corporate and Premium Sales Department at 1-800-221-7945, extension 5442, or by email at MacmillanSpecialMarkets@macmillan.com.

First Edition: 2024

10 9 8 7 6 5 4 3 2 1

For my mother and father

I met one man who was wounded in love,
I met another man who was wounded in hatred.

—Bob Dylan, "A Hard Rain's A-Gonna Fall"

PART I

2017

Dean was asleep on the carpet in Daniel's bedroom, a yellow toy truck in his hand, when Daniel woke. He threw on sweatpants and knelt near the boy, who was curled on his side in blue pajamas and felt slippers still damp at the toes from the dewy grass. He placed his hand on Dean's arm.

"Hey Deano."

The boy took a deeper breath and straightened his legs. A cloudy memory of his own son waking at this age rose up through the decades, and Daniel tried to burnish it: gray early light from the north-facing window above the bed in Forest's old room, dark thumb of ocean visible up the beach between half-open drapes. He nudged at it, but the old memory retreated.

Dean's eyes opened, and he regarded Daniel as if waiting for a response to something he'd said before going to sleep.

Daniel said, "What are you doing here, buddy?"

"I came to see you."

"Where's your grampa?"

"Asleep."

"Are you okay? Everything okay?"

Dean nodded. "I couldn't find anything for breakfast."

"Okay, let's get you something to eat. Then we'll go up and see if Grampa Jack is awake."

Dean followed him down the hall and into the kitchen, carrying his truck. The boy and his mother and grandfather had moved into the main house up the hill eight months earlier, and Dean had taken to visiting Daniel, who lived in what had formerly been a guesthouse on the

Beverly Hills estate of his late friend, Cameron Cooper. Daniel's fondness for Dean's visits made him more willing to ignore the questionable level of supervision the boy received from his grandfather when his mother and the part-time nanny weren't around. Jack was a little older than Daniel, and they had begun a guarded minor friendship, with Jack occasionally stopping down for a drink in the evening when his daughter or the nanny were there to look after Dean. Daniel still had not met Dean's mother, Celia Dressler. She was a young movie star fresh out of rehab number two and a round of tabloid thrashings, and was lately off shooting some epic film that Jack said was supposed to reinvent her career. When she was home Dean stayed up the hill.

The first time Dean had appeared at Daniel's was a month after they'd moved in. Daniel was on his patio reading when the gate in his fence rattled, and he looked up from his book, stabbed by the thought of Cam. No one had used that gate since Cam's death two years earlier, and now someone was fumbling with the pull-chain on the other side. The latch finally disengaged, freeing the gate onto its rusty hinges, and it pushed slowly open. Daniel waited to see who would step through. For a few seconds nothing happened, then a small white disc of a face emerged around the edge. The boy's eyes searched the yard, and when he saw Daniel he pounced through the gate and ran smiling toward him, blond hair bouncing in stride. He looked as though he would leap into Daniel's lap when he got there, but he pulled up short, stopping at the edge of the brick patio and staring, his smile faltering.

"Hi there," Daniel said.

"I forgot your name," the boy said.

"My name's Daniel, and I don't think you forgot it, because I don't think we've met. What's your name?"

"Dean." He looked perplexed. "I thought I remembered you."

"Are you Jack's grandson? Do you live up the hill?"

"Yes. In our new house."

"What brings you down here, Dean?"

"Nothing. I just came."

"Does someone know you're here?"

The boy stared long at him, and his mischievous smile reappeared.

"I'm guessing that's a no. Why don't we head on back up there, okay? I'll take you."

"Do you know my mom?"

"No. I know who she is, but we haven't met. I have met your grand-father."

"Have you lived here a long time?"

"Yes, quite a while."

"But you used to live somewhere else?"

"Well, I guess I did. I lived in a lot of other places when I was younger."

"Closer to the ocean."

"Sure, I lived in Malibu for a while. I grew up across the country, though, in a town called Ithaca with no ocean at all. Let's go, my friend." Daniel stood and Dean took his hand unprompted. They walked back out the gate and sixty yards up the grass hill to the main house.

That first time, Jack had played it off as if losing track of Dean was an anomalous occurrence, but as time went on Dean's visits continued, ramping up to once or twice a week after his mother moved out to the location in Arizona. When Daniel brought him back, Jack often seemed unaware he'd been gone. Sometimes he'd clearly been passed out. So Daniel started letting Dean stay a while. He would send Jack a text to let him know Dean was there, and they would listen to music together or Dean would play with a toy he'd brought while Daniel read. They had marathon Nerf basketball battles—one-on-one and HORSE—the only toy Daniel had in the house. The kid was clearly lonely.

"You like eggs?" Daniel asked when they got to the kitchen. This was the first time Dean had shown up in the morning.

Dean shook his head. "Cereal."

"Well, I don't keep cereal around. What about some toast with pea-nut butter?"

"Okay." Dean went into the living room and pulled the mini Nerf basketball from between the couch and the side table. "Rematch!" he called, shooting for the basket clamped to the kitchen counter. The shot missed and Dean scooped the ball up, did a spin move, and dunked it. "Want to play HORSE?"

"I'm going to fix breakfast, we'll play later."

Daniel made the toast and poured a glass of milk to go with it, then made coffee while Dean ate.

"Doesn't your grampa usually get you breakfast?"

"Yeah. But when I can't wake him up I just get my own cereal. We have no food right now."

"You tried to wake him and couldn't?"

"Yeah. He's really hard to wake up. Not always, but sometimes, especially when he sleeps on the couch."

"Okay, well, once you're finished I'll walk you back up there and we can check on him. Make sure everything is all right."

But Jack showed up a minute later, knocking on the sliding glass door in the living room, which was visible from the kitchen counter. He slid the door open and spoke to Dean without acknowledging Daniel, "There you are, kiddo! I've been looking for you. I didn't get a text from Daniel so I got worried."

"He was here when I woke up," Daniel said. "He said you were asleep. He was hungry, so . . ."

Jack ruffled Dean's hair. "You should have woke me, I would have got you your breakfast." He still hadn't looked at Daniel.

"Coffee?" Daniel said, already pouring a cup.

Jack shrugged and accepted the coffee. When he turned his face to Daniel his expression sagged off the tentpoles of cheer he'd propped under his hungover features. He was still waking up. "Thanks."

Jack was a skinny old man whose face showed his age. He wore tan work boots, old jeans, and a threadbare gray T-shirt. When they'd first met, Daniel had felt a flash of kinship: another aging product of sixties counterculture. Daniel could always tell. They were from different cloth, but they'd been cut by the same scissors.

Jack sat at the counter next to his grandson. "You ready for your big day on Monday?"

Dean nodded solemnly, chewing.

"What's the big day?" Daniel asked.

"First day of first grade," Jack said. "Right, bud?"

Dean nodded again. He gulped the last of his milk.

"That's exciting," Daniel said. "You're going to have a great time."

Dean took a moment to swallow and then looked at Daniel. "Do you remember your first day of real school?"

Daniel laughed. "I'd like to say yes, Deano, but it was so long ago. I guess I don't."

"How long ago?"

"Well, more than sixty years. That's ten times as long as you've been alive."

Dean's eyes widened and he smiled, pleased with the thought of such an incomprehensible span of time. "My mom's coming home Sunday."

"That's great. Are you excited to see her?"

The solemn nod again, his smile poking through it.

Jack said, "She's coming home for one night so she can drop him at school Monday. Then she's got to get back to Arizona."

"They almost done shooting?"

"I don't know. The schedule keeps mushrooming. The director, who's also the writer, is some crazy genius. He keeps rewriting, adding stuff. Five months they've been out there. I guess there's starting to be grumbling among the cast. But Celia, she's drunk the Kool-Aid."

When Dean finished eating, Jack took him back out the patio door and through the gate in the yard. Daniel lost sight of them for a moment behind the fence, and then they reappeared moving up the grassy hill, holding hands. When they topped the rise they disappeared onto the flagstone pool deck of the main house.

BLADES OF SUNLIGHT lacerated the floors under the windows, but otherwise the shades in the small bungalow defended valiantly against the desert morning. Celia sat at the vanity and stared at herself in the mirror. She pulled her pale streaked hair back from her face and examined first one cheekbone, then the other, trying to approximate the camera's pitiless gaze and find the best angles on which to present her face.

The core fear gripped her in the usual way—commonplace enough that at first she sighed and tried to shrug it off, but commonplace or no it did not relent, nor did the litany of ancillary fears it generated. For one, that she was in over her head. In truth, even when she'd been making shlock for adolescents she'd felt in over her head, but now, as the lead in Miles Rossinger's "surrealist, sci-fi *Anna Karenina* reboot," as he referred to it, she was surely not good enough. How could she be? She'd never been all that good to begin with, though recently she'd taken to studying with some good teachers instead of winging it based on grade-school drama class. Miles's constant praise of her performance felt nice when she heard it on set, but rang hollow in memory when she replayed it. And often she thought she saw pity, or contempt (what was the difference, really?), in the eyes of the crew when she moved among them. These were artists. They were Miles's people, whether they liked it or not. She was going to make an incredible fool of herself when this film came out. If that had been her only fear, she would have been fine. The fear of making a fool of oneself was the first thing an actor learned to ignore. But the list went on: Everyone hated her, possibly. The crew, the rest of the cast, her driver, the kid who brought her lunch and bottles of water, the girl who made sure her costume wasn't sticking to her in weird ways between shots in the heat, whose name she kept forgetting. Her son, for being away from him. Not Miles, though. She knew he didn't hate her. But she also knew that everyone outside his inner circle was beginning to hate *him,* if they hadn't from the start, so his friendship wasn't all that reassuring except that he was in charge. Of course nobody actually *acted* like they hated her, but you couldn't trust people to act the way they felt.

Then there was the core fear, the thing that sat at her center, source unknown, nurturing and deploying these lesser emissaries against her. Its unfathomed mass rode inside her always, weighing her down, like a gigantic, immovably dense meteor lying deep in its own prehistoric crater behind the display glass she'd constructed around it. It was so heavy that she was sometimes surprised when her body actually moved in immediate response to signals from her brain. But her body did move, her brain worked, her mouth said the things she told it to, and she was miraculously able to function well enough that she occasionally forgot about the presence inside her for extended periods of time. Right now was not one of those times.

She continued staring at herself in the mirror, tilting and frowning, imagining her face translated through the camera. "Stop it," she said to herself, plucking her cigarette from the ashtray and drawing on it. These kinds of vain exercises were not helpful to technique, and her acting coach had advised her against them, but she'd been doing them since she was a child and found it hard to give them up. Familiar routines sanded some of the rough edges off her anxiety and allowed her to skate through a few moments without wondering what to do next. The knock on the door startled her, though she'd known it was coming. Leo, her driver, always knocked precisely on time.

"Ready to go," he said softly through the door.

"Coming, Leo," she said. "Three minutes." Maybe a one-minute meditation, she thought, something her therapist had recommended. But sitting for even twenty seconds with her eyes closed only gave the fear space to find a fissure, and it roiled into her mind and slurried her thoughts violently. A gout of anger filled her lungs. She rose, walked to the sofa, and in a strange, almost serene rage began to pound one of the cushions with her right fist, as hard as she could, gritting her teeth and throwing her weight behind it, grunting with the effort.

"You okay?" Leo asked from beyond the door.

She'd assumed he'd gone back to the car. She didn't answer him, but went to the mirror, straightened her blouse and her hair, and walked to the door.

The trip to set passed in silence as usual. Celia always sat on the left side, to enhance privacy, and Leo remained just a large head with close-cropped black hair on the plateau of his wide white-shirted shoulders, occasionally a sliver of profile when he glanced in his side mirror. She rode staring out the window at the desert. Even with the SUV's tinted windows and her own dark sunglasses, she felt the unfettered sunlight yanking at her, threatening her cohesion. She was like a balloon rising toward the edge of the atmosphere. Maybe that was just what she needed: to let herself be torn asunder and find out what was underneath. Miles and his little group of loyalists—the Cabal, as some of the cast had started calling them—were planning a trip to some mountain to take mushrooms that weekend, and he was trying to convince her to go. *Torn asunder,* she thought.

"I just got out of my second rehab last year, remember?" she had told him.

He'd said, "I know. But it's mushrooms; it's different. In some places they use them to *treat* addiction."

"Any substance can break down my inhibitions and get me started again, so I've learned."

"I'll make sure you don't take anything else, I promise."

But to her own relief she'd said no. Every molecule in her brain had been lined up to accept the invitation, but something had welled from underneath, from someplace in her muscles, and caused her larynx to say, "No thanks, I'd better not. I'm going home Sunday so I can take my son to his first day of school on Monday. I'd rather be clearheaded for that."

It was all guys anyway, Miles's cabal, a nebulous little amoeba of male ego-stroking, one-upmanship, and phony mysteriousness. It included her costar, Roland Vance. He was a twenty-two-year-old model turned actor who treated her as if she were some grande dame just because he'd grown up on her movies. You're only six fucking years younger than me, she wanted to tell him. Give it a rest. He was a little dim-witted, but strangely good when the cameras rolled. Where did he find the depth, she wondered, in the vacuum of his personality?

Not all the mysteriousness was phony. Not Miles's. He was the genu-ine article, and people sensed it. He'd spent his life generating difficult art that somehow compelled the attention of mass audiences. He'd walked around for so long carrying his astringent magnetism that he'd relaxed into it. He serenely ignored those who were attracted to him, which was most people, so as not to waste time on their insecurity. This was why so many ended up resenting him, though even those who resented him usually tossed their resentment aside when he bestowed his treasured attention on them. When he wanted someone's company, he simply al-lowed them to exist in his sphere. If they interested him he would grant them a peek into his depth—the thing that everyone wanted from him, whether they knew it or not—a glimpse of the genuinely troubled soul who begot the work. It was hard to imagine him ever being actually im-pressed with anyone. Celia knew that the solicitous attention he paid her was unusual, and while it did make her feel special, it also scared her. She felt she couldn't possibly deserve it, and he couldn't possibly be fooled by her. Not him. So he must be faking it. When she was with him, though, she never sensed any falsehood in him; he seemed con-stitutionally incapable of blowing smoke up any ass, even one he was trying to get inside. But when she was alone she couldn't help doubting. The scarier thought, the one that had been stalking her from afar, was that she wasn't who she thought she was, but some other woman, some-one only Miles could see.

The SUV crunched up the long dirt driveway to the location, which was an abandoned cinder-block compound on a remote hill in the southern Arizona desert. A wealthy failed visionary had built it as a re-search center of some kind decades earlier, but ran out of either money or inclination before construction was finished. It had never been used. There was a main building, virtually complete, one wing of which now housed all of the equipment and generators. They had sealed off the section of the building where they were filming for air-conditioning, but a couple of weeks earlier the AC units for that area had gone down. Miles kept saying they were in line to be fixed and they kept not being fixed. There was a rumor that he felt the air-conditioned spaces were detracting from the atmosphere of hardship necessary to the film, and was holding up the repairs intentionally. People who needed cooling off now had to go to the trailers—and the trailers were another controversy. Celia was the only cast member who had her own trailer. Everyone else was assigned to a trailer shared with two to five others. It was unusual, but Miles was known for it. No one complained in front of her, but she knew it was an issue for some. If anyone had asked her ahead of time to share a trailer, she would have been fine with it, but no one had asked. She understood that people assumed she'd insisted on it. As filming had ballooned past the original schedule, it had created a quiet rift between her and the rest of the cast. She felt sheepish, but not sheepish enough to relinquish the privacy she'd come to cherish.

As she got out of the SUV, Celia waved to George Hughes, one of the supporting actors, who was sitting in his car with the engine running reading a book. He lifted two fingers and smiled. There had been a shouting match between Miles and Hughes the week before, the source of which Celia wasn't sure of, though tension between them had been palpable for a while. Since then Hughes had kept more to himself.

Other than the main building, the compound had four outbuildings on a starfish of paved roads draped over the top of the rocky hillock that sat at the foot of a cluster of small mountains, equally treeless and blunt, from which nothing but empty desert was visible all around. Somehow, the main driveway had never gotten paved. The farthest two outbuildings had been painted and built out by production designers to look like strange futuristic dwellings, standing taller now, with tiny oval windows and giant purple shoehorn-shaped structures jutting from their roofs, their sides sculpted to taper gently into the earth. They looked from afar like some breed of colossal alien barnacle latched onto the hill. The color had been chosen to match the yawning purple that the rock faces of the taller mountains to the west assumed in the evenings, when the sun set behind them. For a little while, at that time of day, the landscape transcended its stark, hostile emptiness and took on an astonishing beauty. If she stood outside the main building at sunset looking in the direction of the outbuildings, it was easy for Celia to feel that she really was on another planet. Most of the shooting was being done in and around these two outbuildings, as well as the interior of the main building, much of which had been renovated as well, for the banquet and throne room scenes. They had cut giant oval windows into two of the walls there to match the tiny ones in the outbuildings.

There was a section of the story where Celia's character and a few others fled the city and traveled to remote wastelands, and this section seemed to be constantly expanding in Miles's mind. So occasionally, without warning, Miles would announce an expedition into the open desert to film something new, and a caravan of three Land Rovers filled with equipment and crew would set off into the outback, the actors huddled in the rear vehicle studying the new pages they'd just been handed, which Miles had probably banged out the night before. They would drive aimlessly until Miles decided they had found the place where he wanted to film, and then pitch a little guerilla camp with raised tarps for shade. These expeditions sometimes lasted all day, and Celia had come to dread them.

She walked through the nascent morning heat to her trailer, where Christie, the first AD, was waiting outside with a clipboard and a scrunched expression that told Celia immediately they were in some kind of rush, and possibly Miles was in a bad mood.

"We've got to do another reshoot."

"Okay," Celia said. "Something from yesterday?"

"No. Let's get you into makeup." Christie turned and led the way toward the makeup trailer next door. Her sensible brown hair swung lightly across her back, and Celia envied her again, as she always did. Christie was smart, cool, in control. Christie was sane and friendly. She was Miles's perfect foil.

"What scene is it?" Celia asked.

"She's here!" Christie called through the door, still walking.

As they arrived at makeup, Celia glanced over her shoulder and saw one of the wardrobe assistants emerge from the building's side door holding a long, gauzy white nightgown and carrying it toward her trailer.

"No." Celia stopped at the makeup trailer's steps. "The bedroom scene again? Just fucking no."

Christie faced her, her expression full of sympathy. "I know," she said. "I had a fight with Miles about it this morning. I told him not to do this to you. I told him we had that scene six ways to Sunday. But he won't listen. He wants it again, in different light, and says we didn't get what he wanted in any of the takes." Christie took Celia's hand. "You can do this. You'll be fine." It was a gallant effort.

Celia shook her head. "I won't do it. It's ridiculous."

"Celia, I already tried for you. I really did. He's not going to change his mind."

Celia felt her voice rising from her stomach, and it felt good. "Tell him *he* can fucking play the scene! Tell him *he* can fuck George on set, and then be told to do it *again,* and *again,* and *again!*" The others in the area had all stopped what they were doing and were standing motionless, and Celia heard ricochets of her shouts coming back at her from the cinder-block wall of the building. There was an unfamiliar energy humming through her arms and chest. "This is bullshit!" she yelled, swinging her arms. "No fucking *way* am I doing that again!" The simple release of volume was a surprising relief, and she was getting ready to yell some more when she noticed that the frozen people around her were not actually staring at her, but past her toward the rear corner of the building. She turned and saw Miles standing there. He began to walk toward her. He was smiling.

When he reached her, he said, "This is it. This is what was missing. I want everything you gave in those earlier takes, plus some of this, this energy right here. Rage. Those other takes were amazing by the way. Truly deep work that could not have been better. It was my fault. I pointed you in a direction, and you took it there, you did everything I asked. But it needs more. I need to see that confused person turn, in the very moment, into the beginnings of this fierce banshee. She has to have this battle with herself and refuse to lose it." He was in his passionate mode, which was so infectious. "Not to rage physically, but to be there in her eyes, in her heart. The harbinger of the warrior she'll become." He held his head cocked and his mouth skewed as if he were barely containing his own artistic elation. He had trimmed his beard close overnight, and this somehow made him more convincing.

Celia shook her head, determined not to get caught up, but her voice when it came was meek. "Miles, please. I can't do it."

"You know that's not true. You can."

Her anger rose up again, and she opened herself gratefully to it. "I *won't*. I wasn't even supposed to have to do all that the first time. You talked me into changing my contract, and I did it because you said it was important. Actually, I don't care that much about the nudity, but how many fucking takes? Come *on*. Why don't *you* do it? Huh? Why don't you get naked in front of everyone, show *your* commitment, *your* strength?"

Miles shrugged. He pulled his T-shirt over his head, undid his belt, kicked off his sneakers, and dropped his jeans to the ground. Then, without so much as a muscle-twitch of hesitation, he took off his boxers and dropped them aside. "Like that?" He smiled.

Celia laughed despite herself.

"We're going to do this scene au naturel," he announced. "Every person in that room, including me, will be naked. Anyone has a problem with that will have to take it up with me."

"That's not necessary," Celia said.

"It is necessary, and it's settled." He turned and walked into the building, leaving his clothes behind in the dirt.

Celia stood breathing, her smile souring. It hadn't actually been funny, but mirth was the only valid response that had presented itself. She looked at Christie, and Christie tilted her head expectantly.

Celia set her features. "Okay," she said. "I guess this is the work, right? I hope you've got enough of those gowns, we don't want another safety pin incident." The original scene had called for George to tear the gown, but when they only had one left, Miles had told him to stop tearing it. After a few takes George had gone ahead and torn the collar anyway, and they had fixed it on the spot with safety pins rather than stop for repairs. On the final take, one of the pins had come open as they rolled around, and it had poked into her back as he lay on top of her. He'd thought her cries of pain were part of her performance and kept on with the scene. By the time they were done, the pin was embedded deep in her shoulder blade. She knew she could have stopped it, but by that point the idea of yet another take was so terrible that she had gritted through it.

"No safety pins this time," Christie said.

GEORGE APPROACHED HER, in costume, his flowing red cape raising wisps of dust as he walked toward the building. Celia was having a cigarette, and was not in her nightgown yet. When he reached her, George said, "I can't believe this. It's fucking insane." He was around sixty, craggy and handsome. His character, Kajika, was one of the king's closest advisors, and was having an affair with Celia's character, Anna, wife of the heir to the throne. Her marriage was amicable but merely a convenience, and her husband had a male lover. Lady Anna's affair with Kajika was unemotional, and she had begun secretly falling in love with the newcomer Varek, Roland's character. She planned to end it with Kajika. The scene in question was their final night together. Kajika's deeper feelings for her were unearthed by her break with him, and the scene was subtle at first but eventually became steamy when she yielded to his advances and gave him his last hurrah. It was a key scene because his jealousy and animosity for her were born in that room, surfacing and surprising her in the brutality of the sex. Later, his bitterness would coagulate and make of him a ruthless enemy who would force her into a terrible choice. The week before, Miles had run them through sixteen complete takes, unwilling to cut during the scene. It had been bizarre and humiliating. Celia had never been through anything like it on a set.

She took a drag and turned her head to blow smoke away from George. "It is what it is. We're pros, right? Miles talked to me about what he wants." Normally Miles liked his dialogue spoken meticulously, but for this he'd told her he didn't care so much about the script. "You and George know the scene by now," he'd said. "Stick to the structure, the blocking, but make it new, make it a little spontaneous."

"He's a fucking sadist," George said, his voice dropping into a growling whisper. "It's some sick addiction to power. I seriously think he's doing this as revenge for my fight with him the other day, and you're just collateral damage."

"Whatever. Let's make it work."

He leaned in close to speak even more softly. "Just so you know, he asked me to be more aggressive, shock you a little. I'll do it, but I'm not comfortable surprising you. I'm going to rip that gown to shreds."

"Thanks." She nodded and looked away again. The heat was intensifying, and she could feel the sheen of sweat on her neck.

He said, "This blows, but let's make it spectacular anyway. We might as well."

When she looked back at him he was offering her a reassuring smile. A pang of gratitude warmed her. "Yes," she said. "Let's."

IT WAS AN effort, not looking at everyone. The room was set up to be her bedchamber, at night after a carnival ball. The cameraman, perched on his stool, had a great belly sagging down over his waist. He was not naked but wore only boxer shorts, sneakers, and shin-high tube socks. Jonas, the gaunt Swedish DP, was manning the handheld himself, standing in the corner fully nude, his pale hipless body like a birch sapling. Miles sat in his chair, leaning back with his ankle crossed over his knee, completely unselfconscious. His body showed its age only in certain places—a wrinkle at his armpit, graying chest hair, dry cracked feet—but he was in remarkable shape without looking like he lifted weights. Yoga, Celia guessed. There were three other crew members— sound and wardrobe—two male and one female, all young and all also naked. Celia was the only clothed person in the room.

"It's actually sort of distracting," she said to Miles.

He smiled and turned one palm upward. "Well, you'll just have to deal."

She sat down at her vanity and picked up a silver hairbrush. She heard Miles and the crew talking behind her but she blocked them out and got lost in the mirror. When she heard him say, "Action," she was already in the reverie that would begin the scene. She started brushing her hair, going over in her mind the events that led Lady Anna to this moment.

The knock on the door came, and Lady Anna turned toward it. "Who is it?"

The scene played out smoothly and well, with little change in the scripted dialogue. It was a very good scene, with its slow-build of tension, her darkly dawning realization that Kajika felt mortally slighted by her and was unwilling to give her up easily. She knew he could find a way to use their affair, and the secret he'd discovered about her and the young Varek, against her.

Toward the end, once she'd begun to give in to his advances, he took the collar of her gown in both hands and tore it wide open, throwing its remnants down at her feet and leaving her naked. Lady Anna was surprised, but she stayed with him and they moved into the lovemaking portion of the scene, the heat between them building mutually until, at a certain point, his passion outpaced hers and she found herself withdrawing from the escalation, though still participating. This was the part Miles had coached her on.

Celia's head was hanging off the far edge of the bed, and when she saw Jonas's skinny bare legs and feet as he approached, she felt as if she were either waking from a dream or descending into one. He crouched on his heels beside the bed, aiming the camera into her face, the tip of his penis hanging just above the floor. George Hughes grunted and rammed his pelvis roughly against her. Her body shook violently. Was she here? Or was she somewhere far off, dreaming this strange scene? Did it matter? She became aware that while her mind was somewhat dispassionately taking in the things visible to her and the sensations affecting her, her mouth was stretched open emitting an eerie keening, the sound a ghostly trapped entity in her chest. Was she possessed? She freed the entity and gave it a name, Anna, though it did not arise from the role she was playing. She let it take over, and the keening became guttural sobbing, hot bitter tears blurring everything, briny on her lips. Distantly, she worried she was ruining the scene. Then Celia clenched her jaw, shut off the tears, braced her body against the thrusts, and opened herself to a soothing deluge of deep, absolute fury.

"Here you go."

The only other female in the room was standing, still naked, by the bed, holding a robe. The take was over, somehow. Celia did not move. She was alone on the bed. Blurred bodies circled lazily, voices gave and responded to simple instructions, props that had been moved were being gathered.

"You okay?"

She was not. She felt calm, but was somehow paralyzed.

"You can put this on now."

"Celia, are you all right?" George asked from the other side of the bed, where her feet were, far away.

Then Miles was by her head, bending and gazing at her. He took the bedspread and gently folded it over her, and the warmth felt good despite the room's heat. He also was still naked. "Thank you," he said. "That was more than I'd hoped for. You, Celia, you are amazing. Thank you." He raised his head and spoke to the room, "If anyone tells me we didn't get that, for any reason, I will well and truly commit homicide." He bent back down toward Celia. "Are you okay? Is there anything you need? Should I get everyone out of here so you can regroup?"

Celia moved her leg and felt her motor function restored. "You could get your dick out of my face, that would be a start," she said. The room broke out in relieved laughter. She sat up, swung her legs over the side of the bed, and took the robe from the girl. She could feel that her legs were still shaky, so she put the robe on without standing. She looked at Miles, and almost found herself infected by the glee in his face. She marshaled her anger, her need for agency. "I'm done for the day," she told him.

He nodded. "Understood."

She stood, knotted the robe, and walked very slowly to the door.

THAT NIGHT, JACK got the nanny over and went down to Daniel's with a bottle of bourbon, his third such visit. The first had been some months earlier, in response to a perfunctory invitation from Daniel. They had been in communication before that whenever Dean would go down, but Daniel hadn't really expected his invitation to be accepted, at least not so quickly. He had phrased it vaguely, so Jack could feel free never to take him up on it, but Jack had gone down that very night, and they'd polished off half a bottle. Now here he was again, carrying, with a smirk, the bottle that bore both their names.

Daniel put on music and offered to break out his seldom used stash of weed, but Jack shook his head and waved his glass. "I'll stick with this. There was a time I liked to smoke, but I don't take to it much anymore." Which got them talking about how much weed had evolved, and led to the topic of the sixties, a subject Daniel had instinctively avoided the first two evenings, knowing it could lead to personal questions.

"Were you out here back then?" Jack asked.

"Yes, mostly. Here in LA."

"Man! What a time. I was up in the Bay for a while, right in the thick of it."

"That must have been something."

Jack nodded and sipped his drink. "Oh yeah. Things ain't what they used to be, are they?"

Daniel said, "At what point in history, exactly, do you think things actually were what they used to be?"

Jack laughed. "You know what I mean."

"Sure I do. And you're not wrong. But guys our age were saying the same thing back in the late sixties, and they were not wrong either."

"Yeah, but back then things were changing in ways that meant something. Now, look at it. Kids growing up glued to screens, living on the internet. Change is driven by technology, not music and drugs and mysticism and free will. Things were exploding when you and me were young, you never knew what would happen next. The world was rushing outward into the universe. Now it's only rushing into incestuous commodification." Jack mimed cartoonish astonishment and pitched his voice to match, channeling an imagined brainwashed millennial. "Oh-em-*gee*! Did you get the newest app?"

"Come on," Daniel said. "Everybody mythologizes their youth. We all get nostalgic for when times were vital and unpredictable, when really it's just us that used to be vital and unpredictable. Plus, who are we to say what's for the better? I stay out of it. I try not to be a commentator, just a neutral observer. Generations remake the world over and over, and it's up to them now."

Jack leaned forward and put his elbows on his knees. "I'm a little older than you. I wasn't just a kid in the sixties and seventies. I was twenty-eight in 1968. I had perspective, and I'm telling you, it wasn't great just because we were young. When I was *actually* young things were sliced too cleanly. People had their sphincters sewn up so tight. But everything changed in the late sixties. Brand-new things were happening. There was magic going on that didn't exist before then. Truth—you know, with a capital T—appeared on the scene, and it has been slowly fading away ever since. I take one look at you and I know you know that."

"I get nervous about the capital T," Daniel said. "Usually means someone's trying to manipulate people, or getting ready to do something crazy."

Something flashed in Jack's eyes that might have been annoyance. "Truth is truth. What you or I think doesn't change it."

Daniel took a breath and smiled, drawing back from the line of the conversation. "Fair enough. It *was* a time, I'll give you that. But it wasn't all good."

"Good? 'Course not! It was the darkest time I've ever lived through, and ever expect to. But good and bad don't mean shit at the end of the day. False morality only ends in stagnation. It's about experience! It's about magic, and truth, which are always both good and bad, or maybe neither. Beyond good and evil! Ain't that what Nietzsche said?"

"I wouldn't know. But I'll drink to it. . . ." Daniel downed the last of his drink. "Amen."

"But now," Jack said. "Shit, now look what's going on. You ain't no goddamn neutral observer. I can tell. I mean, look at this motherfucker we have in the White House now. Don't tell me you have no opinion on him. Fucking orange demon pig that he is."

"Well, yes. He's pretty awful. When I think of him, in that office, with all that power . . ." Daniel shook his head and snorted. "We really are a bunch of first-class assholes, is what I think when I see him. Americans, I mean."

"I'd like to grab him by his comb-over and cut his throat with a rusty sawblade, watch him bleed out. I'd like to see the fucking life drain from his eyes while he tries to scream from the bleeding gash in his neck."

Daniel recoiled from the image, looking at Jack. The older man's features had constricted into a paroxysm of dreamy rage. He spoke evenly, and there was nothing there to mitigate, to indicate that he was being fleetingly hyperbolic. He looked, in that moment, like someone who would like nothing better than to do the very thing he was describing.

"I wonder if there's a way to get you in a room with him," Daniel said, but Jack didn't laugh. "You probably shouldn't go saying that in front of Siri, though."

"Who?"

"Oh, I just mean our iPhones might be listening, so watch out."

Now Jack smiled. "Let 'em listen. Fucking NSA. Let 'em come get me." He laughed abruptly, the sound rising out of him in a strange loud burp, unmodulated, like something provoked by an electric shock. It made Daniel uneasy. When this odd sound trailed off, Jack pulled his phone from his pocket and held down its button. Siri's voice said, *How can I help you?* Jack said, "You can tell Trump, that demon, that I'm waiting for him. Come and get me, motherfucker. I'll snap you in two and fuck both halves."

I'm sorry, I didn't understand, Siri's voice said.

"Like fuck you didn't."

Daniel could think of no response and so he let the alcohol wash him into insincere laughter. And then suddenly it really was funny, and they shared a good deep belly laugh that swept aside the uneasiness.

The Stones' "Ventilator Blues" came up on Daniel's shuffled Big Playlist, a compendium of six decades of music he loved. The sexy, malevolent guitar riff snaked through the room.

"Oh, man," Jack said. "I love this tune. You got a lot of weird music, but the old stuff you got is the good stuff, for sure."

"Yeah, it's pretty great," Daniel said, as Jagger began, *When your spine is cracking. . . .*

"One thing I wondered though. All these songs going by, I ain't heard any Grateful Dead. I figure with the time you come from you'd have some Dead."

Daniel shrugged. "Not really a fan. Never caught the bug."

"You ever see them live?"

Daniel paused, pouring himself another finger of bourbon. He looked at Jack and shook his head. "Nope, never did."

"I don't believe it. You were in California all through the late sixties and seventies and never saw the Dead?"

"Like I said, not really my thing."

Jack picked his feet up off the coffee table in a dramatic motion and set them down on the floor, leaning forward. He lowered his chin and grinned, fixing Daniel with a jaunty stare. "What about females, son? You got a girlfriend, a woman around?"

"Sixty-eight and single," Daniel said with a resigned laugh. "I have an ex-wife, but we've been divorced since the eighties."

"Kids?"

"I have a son, Forest. He's forty-one."

"That's good. It's important to have family. Best thing I ever did was mend my relationship with Celia. Begin it, more like. I didn't know her much when she was a kid. Lucky for me she's a forgiving type."

"Sounds familiar. Minus the forgiveness, maybe. But me and Forest are sort of okay now, I guess."

"But don't tell me you've been single since the eighties. There must have been women in between."

"Sure, a few. Not many. I had one serious girlfriend more recently, but it didn't work out. We're still friendly. She's closer to my son's age than mine, so it probably wasn't realistic."

"You love her?"

Daniel threw back his bourbon and shook his head. He spoke through the burn. "Shit, I don't know, Jack. Maybe I could have, but we didn't get there, not quite."

"How many times you been in love?"

"For real? Maybe only once."

"Your ex-wife?"

"No, not her. We were good together, for a while, but it wasn't love."

"Someone farther back, huh? Kid stuff?"

"Yeah," Daniel said. "Kid stuff." Jack's questions were rubbing him wrong. He felt prodded. He realized he wasn't interested in Jack in the ways Jack seemed interested in him. "Listen, man, I have some things to do in the morning."

"Throwin' me out?" Jack said, raising his eyebrows in mock challenge. "I guess I'm boring you." Then his face darkened, the challenge sliding free, for a second, from the humor that had leavened it.

Daniel's irritation grew, and he smiled. "Not at all. I'm just a bad sleeper to begin with, and I have stuff happening in the morning."

Jack's expression, like an opposing magnet, flipped suddenly from aggression back to joviality. "Comprende, partner. Good rapping." He stood, grabbed the bottle from the table, and went to the sliding door. "Catch you on the flip side."

THE NEXT DAY, Daniel ate a solitary late breakfast and cleaned his house. After cleaning, he sat on his patio drinking coffee and sweeping his interior fragments into a semi-functional heap. Almost two years earlier he'd retired from his second-act career as a schoolteacher at a private school in Inglewood that was funded through Cam's foundation, and he'd regretted the decision very quickly. But the school had already activated his pension and replaced him. He now spent three afternoons a week tutoring in an after-school program run by a former student, but his mornings were always vacant.

There was a fractured brand of loneliness triggered in him by certain overcast days in Los Angeles, as if this specific unbroken shade of gray-white overhead created a metaphysical vacuum, diffusing him thinly across his life. The hangover didn't help. He thought of his dinner with his ex-wife the week before. He and Amelia had been divorced a very long time, and finally had a good relationship. A couple of times a year they would have dinner and talk about their son, Forest, and reminisce. She had become a producer and studio executive in her father's footsteps, and always took Daniel to restaurants known mostly to the famous and plugged-in, places that were on the verge of becoming trendy but hadn't yet been ruined by word of mouth. Daniel didn't like these restaurants, and always made a point of dressing as scruffily as possible. Once he'd asked her why she didn't mind being seen with him among her colleagues and the celebrities that frequented these places, and she'd admitted that in fact that was part of the point. The mystery of an unknown face, especially an aging one who couldn't be some up-and-comer, added a kind of street cred to her image. Supplying her with street cred had been an important part of his role from the beginning, back when he'd been a briefly famous outsider artist. It was even possible there were people left here and there who knew who he was, though he hadn't made a piece of art in decades, and no one talked about his work or his past anymore outside of the occasional mention of him as an influence.

He knew that the real reason for Amelia's dinner invitation had been to make him swear not to miss their son's art opening. It wasn't that she thought Daniel would forget, but that she knew how much he would dread such an event. He'd given her his word, and had since been trying to put it out of his head.

Now the day was here, and Daniel could no longer avoid his dread. He hated going places where people might know of his earlier incarnations. He hated having to answer for his former selves. And he hated being alone in crowds. Amelia would be there, but she'd have her husband with her, the man his son called Dad. Daniel was Pop. Agreeing to that state of affairs early on was just another in the list of ways he'd failed his son. Ronald, the stepfather, was a decent guy, and had always done well by Forest. He had written Daniel off years earlier, during the bad time, and when Daniel had pulled his shit together he'd curbed his distaste gradually but never moved past neutral tolerance. Daniel couldn't blame him. So he'd be on his own at this event. He imagined the scene: standing in front of the artwork studiously (he had no idea what his son's work even looked like now; it had been sixteen years since Forest had finished art school and had his last student exhibition), shuffling back and forth to the bar for drinks, a short interaction with Amelia and Ronald, an awkward proffer of congratulations to his son, and a hasty exit filled with shame and relief, all while avoiding anyone who seemed to glance knowingly his way.

He was glad to look forward to his afternoon at the tutoring program, though on Fridays the kids tended to be especially distracted. He left home an hour before he had to be there, to account for traffic, but the traffic was not at peak and he arrived at the community center in Inglewood almost thirty minutes early. Sitting on the front steps smoking a cigarette was his former student Rashid, who had founded the program with Daniel's help.

"Hey Mr. T.," Rashid said, stubbing out his Marlboro but holding onto the butt for disposal inside. Rashid, like all Daniel's more recent students, was too young to fully appreciate that the name Mr. T. was already taken.

"Hey Rashid. You don't want the kids to see you smoking," Daniel said.

Rashid looked at his watch. "It's early enough," he said, standing up. "Can we talk for a minute? I have a situation I want to run by you."

"Sure."

They went into a small common room with an electric coffee urn and two sofas. In the far corner there were a few filing cabinets, one of which housed the program's paperwork. There was no office dedicated to it, but this room was hardly ever used except by the few center employees who drank the coffee. Rashid closed the door and put his laptop bag on a table by the cabinets. He popped a couple of mints into his mouth from his pocket. "It's about Gerald," he said.

Gerald was Rashid's younger half brother. Rashid had been Daniel's student eight years earlier, for two years, and through their association Daniel had met and gotten close with Rashid's mother, Tanya. After Rashid graduated, Daniel and Tanya had become a couple for almost four years. They had stayed mostly friendly when the relationship had broken up a year and a half earlier. So Daniel was close to the family, borderline stepdad, though he and Tanya had never officially lived together. Gerald was now a junior at the school.

Rashid sat, and Daniel sat facing him.

"Is he okay?"

"Sort of. He's having a hard time with his dad, and my mom's not really helping."

Gerald's father, Raymond, a Jamaican EMT, shared custody of Gerald, but had lost interest in Rashid after he and Tanya split. Rashid's father, who was Algerian, had dropped out of the picture before Rashid really knew him.

"What's going on?" Daniel asked.

"He finally came out to Raymond."

"I guess I didn't know he hadn't."

"Yeah, it was a big deal, and Raymond didn't take it well. He's blaming my mom and they're fighting a lot."

"Blaming her for Gerald being gay?"

"I guess so. Or something . . . When he first found out he smacked Gerald, which I don't think he's ever done before. He's calmed down at this point, but my mom has gone straight to DEFCON one, and she's saying Gerald has to cut Raymond off, not see him, and Gerald doesn't want that. He's kind of stuck in the middle."

"But he's staying with your mom still."

"Yeah, but they're having big fights and Gerald is fucking miserable. I'm wondering if you could talk to her."

"What would I say? It is definitely not my business."

"What about Gerald? Can he call you? He needs another adult to talk to, and I don't count."

"Yes, of course. Why wouldn't that be fine?"

"He doesn't feel comfortable. Like it might be an overstep after all this time."

"No way. Come on."

"I told him, but he doesn't see you regularly like I do."

Daniel felt a flash of guilt. When he and Tanya had broken up, Gerald had been angry and confused and had blamed his mother. Daniel had tried to shoulder the responsibility, but Gerald seemed determined to absolve him completely, no matter what he said. Daniel still remembered Gerald insisting on coming over after the breakup. Tanya had dropped him off and Daniel had spent the evening trying to calm him down, saying they were only taking a little space and getting perspective, and either way he and Gerald would still be friends. Gerald had slept that night in what had become his bed in Daniel's guest room, but had never come over again. In the midst of all his turmoil with his mother it had seemed right to stay away and let Tanya work it out with him over time. Daniel hadn't known what else to do.

"I'd be happy to talk to Gerald," he said, "though I don't know what I can do about this situation."

Rashid hung his head, then looked up again. "If I got my mom to call you, would you see if you could get her to back off? She needs to let Gerald start making his own decisions. Her way will make things worse for Gerald with Raymond, in the long run. She needs to let them deal with it between the two of them, but she won't listen to me, and she damn sure won't listen to Gerald."

Daniel paused. "I could try, if it felt right. I can't promise how that conversation might go. She's not exactly disposed to me as a source of life-wisdom."

"I get that." Rashid smiled.

"Was Gerald hurt? When Raymond hit him? Is he okay?"

"He's fine now. It was a shock, for all of us, and it actually did leave a mark for a couple of days. So my mom's got a point, but still, she needs to defer to Gerald this time. Raymond has never done anything like this before, and I don't think he'll do it again. He's been openly remorseful, which is also way out of character for him, and a good sign I think."

Daniel pursed his lips and nodded. His dealings with Raymond over the years had been minimal, but they'd always gotten along. "Okay. Whatever I can do, I will."

After the afternoon working with a few kids, on his way home his phone rang through the car's Bluetooth. It was Tanya.

"Daniel, how are you?"

"Good," he said.

"Rashid said he talked to you about Gerald today, and Raymond."

"Yes."

"Did he tell you Raymond hit him?"

"Yes."

"This is why he kept it from him all this time. Because he knew how he'd react, and sure enough. Though I never thought he'd get physical. Now Ger's talking about wanting to go live with Raymond, for god's sake. Am I *crazy*? How did I become the bad guy here? There is no way I'm allowing that, not right now."

"Rashid said you're forbidding him seeing Raymond altogether."

"What am I supposed to do? Raymond's lucky I haven't gone to the police."

"Maybe there's a middle ground. He's probably only talking about moving out because you're confining him. If you let them visit he'll probably calm down."

"In a fucking pig's eye! Raymond doesn't get to do that and then we pretend everything is fine."

Daniel could hear the stubbornness in her tone and knew he could push no further. She had no intention of being moved, least of all by him. "Well, I see your point. Hopefully it'll all calm down before too long. Take it easy on the kid, though. Rashid said he's having a rough time all around."

"*Me* take it easy on him?"

"He's seventeen, Tanya. He's almost grown."

"Don't fucking lecture me."

"I wouldn't dream of it."

"I know how old Gerald is. But I'm still the one who knows what's best. And right now Raymond lost his privileges."

Daniel sighed, but quietly enough so she wouldn't hear. "I'm sure you're doing the right thing. The quality of your parenting is not in question, not by me, not ever. You know that."

"How about we leave it at that. I do appreciate your concern for him, Daniel. So thanks. But we'll be fine."

"Okay. Just so you know, Rashid said Gerald might call me. I don't want to overstep, but I told him that would be okay."

"Gerald is free to talk to whomever he wants. He's not a prisoner. He still misses you anyway, though he won't say so."

A silence ensued. Then Daniel said, "You know, I'm going to Forest's art opening tonight. He's got a show at a major gallery."

"Give him my congratulations, if he even knows who I am."

Though they'd dated for years, Tanya had never met Forest, and it had been a sore point. Daniel had been about to ask if she would go with him, just to have company, but he thought better of it. "I'll tell him," he said.

LEAVING SET, SHE watched the stand of buildings recede from the cool interior of the car. The desert, doubly tinted by the window and her sunglasses, now looked almost temperate, though she'd just spent the morning in its stifling heat. The darkened room where they'd shot the scene had been only incrementally cooler than outside. Celia tried to fathom exactly what had happened in that room. She had lost a few seconds (minutes?) of time. She tried to pierce the elision in her memory, but couldn't. She felt the old fear swelling differently, as if beginning to come into focus, its cloudy surface polished somehow.

"What time is it?" she asked Leo.

"Just after eleven," he said.

"Oh. It's early."

"You already done for the day?"

"Yeah, I guess so." The prospect of spending the day in her room behind drawn shades seemed grim suddenly.

"That'll be nice to relax a bit."

"Yeah." She paused, looking out the window, not wanting to end the conversation yet, even though she'd virtually ignored this man for months. "What about you? You have other duties?"

He shrugged. "Not really. You are my duties. I'll be available in case you need to go anywhere." She knew this already.

"You staying nearby?"

"No, there is no nearby. A bunch of us, drivers and crew, are staying at a Comfort Suites down by Bisbee. It's nice."

"Is that far?"

"Yeah, it's a good distance. I make it in under two hours."

"You must be up early in the mornings."

He shrugged again, his broad shoulders straining at the white fabric of his shirt. "Part of the job."

"Leo, is there anything to do in Bisbee? I'm sort of dreading a whole day in my hotel room."

"Yeah, there's stuff to do. It's a little deserted, but it's a tourist town.

There's shops and restaurants and art galleries and stuff. It's a nice little town. It's cooler there too. It has some elevation."

"Sounds great, let's go there."

"You got it. Want to stop off at your hotel on the way?"

"Nope. There's nothing I need from there. Why don't you put on some music."

"What kind of music? I have a lot."

"Anything, whatever you like to listen to."

Once the music was on, they fell mostly silent for the drive. Celia looked out the window at the desert. She felt her customary cluster of anxieties, but also the creeping worm of something else. Some imminence that threatened her.

As they pulled into Bisbee, the road skirted a colossal red wound in the planet, fenced off from the passing cars, a yawning canyon whose evenly tiered walls and bright red earth spoke of violent origins. "Oh, wow," Celia said.

"Yeah, that's the copper mine."

"It shouldn't be so beautiful."

"I know, strange, right?"

Around a corner they dropped into the heart of old Bisbee, hidden completely from the giant mine. It was as advertised, a little tourist and vacation town. The main business district was populated by old brick buildings surprisingly close together, some of the streets as narrow as alleys. John Prine was singing from the stereo, *Pretty good, not bad, I can't complain.*

"You tried any of these restaurants?" Celia asked.

"Yeah, a couple."

"Take me to your favorite."

"Well, it's pretty basic. I think there are nicer places."

"Basic is good."

They pulled up in front of a little coffee shop diner. "This is it," he said.

"Let me buy you lunch."

"Oh, I can just bring something out to the car."

"Don't be crazy. I don't want to eat alone. Come in with me, will you?"

He said, "You're the boss," and smiled over his shoulder.

Leo had a wife and a young son. He was an aspiring singer-songwriter. He lived in Silver Lake, and played open mics and occasional paid gigs. He supported his family by driving, and used his meager disposable income renting studio time, making demos of his songs to send around to record companies. He was thirty-one, three years older than Celia. He was a big guy, slightly heavy but with the height and build to carry it well. His white dress shirt strained at its buttons across his chest and stomach. They ate egg-and-potato skillets with tall glasses of ice water that were kept topped off by the flustered young waitress, who had recognized Celia.

Exchanging small talk over a meal was somehow exactly what she needed. She could feel herself subsiding, skating slowly onto safer ice. Leo's dark face and tranquil brown eyes cast a beam of calm, enhanced by his deep voice and unaffected demeanor. Celia wasn't used to people, especially relative strangers, being easy around her. It was comforting.

"God," she said, washing down a bite with water, "you're a musician! I am such an idiot."

"What do you mean?"

"I mean, I just assumed, since you were a driver, that you were *just* a driver. Not that there would be anything wrong with that. I mean . . . I don't know. . . ."

"That doesn't make you an idiot. We all make those kinds of assumptions."

"Maybe you're right, but I don't like how easily I forget that there's usually—not usually, always!—more to the picture than meets the eye."

"Hey hey, my my."

"What?"

"Neil Young?"

"Oh, right."

Leo's voice rose into a fine imitation of Neil Young's quaver. "*Rooock and roll can never die. . . .*"

Celia laughed. "You sound just like him."

"You should hear me sing for real."

"I'd like to. Got any of your stuff on that iPod?"

"Actually no. I keep my own stuff on my computer. I don't listen to it much. It's back in my room."

"Let's go listen to it. It's not far, right?"

"No, not far."

They drove a couple of minutes south from downtown and pulled off the highway again into his motel. He parked around the back of the building and they entered through a rear door using his key card. The room was standard chain-generic, but had a nice view of the mountains. It was filled with signs of long-term habitation, since they'd been filming there for almost five months, off and on. There was a stack of books by the bed, more books and magazines in the small sitting area, a laptop plugged in at the desk, and a beautiful blond-wood acoustic guitar on a stand in the corner.

"You've got your guitar."

He smiled. "I don't leave home without it."

He gathered a pile of laundry that was by the wall near the sitting area and carried it to the far side of the bed, where he dropped it out of sight.

"Oh, don't worry."

"Least I could do. Have a seat, I'll set you up. I don't have any speakers, so you'll have to use my headphones."

She sat in the lone armchair and he brought over the laptop and a big pair of headphones. For the first time since they'd sat down to lunch, Celia felt awkward. She was thankful for his company, but it was strange, suddenly, to be in his hotel room.

"What are you going to play for me?"

"I have a song in mind." He sat on the edge of the bed and searched on the computer for a moment. He switched on the headphones. "Okay, put these on."

Celia put them on and felt the soft pull on her eardrums from the noise-canceling. There was a slow, dark, three-chord intro on acoustic guitar, and then the rest of a full band kicked in. The production was excellent, crystalline. She smiled and nodded at him, but when the lyrics began she felt the expression fall from her face. The voice pierced her almost painfully with its depth and sharpness. Could it really be him? She closed her eyes and listened to the first verse. When she opened them again Leo had gone into the bathroom. The song was a bluesy dirge in the verses, a lament for the nation and the world, that introduced multiple characters and took them through tough times, and then the chorus, instead of doubling down on politics, let in some major-key light and turned personal—a first-person evocation of redemptive love. Celia felt slightly ridiculous as she lifted the collar of her shirt to wipe at her tears, hoping he wouldn't come out of the bathroom and notice. Then the song ascended into an unexpected, almost jazzy bridge that ramped up the energy as if toward a great crescendo but fell, just short of it, back into the darkness of the dirge, and a final mournful verse that circled back on the beginning. It was a great song. As the ending approached, Leo emerged from the bathroom. He sat on the edge of the bed again. She took off the headphones. The song had pulled her into its sphere, and she felt euphoric, exhilarated at being shifted outside herself.

"Oh my god," she said.

"You liked it?"

She was about to go giddy with bubbling praise, but suddenly that seemed inadequate. She set her jaw and nodded, hoping she didn't look too serious. "Leo, what the fuck? You're a real artist. That's an amazing song."

He smiled and put his palm on his own chest. "Thank you. It's probably my best song."

She stared at him with a sense almost of awe. She'd been in the presence of people who'd written songs like that before, but always with their giant wagonloads of baggage, the deformities of fame.

"You play that for music people and they don't want you?"

"They like it, and I've gotten some really good feedback. A few have met with me. The closest I've gotten is they want to buy that song, and a few others, let stars record them. I've always said no to that. The offers have been generous, but they're mine."

"You're an amazing singer. Who's going to sing them better than that?"

"Someone younger, skinnier, more glamorous. Someone already famous, I guess."

"Yeah, fuck that. You hold out. Don't let them ruin your stuff."

"My wife is starting to think I ought to sell. It's been a while now I've been trying. And it *would* be an honor, I mean, depending on who sings them, I guess. Having a little money would be nice too."

Celia dropped back into her own mind then, and so complete had her immersion in his music been that she was momentarily shocked by the magnitude of her native desperation. *What is wrong with me?* She reached out and gripped his leg. "Not that song, though," she said. "Whatever you do, don't sell that one." Once her hand was on him, the movement of her body out of the chair was so fluid and propulsive that she barely felt it happening. She was suddenly sitting astride him on the bed, kissing him.

There was only one moment of real vacillation: She pulled her face away from his and saw in his eyes the panic of a husband and father teetering on the lip of infidelity. He looked shocked. She sat up, still on top of him. She rebuked the part of herself that had waylaid him, the desperate child who needed to fuck her driver to escape herself. She almost sprung off him; the muscles in her legs tightened on the verge of it, but in that moment something else happened. The clear-thinking part of her, the woman who recoiled from the behavior of the manic child, looked at him and saw a man of depth, someone she wanted to know, to be known by. And she watched it happen for him too, as he slid free of the fantasy of fucking his movie-star client—a fantasy he might ultimately have rejected—and saw her. And so it was she, the rueful, frightened, sober young woman, who leaned slowly back down, holding his gaze with her own, and began kissing him again.

Celia had scarcely been with anyone for real since Dean was born. She'd fucked plenty of guys; that was one of the things she did to keep her sanity—though her therapist insisted it didn't help, that the consolation she got from it was an illusion. But really being with a man, for a night or even a moment, she'd mostly avoided that since Darren had left her. The ending with Darren had been a roiling, lurid nightmare. They'd been so good when they started, just two beautiful hedonist kids joining forces and delving into each other to escape the prismatic scrutiny their budding fame subjected them to. How had it gotten to where it ended? Subsequently, Darren's fame had continued expanding into a universe all its own. Their relationship and public troubles were his big bang. After they split for good, his face had become an apparition floating in the mind of the world, a paradigm signifying masculine beauty, while she had somehow come to signify only despoiled youth.

Celia had been so angry when the tabloid photos surfaced of him and a costar that she'd leaked details of his drug use and lifestyle. There had even been a public physical altercation in which she'd thrown a full bottle of kombucha at him and injured him. Amid that maelstrom, when the two of them (three if you counted Georgia Winstead, the other woman) had been in the headlines every day, the pregnancy had reared up like some vulgar and unnecessary plot twist. In her anger she had sworn that the baby wasn't his. He had sued her for a paternity test, and by the time she submitted to it she'd been prepared to fall back into his arms if he'd have her. The fight had run its course and so had her rage. But she'd been shocked to discover that, in fact, Darren was not the father. There had been a guy at a party, she remembered—a meaningless thing, not like the months-long affair between Darren and Georgia. So that was it. No more Darren. No more public sympathy for his cheating. Since then it had been just her and Dean, and her father, who had shown up when Dean was a baby offering to help. She'd known that Jack's offer was born of need and not magnanimity, but she hadn't cared. She'd needed not to be alone in that time, and he had been there. He loved Dean and he never judged her, that was all that mattered. Other than the scary six-month relapse a year earlier, she'd been sober all Dean's life, but she allowed herself these carnal indiscretions. There'd been no one famous, no confusing power dynamics. Just boring little sex machines.

But now here was poor Leo, lying under her, blindly drawn into her vortex. His body was big, and had a slight softness to it, a layer of fat over strong muscle, which was something absolutely new to Celia. She realized she'd never been with a man who wasn't skinny, and lately it had all been boys who trumpeted their micro-fractional body fat and their muscle-targeting workout regimens. Celia and Leo moved up to the pillows and lay side by side, taking a break from kissing.

"I shouldn't do this," he said.

Celia nodded, looking into his eyes. She understood from his inflection that he wasn't truly hesitating but merely coming to terms with an event whose momentum had already captured him, even if he didn't quite know it yet. If he was going to turn back, he would need her help. Looking at him, she felt a fluid calm that was such a relief to her scorched mind that it paralyzed her. She wasn't going to speak and risk losing it.

"I've never . . ." He stopped.

She nodded again, almost spoke, and then didn't. His brow gathered into a pair of vertical furrows. He was pleading with her, she realized, but her serenity was undisturbed, even began to swell. She found him beautiful. She thought of his song, his voice, and sat up. Mercilessly, she pulled off her shirt.

AFTERWARD, SHE SAID to him, "Are you going to be tortured by this? Don't be tortured."

Leo continued staring at the ceiling and took a breath. "I'll try not to be." He stood and went into the bathroom. When the door clicked, a ponderous charge throbbed in Celia's chest. Empty rooms inflated her emptiness. Crowded rooms oppressed her erratic mind. One-on-one contact frightened her. But Leo didn't frighten her, she thought. That fact itself scared her. She wasn't even sure it was true. Could it be true? The only person she knew whose presence didn't quicken her fear even a little was her son. Darren too, maybe. She resolved to pay attention, to try and gauge whether the air changed when Leo returned from the bathroom.

She crawled halfway out of the bed on her hands to reach her bag by the chair and dragged it over. She pulled out her cigarettes and lit one. She looked at her phone, but there were no messages. She smoked and stared at the screen blindly, and when she heard the bathroom door open she put the phone down. He came back in and sure enough changed the air. Not with fear, though, but something else. He pulled on his underwear and a T-shirt and walked over and opened a window.

"Sorry," she said, indicating her cigarette. "Hope you don't mind."

"No big deal." Instead of putting on his pants, he handed her a glass to use as an ashtray and lay back down beside her.

"You want one?"

"No thanks. I quit a couple of years ago."

She said, "My last remaining vice, unless you count sex. I don't even drink coffee, on my shrink's orders."

"Well, I drink coffee, but I gave everything else up too. I'm sober seven years."

Celia looked at him. His thick dark hairline burdened his furrowed brow. His handsome face shouldered its slight extra weight comfortably. "Seriously? What was your thing?"

"Booze and opiates, mostly."

"A cokehead and a junkie. What are the odds?"

"Actually, I think it was a factor when they hired me. They asked me to sort of . . . keep an eye on you. Let them know if you seemed like you were using or drinking."

"Who's they?"

"Nobody. Some studio lackey."

"What did they say about fucking me?"

He smiled. "That didn't come up."

She put the cigarette out in the glass. She thought about the drive back to her room at the spa, looking forward to the scenery they'd passed on the way down, if they left before dark. Then she thought about another night alone in that room.

"Can I stay here tonight?"

"If you don't show up at the spa, they're going to wonder. They're going to call me if they can't find you."

"We can think of something."

He nodded.

She said, "You're thinking of your wife."

"I'm not thinking about her, actually. I'm not letting myself go there, not yet. But thanks a lot for bringing it up."

"Sorry."

"You know what she said to me recently?"

Celia shook her head.

"We were talking about Augustus, our baby, growing up, like someday he'll be in high school, someday he'll be in college, someday he'll be a man. And she said, 'What happens to me during all of that?' I asked her what she meant, and she said, 'While he's becoming a man, what am I becoming?' I didn't know what to say. 'All that time,' she said, 'it's *his* time. It belongs to *him*. What about *my* time?' That's what she said."

"It sounds like a fair question to me," Celia said.

"You have a kid. Do you ask yourself questions like that?"

She pondered a moment. "I guess not. But like it or not, I'm given a different set of rules. A lot of my time isn't mine, but it's not Dean who takes it from me. I wish I had more time to give to him. I have different issues, but dread of anonymous stagnation seems not to be one of them. Public stagnation maybe. Is that worse? Who fucking knows. Plus, I've got real work now. I'm becoming Lady Anna at the moment, and that's quite enough for me."

"So," Leo said, "here's what I thought. Aside from the fact that I can't decide for her what or who she should become while our son grows up, it occurred to me the next day that she didn't say *we*. She said *me*. I mean, when two people are married, isn't it a team effort? Shouldn't she see that this question applies to me as much as it does to her? I'm out here chauffeuring people around to put food on the table, and I'm not getting any younger, either."

Celia looked away from him. She noticed a diagonal crack in the drywall and her eyes followed it down to the baseboard. "I'm not qualified to weigh in on that particular discussion."

"Shit, sorry. You don't need me airing my marriage out with you."

"Well, that's actually true. But don't worry about it, I don't mind. Maybe we should head back to the spa."

He seemed relieved. "Okay. You want a shower first or anything?"

"I can shower there."

When they arrived at the spa, however, Celia did not get out of the car. They had spent the ride talking about their respective paths to sobriety, trading war stories at first and then rehab stories. This led somehow naturally to a discussion of relationships, with Leo gingerly exposing more fragments of his strained marriage and Celia speaking about Darren. Leo had the decency and maturity to act as though Darren were just an ex, not digging for the kinds of detail people couldn't help wanting. She realized she had never spoken freely about Darren with anyone except her therapist. After sobering up she'd had to distance herself from many of the friends she used to party with, and none of her friends could discuss Darren normally anyway, even the famous ones. When she brought him up with Frida or Chelsea or Rafe their eyes always narrowed with false earnestness, and their voices deepened warily, masking their hunger for gossip on Darren Styles. They were sympathetic and supportive, but always so careful not to say anything that might stem the flow of information.

"Was it Love, capital L?" Leo had asked her.

Celia was taken aback by the question but found herself answering quickly, in a low involuntary moan, her head nodding along with the chant as she looked out through the arid dusk, "It was it was it was it was. . . ."

"I'm sorry about that. It's a tough thing to lose."

"You know about that? Losing love?"

He smiled. "Not really, no. I'm imagining. There was a girl I was close to in rehab, in a romantic way, who went back out pretty quickly and died of an OD. It was very sad, but I can't say it was true love or anything."

"That is sad. I'm sorry. It's much sadder, really. Darren didn't die."

"Is it really easier, to have him walking around in the world, reminding you, and then marrying someone else?"

She laughed. "I didn't say it was easier. But less sad, for sure."

He nodded. Celia did not ask about his wife, and whether he loved her with a capital L. Strangely, she assumed he did.

When they pulled up in front of her bungalow it was almost full dark, the desert night having risen like vapor from the sand and sage.

"Want to come in?" she asked.

"Might not be a good idea," he said, and she could hear in his voice his powerful desire to do it. She waited, but he did not shut off the engine. She found she wanted to stay in the car with him.

Thinking of the gloomy interior of her empty room, she said, "Will you drive me to Los Angeles?"

"If you want me to, it's my job."

"No, you're not obligated. I won't order you. Leo, will *you* drive me there, to my son, right now? Say no if you'd rather not."

The pause he took before answering was so sweet to her. She became enchanted with the pause, watching his breath deepen, at first staring at her and then turning his gaze out the windshield in contemplation. It didn't matter what he answered, the pause was enough.

"It'll be morning by the time we get there."

"I know. Can you make it that long?"

"I can make it. I'm a machine."

They fell silent again for a moment before he slipped the car into reverse.

DANIEL SKIPPED THE valet parking in front of the gallery and left his Toyota on a side street. He walked through a gas station rounding the corner onto Highland. Down the block, as he neared the white box of the building that housed the gallery, he could see people entering, red-jacketed valets jogging back from the parking lot. Somehow Forest had gotten a show at this upper-echelon spot. Possibly his mother's influence had played a role. Daniel experienced a mild seizure in his chest. He couldn't remember the last time he'd been in an art gallery. When he got close, he could see through the tall front windows into the vaulted white space: a display case, large and stark, filled with slender people in muted hues. His first impression: the work on the walls was big, with scattered daubs of color popping from grayscale backgrounds. He gave his name at the door and entered, and moments later his stress over the press of bodies and the ricocheting hubbub of voices fell away as he stood in front of a huge painting facing the entrance. It seemed at first to be an Impressionistic rendering of a group of bright-robed figures struggling through a sandstorm at night. It took a few seconds for the eye to register that the background was a black-and-white photograph over which paint had been applied—in some places a translucent stormy gray wash through which the images underneath could be made out, and in others thick and in bright colors from which the ghostly figures materialized, echoing and usurping the underlying images. The base picture, what was visible of it, was a bird's-eye view of a crowded party, people with drinks and cigarettes packed into a large living room, furniture all moved back to the walls and a makeshift stage set up, the instruments waiting on stands for the band to return from a break. As he looked at the part of the stage that was visible beneath the paint, he recognized a sculpture of a black helix in the corner, and realized the picture was from inside the house he and Amelia had lived in, the house in Malibu where Forest had spent his childhood. It must have been taken from the second-floor landing that overlooked the room.

All the paintings used the same technique, but they were startlingly various in their coloring and execution. In each one, the painted imagery was haunting and beautiful, set in dreamlike relationship to the black-and-white photograph below. Sometimes the photographs were so heavily painted that they were almost indecipherable, with only a few details showing through, and sometimes only touched here and there with mists and pinpoints of color. The overall effect was of a duality of worlds, permeating and interacting with each other, but not in any simple or fantastical sense. These were not invisible fairies and nymphs, but an acknowledgment, thought Daniel, that in every moment, as we smile and drink and talk and vacation and surf, as we fight and earn and watch each other die, there is human truth, there is merciless beauty and sorrow, there is lonely questing. Daniel was transported with pride and trepidation. The work was executed with such assurance, such depth, that he wanted to cry out at the fact that he did not know his own son.

He saw Forest at the back of the room, being regaled by a group of grand-looking folks. He felt ashen and could not think of how to approach, or what he might say if he did. He went to the bar for a drink, then carried it around and looked again at each of the paintings. He had still not spoken a word to anyone, and he realized that his fears of being recognized were probably grandiose paranoia.

As he stood regarding one of the smaller pieces, Amelia appeared at his shoulder.

"Didn't I tell you?"

"Yes, you did."

"You didn't even listen. I watched it go right through your head without disturbing a single synapse when I told you Forest's work was good."

Daniel paused. She was right. He barely remembered her saying it. "Well, you're his mother."

"Yes. And you are his father."

"Amelia."

"Go and talk to him."

"He's busy. I'll wait."

"If you wait, you won't do it."

"I don't think he likes me much."

She made a quarter turn and faced him directly. "He's not obligated to like you. But tonight, he needs you to talk to him. I know this."

"He said this?"

She gave an exasperated laugh and looked away. "Don't be an idiot."

They both turned back to the painting. It was a photograph of a woman seen from behind, sitting naked on the side of a bed leaning forward, her feet on the floor and her head in her hands. The knobs of her spine formed the centerline of the piece over the swirled bedcovers. Painted sections encroached on both sides like a parted sea closing back in, dark, with waves of red and swarms of blue eel-like presences. Above her head, the two painted sections converged in a splash of white.

"How's Ronald?"

"Ronald is fine. I am fine. Work is fine. The weather is fine. Talk to your son." She walked away.

Daniel steeled himself, turned, and moved toward the corner where he'd seen Forest. But Forest was no longer there, and he wandered around some more, scanning the room. He stopped again in front of the giant painting by the entrance.

"Gorgeous, isn't it?"

Daniel faced the voice and had to drop his gaze when he saw how small the man was. He was thin and silver-haired, impeccable in a black cashmere blazer with a royal-blue pocket square. His head reached only to the middle of Daniel's ribs, and his dark eyes looked up with great stillness.

"Yes, it is," Daniel said, looking back to the painting.

"Daniel Tunison. Am I right?"

Daniel sighed and glanced at the man.

"I was hoping I'd get a chance to speak with you tonight. Charles Foreman." He offered his hand, and Daniel shook it without otherwise responding. This was the man whose name was on the gallery. "I hope you won't mind me saying, I'm an admirer of your work."

"Thank you," Daniel said. "But that's in the past. I'm just a retired schoolteacher."

"And father of another prodigious artist. Your son's work has been something of a revelation for me. I was in danger of forgetting my reasons for being in this business."

"Looks like you've done pretty well on all fronts, in this business," Daniel said, sweeping a hand to indicate the opulent gallery.

"I've been successful, but success has a way of insulating itself, of perpetuating itself to the detriment, really, of all else. This show has rekindled my sense of wonderment."

Daniel nodded.

Foreman continued, "It's the same sort of wonderment I felt when I first stood under *Thorn Tree*. I saw it in the desert, you know. I was one of the early pilgrims. You were still working on it. I was in school, and we heard rumors of a monastic desert artist creating something phenomenal. This was before it was in the guidebooks, even before the piece in *LA Weekly*. We spoke to someone who had met someone who claimed to have been there. We followed secondhand directions, and it took us all day to find it. We actually had decided to head home, thinking it was a hoax, when we saw the miniature windmill we'd been told about. The door to that roofless barn was open and we went in. We respected the sign that said no photos, even though we did have a camera with us. We'd been wandering around under it for maybe half an hour, mouths agape and necks aching from looking up, when you came in. You were carrying a crate, and you were so tall, this bronzed, dusty pillar of sinew with haunted eyes. I fell in love with you immediately. You very politely asked us to go outside. I tried to express my admiration to you, and you just repeated your request that we leave. And so we did."

Daniel smiled. He'd heard versions of this story before, and he never knew what to do with them. People were signifying some sort of connection with him that he did not reciprocate. "I guess I can't do the same now, since you own this place."

Foreman laughed. "I suppose not. I won't disturb you further, just wanted to make myself known to you. If you still make things, I would be honored to see them at any time, by the way, purely as an admirer."

"I don't."

"Ah, well . . ." He nodded, to indicate he knew this already.

"I'm looking for Forest."

"He's taking some respite from the crowd in my office. I can show you to him."

Daniel followed Foreman through the gallery to the rear of the space, impressed by the way he kept a steady pace while silently acknowledging people he knew as he passed them. Daniel felt the perennial fear and excitement of seeing Forest. It was impossible to know whether he would encounter Forest the mellow and friendly, if distant, son, or Forest the burr of resentment, tossing rapid-fire barbs. They went down a short hallway and Foreman opened the door at the end. It was a spacious office with a sitting area on one side where four people were gathered. Forest was on the sofa smoking a cigarette, and next to him was a girl so beautiful that Daniel's eyes caromed almost painfully off her and roamed the room, struggling for composure while tethered to her pale-legged form as if by elastic. She was maybe twenty, and her eyes lazed through empty air around her with practiced detachment. The other two were men Forest's age, with fashionable beards and suit jackets over jeans.

"Hey Pop," Forest said, staying seated.

"Forest, your show is fantastic."

"Glad you like it. Thanks for coming."

"I mean it," Daniel said, feeling the inadequacy of his words. "I love these paintings." He pulled up short of the presumptuousness of saying he was proud. There was an awkward pause.

"Guys, this is my father." The others nodded in silent greeting.

The girl furrowed her brow. "Your father?"

Forest smiled. "It's confusing, I know. I call Ronald Dad, but he's my stepfather, actually. Daniel here is the only person ever to impregnate my mother." Another silence. "Pop, this is Tamara." The girl smiled. "And this is Jeff, and maybe you remember Matty Jones."

The man on the right looked at Daniel, smiling. "Hey Pop."

"Oh my god, Matty." Daniel stepped forward and shook his hand. "How long has it been? You were just a kid last time I saw you."

"Yeah, it's been a while."

Matty was a grade-school friend of Forest's, and the two of them used to spend nights at Daniel's sometimes, in the early days of his res-urrection. There had been a few good years when Forest had received him back openly, but by the time he went to college the connection had been lost. His son's childhood resentment, which he'd set aside in his boyish relief at Daniel's reappearance, had curdled into adult judgment, and Daniel hadn't known what to do but respect Forest's stated wish to be left alone.

Foreman, who had been standing by the door, said, "Forest, I'm heading back out there. The show is bowling everyone over. The word *success* doesn't do it justice. Stay back here as long as you like, and I'll see you at the dinner." He looked at Daniel. "Good to finally meet you, Mr. Tunison."

Daniel nodded. "Likewise."

"You should come to the dinner, Pop," Forest said. "There's room— right, Charles?"

"Absolutely, please come," Foreman said, stepping into the hall and shutting the door behind him.

"Thanks, but I wouldn't want things to be awkward for your mother or Ronald."

"Come on, you have dinner with Mom all the time, and Dad couldn't care less. Nothing disturbs planet Ronald."

"Well, it's not exactly my scene." The only thing Daniel could imag-ine being more averse to than a large art-world gathering was a small art-world gathering.

"Not your scene? It's precisely your scene. You guys might not know, but Pop here was a famous artist in his day."

"Not really famous. And that was a long time ago."

"Charles remembers you. He probably fawned over you out there, didn't he? I think he might have taken me on just for the chance to meet you."

Daniel became flustered. "Not a chance. Your work . . . I mean, Forest, these paintings . . ."

Forest fell quiet, staring.

"They're astonishing," Daniel said.

His son's face released itself into a genuine smile, a total shift. "Thanks, Pop. Thank you. Means a lot."

Daniel's eyes stung. "You really want me at this dinner?"

"Yes, I really do."

"Then I'll come, of course."

1968-1969

Daniel met Rachel Cullen in September of 1968 at a party thrown by some fellow art students. There was a band playing, made up of erstwhile painters. Everyone wanted to be a musician in those days. Music was having its moment; it was the art form most likely to change the world, and even movie stars were prostrating themselves at the feet of rock stars. His first glimpse of her was of the side of her head as she entered the room talking over her shoulder to the person behind her. Her wavy auburn hair fell to her ribs, and she wore cutoff jeans and leather sandals. Her tan legs held his eyes for a moment, and then she turned into the room laughing and her face sliced a clean gash in his chest. It wasn't some generic hormonal reaction to beauty. She was beautiful, but her beauty was not extreme. It was something about her particular features, about the person who inhabited them. He came to believe for a long time afterward that they'd known each other in past lives, that he'd recognized her instantly. Now he was less sure of that, as he was of everything.

He didn't speak to her for a couple of hours, but he traced her whereabouts as the party progressed, watching her through doorways and across rooms. Whenever he'd lose track of her, he would take a spin around the party to make sure she hadn't left, but he couldn't bring himself to just walk up and say something.

Then, when he was standing at the back of the living room as the band finished a set, she sat down on the sofa near him, by herself. The small sofa was roofed by a bunk bed that arched over it, the lower bunk removed. She was only three steps away, and unoccupied, so he gathered himself and walked over.

"How do you like the band?" he asked, leaning over to talk under the bed.

"Not bad," she said, giving him a smile as if they were picking up the thread of a previous conversation. "The drummer especially." A girl sat down on her other side, taking the seat that Daniel had been eyeing.

"Yeah. He's great. He's a friend of mine." Daniel felt stupid, but he blundered on. "My name's Daniel."

"Rachel," she said. She stood up to talk more directly. She regarded him seriously, neither trying to impress nor rebuff him, and this stilled his uneasiness. Through the set break, they leaned with cans of beer against the ladder of the bunk bed. Her gaze didn't shy from his, and their conversation became an eye of calm in the escalating chaos of the party. When the band started playing again, they had to lean close in order to hear each other, and when the music got especially loud she would let her cheek touch his as she spoke into his ear. It would have made sense to suggest moving to a quieter place, but Daniel liked the way they were pressed close by the noise and the dancers.

They talked of mundane things, the stuff of any first meeting, but moments of eye contact and brushes of skin and small smiles began to organize themselves into a second, deeper conversation that ran parallel, in which they gradually acknowledged mutual attraction. A vein of bright irony shone through her tone, communicating cheerful disdain for the niceties they were observing. Daniel tried to mirror it back to her when he answered her questions, but was unsure whether he was succeeding. She asked him about where he was from and what his family was like, and he told her the facts without embellishment: upstate New York, his parents both college professors—his father an engineer and his mother chair of the History Department.

He left out his brother, Eugene, who had been killed in the war only six months earlier. This was not a tactic; he simply didn't yet know how to talk about it. Gene had enlisted in part as an act of rebellion, a break with their parents. Gene had died a hero, with posthumous medals and letters testifying to his bravery from his comrades and commanding officer, but their mother had prevented any military honors and symbols from being part of his funeral.

"What about you?" Daniel asked, and Rachel shrugged.

She gave him her serious stare again for a moment, letting her long hair frame her eyes. The matter-of-fact intelligence in her expression, absent any challenge, was something new to him, having grown up around people who wielded their brilliance like nunchucks. "What about me?"

"I mean, where are you from?"

"Nowhere," she said.

"Sounds interesting. What's it like there?"

She smiled. "Well, it's almost exactly like Tucson, Arizona. You have any siblings?"

Daniel looked away as the band introduced a guest guitarist. "Older brother," he said, before turning back to her. "You have any?" But the band had launched into a loud fuzzed blues and she shook her head in the din.

"What?"

He leaned close to her ear, his skin touching hers for exactly the fifth time, but the first time initiated by him, and repeated the question. She didn't speak. She turned her head and kissed the spot where their cheeks had touched. It was the same spot where anyone might kiss him platonically hello or goodbye, but she left her lips on him for a moment, and the lingering made him suddenly hard. He felt coolness on his skin as she inhaled through her nose. She slid her lips to his ear and said, "Want to take a walk?"

They walked east, away from the ocean, through small residential streets and then along the main Venice canal, crossing it on an arched white footbridge, and Daniel fell in love. He'd been in California for a year, but it still held that mythic quality some Easterners imbue it with. The silhouette of a palm tree against the night sky, edge-dusted with moonlight, was all it took to douse his mind in a wash of magic. Dropping his gaze and seeing that same moonlight on scattered trash and rolls of discarded wire fencing did not diminish the effect, and when he brought his eyes back to see it play off Rachel's brown shoulder and the faded red pattern of her tank top, he was utterly gone. But with her it wasn't magic, he realized as they walked and kept talking. It was something simpler about her that drew him in. She managed to seem unbound by conventionality without needing to put on bohemian airs. She spoke directly to him, and her voice was free of the false breathlessness so pervasive among his crowd.

Daniel, in contrast, was barely able to rein in his own very real breathlessness. His lungs felt filled with helium. A part of his brain could do nothing but run the memory of her kissing him at the party over and over. Walking next to her felt both ecstatic and torturous. She sounded completely calm and centered, and seemed not to be suffering the same torment he was: seeing her hand swinging at her side and wanting to take it in his, seeing the shallow curve of her narrow neck and wanting to trace it with his lips, battling heroically to keep these thoughts on the romantic side of the berm that separated them from indecency—because there was more he wanted, and he was afraid his vibe would drive her off if he allowed himself to imagine sliding his hand up her leg and inside the bottom of her shorts and . . . *Stop*. He wanted to keep his thoughts respectful, even if they weren't completely in his control. Finally, he overcame his cowardice and, as she was in the middle of talking about a class in American poetry she was looking forward to, he took her hand. She stopped walking, fell immediately silent, and turned toward him, as if the contact had flipped a switch. She still radiated calm as she smiled and took a small step, covering half the distance between them. But when he kissed her he felt his own feral hunger equaled in her suddenly writhing body. There was no series of pecks leading them into that first kiss, just a smooth fury that overtook them both, a slow, wide-mouthed welcoming, more like a reunion than an introduction.

The initial rush of the kiss swept Daniel up and emptied his mind, but the thing that struck him as he regained the power of thought—still kissing her—was that he wasn't crazy. This thing, whatever it was, was happening. The thoughts he'd been shoving aside since they'd started walking, to protect himself from foolishness and fantasy, had not been foolish after all. He could feel it.

What if you're still being foolish? a jaded voice whispered. *What if she's just some fast girl who hates spending the night alone?* He pulled his head back to study her, breaking the spell for a moment. What he saw was a face filled with a question. He smiled to reassure her, and formulated his own question, because he felt he had to know. They stared at each other while he gathered his courage. All his insecurity seemed freighted in the question, and asking it felt like a wild and ill-advised exposure. If she scoffed or balked . . .

"Is this real?"

They were still embracing, their pelvises touching but their shoulders and heads apart. She stood contemplating, maybe deciding whether he was really asking what he seemed to be asking. After a moment she pursed her lips and inhaled deeply. "I sure hope so." Her face released into a smile and she kissed him again.

THEY GREW CLOSER through the fall and winter, but the California spring became their season. It was nothing like the northeastern spring Daniel knew. There was no snowmelt, no thawing brown yards turning green, no burgeoning of leaves in the forests giving fuller voice to the wind. Spring in LA was subtler, but it was theirs. Everything, in fact, was theirs. Daniel had always figured that when people fell in love they retreated into a smaller world all their own, but he and Rachel, in their ongoing exploration of each other, expanded, gaining a mysterious kind of ownership over everything. Only other people were excluded. The sidewalks and streets and highways, the walkways through the lawns and quadrangles on campus, the halls and stairways in their dorms, all seemed perfectly laid out to carry them to the places they needed to go together, and more importantly to guide them back to each other smoothly and quickly whenever they'd been forced apart. The city was theirs, the coffee shops where they ate and the tables they ate at were theirs, the wind that hit them when they opened the door of the coffee shop and stepped outside was theirs, sweetly whipping Rachel's hair for Daniel. This ownership had no whiff of commodity to it, and extended to items of property. Daniel's car, a seven-year-old brown Ford Fairlane, became theirs, just another part of their vast communal world. The clothes on Daniel's body were now theirs, not his, and when

Rachel hooked a finger into the belt loop of his jeans she had perfect sovereignty over every stitch in them, as did he when he slid her shirt up her waist. Their bodies, even, maybe especially.

This fusion of lives and worlds and bodies, this joint dominion, happened spontaneously, independent of the much slower process through which they began to know each other. So for a time, it was confusing for Daniel to be so inextricably linked to a person he didn't really know. As they grew closer, he began to see that her foundation of calm engagement was actually a barrier that shielded a shifting and secret province whose substance he couldn't discern. The barrier was thick and intricate, but there were fissures in it that caught the light occasionally. In those moments she seemed, unaccountably, on the verge of something drastic, like screaming or lashing out or maybe just walking away from him. But she never did. She would squeeze him and hide her face from him, and when it reappeared she'd be smiling. There was a gloom that descended on her sometimes after they made love, which she would not talk about with him. She allowed him to see it, shared morsels of it with him through her eyes, but quietly shook her head when he tried to ask what was wrong. She would roll away, pulling his arm over her, and breathe deeply. Then, after a minute, she would light a cigarette and sit up and flip the record on the turntable over. Daniel didn't press because he knew they had forever.

The school year ended in May and the bookstore cut back to summer staff, which meant he was out of a job. He and Rachel moved into a tiny room together in a house in Venice, where the scene of artists and students to which they'd become attached was centered. It was cheap, but he was almost completely broke, and she took the last of her money out of the bank to pay up front for the whole summer.

"That way, we'll be free," she said. "We at least won't have to worry about a roof over our heads."

The house had three other residents. Phil and Stephen were students, wild-haired lit majors slowly pursuing degrees to avoid the draft. The other, and de facto house leader, was Neil Tallman, known to most as Tall Man, though he was not as tall as Daniel. Tall Man styled himself a free-spirit surfer and lay shaman, dispensing earthy, profanity-strewn wisdom to his mostly younger acolytes. He was a drug dealer by trade, though he would have bristled at the title. He thought of drugs as a minor side gig that paid for his free-spirit life. He was not someone who always had drugs and customers around, but he knew people who were plugged into pot and pill pipelines, and when someone wanted to buy a large amount of something, he would procure it for them at a markup. Though he was a surfer, he seemed not to have any surfing friends. It was something he did alone, a kind of sacrament that he never defiled by discussing it or sharing it with anyone. He had an old pickup in the driveway that he took to the beach most mornings.

Daniel and Rachel spent the first couple of weeks there mostly holed up in their room, making love and talking. Rachel was taking two summer classes, so when she was away at campus Daniel looked for part-time work. The idea of a full-time job, which would take him away from her five days a week, was unthinkable. When he wasn't job hunting, he sat around with Phil and Stephen, smoking pot and talking about music and Russian literature. During one such afternoon, Tall Man came out from the back of the house, where he inhabited the master bedroom. He didn't generally hang in the living room unless there was company or a party. His bedroom had its own bathroom and was located at the end of a long hall behind the kitchen, so his world was complete in those three spaces. He and his customers often came and went through the back door, unseen by Daniel and the others.

"Boys, what's the grass situation?" Tall Man said, standing under the hallway transom. He wore only his Fruit-of-the-Looms and an open linen shirt that looked Moroccan. His flat stomach was tan, and his legs were thickly muscled. His looks were a definite part of his mystique—long sun-bleached hair a few shades lighter than the beard that augmented his rough-hewn features—as was the fact that he spent most of his time alone despite those looks. Occasionally the morning after a party a woman would emerge from his room, but never the same one twice.

Phil pointed at the coffee table. "Those two roaches are the entire situation."

Tall Man walked over and stooped to the table, plucking one of the roaches from its groove in the ashtray. "Shit," he said. He picked up a lighter and sparked it, drew a few puffs until it endangered his fingers, and stubbed it out again. "We'll have some more by tomorrow. You boys got any cash to kick in?"

They all shook their heads.

"I'm still looking for work," Daniel said.

"I'm not worried about you, Danny. You and your queen are paid up on rent at least. These two fuckers are behind." His tone was fond, but he looked at Stephen squarely.

"Just a temporary lapse in cash flow, Tall," Stephen said. "We'll have it for you soon."

"I don't give a fuck about what you *will* do. Don't you know tomorrow never happens? Talk to me when my palm is green."

"Yes, will do. I mean . . . okay."

"Daniel," Tall Man said, "will you come back to my room for a minute? I want to ask you something of a private nature."

"Sure." Daniel stood. He'd never been into Tall Man's bedroom before.

The room was strung with red Christmas lights, but they were not lit. An Indian tapestry hung over the rear window in place of a curtain, and a corner of it had been pulled up and tucked over the top to let daylight in. There was no dresser, but a small sitting area with a table, an old love seat, and a chair. The room was much neater than Daniel had expected. A bedside table held a small shelf of books and a statue of Buddha. Tall Man sat in the chair and motioned toward the love seat. Daniel sat.

"You and Rachel liking it here?" Tall Man leaned forward over his knees, which brought his face into the shaft of light from the window. He had tough, almost-handsome features that were made striking by their canny inhabitant and their attachment to an extremely beautiful body.

"Yeah, it's great."

He nodded. "Good. You guys are a pair of good ghosts. You bring the vibe here up. It's good to have you." Tall Man sometimes referred to people as ghosts. The term he used more often was "bad ghost," meaning someone he didn't like or was suspicious of. "How's your job hunt going?"

"Well, haven't found anything yet. Anything I want, that is."

"It's important not to do something you hate, if you can avoid it. I might have something for you. Something you could do for me that would be worth some money. Also, it'll be good for the whole scene. People will thank you."

Daniel sat silent for a moment. It was exciting to be receiving a business proposition from Tall Man. "What is it?"

"Okay, so. I need to go up to San Francisco and trade one thing for another thing and then bring it back. The thing is, and please keep this to yourself, I'm on parole. So a road trip with weight would be a big risk for me. I'm careful whenever I do stuff here—I never have anything big in my possession for more than a few hours. Now, the drive is probably not a huge deal, you know, just observe traffic laws and don't be stupid, but even so I can't see risking that big a chunk of time. For you, nice college kid with no record, it's less of a thing. Not saying it isn't still a risk, of course. Which is why I'd remunerate you pretty sweetly. You could spend the rest of the summer balling and partying, no more worries."

Daniel thought for a moment. "What exactly are we talking about here?"

"I've got a line on some Owsley acid"—his face broke into a reverent smile and he rolled his eyes toward heaven, laughing softly—"fucking holy grail shit, my friend. Make the shit going around here seem like kiddie vitamins. But these people I'm talking to, they don't want money for some fucking reason, they want grass, a lot of it. Actually that's a good thing, because I can get grass fronted easier than cash. So I've got to get some weight to them by next week and they'll lay the shit on me. Enough to keep all of Venice flying all summer."

"Wow," Daniel said. "I haven't even tried acid yet."

"Wait till we get the Owsley. Do it up right."

"So, I'd be driving up to the Bay with a car full of grass, and back with a car full of acid?"

"Yeah, but the great thing is that the acid is in liquid form and takes up no space at all. You can have it in a couple of rubbing alcohol bottles in the trunk or whatever, and even if you got pulled over they wouldn't know what they were looking at."

Daniel's heart was surging. "I'm going to have to think about this before I answer."

"Yeah, of course. I'm asking you because I know people, I'm one people-knowing motherfucker, and I know you're someone I can trust, someone who can handle himself with seriousness. Those two loveable fucks out there, I wouldn't put this in their hands. You dig? But don't say anything to them, or anyone. This is top secret at this point."

"I'll need to talk to Rachel, I think. I can't have a secret from her. We're not like that."

Tall Man nodded quickly and flapped his hand. "Of course. Rachel's cool as rain. She does not worry me. But no one else."

"Absolutely. I get it." Daniel sat nodding, and a long moment passed in silence.

Then Tall Man grinned, his big mouth and perfect teeth taking over the bushy lower half of his face. "I love this about you, man."

"Love what?"

"You're about to get up and walk out of here."

"I mean, not necessarily, if there's something else."

Tall Man laughed. "Something else? I love it!" His eyes were bright, and Daniel grew apprehensive, thinking he might have offended him somehow. "You can't think of what else we might have to discuss, can you?"

"I guess there's a lot, but first I need to decide if I'll do it, right?"

"Yeah, brother, that's the truth." He calmed and looked directly at Daniel. "The thing I love about you is that you have not asked what your end is. It's not even something you need to know to help you make your decision. That tells me two things. One, that this trip would not be about the money for you—which is a good policy for life in general. And two, that you've already decided, whether you know it or not. I don't know what that decision is, but you've already made it."

"Well, I just assumed whatever my end was would be fair."

"And it will be." He reached forward, put his hand on Daniel's knee, like a parent with a child. "Go." He waved his other hand. "Talk to Rachel. Let me know by tomorrow."

Daniel went down the long hall to the living room, and saw through the front window that the Ford was parked at the curb, which meant Rachel was back. He stepped into the shorter second hallway and opened their bedroom door. She was sitting on a steamer trunk by the window looking out onto the alley at the side of the house. She didn't turn, but she'd heard him enter. Daniel took in the soft drape of her hair down her back and the slight impression her cutoffs made across her thigh in the sunlight. One bare foot was drawn up onto the trunk so she could sit sideways.

"Hey," Daniel said.

"Come look at this cat," she said. "She's beautiful." She spun her head and smiled over her shoulder and her joy at seeing him was so natural that it registered as a quality of her being rather than a reaction to his arrival. As Daniel walked to her, she turned back to look out the window. He perched behind her and sunk his face into the crook of her neck and breathed, smiling, into her warm skin. "See," she said. "She's so serene and regal, like queen of the urban jungle."

"Uh-huh." Daniel didn't raise his face, preferring her skin to the cat. "I might have found a job," he said.

THEY LEFT AT sunrise two days later, and took the inland route, figuring the less time on the road the better with two duffel bags of pot in the trunk of the Fairlane. She wouldn't even entertain the idea of him going alone. Tall Man said it was good; a couple would be less suspicious to a cop. Daniel had cut his hair short, and Rachel dressed like a sorority maiden and wore a makeshift engagement ring. They took Highway 99 through Bakersfield and Fresno, made a left at Stockton, and crossed the Bay Bridge into San Francisco from Oakland. Tall Man had made Daniel memorize the route from the bridge to the house where they were to meet a man named Ron Ron, someone Tall Man had been in prison with. "A good cat," Tall Man had said. "Not a violent cell in his body, so don't worry about the prison thing. If it hadn't been for me and a couple others, Ron Ron would never have survived that place."

The house was a small cube, and had an empty concrete parking spot paved into its tiny dirt yard. Daniel pulled into the spot. The place looked uninhabited, with broken gutters sagging from the eaves and no light showing through the gaps in the blinds. Rachel waited in the car while he went and knocked on the screen door.

The door behind it opened and a stunned face appeared there, shaded by the screen, a skinny dude whose mid-length blond hair showed no signs of care and whose eyes bulged as if in mortal fear. When he spoke, though, his voice was steady and it was clear he was merely possessed of fearful features.

"Hey there. What can I do for you?"

"I'm looking for Ron Ron."

"He's not here. What can *he* do for you?"

"He's expecting me, I believe. I came up from LA."

The guy paused, staring, and then his eyes, impossibly, widened. "You Danny?"

"Daniel, yes."

"Neil's friend?"

"Yes, right."

"I'm Ron Ron. Shit. I didn't know if you were coming. You want to come in?"

"My girlfriend is in the car, I'll get her."

Ron Ron glanced over his shoulder into the dimmed room behind him. "Never mind, we're not staying." His voice dropped. "You have shit *with* you?"

Daniel nodded, eyeing Ron Ron for signs of major intoxication. It was hard to tell with a face like that.

"Okay, fuck. Just wait in the car. I'll get my stuff and we can drive out."

"Drive out where?"

"North. Out to where the people are. The people we're meeting."

Daniel walked back to the car.

They drove through the city and across the Golden Gate, while Ron Ron expounded on their destination.

"The ranch is incredible," he said. "I stay out there sometimes myself, but my old lady doesn't want to bring the kid there, so we're staying in town. I don't know what her problem with it is. There's other kids there. But she's hung up or something. It's like, this *scene,* man. The people there are bringing themselves back in tune with nature, the land, a real community. Not a fucking *commune,* man, nothing like that. It's absolutely free, not some creepy place with council meetings and shit, I've seen one of those, not fun. This is true freedom, no rules, no regrets, no hang-ups." His voice, during this speech, became sweet and soft, and Daniel could see him in the mirror smiling out his window like a contented child, his pasty skin gone ruddy with fervor.

"And these are the people who have the acid?"

"Yeah. Well, like one of them is tight with Bear's guy, and he keeps them supplied."

"Who's the Bear?"

Ron Ron looked at Daniel in the mirror. "Owsley, man."

"Oh. I wasn't sure Owsley was even a person."

"The thing is they don't ever sell the stuff. They don't believe in exchanging money for it; they think it, you know, sullies the trip with the national karma, which is not too clean currently."

"And that's why we've got a trunk full of weed."

"Right on."

After Ron Ron's description, Daniel had pictured some bucolic utopia, hippies on horseback raising sheep, but when they arrived it was just a small clapboard house on a large piece of property. There were no outbuildings but there was a cluster of tents and lean-tos off to the left, under a giant oak with a diagonal white scar across its middle, an old healed lightning strike that had made the tree list sideways, swooning toward the house. There were people here and there, some sitting on the ground by the tents. A guy rounded the corner of the house and entered through the front door, which stood fully open. None of them seemed interested in the Ford bouncing downhill toward them on the curving dirt drive. Two old cars and a van were parked in haphazard configuration on the right side, and Daniel pulled in behind them.

Daniel and Rachel followed Ron Ron up to the house and through the doorway. The interior was sparsely furnished and messy, with clothing and blankets strewn throughout the living room. Through a doorway they could see a guy with his back to them, doing dishes at the kitchen sink. A barefoot girl in a long blue cotton skirt and loose black T-shirt came out of a side room and gave them a beaming smile as she passed and went outside. Ron Ron made a right down a short hallway. They passed the bathroom and he knocked on a door at the end. When there was no answer he knocked again, more loudly. He tried the knob, but the door evidently was locked.

"Wouldn't expect a locked door in a place like this," Rachel said.

"I told you," said Ron Ron, "it ain't no commune, just a scene. That's Cam's room. He owns the place, and he's the one knows Bear's people."

As they reentered the living room, a bearded guy came through the front door. He wore a threadbare gold-button navy blazer with no shirt underneath, and gym shorts. He smiled. "What's up, brother?" he said to Ron Ron.

"Hey my man. Is Cam around?"

He placed his hands in the side pockets of his blazer and looked thoughtful for a moment, like a man on the veranda of his country club who's just realized he forgot his pipe. "I don't think so. He's still up north."

"Aw fuck. Like, when's he coming back? These guys need to talk to him."

"Okay. Who do we have here?"

"I'm Daniel, and this is Rachel."

The guy extended a long arm, the jacket's sleeve riding up to the middle of his brown forearm. "Hey there, my name's Win." When Daniel shook his hand, he found himself pulled into a tight embrace. Then Win let him go and hugged Rachel. "Really good to have you guys here. First time at the ranch?"

"Yeah. We just came up from LA."

"That's amazing. You know Cam from down there?"

"We've never met him."

"They're here on a transactional basis," Ron Ron said. "Dig?"

"Okay, right, I hear you."

"So when's Cam gonna be back?"

"He'll be back by tonight for sure. He wouldn't miss tonight."

"What's tonight?" Daniel asked.

Win raised his eyebrows and stared at him. "What's tonight? You serious? The Dead are playing the Fillmore!"

"Oh." Daniel nodded.

This sent Win into a whooping peal of laughter. "*Oh!*" He screwed his face into a mask of comic seriousness, stiffening his neck—"Oh"— and then he broke out laughing again. "*Oh* is right! *Oh,* you guys got here on the right fucking night. Wow, are you in for it!"

Daniel smiled. "That sounds great, but we're here just for a short time. We need to do our thing and get back to LA."

"Nonsense. My friends"—Win placed a hand on Daniel's shoulder and one on Rachel's—"you did not come here by coincidence. You did not come all this way, chancing to arrive on this very day, to not go to the center of the blessed goddamn universe with us. I won't hear of it. You're here, you're coming. End of story."

Daniel looked at Rachel, and she shrugged and smiled. They followed Win outside to the tents and sat down on the grass with the others. They were given fried rice cooked over a firepit, joints made the rounds, and the afternoon proceeded toward twilight. The ranch, which had seemed so dingy and disappointing when they first pulled in, did begin to reveal a kind of enchantment. The people there had clearly knitted themselves into a tribe. Their smiles were ready and immediate, and there was little of the ego-posturing that permeated the scene in Venice. They drifted among each other under that swooning tree and the sudden cobalt of the early evening sky: thick-maned men in jeans and beads, willowy women shorn of inhibition, whispering through the grass, all touching each other easily, draping themselves over each other on the warm earth.

Farther down the hill, where another flat area bordered the forest,

there was a second group of tents with its own firepit. The people moving among those tents were all dressed in gauzy white, and the women
wore white scarves on their heads. At one point Daniel saw them gather
cross-legged into a circle and hold hands.

"What's going on down there?" he asked Win. "Are they part of your
group too?"

"Yes and no," Win said. "That's Hugo and his people. He showed
up here a couple of months ago with three others, and some of the
people here have joined them. They used to mingle but they've started
keeping to themselves, which creates a weird vibe. People are saying it
might be time for them to move on, but far as I'm concerned they're not
hurting anyone."

"Is he, like, a guru or something?"

"He's got a lot of ideas. I've talked to him quite a bit, but his movie
doesn't do it for me. It's very detailed, but somehow manages to be vague
also. Something to do with learning to manage your future reincarna-
tions. I don't know, everyone's got their own trip these days, and if it
makes them happy then why not. They're doing all their stuff separately
though, which they didn't used to. They're even tripping separately, in
some kind of controlled or structured way. You won't see them coming
to the show tonight. Go on down there if you're interested. Hugo is
happy to talk to anyone who wants to listen."

"I'll skip it," Daniel said. "I don't look good in white."

The thing that enchanted Daniel most about that afternoon was
not the ranch itself, or the people there, but the effect the place seemed
to have on Rachel. Some essential tension drained out of her, and her
limbs began to move smoothly, lither and slower even in tiny actions like
pushing hair behind her ear or brushing a leaf from her skirt. Her face,
which normally projected that calm which Daniel had come to understand was a layer of protection, took on a truer calmness. He knew that
whatever mysterious province she was protecting was still there, but in
that place it lost its power. They reclined on the grass and she laid her
head against his breastbone after they finished eating and smoking. A
jet sketched its contrail slowly onto the sky over them, and when Daniel
started to speak Rachel said, "Shh, I'm listening to your heart." After

a moment she lifted her head and propped herself up, looking down into his face. Her hair curtained them from the hillside, and her eyes gazed into his. A single heavy drop landed on his cheek, and then with no sound or change in her expression, just tears flowing out of her, she was crying. Daniel was about to ask what was wrong and she kissed him to stop him, then pulled back and looked at him again. She seemed to be searching him. They had been madly exploring each other for eight months, discovering great tracts of new territory together and planting the flag of their love across all of them, but this was something different. This was a moment of interrogation. This was an unfamiliar, embryonic trust, dawning in her and needing to assess his worthiness. He held her eyes. She nodded once, seriously, as if an agreement had been reached, then laid her head back on his chest.

The scene there made the world of strife seem very far away, though of course it was not. There was a young man named Fritz in an oxford shirt whose head was bandaged, a seeming newcomer. Faded yellow bruising trickled down out of the bandage and across the left side of his face. He'd been beaten by police at a protest in Berkeley. He was attached to a blond girl in a yellow African shirt, a resident of the ranch, who lay with her head in his lap. He got into what passed for a debate with Win and a couple of other residents, over whether there was any real importance to concerts and events like the one coming up that night.

"It's all well and good," Fritz said, "to turn on and drop out. But how far out? Look across the Bay. There are fucking troops in the streets. They're killing people. America is under attack from within, from the top. We can't sit back and do nothing."

"You forgot the middle part," said Win. "The most important part. Tune in. Once you're tuned in, to the true present reality, to the universal trip, you're in a position to change the world from *within*."

"Tell that to James Rector. Tell that to his family."

"Listen, my friend," Win said, "I'm not denigrating your efforts, am I? I'm not saying you're not doing important stuff. I have nothing but respect for all of you over there. Some of the people here were there on bloody Thursday with you, and most of us were at the big protest last week. We get it. But what we're doing is powerful too. Don't dismiss our movie because your own seems so important. That's myopia. That's contempt prior to investigation, a big no-no for the rational man, right? Once you turn on with us tonight, and hit the show, then at least you'll know what it's all about. Talk to me tomorrow."

Fritz smiled. "Don't get me wrong. I'm totally open, and I've got nothing against fun. I need a little break from all that terrible craziness over there."

"Time for some good craziness!" Win said. "Shhh . . ." He stood and held his hands out for quiet, lifting his head toward the top of the rise as if scenting something on the air. "He's here."

A moment later, headlights topped the hill and an old green pickup grumbled down the driveway in the early dusk. It pulled to a stop with a honk of brakes in front of the house, and a man with close-cropped brown hair got out. He was tall, clean-shaven, dressed in a plain white T-shirt and blue jeans. He stretched his body full-length toward the sky, clasping his hands above his head, then leaned in and pulled a canvas rucksack from the cab. He waved a greeting at the people on the hill and walked into the house.

"Can you tell him these guys are here," Ron Ron said to Win. "Maybe we should go in and talk to him."

"Keep your shirt on," Win said. "He just got home, let him settle in. He'll be out when he's ready."

It was half an hour before the man reappeared from the house, his hair wet from a shower and a blue crew-neck sweatshirt on against the cooling air. He sauntered over to the group. Everyone seemed to be watching him, but he affected nonchalance and said, "Howdy people," as he sat near Win in the grass. He was a little older than most of the others, past thirty, but he still had the rangy body of a teenager. His face was long and tanned.

"Cam," said Win, "this is Rachel and Daniel. Ron Ron brought 'em out."

"Hey," Cam said. He nodded and made eye contact first with Daniel, then with Rachel. "Welcome."

"You remember I told you a while back I knew a guy in LA?" Ron Ron said. "These are his people."

"Well, I hope they're their own people," Cam said.

"I mean, you know, they're representing him."

"Who's this guy again?"

"My friend, who wanted to do that exchange. We talked about it."

Cam nodded, but it was unclear whether he recalled the conversation. "You guys coming to the show with us tonight?" he asked Daniel.

Daniel smiled. "Win hasn't given us much of a choice."

"You won't be sorry. People, it's time to start heading in town. How about it?"

Murmurs of assent from the group, and they began standing, reaching into tents for jackets, pulling on shoes.

"You guys want to come inside for a minute?" Cam said.

Daniel, Rachel, Ron Ron, and Win followed him into the house and down the hall to his bedroom. Win shut the door behind them and Cam picked up a fatigue jacket and the rucksack. "So what's the deal here? You guys are here to trade weed for vitamins, right?"

"Yeah," Ron Ron said. "You remember. We talked about it last month."

"Yes," Cam said. "I remember the conversation. But at the time it seemed hypothetical. The amounts we discussed could take a while to come by. A day or two at least, maybe more."

"When can you let us know the time frame?" Daniel asked.

Cam sighed and looked at the ceiling. He seemed put-upon by the prospect of the deal. "I can try to talk to my guy tonight. Might have an idea by tomorrow."

"We can wait that long, but I'd have to check with my friend to see if longer would be an issue."

"Come to the show tonight, we'll have us a time. Forget the rest till tomorrow." He was rummaging in his bag, and he pulled out a small mason jar with two inches of clear liquid in it. "We've got all we need right here."

"One thing," Daniel said. "We've . . ." He hesitated. "We've got a trunk full of stuff that doesn't belong to me, and I don't want it sitting around on the street or wherever. I'm responsible for it. I need to keep it safe."

Cam opened the jar and touched the tip of his finger to the surface of the liquid, then sucked it. "Bring it in here. We'll lock the door. It'll be safe." He held the jar toward Win.

Win shook his head. "I like to go closer to showtime, so I come up during the first set." He looked at Daniel and Rachel. "You guys first timers?"

Daniel nodded.

"Halle-fucking-lujah. Stick with me, I'll make sure you don't get lost."

"Win is the best guide around," Cam said. "Follow his lead."

When they stepped out the front door onto the porch, Daniel's eyes lifted from the weathered planks in front of the transom, and Rachel was there ahead of him, stopped at the porch's edge facing the grassy hill above which light still paled the western sky enough to obscure the stars. Her hair and the reddish cotton fabric of her skirt rippled together in the breeze, and seeing this, with the green hillside beyond and the tribe of hippies trailing across toward the vehicles, Daniel experienced a moment of wholeness. This was not the hermetic wholeness their relationship had so far produced in him, which excluded others, but something bigger, something utterly tranquil that encompassed all souls and the world.

Past Rachel's shoulder he saw a shirtless, shaggy, mantis-like guy loping toward them on legs so long and skinny they seemed in danger of breaking or collapsing with every step, though he moved easily. He carried a leather bag and his musing eyes were raised to the darker eastern sky above the house, behind Daniel. He crossed in front of the porch and vaulted into the back of the pickup truck where three others already sat. The evening flashed with group laughter. Rachel turned and saw Daniel standing behind her, and her smile joined in.

Daniel opened the trunk of his car. He and Cam pulled out the two brown duffels and carried them inside. Tall Man had done such a good job sealing the pot in plastic that the smell was virtually undetectable. When they got into Cam's room, Cam pushed the bag he was carrying under the bed with his foot. Daniel set his down on the floor.

"Is that a safe spot for them?" he asked.

"Safe as any, I guess." Cam used his foot to shove the second bag under the bed with its partner.

"No offense," Daniel said, "but I'm uneasy about this."

"Understandable. I don't know what to tell you. I think they're safe here. No one knows why you're here except Win and Ron Ron. Win I trust with my life. Ron Ron, I don't know him that well. He comes around now and then but he's not really with us."

"My friend who sent me says he's trustworthy."

"Well, that's your business, I guess. We've never had any issues of that kind, with anyone here. Even if they knew this shit was here they wouldn't take it."

"But you keep your door locked when you're not here."

"Hey man, it's a fucking zoo around here. That's just a reminder to people to respect my space. I have some prerogatives as the owner of this joint, and one of them is to have my own private space. Nobody here would ever steal anything from me, but they might want to fuck on a bed instead of a sleeping bag, and I'm a little particular about that kind of thing."

Daniel stood thinking. It felt like a mistake to leave the stuff unattended in a stranger's house.

"Listen," Cam said, "you want to stand guard over it the whole time you're here, that's fine, be my guest. But this train is leaving the station now. I'm heading into town for the show, and I'll be high in half an hour, so come or don't come, up to you." He held up the key and headed for the door.

"Okay, I'm coming," Daniel said, stepping into the hall.

Cam smiled as he spun the lock on the bedroom door. He glanced at Daniel. "You've chosen well, my son."

WIN RODE INTO town with Daniel and Rachel, squeezed into the back seat with Fritz and his girlfriend, Sarah. When they parked near the Fillmore he pulled the mason jar from a satchel he carried. "Ready ignition," he said, uncapping it.

Daniel observed the care with which Sarah dipped her finger into the liquid, only touching the tip to the surface. Then when Fritz dipped she admonished him to be careful. Win held the jar out over the front seat. Daniel looked at Rachel. She seemed excited, but he felt a knot of apprehension in his stomach. "This can be pretty serious business, I've heard," he said.

"We're serious people," she said. "We can handle it."

Win leaned forward over the back of the seat, so his face was between them. "Momentous, yes. Serious, no. At least not in some archaic, boxed-in way. When a man is freed from a prison cell and sees the sky for the first time in his life, that's serious, in many ways. But it's cause for celebration too. This is adventure, that's all. It's discovery." His eyes flashed first at Daniel and then at Rachel, and he dipped the whole tip of his index finger into the liquid and put it into his mouth. "I'll be there with you," he said. "I won't abandon you. This is what I do, I'm a guide."

Daniel dipped just the upper pad of his finger and sucked on it, and Rachel did the same. They got out of the car and walked to the venue. Win pointed at the four of them when they were at the front, and the guy manning the door waved them in.

Daniel had never been much of a drug taker. Even in the current cultural zeitgeist, he did not feel drawn to it. He had smoked enough pot in his life to have had some mild extra-corporeal experiences, that sense of the bindings between mind and body slackening. He expected LSD to be some amplified version of that, but when it began to take hold, it was something else entirely. The initial sensation arose out of unmapped territory, and would in itself have been sufficient to qualify as a revelation: Everything—people, walls, clothing, air—seemed lit softly from within. The psychic region generating this sudden new perspective was unfamiliar, but not alien; it was identifiable as a natural part of himself, as if he'd been walking around with one eye closed and was only now experiencing depth perception. Some of the faces he looked at, as they stood watching the crowd shift and pulse around them in the venue's lobby, were open and cognizant, residing securely in the deeper perspective he was just discovering, but many wore the rigid expressions of the still-blinkered. He felt a fond condescension toward these, having so recently been one of them. A thought suddenly worried him. He looked to Rachel to gauge her headspace, and found her beaming directly at him. Their moment of eye contact sent a shaft of warmth through him. They were in the same territory.

"How you guys doing?" Win asked.

"Spectacular," Rachel said.

"Yeah," said Daniel, nodding. He could think of nothing else.

"Nice. We're in it now, but this is just the beginning. This is the breeze before the typhoon."

This surprised Daniel, since it seemed it had been a while since they took it. "How much longer until the full effect?" he asked.

"Well, there's no set of traditionally predictable effects, unlike most other drugs. But generally, the intensity continues to escalate for the first few hours."

Rachel seemed unfazed by this information, but Daniel was taken aback, since there was at the moment a fairly potent surging energy inside his chest whose heft and power made him feel suddenly small. It triggered a vivid memory of being rolled by a big wave while body-surfing.

"Yeah, yeah, yeah," Win said, placing his hands on Daniel's shoulders, "you got this. It is all part of *you*. You've got to liberate your spirit of adventure, that's all." He was looking into Daniel's eyes, and had clearly sensed his apprehension. "You want to see something? I think you're ready for this. I'm going to show you something. Are you ready? You need to be absolutely ready."

Daniel nodded.

Win was still wearing the blue blazer with no shirt underneath, buttoned across his lean midriff. He undid the button and flung open both sides of the jacket, and the entire lining was painted with intricate patterns in dayglow colors, a sudden smorgasbord for Daniel's newly scrubbed eyeballs. The colors erupted through him with something akin to perfect comic timing. Daniel burst into spontaneous gut-laughter, as the patterns on the fabric began to throb and slither merrily. Then all three of them were laughing, and the laughter felt so exquisite he abandoned himself to it. It washed away all his fear. Win howled wolflike at the high ceiling and said, "Let's head in there!" He danced away toward the interior, and Rachel and Daniel followed.

They found a group of people from the ranch sitting down near the front and joined them. When the band took the stage the crowd cheered and rose to its feet. The musicians grinned and went quickly about getting their instruments ready, a couple of them giving little waves to the audience. There was no rock-star posturing, just a group of guys who were going to play some music, but when they started, the first chord battered Daniel's chest, resonating weightily through the building, and the sound immediately became an entity unto itself. Daniel had heard some Grateful Dead songs on the radio and on people's stereos, some of it sweet and joyful, some a bit strange, but this was bigger, much bigger: a raw, taut web of musical clamor, frayed at the edges and very much alive. The first song had quiet, morose verses between slowly escalating frenetic guitar interludes. It was a song filled with existential sorrow, a postapocalyptic lament that closed with the line, "*I guess it doesn't matter anyway!*"

The second song was readily identifiable as a country tune, the lyrics about a card game and a shoot-out, but was played with such frantic energy that it became something darker, now matching the smirking menace of its murder-strewn lyrics: a microcosm of the weird and violent American core. The people around them were dancing and sweating and whipping their manes madly. Daniel bobbed to the beat, but otherwise stood still, letting the acetylene din burn through him. Rachel danced near him, somewhat tentatively compared to those around her. When they started the third song, Win turned from his unbridled dancing to Daniel and Rachel and said, "Listen carefully to this one. It's advice for later in the show, later in the trip." This one was a more identifiable example of current psychedelic rock, a lilting, musing song whose tempo sped and slowed in fits and starts. The lyrics, what he could make out of them, didn't seem particularly wise or advice-laden to Daniel. The first verse registered only as psychedelic gibberish and slipped immediately from his memory, but some of the later lyrics were at least interesting. The first chorus slowed down to sing, "*Everywhere*

I go, the people all know, everyone's doing that rag," then repeated it double-time. After some more psychedelic arcana, Daniel took in one of the later verses:

"Don't neglect to pick up what your share is
All the winter birds are winging home now
Hey Love, go and look around you
Nothing out there you haven't seen before now."

Then the chorus, whose lyrics changed each time: *"But you can wade in the water, and never get wet, if you keep on doing that rag."* Win smiled at Daniel then, tapping the side of his head with a finger.

As the show progressed, Daniel mostly lost track of the songs during the extended instrumental jams. He began to dance halfheartedly, off and on, along with the rest, but still watched the stage. The music was big and messy, with veins of crystalline insight emerging through the lead guitar. The band members sweated and grimaced and smiled and continued to delve deeper into their powerful sound. They morphed in Daniel's mind into a group of miners, deep underground, swinging their pickaxes frantically at the dark rock around them, chunks of ore flying everywhere, and then in the quieter sections they smelted the ore for its bright treasure, isolating it and crafting it into dazzling shapes.

He took all this in for a while purely as a viewer, appreciating, until the moment when it occurred to him that the substance from which they chipped their ore, the dark rock of the mine, was reality itself. It included him, and this thought, coming at a particularly crazy moment in a particularly dark and heavy jam, scared him. It was one thing to be a bystander, an audience to chaos, and another to be implicated in it. His heart felt wild in his chest, and he looked around for Rachel, but she wasn't in sight. No one in the crowd was looking at him, all seemed sunk in their own caverns. He felt he was losing psychic traction, and the towering wave of the drug and the music loomed over him. Then he saw Win in front of him, and Win turned and made eye contact. When he caught Daniel's expression, he tapped the side of his head twice, as he'd done earlier in the show, and went back to his dancing. Daniel re-membered the line from the earlier song, *You can wade in the water, and never get wet, if you keep on doing that rag.* Without hesitation he dropped into the driving beat and started to dance in earnest, feeling somehow that everything was at stake.

By the time the jam quieted into near silence, he had regained traction, had taken it back for himself, and he felt good, strong. He stopped dancing for a moment and filled his lungs, looking up at the ceiling. When his gaze dropped again, Cam wandered out of the crowd toward him, and when they saw each other something happened. Cam's face was all at once the face of an ancient friend, someone who had stood by his side through lifetimes, someone he loved instinctively and without impediment. Cam smiled and stepped up to Daniel and they embraced, then he looked again into Daniel's eyes and nodded. "Yup," he said. "We're fine. We're golden." Cam walked on through the crowd, but Daniel felt the connection between them continuing, unbroken. It conferred on him a deep sense of calm, a calm atop the crest of that monstrous high.

The band was taking a long interlude between songs, tuning. In his place of power and calm, Daniel stood, taking in the scene. He saw Rachel's hair through the crowd, moving his way, and his heart swelled. He smiled broadly in greeting as she stepped between two men into the small clearing he inhabited. But her expression pierced his calm like a bullet. She looked terrified, her skin blotchy and her eyes screwed back in confusion. When she saw him she rushed to him and clung to his body.

"Hey," Daniel said. "What's wrong, love? Are you okay?"

She didn't speak for a moment, just squeezed him hard and hid her face in his shirt.

"I'm here, baby. You're okay," he said, not knowing what to do.

"I need to leave here," she said. "Can we go?"

"You sure?" The band started another song, and her answer was lost, but she pulled her face back and looked imploringly at him.

She put her mouth to his ear. Her voice was high and quavering. "I really need to leave. Please."

"Okay," Daniel said. "Let's go."

He led her through the crowd, telling Cam in passing that they'd meet him after, and then walked out into the street. When the door shut behind them, the change of atmosphere from the frenzy of the interior to the relative quiet of the street was profound. A few people stood around in front of the venue, the city's lights and surfaces gleamed, a traffic signal down the block mutely converted red to green. The growl of a passing car was like a contented snore. The music was muffled but still audible, pulsing behind them. Hard to imagine that simple building could contain what was going on inside it. Like a thunderstorm trapped in a cardboard box. Daniel felt the night sky's remote gaze upon him, his head newly cracked open to understand its enormity. He tried to focus on Rachel, which wasn't easy. She snapped her eyes around like some small frightened creature.

"Did something happen?"

She nodded.

"Tell me."

"I saw someone in there. Someone I know from before."

"Before? You mean from back home?"

"Yes."

"Who was it?"

"Can we just walk a bit? I want to walk."

"Sure."

Once they had rounded a couple of corners, with Daniel squeezing her shoulder, she began to speak again. She shrugged off his arm and did not look at him as they walked.

"I never told you about Johnny. He was my . . . We were together for a while, in Tucson, before I came out to LA."

"When you were in high school?"

She nodded. "He was a little older, and we got involved, and it turned out he was not a good man." She looked up at the sky for the first time since they'd walked outside, and her breath deepened. "I've avoided telling you about him. Some bad things happened, and it's hard to talk about. He manipulated me, emotionally at first, then physically. When I tried to break it off he started threatening me. And for some fucking reason it worked, I stayed with him. I was too ashamed to tell anyone who might help me."

"God," Daniel said. "That sounds awful."

"And it got . . . worse." She turned her head away from him. She looked lost. They had reached the middle of a residential block, with chipped white houses crowded close, apartment buildings at the corners. She walked unsteadily over to the stoop of a house whose lights were off and sat down. Daniel stood facing her.

"When I finally got the courage to make a real break from him, he . . . imprisoned me. . . . God, I've never used that word before. He tied me up. He had me tied to his bed for days. My mother was so used to me being gone that she never noticed. And I never told her."

"Jesus." Daniel's heart forged ahead painfully. The pictures her story created in his head were insupportable. The acid high, which until then had seemed organic within him, even in its extremity, now felt gratuitous and obtrusive. He wished he could dismount from it.

Rachel looked at him with sudden fierceness, holding his eyes. "He committed crimes against me. And when he realized that what he was doing meant he could never keep me, his motive shifted to revenge, and he let a friend come over and do things too."

"He ought to be in prison," Daniel said.

"I went to the police. Two days after he let me go I went in and sat with a detective and told him the story. Once he found out Johnny was my boyfriend, he advised me to forget it and move on, cases like this were hard to prove and prosecute. Best to just go on with my life, he said."

A bolt of rage shot through Daniel's chest. "He should pay. He has to pay."

She shook her head. "No. Please. I need to move away from him now, put it in the past."

"Did he see you?"

She paused, then nodded. "He actually came up to me."

"What did he say?"

"He just said hi, like nothing had ever happened. He introduced me to the guy he was with, as if we'd never met, but it was the same guy who had come in when I was tied up! Like an idiot I shook his fucking hand, said hi to both of them. Then I made some excuse and went to find you."

Daniel sat down next to her and they looked at the sky together. He could feel the jagged edges of the broken armor she'd built around this event keeping him at bay, and he resisted touching her. Here it was, the thing he'd sensed under her veneer. It was not a vague or amorphous personality trait but a trauma. The rhythm of their breathing fell briefly into unison.

"You never told anyone else?" he asked.

"Just that detective, and now you."

Daniel felt as if the conversation were happening underwater in a fast-moving stream. The disconnection between the subject matter, the somber tone it demanded, and the coursing rush of the drug, which was showing no signs of ebbing, were surreal. The rush manifested now as a powerful current against his back, and he braced himself and tried to resist it, staying present with Rachel on the stoop. His thoughts began squalling past nonsensically, ripped free from reason and language. *Wade in the water,* he remembered. . . .

"Let's keep walking," he said. "Don't you feel like being in motion?"

She looked at him, and her sudden smile was a balm on the turmoil in his mind. "I do," she said. "Goddamn it, yes."

He stopped bracing against the current and moved with it, and the chaos eased as he joined it. They walked through the city for a long time not speaking, just observing and communing silently over the things they saw. They didn't stay on the wider avenues more than a block at a time, opting for side streets. Every time they turned a corner from a populated avenue onto a smaller empty street there was a sense of latent adventure, new territory. On one side street they stopped near a tiny crooked tree. It looked as though it had been planted sideways, or knocked off-balance, and then slowly corrected as it grew to extend vertical, so there was a bend in its trunk. Rachel looked at Daniel, and he knew they were both feeling compassion for this poorly trans-planted entity that seemed to be wondering how it had come to be in this strange place surrounded by alien flatness in every direction except up, the direction in which it strove. Rachel tenderly touched its leaves and its slender trunk before they moved on. The longer they went with-out words the deeper their mutual experience felt. The cool air and the night sky, the sounds of car engines, horns, music escaping from an upper floor, all moved through Daniel and Rachel simultaneously, stitching them invisibly to each other; they engaged the world together as it passed them. They came upon the spectacle of a group of young hippies struggling to carry a giant sofa up the front steps of a house with a girl yelling directions at them, and Daniel joined the boys under it while Rachel watched, smiling. As he helped them carry it up the steps and then through the double front door into the ground-floor apartment, he felt strength coursing through him, and he knew Rachel felt it too. Either one of them could have carried that couch with one hand by themselves, twirled it like a basketball. When he stepped back out to the top of the stoop, huffing happily, and saw her on the sidewalk, they laughed spontaneously at the wonder of finding each other again.

The front of an open grocery store, with boxes of fruit displayed on canted stands under a wavelike string of incandescent bulbs, made them both smile when they turned a corner and beheld it. No customers marred the scene, and the boxes of oranges, grapefruits, berries, and bananas glowed together like the deconstructed features of a face, the two bright symmetrical open doorways into the store becoming the eyes, the sidewalk and curb a pair of inscrutable lips. Daniel moved as if beckoned to a box of oranges and selected one, went inside and paid for it. The counter man did not return his smile, which was somehow as it should be. They continued to walk as he peeled the orange and pulled it into two halves. The soft membrane of the first slice cooled Daniel's tongue, and when he broke it with his teeth the taste hurt him with joy. They stopped walking in reverence for the act of consuming the orange, moaning and grunting as they ate, and when they started moving again they also began to speak, very naturally, and now they simply talked about the night, the city, the acid, the music they'd heard. Also about human existence and its beginnings and endings, the continuum of consciousness, school, oceans, but never about the improbability of their strange connection, the thought of which trailed them like a giant shivering soap bubble.

At a certain point there was a crowd in the street, a big cheerful crowd, and it took a few moments to realize that they had arrived back at the Fillmore, and the concert was letting out. Daniel saw trepidation in Rachel's face, but she was no longer ruled by it.

"You okay?" Daniel asked, as they approached the scene.

"Yes, but let's not stay here."

"Well, the car is right there." Daniel pointed across the street. "Let's see if we can find Win or Cam."

"Can you give me the keys and I'll wait in the car?"

He watched her cross the street. She got into the passenger seat and locked the door. He waded into the crowd and was immediately awash in the roiling energy of the show and its audience. It was an ecstatic energy, and compelling, but after their quiet harmonious walk it was also intrusive. He felt like a deserter having stumbled again upon his regiment when Cam materialized out of the crowd and said, "Hey! Where have you been?"

"Just checking out the neighborhood a bit."

"How'd you like the show?"

"It was intense. They're something."

Cam laughed. "They *are*, aren't they? They are *something!*"

"It took me a while to realize. They are not messing around."

"Nope." Cam looked past Daniel's shoulder grandly, as if at some numinous horizon, then shook his head and smiled again. "You're in luck, by the way. Someone's going to come by the ranch in a bit and bring what you need. A lot of people are headed back there. We're having a thing."

"Great. Is Win around? Does he need a ride back?"

"He left already, with some others."

"I don't remember how to get there."

"Where are you parked?"

Daniel turned and pointed to his car. He could see Rachel staring blankly at the crowd. She had lost sight of him.

"Wait there," Cam said. "I'll pull my truck around and you can follow me."

Daniel got in the car with Rachel. She had lit a cigarette, and she handed it to him. The bite of the smoke was beautiful on his charged nerve endings, almost thirst quenching. They rolled the windows down and passed it back and forth hungrily, but when it was finished they didn't crave more. It was some time before Cam's old pickup rumbled up next to them, a girl in the cab with him and two guys sitting in the bed.

"Join the convoy," Cam said, and the car behind him left a space for Daniel to pull in. There were two other cars also following Cam, and the drive seemed to last a long time. Daniel dropped into a psychic tunnel, his eyes coupled to Cam's taillights, easing the wheel around and marshaling his concentration to operate the car. Any glance at the scenery slipping past crowded and confused his vision, threatening to untether him from the task at hand, so he concentrated on the taillights and nothing else. Rachel seemed to sense his need for focus and didn't speak. He was relieved that he could feel a distant tapering of the high, a promise of future abatement more than an actual abatement. The revelation of Rachel's story had created a rift between himself and his experience that he understood had circumscribed the possibilities of the trip. The potential ignited in that crowd, with that music carrying them all forward together, had been electrifying. But the quieter binary communion as he and Rachel had walked through the nighttime city had compensated for whatever they'd missed at the concert. It had been a gift, one he knew would stay with him when he came down, and he was ready for that return to earth.

When they got to the ranch, Daniel parked with Cam near the house, and the other cars peeled off and parked in the grass by the tents near a larger group of vehicles. The two guys in the bed of Cam's truck vaulted out and jogged toward the party. A new fire climbed and leapt from a pyramid of old planks in the firepit, and there were three times as many people as there had been earlier. A car radio was playing music, and people were lugging amplifiers from the house toward the tents and teepees. Cam got out and beckoned to Daniel. Daniel and Rachel followed Cam to the porch, along with the girl who had ridden with him. "Let's go in and talk this thing through, so we'll be ready when he gets here," Cam said. The four of them went into his bedroom, which he opened with the key. Cam pulled the bags of pot from under the bed. "Okay if I crack one of these open and inspect the quality?"

"Of course," Daniel said.

"This is Stacy, by the way."

The girl smiled at them. "Daniel and Rachel," said Daniel. "Good to meet you."

Cam sat on the edge of the bed and unzipped the top of one of the duffels. Inside was a hump of black plastic and duct tape. He ripped a hole in the plastic and extracted a small handful of buds. He sniffed them and frowned approvingly. "Let's see how it tastes. We won't feel much with the acid still going, but maybe something." He picked up a pipe from his bedside table and put some in it. Daniel sat in a chair across from the bed, and Rachel sat on the floor leaning against his legs. When Cam passed the pipe to them, blowing out his hit, he raised his eyebrows at Rachel.

"You okay? You look like you've been through the wringer."

"I'm okay," she said. "I had a bit of a hard time before, but I'm okay now."

"Good," said Cam. "You need anything, you just ask. Whatever your head or heart might need, if we have it, it's yours."

Rachel said, "Thank you." Her smile was beginning to look more relaxed. Cam's presence itself seemed to have a calming influence, which Daniel also felt.

Rachel shook her head at the pipe, but Daniel took a hit. Once again he liked the feel of the smoke in his throat, but otherwise it had no discernible effect.

"Looks like we have ourselves a deal," Cam said. "Although it's going to be harder for you to test our product, unless you want to fly off on another trip."

This had never occurred to Daniel, and seemed absurd to consider, both because another trip right now was out of the question and because the idea of mistrusting Cam was itself ridiculous. "I trust you," Daniel said.

Cam offered a wide smile. "I know you do." Again, Daniel felt that powerful sense of a long-established friendship, bordering on kinship. "I feel it too," Cam said. "There is trust here, among us."

A long silence ensued as they all smiled, and Daniel could feel the first hint of self-consciousness beginning to creep in at the edge of his mind just when Stacy, who was smiling more brightly than any of them, exclaimed, in a deep southern accent that caught Daniel by surprise, "Far *out,* y'all!" This sent the four of them into an attack of laughter that grew and throbbed, feeding on itself and assuming visible form in the air: a glaucous rhythmic amoeba.

"How about we head out to the party?" Cam said.

Rachel looked up at Daniel, her uneasy eyes diverging from her laughing mouth. She turned back to Cam. "Could we maybe stay in here? I'm not feeling up for another crowd right now."

"Of course. Like I said, anything you need."

THEY'D BEEN IN the room almost an hour, listening to music on Cam's stereo, when the door opened again and Cam came in with a tall, hunched man. He wore glasses and had a pinched face too small for his body. "Guys," said Cam, "this is Howard."

The man nodded distractedly and said in a faint nasal voice, "Pleasure." He pulled from his satchel a large mason jar filled with clear liquid, and handed it to Daniel with no preliminaries. Daniel held the jar and looked at it.

Cam said, "That's full strength, like what we had earlier. One tiny drop is plenty."

"My friend thought it would be a couple of jars," Daniel said.

"This is the amount we had discussed. Believe me, you'll all be happy."

"Thank you," Daniel said to Howard. He pointed at the two duffel bags by the bed. "There's my end, in those bags." But Howard just gave a distant nod and walked out without even looking at the bags.

When he was gone, Daniel said, "Is that guy all there?"

Cam said, "Oh, Howard is all there, he's just not all *here*. He has covered distances that you and I can't conceive of, and has given up the pretense of fully returning. He's made himself at home out there."

Daniel found himself nodding along, not really comprehending.

"How you feeling?" Cam asked Rachel. "Think you want to join the party now?"

"I'm okay, but I think I'd better not. I think it might be best if we left, got on our way back home."

Daniel looked at her, surprised. Her eyes caromed off his and wandered the room, then she looked back at him and he saw gravity there. He said, "We'd better go. My guy is nervous and waiting, so we should hit the road."

Rachel said, "Can we come back and visit? Another time when there's no deal happening and we can just enjoy the scene?"

"Anytime." Cam shifted his gaze from her to Daniel. "You guys are welcome here whenever you want. Just show up." He walked to his bedside and opened a drawer. He returned with two white pills. "When the acid wears off you might need these for the drive, to keep you alert."

He gave them to Daniel, and Daniel put them in his pocket. Cam hugged him and said, "Be safe, my friend."

"I will. Thanks."

"We'll see each other soon. I'm sure of it."

DANIEL'S ABILITY TO drive normally had mostly returned when they got on the road. He felt able to hold a conversation and maneuver through turns and signs and highway ramps without much trouble, although the acid still pervaded the planes of his perception. Even so, they didn't speak for some time. The motion of the car, the night air swirling through, with occasional physical contact when they reached across the seat to caress a hand or a shoulder, were all the communication they needed for a while. They crossed the Golden Gate and felt the cool blossom of expanding space in the dark sea air around them. Now Rachel had to give him directions from the map to get through the city. They had decided to follow the coast this time, with the jar of LSD safely wrapped and wedged in the back of the trunk with some old paintbrushes Cam had given them. If it was found they would say it was paint thinner. If they didn't have the energy for the whole drive they would stop somewhere and catch a couple of hours' sleep in the car.

After an hour of mostly silence, as they were finishing making their way through the city, Rachel said, "He was there."

"Who was there?"

"Johnny. He was at the ranch, just now."

Daniel glanced over at her, but her eyes stared coolly ahead. "How did you see him? We didn't even go outside."

"He was one of the guys in the back of Cam's truck."

"God. Why didn't you tell me?"

"I didn't want there to be any trouble. That's why I didn't want to go outside."

Daniel tried to remember the guys in the back of the pickup, but his concentration had been so consumed with driving that every-thing else seemed a blur. His memory conjured a picture of one guy with very long shaggy brown hair wearing a tan suede jacket, and another with short hair in a gray leather hat. Their faces wouldn't materialize.

After a minute Daniel said, "I guess it's good we got out of there."

"Yes."

Then something occurred to him. "But, should we leave him there? Shouldn't we have said something to Cam? What if he does something to someone there."

Rachel shook her head. "I don't think he's some career rapist. What he did to me had to do with this . . ." She took a breath, searching for the words. ". . . unwholesome synergy he and I had, which caused him to become fixated on me and brought out the absolute worst in him."

"So it wasn't really his fault? He was just a victim of his own too-great passion?"

"Don't do that, Daniel. Please."

"Sorry."

"Let's just move away from him, from all of that."

"Yes. Okay."

They fell silent. They were coming out the other side of the city onto the road that followed the coast. After a few minutes of rushing air and the occasional gasps of cars passing in the other direction, she said, "I've always inspired fixation in boys, since I was a girl. I don't know what it is. I realize it gives me power, but it's a power I've never wanted, and have no idea how to wield." She extended her tanned arm out the window and drew patterns in the wind. "You're just the first one whose fixation has been reciprocated."

They almost forgot about gas, and were close to empty when Daniel noticed the gauge. They found an all-night filling station in Santa Cruz and bought ice cream sandwiches out of the tiny freezer inside after topping off the tank. They finished them in the car before starting the engine again, and then shared a cigarette as they drove on. They came to a section where the road soared above the ocean, and the great water's proximity beyond the cliffs lent new depth to their vision and their accord.

"Let's stop for a bit," Rachel said. "Somewhere along here, before the sun comes up. I want to hear the ocean."

Daniel pulled into a turnout with a small parking area and shut off the car. When they got out they could see a trailhead in the starlight, leading toward the sea. It passed first through a tunnel of tall bushes and trees before opening into a meadow on a high plateau above the water. There was enough light to silver the tops of the bushes and grass, so they could see the dark gap of the trail, but not enough to make out the footing, so they made their way carefully, holding hands. When they looked up to the west, they saw ahead of them the silhouette of a giant tree standing alone against the stars, near the cliff's edge. The trail led straight for it, and they walked until they had to duck to go under the ends of the long inland branches, and then stood straight under the dense canopy. The area under the tree was darker, and was its own distinct world, a place of great safety and calm, and standing in it made the tree seem a paternal figure. No ill could befall them under this tree's protection.

They sat down against the trunk facing west. They could see under the tips of the branches a few faint stars above the sighing blackness that represented the ocean. The sound of the water's measured breath rose up to them from the base of the cliff. Daniel and Rachel fell into a long conversation where once again they skirted and evaded the topic of whatever was evolving between them, while delving into other weighty ideas. With the acid gradually releasing them from its fever, they became minutely aware of the chemical nature of their existence, of their bodies and the progress of them through time and space. They perceived, and discussed, this central predicament of human life: existing as a boundlessly ambitious and seemingly infinite consciousness wedged into a magnificent mechanism ripening inexorably toward its own demise. Would there be more, after the body's end? The inevitable question was not, on that night, an ominous one. Asking was an adventure that knowing might have diminished. They agreed that more seemed very likely.

"I want to be out under the sky for a bit," Rachel said. "Will you wait here for me?"

"I'll come with you."

"No. I want to see how I feel under the sky alone, away from our cocoon, and our tree. Just to see."

"Okay." He found he did not want to be apart from her. He felt so utterly quenched in their cocoon that her desire to step away from it startled him.

She must have caught something in his voice, some fear, because she leaned in and gave his neck a long kiss. "You," she whispered into his skin, "are for me." Then she stood and faced him. "I shall return," she said, and Daniel felt a warmth soak into him, subsuming his fear. She raised her chin as if in soliloquy, *"And realize once more my thousand dreams."* Daniel smiled. He could tell it was one of her remembered lines of poetry. "Wait for me, Daniel," she said. "Right here."

"I'll be here."

He watched her pick her way over the roots northward, toward where they'd seen another fork of the trail turn and run parallel to the cliff. His eyes were fully adjusted now, and he could see the reddish color of her skirt as she passed under the edge of the tree's canopy and stepped into the open night.

He turned back to face the vast black table of the Pacific, which from his vantage was bordered above by stars and branches, and below by the silver lip of the cliff. He closed his eyes for a moment, and the life of the tree, whose hard trunk was pressed against his spine, poured through him, and continued pouring through him when he reopened his eyes. It came in waves that merged with the sound of the waves from the beach below. The tree expanded into him and he into it. He could feel its trunk and topmost branches reaching upward, its roots burrowing down and gripping the earth, the stratified interior rings, the veins and skin of each leaf carrying nourishment and respiring oxygen into the darkness. He could feel birds sleeping in its hollows and insects meandering through the furrows in its bark. And then with a breath he moved deeper, and felt the tree growing beyond itself, into the sky, into the distant reaches of the earth's crust, until he understood he was experiencing not just the tree's living body but the lush untroubled immensity of its conscious-ness, which was not subject to the vicissitudes and ephemerality native to human awareness. The tree had been growing here on this cliff for centuries, and its inner life was a majestic and fully articulated expan-sion of its corporeal form, an image of what it might achieve if it were able to grow forever. In its soul, the tree's branches were woven intri-cately into the stars, and its roots enfolded half the earth.

When light began to infiltrate the western strip of sky in front of Daniel, he turned his head and realized that morning was arriving out-side the canopy of branches. The sky behind him was bright with the sun's imminence. He could not have said how long he'd been sitting there, merging with that tree. Possibly, he thought, the tree's relation-ship with time's passage was so different from his own as to erase tem-poral awareness. It might have been two minutes or two hours, and only the angle of the light made anything longer or shorter unlikely.

He didn't see Rachel. He lifted his chin and parted his lips, but some-how the idea of calling to her and disturbing the hush of that place was unthinkable. He was about to rise and go looking for her when he remembered what she'd said—*wait for me*. His faith in her return was complete; he still felt the warmth of it in his chest. He leaned back against the trunk and closed his eyes. The LSD was virtually gone now, and his eyelids relished their new weight.

* * *

HE DIDN'T FEEL as though he'd slept, but rather passed briefly alongside consciousness, and when he was jostled back in by the tip of a baton shaking his shoulder, something crucial cracked, though in the moment he didn't yet know it. The things that followed had no place in his life. It all happened in a fractured new plane that had no right to exist. It was wrong. He'd ended up on the wrong side of the crack, in a reality that slowly revealed itself to be counterfeit. The policeman who woke him and asked what he was doing there seemed at first to belong to the same world Daniel had passed out of, and he answered calmly, "Waiting for my girlfriend."

"Who's your girlfriend?"

"Rachel. She's around here somewhere."

"What's she look like?"

"Tall, brown hair."

"What's she wearing?"

"Red skirt, white shirt."

"Okay, just sit still a second." The cop stepped away and called out to another policeman, who came in under the tree. When they were both in front of him, the cop said, "You're going to need to come with us."

Daniel suddenly remembered the acid in the trunk of the car and was stabbed with fear. "Why do I have to go with you? I need to wait here."

"Get up," said the cop, pulling handcuffs from his belt.

Daniel complied, and they put the cuffs on and led him out to the parking area. Sitting in the back seat of the police car, which was parked behind his own, with the lights of an ambulance flashing through the window and glinting off the rear bumper of his Ford, he assumed they'd somehow found the LSD and known what it was, and he was probably on his way to jail. He was trying to think of ways to make sure Rachel was left out of the legal trouble when he saw the medics carry the stretcher through the bushes from the trail. It was then that Daniel began to sense the fracture that had occurred. A body on the stretcher was covered completely. Daniel started knocking his head against the window to get the attention of the one cop he could see. The man turned halfway around and looked at Daniel.

"Who is that?" Daniel asked.

The cop just shook his head and turned away again.

None of this had any place in Daniel's life, though eventually, of course, it became his life.

2017

Dean's bedroom was cornflower blue with clouds painted on the ceiling. Bins of toys lined one wall, and a picture of a giant robot hung over his bed. He lay splayed on his back, his arms thrown above his head, and at the sight of his face Celia felt a happy sob burrow under her lungs. She knelt by the bed and waited a minute before touching him, letting the sight of him wash through her. She put her palm on his chest and rubbed softly. When he opened his eyes, he did not exclaim or cry out, but just rolled and crawled sleepily into her arms, hanging himself over her shoulders. She felt his embrace slowly yield as he fell again into sleep. She laid him back down, kissed him, and whispered, "I'll be here when you wake up, nugget."

She'd left Leo in a chair on the rear patio, and she made her way back there. Her father was still asleep behind his closed bedroom door. A couple of empty beer cans and a half-full bottle of bourbon decorated the table in the den along with dirty dishes, a used glass ashtray, and a pack of Camels. Leo hadn't said anything when they'd come in, but Celia had felt something plummet inside her when she'd seen the aftermath of Jack's night. This was the first time she'd shown up unscheduled, and she hadn't seen this before. When she was around, he did his drinking in his room, at night. Signs of it were kept out of sight. For the first few years he'd been with her he hadn't let her see him drinking at all, out of respect for her sobriety. Since they'd moved into this big house he'd been slightly more open about it. Celia hadn't considered it an issue, but she was rethinking.

She went out to the patio through a side door and crossed to where Leo sat. He smiled at her. "How's your boy?" he asked.

"He's fine, still sleeping." They were both groggy from the all-night drive. They'd stopped once, for food and gas, and had made love again in the car before getting back on the highway. This had unknotted their awkwardness, and now in their fatigue they had fallen into the fragile familiarity of new lovers. "Come on in the kitchen," she said. "We can get a snack, then I'll show you the guest room. It's better if you don't sleep in my room." He nodded, understanding. "I'm going to stay awake till Dean wakes up and get him breakfast." They went into the kitchen and ate bowls of Dean's Lucky Charms, greedily slurping the milk and laughing softly at the sounds and the pleasure of the sugar.

There were two extra bedrooms in the house, but only one was so far equipped with a bed, and Celia led Leo past Dean's room to it. The bed was made, and she went to the window and pulled the blind. "Sleep as long as you like," she said. "There's a bathroom just to the left in the hall."

"Okay, thanks." He sat on the bed and smiled at her. "What did your text to the boss say?"

"Just that something came up with my son and I had to come home, and that you were driving me. I said I'd be back after the weekend."

"All right."

She went to him very naturally and kissed him. "Get some rest," she said.

Celia walked into the den and carried the bottle and the cans from the coffee table into the kitchen. She cleaned up the rest of the mess— the full ashtray, scattered magazines, a used glass, plate and fork, some clothing of her father's—and as she cleaned, her anger built. Was this how Jack lived when left to himself? Was Dean subjected to this constantly? There were red-brown spots of food on the table and she got a sponge and some Windex. She ground her teeth as she scrubbed the spatters of spaghetti sauce from the glass, applying her anger to the task. She put the three remote controls back into the wooden tray that held them. She stood, looked at the room, and breathed a big shaky sigh. "Not fucking okay," she hissed, then went into the kitchen to wait.

She had the TV on and was watching CNN an hour and a half later when Dean shuffled in wearing his blue pajamas.

"Hi nugget," she said, muting the TV. "How'd you sleep?"

He was silent a moment. "I thought I dreamed that you were here."

"Nope, I'm really here."

She stood as he walked to her, and he embraced her again, holding tightly, his head molding into her belly.

"You want some eggs?"

"Cereal is fine."

"I want to make you something. Either eggs or oatmeal, which one?"

"Okay, oatmeal."

He sat at his normal spot at the bright wooden table. There was no juice in the fridge, and just enough milk left for the oatmeal, so she drew him a glass of water and he took one small sip. When the oatmeal was ready, with milk and brown sugar, she sat across from him and watched him eat.

He said, "I thought you were coming tomorrow. That's what you said."

"I decided to come a day early because work let me. I drove all night to get here."

"You did?"

"Well, my driver, Leo, drove me. We drove together. He's here, sleeping in the guest room."

Dean's face scrunched as he lowered his spoon. "Why's he sleeping here?"

"He was so tired when we got here that he just needed to lie down. He's a nice guy. You'll meet him probably, when he wakes up."

Dean nodded and kept eating. She loved watching him eat. It was more than just seeing the animal pleasure in his face as he chewed and swallowed, the movements of his jaw, the smiles he'd flash her between bites—though these things were beautiful. It was imagining the food breaking down in his stomach, its nutrients spreading through his organs and cells, giving him life, helping him grow, sustaining and nourishing him. She could sense the whole process, and it smoothed and calmed the world for her. It was something unassailable, something upon which no neurotic negative projections survived. It drew her away from the fear more dependably than anything else.

She waited until he'd finished, then asked him, "Does Grampa Jack sleep in a lot?"

"Yeah." Dean nodded. When he saw her face he added, "Not all the time."

"Is he usually still asleep when you wake up?"

Dean shrugged. "Sometimes. But it's okay, I just get cereal and watch cartoons. Or I go down to Daniel's house, and he makes me toast with peanut butter."

"Daniel's house? You mean down the hill?"

"Yeah. He's nice. Him and Grampa Jack are friends."

"Do you go down there a lot?"

"No."

Dean had sensed her displeasure and his face went long. He didn't want to add to it. He pursed his lips as if to keep himself from talking.

"It's okay, Deany. Don't worry, you didn't do anything wrong. Okay?"

He nodded.

"You like Daniel?"

He nodded again. "He listens to music all the time."

"That's nice. Is it good music? You like it?"

"Yeah."

"What kind of music?"

Dean smiled. "Daniel says music is injured by categorization."

Celia laughed. "Is that right?"

"Yup," Dean said, and began laughing too. She poked his shoulder and he dissolved.

"You silly nugget."

LATER THAT MORNING, Celia was sitting by the pool with Leo and Dean. Jack had given a sullen greeting when he emerged and then claimed to have errands and went out in his car. Leo was in the pool with Dean, letting him dive off his shoulders while Celia watched from the shade of an umbrella. From down the hill, she began to hear strange music, a drifting, high falsetto singing beautifully, words that couldn't quite be made out. She focused her ear on it, but the words remained obscure.

"Leo," she said, getting up, "I'm going down the hill for a minute. You'll be okay with Dean?"

"Sure, of course."

"Are you going to Daniel's?" Dean asked. "Can I come?"

"Not right now, sweetie. You stay here with Leo."

Instead of walking straight down the grassy hill, she took the flagstone path that wound from the side of the house. The section of it that went along the curving driveway was separated from it by a tall hedge, then halfway down the path turned right and led to the guesthouse. There was a paneled wooden gate to the house's small backyard, but Celia followed the path around to the front door and rang the bell. The music was louder here, the song hauntingly beautiful, but she could still not make out the lyrics. The singer was emitting long high syllables in slow rhythms, as if the meaning were contained not in the words but in the melody. She wondered whether the bell could be heard over the music. She was about to ring again when the door opened.

He was a tall, gaunt older man. His silver hair was cut close to his head, and his long-lined face was tan and clean shaven. Celia felt a charge of anxiety in her chest, realizing she hadn't thought what to say.

"Hi," he said, smiling. His eyes were large and lent sadness to his smile. When she met his gaze Celia felt slightly eased.

"Hi, I'm Celia, from up the hill." She pointed in the direction of her house.

"I know. Hi, Daniel." He offered his hand and she shook it. "What can I do for you?"

"Nothing really. I just wanted to meet, maybe talk for a second."

"Come on in," he said, walking back into the house and leaving the door open for her.

She followed him in to where he'd turned a corner into the living area. He was near the stereo, leaning over. The music went off.

"What was that you were listening to?" she asked. "I couldn't make out any of the words, but it was beautiful."

"That's because he's singing in Icelandic. They're called Sigur Rós."

"Oh I've heard of them. Do you know what that song is about? It sounded sad."

"No idea. I've thought about looking up translations of the lyrics, but I've gotten used to not knowing and I don't want to spoil the sort of ethereal obscurity."

Celia smiled. "So, I understand my son has been coming down here sometimes?"

"Yeah, once in a while. He just shows up." He sat down in a large stuffed chair and crossed one bare foot over his knee. "He's a good kid."

Celia had been apprehensive. She had walked in with her antennae raised, ready to suss out the stranger who had been spending time with her boy. But something about this man put her at ease. She knew she'd still go through the motions and ask him the questions she wanted to ask, but she was no longer suspicious of him. This surprised her.

"He said you're feeding him sometimes?"

"Just once, when he appeared in the morning and he was hungry. I made him some toast. I hope I didn't overstep. I'm on my own so much down here, I forget how things work."

"No, it's fine, I guess. I don't really like the idea that he couldn't find food at home, or that my father is sleeping in and letting him fend for himself. But that's not your issue."

Daniel shrugged and turned his head to the side, staring out into the yard. Celia admired the lines of his profile. He was still a handsome man, and must have cut a figure in his day.

"What do you do, Daniel?"

"I'm retired. I was a schoolteacher. High school English."

"That's great. English teachers are always the cool ones."

"I guess so."

"Well, mine were."

There was a pause. "Listen," he said, "you want me not to have Dean over? I get it if that's what you're here for."

"I don't know what I want. I heard he'd been coming down here, and I've never even met you. That didn't feel right. Now that I have, maybe I won't mind. But I guess I just don't know yet. Dean says you're friendly with my father?"

"A little. He comes down for a drink every once in a while. Dean comes with him sometimes."

"Well, obviously if he's with Jack it's fine. I guess maybe, for the time being, you could just bring Dean back if he wanders down. I don't want to seem suspicious or anything. . . . It's not that you've done anything wrong."

"Absolutely understood," Daniel said. "I don't take it the wrong way at all."

"Thank you." Celia shifted in her seat, about to stand, but settled back again. "Can I ask you something?"

"Sure."

"Do you think Jack is okay to be caring for Dean? I'm not sure what it's like when I'm away."

Daniel took a breath. "Jack loves the kid, for sure. And he's family. That's important."

Celia nodded and waited.

"But he drinks a bit. And when Dean wanders down here he sometimes doesn't notice for hours. Since you're asking my opinion, Dean's a little young for that kind of autonomy."

"Yes. It's only since I've been filming this movie that I've ever been away from Dean for long. In the past, Jack just did day-to-day stuff. When we were co-parenting, so to speak, it always worked well."

"Maybe Jack could stand to have some more help. There's a nanny some of the time, right? Maybe she could stay at the house full-time when you're out of town."

She nodded again. "Probably a good idea. I'll have to figure out how to bring it up with Jack. He's not crazy about being critiqued."

Daniel smiled.

"Obviously these are not your problems. Sorry." Celia stood.

"Dean's a great kid. He's always a pleasure to have around."

"Thanks. I appreciate you talking to me. Can I give you my cell number? In case you ever need to reach me?"

Daniel pulled his phone from his pocket. "Sure. We are neighbors, after all. I'll give you mine too."

Celia went out the sliding door on the way back, through the yard and straight up the hill to the pool. Leo and Dean were out of the pool, and Leo was drying him off. They were talking, laughing softly.

"Was Daniel there, Mom?" Dean's hair was frazzled from the towel, and he smiled, knowing he looked funny.

"Yes, honey."

"Did you like him?"

"I liked him a lot. He's a nice man."

Dean gave a single nod, to show he approved. "I'm going to go put clothes on," he said, and went into the house. Her father's car appeared for a moment in the section of driveway visible from the pool deck, then rounded the house to the parking area.

"Will you hang for another minute?" Celia said to Leo. "I want to talk to my father."

"I'll go get dressed." He went off toward the room he'd slept in. She watched him walk away in the old bathing suit of Jack's he was wearing, which was small on him. It accentuated his weight, but he didn't seem at all self-conscious. This quality in him struck her powerfully, and made the things they'd done together seem suddenly realer. Her mind was so automatically attuned to how she looked, to how everyone looked, that just seeing someone comfortable in his own imperfect skin was a minor revelation. She wanted to follow him into the guest room and close the door behind them.

She went to the kitchen, where Jack was putting groceries away.

"I let the food situation get a little thin," Jack said when she walked in.

"Thanks for shopping," she said.

"Uh-huh." He put milk and yogurt into the fridge and began putting boxes and cans into the pantry cupboards.

"I went down and met Daniel, our neighbor."

"Oh yeah? Good."

"Dean said he goes down there sometimes, so I decided to introduce myself."

She saw him register her tone. "Dean just likes to explore, and Daniel is a good guy. There's nothing to worry about." He turned and faced her across the butcher-block island.

"I'm not worried, but you know . . . he is a stranger."

"Not to me. I'm friendly with him." His features fell into the stubborn look he reserved for arguments he didn't plan on losing.

She didn't feel like challenging him. Later, she thought. "He said he was a schoolteacher?"

Jack smiled. "He's being modest. He was a teacher, but before that, in the seventies, he was a famous artist. He made some huge sculptures that were in some high-end places. And his ex-wife is Amelia Stander."

"Poseidon Pictures? That Amelia Stander?"

"Yup. They were legendary for their parties back in the day, had a pad in Malibu and everyone in Hollywood used to go. There was a big story about how he went and destroyed one of his own art pieces because he didn't like the guy who had bought it or something. He fucking blew it up! Dynamited it! How's that for wild? He was arrested for it, and that's when the two of them split up, I think."

"Wow. He told you all this?"

"No, he didn't tell me anything. I googled him. But now he's quiet as can be. He's a different guy than he was back then, I'm guessing. He went and became a teacher later on. Taught kids in some free school in Inglewood, I think. Well, you met him. You can tell he's a solid citizen."

"I'm sure he's a great guy. But I told him that for the time being I didn't want Dean down there without you. He understands. Maybe once I know him better."

Jack looked at her as if humoring someone fragile. "Sure, whatever you say."

She felt a shaft of irritation. "I also cleaned up your mess from last night."

He raised his eyebrows, affecting nonchalance. "Thanks."

"You know it's not okay to be drunk around Dean."

"I wasn't drunk. And he was asleep anyway."

"If I hadn't been here he would have seen all that when he got up. That's not okay with me. And we don't smoke in the house."

"Aye-aye, skipper. A one-time thing. Sorry."

"I'm serious, Jack."

"I know," he said. "I get it. Okay? I'll do better."

Celia nodded. As he turned to go, she was about to mention the possibility of a live-in nanny, but pulled back from it. She would look into it first, get it set up. Her relationship with her father was built more like a work friendship than parent-child. They distantly cohabitated and took turns caring for Dean, but when the catalyst of the boy wasn't around their intimacy had major limitations, and she was forced to realize that after five years she still didn't really know him. Dean had been half a year old when Jack first showed up. Celia had been stricken over the breakup with Darren, still newly sober, and utterly petrified of the tiny sudden person whose life was solely her responsibility, and here was the father she remembered from a few visits earlier in life—the quiet man who in her memory had stared at her with such love that she quit believing her mother's sneering denigrations of him. When she was nine, on their second meeting, he had taken her to a small amusement park. Etched on her brain was the giant hot dog he bought her, with every fixing she wanted, followed by soft serve ice cream with sprinkles. She'd been shocked when he said yes to everything she asked for; her mother didn't allow fatty foods or sweets, concerned with her weight and complexion on auditions. Diana called Jack *Mr. Lost Weekend.* "He's nothing but a mistake I made before I stopped drinking," she told Celia, "a vagrant I met in a bar." But Jack had told Celia he loved her, and she had believed him. After a few sporadic visits over a single year, he disappeared again.

When he showed up after Dean was born, Celia had been teetering on a few different brinks, and since she had no family left who cared about her, she'd let him move in almost immediately. He had promised to love and help care for Dean, and he'd done that. Celia was grateful, but an empty space still hovered between them that their shared love of Dean couldn't quite fill.

She went to Dean's room, where she found him playing with the gigantic Lego robot Jack had bought him for his birthday in July. She stood in the doorway watching him, and after a moment he looked up. His expression was like a grown man's, someone who's been interrupted during a crucial task.

"What's up?" he asked.

"Nothing, just came to see what you were up to."

"Playing," he said.

"I see."

When he saw she wasn't leaving, he placed the small action figure he was holding into a compartment in the robot and closed the cover. "Is Leo going to stay with us now?"

"No, honey, not for long. But Brenda might start staying with you and Grampa Jack when I'm not around. How would you feel about that?"

He considered this. "Good, I guess."

"You like Brenda, right?"

"Yeah." Dean smiled.

"Okay, good. I don't know for sure yet. If Brenda can't do it, I might need to get someone else who knows how to help out like that."

"Okay," he said, and made a show of shrugging. "I don't care."

"And then I'll be done with this movie and I'll be home all the time again. Won't that be nice?"

"When?"

"Not too long now, Deany, but I don't know for sure how long. We're getting close to being done."

Celia heard the door to the guest room open down the hall and turned to see Leo emerge. He walked over.

"Dean was just asking if you'd be staying another night with us," she said.

"I guess I'd better not." Leo stepped forward to where he could see Dean through the door. "I had such a good time with you today, buddy. But I have a son also, and I should get home to see him."

"What's his name?"

"His name is Augustus. We call him Gus."

"How old is he?"

"He's young, almost one. He hasn't even learned to talk yet."

Dean smiled at the news of his superiority. "Gus Gus bo-bus," he said, high-fiving Leo goodbye.

Celia walked Leo to the front door.

"You going to fly back Monday, like you originally planned?" Leo asked. "If so, I can drive back tomorrow and be there to pick you up at the airport."

"Why don't we drive back together," she said, trying to make it sound like a logical solution rather than an invitation. "After I drop Dean at school Monday morning I'm free, and I wasn't supposed to be on set that day anyway."

Leo looked at her, the magnitude of his conflict expanding behind his eyes. His face visibly drained, as if he were about to vomit, but he answered quickly and there was guilty relief in his smile. "Yeah, sure. Pick you up here?"

"Say nine-thirty a.m.?"

He nodded, hesitating before turning to leave.

She took his hand. "I'm sorry," she said.

"For what?"

"For making things difficult for you."

"That's not on you."

"You want me to cool it, anytime, just say so."

She saw his eyes roll in a silent groan and his head begin to turn toward the open door as if to rush off, but he turned back abruptly and almost violently kissed her. She rubbed the burn of his stubble around her mouth as he climbed into the SUV and drove off.

"Makin' it with the driver now?" It was her father, wandering in from the kitchen.

Celia was flustered and quickly angry. "Don't fucking spy on me."

"Hey, I got no judgment, you know that."

"By the way, I'm going to see if Brenda can stay in the guest room when I'm out of town. You could use some full-time help around here I think." She stared straight at him, daring him to challenge her in that moment, but he just raised his eyebrows and crimped his mouth.

"Whatever you think," he said. "You're the boss."

CELIA AND LEO arrived in Bisbee on Monday in time to have dinner at a small Vietnamese restaurant. They'd decided to stay at Leo's hotel since it would be easier to slip her in there unnoticed. The spa was filled with other cast members. After they ate, it was still twilight, and they took a walk up through the town. The main thoroughfare wound among the foothills the town was built on, meandering toward the mountains behind. When they'd cleared the downtown area, where a quarter of the storefronts were vacant, the road grew steeper, forking a couple of times, and ran first through a patch of small motels and then into the residential hillsides. Car traffic along the road was sparse, and foot traffic almost nonexistent. One man passed them, walking a small white dog down the hill. He was young, heavy, his dark hair slicked sideways across his skull, and he nodded at them without speaking when Celia bent down to greet the dog.

Farther up, they topped a small rise and stopped to look back. The stars were out now over the town. Celia slipped her arm around Leo's waist, and he kissed her for a moment.

"What did you think of me before?" she asked him when they'd started walking back downhill.

"Before what?"

"Ha. Seriously, the straight dope."

"I thought you were someone who was surviving as best she could."

"A survivor," she said. "A prime example of deep jading, maybe? A cold bitch lost to her softer virtues?"

"No. A person in some kind of trouble, grappling with fears. I know courage when I see it."

"And I know bullshit when I hear it."

He stopped walking and took her arm. "Hey," he said. She faced him. "Don't say that because it'll never be true. Got me? You may know bullshit, but sincerity is not your mother tongue, so listen. Celia, I saw *you* in there, before, same as I do now."

Celia believed him. She heard her own suddenly tiny voice as if from a distance: "Do you think others do too?" She dreaded both answers, and took a quick breath as if to suck the question back in.

Leo looked away up the hill, and then back, before speaking. "What does it matter?"

"I wish it didn't." She hung her head for a moment and mustered her full voice, her practical face. "Oh, how could you understand?"

He smiled abruptly. "Don't give me that shit," he said.

He was looking into her eyes, and Celia felt a flash of elation so powerful it brought an absurd urge to strike him. She laughed and kissed him instead. It was for real, this kiss. Kisses tended to be lovely negotiations, disjointed constructions however pleasurable, different for each participant. But this was a new, complete thing, singular and solely theirs, like a child.

They walked in silence for a while, their way lit both by streetlights and the sprawling southern sky before them. "Still think I'm in trouble?" she asked him.

"What do you mean?"

"'A person in trouble.' That's how you described me. Has getting to know me confirmed or tempered that verdict?"

"I don't know. Have I really gotten to know you?"

"You've started to."

"Which, since we're doing straight dope, gives you more reason to shield your trouble from me. I mean, sure, the parts of you I'm seeing are parts I would never otherwise have encountered, but the trouble, if I didn't imagine it, must still be there." He grinned at her. "Unless a couple of days with me has cured all your ills."

She smiled back. "Is that so far-fetched?"

"Yes," he said, dropping the joke.

She turned away, walking faster. She found herself suddenly furious that he had ruined the moment.

"Hey, I didn't mean it like that. What I mean to say is I don't need you to be untroubled."

"It's fine, let's just drop it."

"No. Look, I don't even *want* you to be untroubled. I'm a fucked-up soul myself, otherwise I wouldn't be cheating. I don't just go around fucking everyone."

"Some of us do. The troubled ones."

"I'm hiding my trouble too. I've spent the past five years married to someone who would so prefer me to be untroubled that it's easier to pretend I am. She met me after I sobered up, so she doesn't know that side of me at all. It's like a fairy tale to her when I talk about it, a myth of my past that couldn't be fully real. She really only sees the healthy me.

She was never drawn to the trouble. She doesn't even want to hear about it, though she wouldn't admit that."

They had stopped walking again, both of them still looking ahead into the star-crazed sky. Celia said, "Okay, so let's do it. Let's each tell about our trouble, what we don't share with others." She heard him take a deep breath. They did not turn toward each other.

"Who goes first?"

"I can," she said.

"I'll go first," he said.

"All right, but no war stories. Something about you, not some random instance of depravity from the past." She faced his profile, and he gathered his thoughts, still looking to the horizon. It occurred to her that this mimicked the classic therapeutic configuration: listener looking at the speaker, speaker looking away.

"Okay, no random acts of depravity." He paused for a long time. "At the base level it's fear. It's all about fear. People ask, 'What are you afraid of?' and that is not an answerable question. Any time I name a source for my fear I feel it as a deflection. I mean, sure, I can get close. You know, as in: I'm afraid of people because someone I trusted fucked with me when I was a child. I was traumatized, yes, and the fear probably began there, I guess. But I don't really know because it seems, now, somehow elemental. It embodies some ancient, sleeping doom, and the only escape is self-destruction. You know? Like, if I become my own doom I've taken that power away from anything else. It's preemptive. At least there's agency in it."

She felt the laughter spill out of her in a rush. Its piercing volume was at odds with the moment and the release it brought. Leo looked at her dumbfounded.

"Get the fuck out of my head, man," Celia said. "I mean, really, it's a little much. Get your own troubles." She saw him catch the camaraderie in her tone, and he laughed. They had started walking again. She said, "I feel like I don't have to take my turn. You just spoke for both of us."

He nodded as if this didn't surprise him. "Well, that is something."

"Is it a cop-out?"

"Not if it's true."

They walked in stride, briefly hearing music trailing down from one of the houses up the hill, a piano ascending to the bridge. A car passed, and when it was gone so was the music. Celia whistled softly, shaking her head, and they went the rest of the way in silence.

DANIEL WOKE ON Sunday with Celia Dressler in his mind. There had been something about her that tugged at him, something in her features and the way she inhabited them that seemed familiar. He initially wrote it off to her fame, but he found himself drifting up from sleep with a picture of her face at a specific moment floating in his mind's eye: She had turned toward the windows, lifted her right hand to tuck her hair behind her ear, and as she'd turned back—her hand still tucking the lock of straight blond hair—she'd given him a small smile and dropped her eyes. It was that moment, the combination of the hand and the smile and the dropping eyes, that tugged most strongly at some distant chamber of his mind. As consciousness congealed, lying in bed, he placed it: Rachel. She had looked, in that moment, strangely like Rachel. He hadn't placed it immediately because Celia, blond and blue-eyed and lightly freckled, did not resemble Rachel in any obvious way. She had chanced to run through a series of motions and expressions that triggered some latent imprint in him and educed an underlying resemblance. Now that he thought of it, the resemblance, though vague, was discernible.

He rose and pulled on a sweatshirt and went to the kitchen. He didn't give Celia much further thought now that he'd figured out what was tugging at him. As he was spreading his toast with peanut butter, Jack knocked on the sliding door. Daniel waved him in, hiding his irritation at having his morning invaded. "What's going on, Jack?" he asked.

Jack said, "Hope it's okay me stopping by."

"Sure," said Daniel, pouring coffee. "Is something up? Dean okay?"

"He's fine. But something is sorta up."

Daniel slid the cup across the counter to Jack and poured one for himself. He felt some resentment that he'd made enough for two cups but now would only get one. "Okay, so what is it?" Daniel asked.

Jack sipped the coffee, pausing deliberately. "I thought we were friends, Danny."

No one called him that. Daniel didn't respond, but looked Jack in the eye.

"Are we friends? Just answer me that."

"I guess so. What's going on?"

"My daughter comes down here to talk to you, and suddenly she thinks we need a live-in nanny. Suddenly I'm not competent to care for my own grandson like I've been doing his whole life. You know anything about that?"

"She asked me questions and I answered them. Mainly she just wanted to meet me, since Dean was hanging out over here. This really has nothing to do with me."

"Did she ask you if you thought I needed help?" Jack's hazel eyes had a piercing interior glow intensified by the sallow, tumid mask of cracks from which they peered, and by the rest of his sagging gray-stubbled face. The ravages of old age were ruthlessly upon him, but his fulgent eyes bore no trace of surrender.

"Jack, don't involve me. What's the big deal anyway? A nanny just makes your life easier, and I'm guessing the expense is not a hardship."

Jack shook his head. He looked away, sipping his coffee. "I didn't think you'd do me like that, man." He turned back and gave Daniel a sharp look, the kind of look men use to intimidate one another. Two stints in prison had made Daniel alert to such looks, but in his own house it was a shock. "I don't like it," said Jack, holding Daniel's gaze. "Not one bit."

A response did not immediately present itself, so Daniel began eating his toast. He now just wanted Jack gone. He kept his mouth full and his eyes averted, trying to think of how to accomplish that. He decided to try placation.

"I said very little to her. I never said you were incompetent. Nothing like that. Whatever I said, I meant no harm." He could feel Jack's eyes still on him, but he didn't engage them.

"Aww, I know you didn't." Jack continued to stare. "You're just trying to help, do what's best for Deano, right?"

Daniel didn't answer. He looked back at Jack, and their eyes met again.

"It's just kind of funny, is all," Jack said.

"Is it?" Daniel felt he'd had enough.

"Yeah. It's funny a guy with a criminal record is saying I shouldn't be alone with my own grandson."

Daniel stood from his barstool, hoping to get Jack moving. "We should leave this here."

"Oh, now you want to leave it? Yeah, I googled you, man. You're a drug dealer and a public nuisance, a felonious vandal, some would say a terrorist."

"Good for you, Jack. You found out my big secret. Which is public knowledge."

"But that first time you went away, they tried to get you for murder and they couldn't. What was that about?"

"I have things to do, if you don't mind."

"Did you do it? Did you kill that girl?"

"What I'm saying is, get out."

"No, you didn't. You ain't the type. You don't have it in you. But you probably feel responsible, don't you? You definitely are *that* type. You loved her, maybe, and she died all messed up on the drugs you gave her. That's got to feel pretty awful, doesn't it?"

Daniel studied him for a second, angry but also curious about the mechanisms driving this sudden shift. Behind Jack's eyes was a viscid malevolence Daniel hadn't encountered before, along with something else he couldn't pin down that had been there all along, something which only now troubled him—an obscured quality that seemed to preclude even the possibility of fear.

Daniel felt, alongside his anger, his own swelling fear, and grew angrier at having tried to placate Jack. It now seemed cowardly. He opened his mouth to say *Get the fuck out of here*, but found himself pressing diplomacy again instead. "I don't know what made you so pissed at me, Jack. I really didn't do a goddamn thing against you."

"Okay, I believe you," Jack said. The malevolence fell from his eyes with weird abruptness. "I had to make sure, right? A guy's got to know who his friends are in this world."

Daniel nodded, not in agreement but automatically, saying, "All right."

"And you're right, a live-in nanny won't be bad to have around. Make my life easier, like you say. She can do more of the busywork. Hopefully it'll be someone new. Wouldn't hurt to get someone easy on the eyes either! Am I right? The nanny we got now ain't much to look at."

Daniel was as apprehensive of this false retreat as he had been of the aggression. "I really do need to get ready to go," he said.

"I thought you were retired."

"I volunteer as a tutor, and I'm helping one of my students with something this weekend, so . . ."

"You know, all that stuff about your past, I actually think it's all really fucking interesting. I mean, what a life you've had! I want to hear more about it."

"Some other time."

"No hard feelings, right? I was just fucking with you," Jack said as he edged out the sliding glass door.

"No. You caught me off guard is all."

"Yeah, which was the point. Anyway, see you."

Daniel slid the door shut and watched Jack stride up the hill. "Holy shit," he said under his breath.

A WHILE LATER, Daniel decided to go out for an early lunch, in part to get his car out of the driveway in case Jack drove by, to uphold the fiction that he had somewhere to be. He parked near a burrito shop he liked. A parking garage down the block from it had been torn down since he'd last been there, and was now a fenced-in construction site, deserted on a Sunday. There were piles of rubble from the old structure and hills of fresh dirt with tracks winding among them, bulldozers, backhoes, and trucks all scattered and idle. Two turquoise porta-johns sat far apart in seemingly random locations. It looked like a sandbox abandoned by giant mad children. There was a closed bank between the site and the burrito shop, and inside it two large TVs had been left on, both playing the same cable news network: split-screen coverage dividing the anchor's bland gray-bearded face from sweeping helicopter shots of a school rooftop, a school where five days earlier, on the other side of the country, sixteen students and a teacher had been killed on the second day of school by a fellow student, someone they'd all known for years. The nation, again, had mad children on the brain.

Usually Daniel would have carried his lunch out and driven the fifteen minutes home to eat on his patio, but for once he didn't want to be alone. He'd been on his own the day the shooting had happened, and hadn't learned of it until a day later, the news arriving matter-of-factly on the car radio as an addendum to a story about the newly ignited gun-control debate, the newscaster's clipped tone assuming prior knowledge. Daniel sat down at the only open table in the tiny restaurant and ate silently with his fellow Americans. Music drifted down from the ceiling, horns and congas and keyboards coaxing Daniel's leg into motion. The two young children of the family that occupied the pair of tables next to him went from jubilant bickering to engrossed silence when their food arrived on a tray delivered by their father with a swooping dramatic flourish. He set it on the table like a magician presenting a conjured bouquet, and they all fell happily to eating. This caused in Daniel a pang that blurred his vision. He looked out the window. The back edge of the cloud cover had become visible to the west; LA's default blue sky was returning. As he stared at the sky out the window a man in baggy jeans stopped on the sidewalk, directly in front of him, and after a moment Daniel drew his attention down from the sky and looked at him. It took a second to register that the disheveled old man raising his palm and grinning sideways at him was Jack. Daniel found himself dumbly waving hello, and Jack walked in.

"What are you doing here?" Daniel asked.

"Howdy friend," Jack said. "You come to this place too? I love this place."

"Been coming here for years," Daniel said.

"Well, glad I ran into you. Hang out and I'll get a burrito and join you."

"I was about to leave."

Jack gave him an inscrutable squint. "Hang out a second, will you. You're only half done, for Jesus' sake."

Daniel dug in and ate quickly while Jack was ordering. He was almost done when the older man got to the table. "You take care of that trouble, with your student?" Jack asked.

"Trouble?"

"Yeah, you said you were helping some kid with a problem."

"I don't think that's what I said."

Jack smiled and raised his partially unwrapped burrito. He opened his mouth bizarrely wide, rubbery excess skin falling back away from his gaping jaw and gathering in folds by his ears. Instead of biting off a corner he slowly inserted the entire end of the burrito into the maw he'd generated. Daniel thought of a snake unhinging its jaw for oversized prey and half expected him to swallow the entire burrito without chewing, foil and all. When he had as much of it inside as physically possible he finally bit down, quickly and cleanly, and began masticating in great, machinelike chomps.

Jack's eyes continued to smile as he chewed. Daniel watched his overextended cheeks and thought of Dizzy Gillespie. When he had most of the bite swallowed, Jack said, "You ever put something that big in your mouth?"

Daniel cocked his head but didn't answer.

"Maybe in the joint? I was inside awhile too, I know what goes on." Something fell into place when Jack said this, and Daniel realized he'd sensed it already. Of course Jack was an ex-con.

"Nobody raped me in prison, if that's what you're asking."

"Hey, it doesn't have to be rape. Nobody would blame you for making your time a little easier, giving it up to the right people. Different rules in there."

"That what you did?"

"Me? Fuck no, I'm no faggot."

Daniel glanced at the family next to them, who were gathering their trash to leave. They affected not to have heard.

"There was this one kid, though," Jack said. "Nice kid, I helped him out and he gave it up for me once in a while. Just hand and mouth stuff, you know, nothing filthy." He shrugged. "You have to make do. He and I got pretty close, actually. But I never touched his dick."

"Jack," Daniel said. "Are you following me?"

"Let me ask you something. You believe in reincarnation?"

Daniel stared.

"You know, past lives? You ever meet someone and feel like you knew them before, in some dream-memory you can't quite access? You know that feeling?"

"I do." Daniel thought of Cam.

"That's how I felt about that kid, Stevie. Stevie Storrow, that was his actual name. Sounds like something out of a poem, right? He was this beautiful half-negro kid, but I swear I knew him in another life—and in that life he was my woman. I don't know where or when or who I was, or any of that shit. I just know he plugged into a place in me reserved for women, and he—or *she*—had been there before."

"That's a nice story."

Jack beamed. "Yeah, it is, in a certain way."

"Maybe in the past life you were *his* woman. Couldn't that be?"

Jack shook his head impassively. "No. Because I have a man spirit and he had a woman spirit, and whatever bodies we have ain't going to change that. That's what fags and dykes are, I think: when someone with a man spirit gets born in a woman's body, or, you know, the other way around."

"Interesting theory. Listen, I have to go." Daniel balled up his foil and napkins.

"Don't you want to know what I was in for?"

"Not really, no."

"Most people's first question, *Whadja do?* Hey, it's only fair, since I know what you did."

"I'm not asking."

"I robbed a bank, if you can believe it. Tried to, anyway."

"Why are you telling me?"

"Shit, friends talking, that's all." Jack kept eating and talked through his food. "Don't worry, Celia knows, I told her everything. I'm a changed man, fully reformed. More than I can say for my poor partner. Old Jules. Security guard put a bullet in his head and he was a goddamn vegetable for a while until he died. He didn't even have bullets in his gun. Fucking security guard also killed a bystander, which for some reason put *me* in prison for longer. I never fired a shot. Try and make sense of that."

"Uh-huh. You didn't answer my first question. Are you following me?"

"What do you want me to say? 'No?' Will you believe me? How about, 'What the fuck are you talking about, you paranoid freak?' Or, 'Yes! I'm tailing your ass all over town for no particular reason?' Maybe I'm hot for you, maybe that's it. Maybe I *am* a faggot."

"It's a simple enough question. I'm not asking why."

Somehow Jack had eaten his entire burrito and was already crumpling the foil onto the tray. "Wow, you really have some issues, don't you? Daniel, buddy, my whole attitude toward you is one of friendship. I know I got a little worked up earlier, but only because I thought you bad-mouthed me to my daughter. That's done, okay? I have only good intentions. I feel for you, brother. Really I do. What happened to you with that girl way back when, that was something awful. You loved her, didn't you? I could tell by the way you reacted before. You really loved that girl. Am I right?" He paused, and his expression morphed smoothly from deadpan sincerity to something realer. "Hey, you ever wonder, speaking of past lives, about where she might have ended up? You ever hope she'll come back to you somehow, in a different body?"

Daniel's head jerked involuntarily. It was as if something had slithered into his marrow.

"Oh-ho-ho-ho," Jack growled, smiling. "'Course you do. I know what that's like. I've been in love with two people in this life, and both of them died. I'm always on the lookout for them. Stevie would be about thirty-four by now, if he reincarnated right away. Though he could be younger too. You ever think you found her again? Your girl? I mean, anyone you've met you think might be her? She'd be what, at most in her late forties now?" Jack's face glowed with a peculiar excitement.

Daniel began to stand, but something solidified in him and he sat back down. He said, "There's no delicate way to put this, Jack. So I'll just be direct, out of respect. Our friendship, such as it is, isn't working out. I don't feel I need to explain myself. It just isn't meant to be, that's all. We can go back to our separate lives in separate houses, just neighbors, and that'll be that. Okay?"

Jack's expression gathered in on itself. Gravely, he held Daniel's gaze. "That stings, buddy. I won't lie."

"You'll live," Daniel said, standing up. "And quit fucking following me." He walked out into the sunshine, his chest burning with the ferocity of animal terror.

Blue sky drowsed over the avenues as he drove east, the westering sun propelling him through the long palm-trunk shadows angled obliquely across the road. He stayed on surface streets, and his heart calmed slowly.

Twice in one day Jack had made him think of Rachel, and she touched him now, as she did from time to time, through everything. Through all the silted layers, the years of agglomerated moments, she still touched him as if through a perforation in a membrane beyond which she continued, disconnected but alongside, not in the form of a memory or group of memories but as an entity, a presence born of those memories. The ghosts of memory, Daniel thought, and Forest's paintings came suddenly to mind, rising not from the mental realm reserved for his son, but from the territory of art. Those bright ghostly figures shrouding and haunting black-and-white reality. Without forethought Daniel made a left, two more lefts around a residential block, and then a right on the avenue and headed back west, toward the ocean.

1972–1975

If he'd been meaning to die, he would not have brought food and water. He would not have gotten himself a new pair of hiking boots and a tiny camp stove and a hat against the sun. If he'd been meaning to die, Daniel always told himself afterward, he would just have done the job. There were plenty of easy ways to check out, and plenty of hard ones too. Death hadn't been his goal, not directly. But, something in him had become unperturbed by the idea. It was merely one of the possible outcomes of walking alone into a vast unpopulated desert with no plan and no map, and at the time what he felt was not a death wish but a cold equanimity toward outcomes. He'd looked at a map ahead of time but not brought it with him. He'd marked a spot on the highway, a certain distance from a certain town, in his mind. And a direction in relation to the highway, about an eighty-degree angle. This would take him through a long stretch of land with no roads and no charted human habitation.

He would have died. The stretch of land he'd chosen was too barren, and the supply of water he'd brought was insufficient. There was a stand of scrub-covered mountains in its center into which he'd walked, where the map had marked a stream that turned out to be dry, and he'd made it across them to the other side where they fell once again into open desert, and there he'd stopped. He was weakening, fully out of water, and he understood that walking out into that shadeless expanse, which he remembered from the map was as long as the one he'd crossed on the way in, would mean certain death. He made camp in the shade of a leaning rock.

If he'd wanted to die, he wouldn't have built fires day and night from dead brush, hoping to signal anyone who might see the flames at night, or the smoke in the day. He hadn't actively wanted to die, but after a couple of days, as his strength failed and his mind began to play tricks on him, he began to acclimate to the idea. He would have died if not for Ben.

Daniel entered consciousness near midday, on his third day in that camp, to the sound of forced air, some kind of bellows, and his first thought when he looked up and saw the face of a horse nosing the ground five yards away, blowing in the dust, was *hallucination*. Then he lowered his chin and saw a dusty boot near his face, and a voice said, "What the hell are you doing out here?"

Daniel said, "Just dying."

The old man sat him up and gave him a drink of water. When Daniel was awake and a little hydrated, he pulled a bag of Brazil nuts from his pocket and dropped a few into Daniel's hand. Daniel put one in his mouth, but it was hard to chew and he spit some of the pieces into his hand and worked on a smaller portion. It took him a minute to get it down.

"We're going to have to leave your things here," the old man said. "My horse'll have trouble enough with the two of us, and I can't walk all the way. She's old like me. I haven't been on her in a year, but when I saw your fires two days runnin' I figured someone might be in trouble. This ain't no place for camping, son. You think you'll be all right on the horse?"

"I don't know."

"We'll make it work. My name's Ben."

"Daniel."

They rode the old horse slowly through the afternoon, and Daniel was in and out of consciousness behind the saddle. Ben tied Daniel to his own body to keep him from falling off. It was near dark when they arrived at a trio of ancient miserable buildings. One was a small unlit bunkhouse, one was a trailer on blocks with a light on inside, and the third was a dilapidated barn around which spiny piles of scrap metal loomed against the low horizon. It was a salvage yard. To the right of the trailer, a long straight dirt driveway ran east, out to a two-lane blacktop that was just visible in the dusk.

Ben led Daniel up the steps into the trailer and sat him at a banquette in the front room. He drew him a glass of water from the sink. "You need to try to eat something, my friend," he said. He pulled a plastic container of refried beans and rice from the small refrigerator and heated it in a pan on the stove. He used a plastic spatula to scrape the mixture onto an orange plate and set it in front of Daniel. Daniel spooned a bite to his mouth, and the food tasted astonishingly good. He chewed the first bite for a long time. It was hard to swallow, but he got it down. After a few bites it became easier. Daniel finished the plate and said, "I'd like to go to sleep now."

Ben led him to the back of the trailer, where there was a small bed crisply made with sheets and a blue camp blanket. He pulled a clean T-shirt and underwear from a shelf and held them out to Daniel. "Change into these, and we'll get you cleaned up tomorrow."

"But, this is your bed, isn't it?"

"It's okay, you take it tonight. There's a couple of cots in the bunkhouse I can use."

Daniel nodded, and his head felt as if it were filled with a liquid much heavier than water. He almost passed out right there on his feet.

THE NEXT DAY, Daniel was surprisingly restored. He ate most of the food in Ben's kitchen, promising to repay him the supplies. Ben said, "I'm just glad you didn't die on me." Ben wanted to give him the bed for another night, but Daniel wouldn't take it. He moved into the little house across from the trailer. There were two squeaky cots with roll-up mattresses, and Ben had laid a sleeping bag on one of them. "I used to have men out here to help with the yard sometimes," he said, "short-term labor, when I was up and running. Now it's just been me for a while. I shut down the business a year ago."

On the second morning, as they ate breakfast, Ben said, "When you're ready to go on to wherever you were headed, I can take you into town, to a phone or whatever you need. My phone line went out a while back and I ain't had cause to fix it."

"I wasn't headed anywhere," Daniel said. "I was leaving everywhere."

"Well, unless you consider this somewhere, you succeeded."

The beans that accompanied his eggs had slices of hot dog in them, and Daniel took another bite to soften the stale bread in his mouth. When he was done chewing, he said, "I just got out of prison."

Ben nodded. "All right."

There was a pause. The old man's features had a gaunt power behind them, his eyes narrow and penetrating, his cheeks drawn so that his mouth, resting in a pensive frown, took up a bit too much space on the lower half of his face.

"Nothing violent. I was in for drugs."

"I didn't ask."

"Well, I didn't want you to worry."

"I ain't worried."

Daniel nodded and began eating again. "I wanted to be up front with you," he said. "I was wondering if I might stay a few days, in your bunkhouse. I could do any work for you that you might need, to earn my keep. And I'd leave whenever you say. I just haven't figured out a destination yet."

Ben stared at him a long time. "I told you, I shut down my business. I don't hire help no more."

"I'm not looking for a job, but I don't want a handout either. I'm just asking for a few days."

The old man drew a breath and shook his head, and Daniel was ready for a flat no. But he said, "There is one thing, but it ain't small, and it ain't easy. Might take a few days."

"What is it?"

"There's still a lot of salable scrap out there, and I've been meaning to get some gathered and sell it off bulk to another yard. I couldn't do it without help. I'll need to fix the flatbed, and you'd be loading it up by hand 'cause there ain't no loader, and then it'll be a pretty long drive. Won't yield much money either, but I could pay you a little once it's done."

Daniel responded without hesitation. "I'll do it. You don't have to pay me. Just a bunk and food would be all I need."

"We'll get your strength up another day or so first. It'll be a bear of a job."

BEN HAD A big wood-bottomed flatbed trailer with iron side panels. One of the sides had fallen off, and they welded it back onto its metal posts and then fastened it by drilling holes and putting in new bolts. They put extra bolts in on the other side too, for good measure, since the load they would be carrying was heavy. Daniel filled it with what he could lift and throw in by hand, sweating freely in the heat and sucking down remarkable amounts of water as he worked. When the trailer was at capacity, they secured the tailgate with heavy chain, hitched it to Ben's truck, and drove a couple of hours to a larger salvage yard in a suburb of Las Vegas. There, since the dumping mechanism on the trailer was broken, the owner ran a long chain around the back of the load, hitched it to a large post, and had Ben drive away from it while Daniel watched to make sure none of the pieces caught on the sides and damaged the trailer. Daniel climbed in and threw out what was left piece by piece.

"I got more," Ben said.

"Bring it on," the owner said.

"I also got a lot that's too big to load by hand, and I sold off my busted loader. If you want to send someone down for it I'd give you a price cut."

The man squinted pensively and finally shook his head. "Not worth it for me. But you bring it and I'll buy it at this price."

"All right."

After two more full loads of small scrap over the next two days, there was still quite a bit left, much of it in bigger pieces. "We could cut some of it up with the torch, or rig up a hoist, but that's plenty for now," Ben said. "If I ever really need the money I'll rent a loader and carry out the rest. This is more than I thought I'd ever get done anyway."

He tried to pay Daniel, but Daniel refused. "A deal is a deal," he said.

"If I could stay on a while longer I'd be grateful. That could be my pay-ment. Whatever else you want me to do around the place also."

The two of them had developed an easy quiet rapport over the days working together, and Ben seemed to have grown to like him. He shrugged and said, "It's no trouble for me if you're in the bunkhouse. There ain't much else to do, but I guess you can stay a bit."

Most days the old man was right, there wasn't much to do. Ben spent most of his time in the trailer with his headphones and his ham radio, talking to people in Chile and Omaha and Alaska. He cared for his dog and the horse, who lived not in the barn but in a small paddock with a makeshift indoor stall attached. Daniel offered to take over caring for the horse, but Ben shook his head. "She's used to me doing it, all her life. She's skittish of anything different. I'm old enough to understand what that's like."

So Daniel spent most of his time on his own in the small bunkhouse, which was much bigger than his prison cell had been. He read what books he could find around the place: a few Western thrillers, nature guides, a vocational textbook for welders. He was used to being in a small space with a limited reading selection, so he didn't feel any bore-dom. In prison, boredom was a dangerous luxury. Over time, he found ways to make himself useful. He took lists to town in Ben's truck and did the shopping, and he put himself in charge of laundry, which Ben protested at first but then acquiesced to. He snuck some variety into the grocery selection, and began to do most of the cooking, which Ben did not protest. He also fixed up the bunkhouse, patching the roof and walls, sweeping out the insects and dust, mopping. They shared the one toilet and cold shower in Ben's trailer because the old outhouse past the bunkhouse was beyond repair.

When he wasn't working or reading, Daniel abandoned thought. Abandoning thought had become his primary endeavor in captivity. He'd learned to just drift off into his own gloom until he reached the edge of it and popped through into an approximation of nothing. Now, in the bunkhouse, there was no one there to see the ruined vacancy in his eyes, which his cellmate Vernon, a strangely thoughtful pimp who had assaulted a cop, had called his "bombed-out look." Generally, his reentry into the world from these sojourns was like waking up in a cold dungeon. There was nothing particularly liberating about them except that they were a temporary hiatus from the dungeon of his mind. The actual prison itself he hadn't wanted to escape. It had seemed like the right place for him. When they let him out, the free world felt unnatural. There was too much accessible space, too much unknown prospect, and so he'd attempted the physical equivalent of his mental sojourns, he'd set out into the biggest patch of nothing he could find on a map.

The day he picked up the pencil was the first time he'd returned from one of his empty reveries and not felt utterly trapped inside himself. Something happened, a tiny difference whose genesis was unclear, and there seemed to be a pinhole in his gloom—distant, but real. He reached without thinking and picked up a pencil which lay on the table by his bunk. He opened the welding textbook to its blank inside cover and began to draw. The image he drew arose not from a process of conception but seemed projected through that distant pinhole from beyond, making of his mind a camera obscura. It was a tree. The tree. The place where she'd told him to wait for her.

That first sketch took him only ten minutes, and then he put the book down. When he looked at the sketch again a short time later, it seemed terribly inadequate. He searched for a larger piece of paper, and finally pulled an old poster from an auto race off the wall and extracted it from the plastic frame. Its back was blank, and he used it to make a larger sketch with the same pencil. The time he spent sketching felt imbued with something other than the gloom that had ruled him for three years, something he couldn't quite identify but which his cells hungered for more of. Still, the final product was discouraging. He spent that afternoon sketching on any blank or semi-blank paper he could find. He made smaller, heavily detailed drawings, he tried giving background to the one on the poster but that just ruined it altogether. He knew he needed it to be bigger, so he brought in some coals from a firepit outside and tried drawing on one of the wooden walls. Given the texture of the surface and the limits of the makeshift charcoal, he could barely tell what he'd drawn. He stopped and went over to the trailer to make dinner for himself and Ben. When they were sitting across from each other eating the pasta and sausage he'd made, Daniel said, "There's something I need to do that I'm going to need supplies for. I know I said I wouldn't need money from you, but if you could loan me a little, I'd pay you back eventually."

"How much you need?"

"I'm not sure yet. I need a couple of rolls of construction paper, some ink markers. Maybe some paint."

Ben nodded, his brow gathering. "What are you doing?"

"I'm making a picture. A big one."

"You an artist or something?"

"No. I just need to make a picture."

By the time he moved from paper to metal, months had gone by, and the inside of the bunkhouse was covered with more than thirty large sketches and paintings of the tree, each one inadequate in its own specific ways. Daniel tried raising the level of detail, he tried cloudy Impressionism, and none of it worked. It wasn't that the pictures weren't good as art. They weren't, but that wasn't the point, somehow. Daniel's skills as an artist were fairly undeveloped, and he didn't expect the drawings to be good. What he did expect from them he couldn't quite determine, but he knew that the drive to keep trying had a goal, and that he'd know it when he reached it. He had cleared the entire floor, and was preparing to tape together a number of sheets of construction paper in order to go bigger, when he caught sight of the welding textbook lying in the corner. He had read the entire thing two months earlier, just passing time, and Ben had a welding rig out in the barn. Daniel walked out the door and over to where the remaining piles and pieces of scrap metal were. He wandered through, inspecting first the larger pieces, envisioning any way he might use them, or parts of them. In his mind he began assembling some of the pieces whose shapes seemed to fit together. Then he dug through what remained of the smaller pieces, dragging some to an open area and laying them out in patterns around each other, forming branches and leaves.

His first attempt at a sculpture took him only two weeks, and was a jumbled assemblage of junk in the vague shape of a tree which would not stand up under the weight of its own pieces. He had put it together lying on its side with supports, and when he tried to pull it upright using the winch on the truck, one of the rebar branches fell off and there was not enough weight in the base to support it. He re-welded the branch and tried to add weight to the base, but it still would not remain upright. He realized he was going to have to anchor it somehow, but by that point he had grown to hate the thing he'd made and he tore it apart and started over.

The second one stood, but only because he anchored it through the side of the barn to a support beam. At one end of the yard was a pile of seven giant metal streetlight poles, each too heavy to move without mechanical help, but Daniel used the torch to cut the thinner arms and support struts from their tops to use as branches. He cut them into pieces and put them back together in curved shapes, adding other scrap as bark and twigs. It was still only a vague impression of a tree, about seven feet high, but Daniel was proud of it for a couple of days, and continued adding detail, cutting an old car hood into flat leaf shapes and spot-welding them to the branches. On the third day, when he stepped out the door of the bunkhouse, he looked at what he'd made and hated it again. It looked like nothing to him. Like junk propped against a building. He tore it down.

This time he took a break. He tried mulling over exactly what he wanted to accomplish, but inactivity only ran him up against the most barren reaches of his mind and spiraled him back into gloom. While he'd been working, physically moving and attaching pieces, envisioning additions, conceiving logistics, there had been a clear, goal-oriented comfort involved, but when he tried to think ahead to the goal itself, to complete in his mind the image of a final product that would satisfy his core, he came up empty, and emptiness was now the enemy. So he simply began working again.

He moved into the barn, so that if it got too tall or unwieldy he could anchor it on multiple sides to the structural beams. This time he started with a larger base. He took the truck and dragged three of the dismembered streetlight poles over into the barn's doorway, took a giant pulley from an old hoist arm and attached it to the central support beam of the barn's roof. There was a large hole in the middle of the roof, giving him plenty of light to work by. Then he ran a cable through the pulley, backed the truck into the doorway and attached it to the winch. He slowly pulled each of the light poles upright. He secured them, clustered together, to the support beam using three lengths of chain, and their tops poked out through the hole in the roof. Using other scrap as filler, he welded the three poles together and put in a series of bolted struts up the entire length. Now he had his trunk.

He began building the branches individually and plotting where he would attach them. When he had eight branches built, he began connecting them to the trunk. Four of them were long—made from the streetlight arms and bunches of rebar welded together, cut and reattached at angles to create the impression of meandering growth—and he hung them from the overhead support beams before welding them onto anchors made of more bent rebar he'd clamped and welded into the body of the trunk. He didn't like how the rebar looked, but planned to cover it later somehow. The other four branches were smaller, and easier to attach, and he raised them higher up the trunk. When he had them all on, he began cutting more leaves out of any pressed steel he could find. Once he had a big bucket of leaves cut, he took them inside the bunkhouse at night and set about filing them by hand into better shapes. The first night he did this he took some of the leaves, after getting the shapes right, and used a hammer and chisel to gouge vein lines into them. In places where the lines went awry, he found himself following whatever logic the missteps indicated, and after a while the patterns he engraved weren't vein lines anymore but runic forms generated by his subconscious. Once this process began, it became his only obsession for a while. He just kept making more leaves, and engraving them in greater and greater detail as his skill with the tools evolved. He created an alphabet of runes and strung them into unknowable words, and sometimes made tiny pictures and patterns. Each design on each leaf seemed to exorcise an individual thought, thoughts that could now go straight from his subconscious to the chisel without troubling his conscious mind. As he went through the process of creating twigs out of braided wire and attaching the leaves to the branches, he found himself aching for the leaf-making, anticipating getting back to it. When he had attached all the leaves he'd made, they filled the branches nicely, and even though he knew that more branches would be necessary to make a place for more leaves, he went back to cutting, filing, and engraving the chips of metal until he ran out of flat steel to cut them from. Another month had gone by, and he had four times as many leaves as he'd made the first time, so reluctantly he went back to constructing more branches.

Ben came in one day to inspect the progress. He looked closely at the base of the trunk, nodding. Daniel watched as Ben's gaze moved up the trunk to the branches, and then to the places where Daniel had set up anchors and chains to hold the whole thing up. He looked also at the new branches that were lying around on the ground, some of them quite large.

"Before this thing gets too heavy," Ben said, "you're going to want to get it anchored better. This old barn will only hold so much. I'd suggest digging a hole and laying in some concrete." He looked up again, toward the top, where the trunk ended abruptly, the higher reaches of the tree still purely imaginary. "Also, looks like if this thing gets as big as it wants to, you might end up going farther through the roof—am I right?"

Daniel looked up. "I guess I hadn't thought about it. You could be right." He shoved his hands into his pockets. "Ben, I can scrap this or move it outside. I didn't mean to take over your barn for good—I'm not thinking ahead much. Sorry."

Ben's smile was quick, as always, a spark of the eyes and mouth that lasted no more than a second, his granite features hardening again so fast that the smile might have been imagined. "What do I need this barn for anyway?" He turned his palms forward. "Nothing. You keep going. Maybe I can be the one to think ahead for you. We could rent a backhoe and dig a hole here"—he pointed to a spot adjacent to the base—"attach some kind of root to the trunk and hoist it in, then fill it with concrete. Once that was done, you could hang whatever you wanted on it. It wouldn't go nowhere. But you oughta start with a good foundation. Right now, if this thing starts to lean even a few inches, it could bring the whole works down."

Daniel nodded.

"We should also pull some of the roof off now, before there's too much here to work around. If you wait too long you'll have to take it off carefully, which we don't have the equipment for. Time to rip it down is now. Then the barn could just be a ready-made scaffold."

"Well, maybe this is a little more than I can chew. I don't have money to rent a backhoe, or any of the other stuff we might need."

"You been helping me out here, without much recompense. Time I started giving you something anyway. And on top of that, I want to help. I want to see what you end up with. Otherwise I'm just rotting away in my trailer."

"I wouldn't say that."

"You don't have to. I said it." Ben laughed, then coughed hard and walked out. "We can take the truck to Rent-A-Center tomorrow," he said over his shoulder.

The next day they drove first to a big home goods store, where Ben loaded a handcart with supplies and equipment, including a Sawzall, a large handheld grinder, ten bags of concrete, three lengths of rope, and a webbed harness.

"What's that for?" Daniel asked, about the harness.

"That's for you. I sure as hell ain't going up on that roof to take it down."

At the front, Ben went to a counter and placed an order for a load of rebar to be delivered. "You're going to need it," he said. "I saw you already used what was lying around."

Then they went to Rent-A-Center and got the backhoe, which was on a trailer that they hooked to Ben's truck. On the way home, the old truck struggled, chugging and straining as it had when they pulled the loads of scrap to the yard near Vegas. "Old Trish'll hang in there, don't you worry," Ben said. "When the chips are down she never fails me."

"How'd your truck get the name Trish?"

"Named her after a girl I knew when I was young. She never wanted me but that didn't stop me from pining after her like a fool. I always had this kind of dream, or like, landscape, in my head—what my life might have been if she'd become my wife. If this truck's any indication, it probably would have turned out pretty good." He laughed loudly, then coughed, rolled down his window, and spat into the desert.

THE EARLY VISITORS were locals who had heard about the tree from the plumber who'd been out to fix the toilet in the trailer. These people were not looking to appreciate art, but merely to see something unique which was rumored to have cropped up near their town. The tree was a curiosity, as was Daniel. The first was the wife of the owner of the grocery store, who drove out with a friend. The two women parked by the trailer and knocked on the door, and when Ben answered they asked if they might take a look at the thing being built in his barn, which from where they stood was partially visible through the open doorway and the now-skeletal roof.

Ben said, "It don't bother me, but you'd better ask Daniel."

"He's the boy staying with you? I see him at the store every week."

"Yes." Ben raised his chin toward the barn. "He's out there working. He's a nice kid, but he can be private. Just go ask him."

Daniel, who had overheard this exchange from inside the barn, stepped into one of the old horse stalls and sat down. He couldn't have said exactly where the urge to hide came from. It wasn't fear or anxiety, but mainly a desire to avoid conversation, especially about the tree. He heard the women wander into the barn and stop near the doorway. One of them gasped.

"Oh my," said the other one. He heard their shoes shuffling around the dirt floor.

"I wonder where he is."

"I don't know."

"We ought to look for him, like Ben said."

"Well, he's not here."

"I'll check out back."

He heard her open the small rear door of the barn and step outside.

Daniel had turned the area behind the barn, where a long, slanted roof jutted from the back creating about thirty square feet of shade, into an outdoor workshop and staging area for the smaller pieces. She was out there for a minute, then reentered.

"He's got a bunch of stuff out there, but I don't see him." She passed very near the wooden fence he was leaning against, and must have seen his shirt through the cracks, because she poked her head into the stall. "Oh lord! I'm sorry. Are we bothering you? We just wanted to see what you're making. Is that all right?"

Daniel stood slowly, acting as if he'd been taking a nap back there. "I guess it's fine," he said. "As long as you don't ask any questions." He waved his hand, miming nonchalance. "But go ahead and look all you want." He walked out the back door into his workshop and shut it behind him. He waited back there until they left.

The presence of strangers in this haven of his was jarring, and the prospect of them requiring something of him alarmed him. But he realized he hadn't minded people seeing the tree. The tree itself seemed to benefit, somehow energetically, from the attention. As visitors became more regular—although there were never very many—he grew accustomed to them, and word of his desire for quiet and privacy also made it into the town's gossip about the place, so people generally left him alone. Often when someone would drive in, Daniel would simply go out back until they left, but if he was in the middle of working on the main body of the tree he would keep working. He would give them some small acknowledgment when they entered, and then ignore them, and found that worked best at minimizing interaction. It was only when people from farther away—the art appreciators—began to show up that he started putting up the signs.

Though these urbane pilgrims were more familiar to him, he usually didn't like their visits. Some of them would approach him with presumptuous intimacy, and begin talking to him as if they were members of the same guild. He could not figure out how to discourage these conversations politely, and when pressed would move quickly from taciturn to irritable. People who considered themselves thoughtful and well-intentioned would find themselves suddenly being asked to leave.

But if they kept quiet and remained unobtrusive, he would continue to work around them for as long as they wanted to stay.

THERE WERE TWO visits that stuck out in his mind, whose details would stay with him through his life after much of the two and a half years he spent building the tree had smeared into a blur.

The first was a group of four who arrived one day in a ragtop Mustang, two long-haired young men and two young women, all with sunglasses and wind-burnished cheeks. They climbed from the car like astronauts from a lander, heads swiveling, casting mirrored gazes all around the property, although the object of their visit stood visible directly in front of them. As they walked to the barn, they exuded the dissolute glamour of rock stars, the scruffy guys slinking skinnily forward in their tight flared jeans and black zipper-boots, the women muss-haired and bare-legged.

Daniel was in his harness halfway up the trunk, welding a curved and polished piece of steel bark onto the main skeleton. He pushed up the visor of the welding helmet and watched them approach through the open arch of the barn entrance. When they stepped into the shade of the barn, one of the guys looked up at him and said, "Hey, man. How you doing?"

Daniel was always wary of matching a casual, friendly tone, for fear of encouraging conversation, so he just nodded.

"This is incredible, man," the guy called up to him. "Really phenomenal, wow!" The other three had begun wandering in a slow circle underneath, looking up into the branches and inspecting some of the work materials that were lying around.

Daniel hadn't finished welding the piece of bark, but it was attached securely enough to leave. He lowered himself until his feet hit the floor and unclipped his harness from the rope.

"Cyrus Foley," the guy who'd been speaking said, extending a hand.

Daniel shook the hand and said, "Hi."

The other guy, completing his circuit around the trunk, came alongside his friend and said, "How long you been working on this?"

"A while," Daniel said, and began to move toward the rear door and escape.

"Mind if we take a picture?"

Daniel spun back, pointing at the wooden sign nailed to the doorframe that read *Quiet Please, no pictures.* "No. Please, no pictures." His tone had gone hostile, his irritation at the request compounded by his hatred of being forced to interact.

The first guy, Foley, slapped his friend's shoulder. "No worries, brother. All good. Pete, let's go have a smoke." He steered his friend out into the dirt yard and they leaned against the car, smoking. This left Daniel alone in the barn with the two women. They were still wandering under the tree staring up at it. Daniel started walking again toward the rear door, and one of them said, "Hey there, can I ask you a question?"

He stopped and faced her, not hiding his irritation. She sauntered over to him, and by the time she arrived in front of him, his irritation had been deeply compromised by the aqueous roll of her hips and the profusion of her bare arms and legs. There was a sly haughtiness in the slant of her head and her pursed lips. Daniel, after almost three years in prison, and a year and a half out here with Ben, had embraced the default celibacy that came with his isolation and his mental state. He never questioned it. But he was still twenty-five years old, and unaccustomed to sights like her. She removed her sunglasses and the haughtiness evaporated. She was younger than him, and her smile was friendly and ingenuous.

"Did you grow up here, in this junkyard?"

"No," Daniel said.

"Been here long?"

"A year and a half."

The other woman sat down on a bucket a few feet away, ignoring the conversation, and propped her foot on her knee, removing her slipper and rooting inside it for a rock. Her cutoffs were very short, and her tank top hung loose in the neck as she leaned forward. Daniel struggled not to stare.

"My name's Greta. What's yours?"

"Daniel." He found himself answering her unhesitatingly. The part of him that recoiled from human contact was still very much present, but had been left stunned, watching from behind a scrim, while the part that now stepped in and pulled the vocal levers was merely a timid vassal of his libido. These dynamics within himself would normally have taken place on oblivious autopilot, but isolation had made him mindful of his own inner workings.

"You do anything besides work on this tree, Daniel?"

"Not really, no."

"How long do you think till it's finished?"

"I don't know. I don't think about it that way."

"You mean, like, it'll never really be finished?"

"It might be, sometime. I just don't think about finishing. When I do, I guess I'll know it." Daniel felt the words tumbling out of his mouth like a sluice of gravel. He wanted to stop them. "I need to get back to work," he said, pointing to the rear door and starting to walk to it.

"You have a workspace back here?" she asked, moving in step with him.

He nodded, speeding his pace.

"Can I come look?"

"Sure," he said, cursing himself silently and helplessly, beguiled.

"I'll be back, Jill," she called to her friend.

She followed him out the door and slowly sidled along the worktable, picking things up and asking him about them: What were they, where would they end up on the tree, was there a master plan somewhere? He answered her in each case as briefly as he could, while moving the next piece of bark he'd fashioned onto the table so he could begin polishing and engraving it.

"If you do finish it, what do you think you'll do with it?" she asked.

"Do with it?"

"I mean, will you try to get it moved somewhere, so people can see it?"

"No."

"Really? What about you? Will you stay here when it's done? Or go somewhere else and build another giant thing?" She was facing him now, as he began brushing the metal hunk with steel wool—something he would normally do only after going at it with the grinder, but the grinder would have made conversation impossible. He was just doing it to busy his hands and distract himself. She was standing close, leaning on the edge of the table, lolling her head to the side so she could look directly into his face. Her unruly blond hair hung down and touched his left hand, which was holding the metal steady. The brush of her hair jolted him, as if in contacting even one tiny part of her he had touched all of her. The cords of her neck drew taut beneath the skin, and the corner of her mouth curled slightly, an incitement.

"You ever come into LA?" she asked.

He stopped. He looked at her and spoke from behind the scrim. "Greta, I'm going to need you to stop asking me questions. Please."

"Oh," she said, and smiled brightly, as if his request pleased her. "Sorry." She clearly understood the potency of her smile and was deploying it against him, but somehow this did not diminish its sway. "I can just be quiet and watch."

Daniel gathered himself and looked away from her. "I think it's best if you and your friends leave," he said. "I'm sorry. It's not personal. I'm just not a sociable person."

She laughed. "You mean, it's not me it's you?"

Daniel smiled at her, and the edge of something in him began to crumble. He felt as though he hadn't smiled in years, and now he wondered if that was so.

"Listen," she said, "no worries. We're not here to fuck up anyone's trip. You want us gone we're gone. But you should really let them take a picture of your tree. Cyrus works for *LA Weekly,* and he could make things happen for you."

"He's a reporter?"

"He's a *writer.* He's done pieces for *Rolling Stone* and all kinds of places. He interviewed Neil Young this year. *LA Weekly* is just his day job. If you sat down with him, he might do a piece on you, too."

Daniel went quickly through the door into the barn, and the first thing he saw was the other man shuffling sideways under the tree with a camera pointed up into the branches.

"Hey! I asked you not to take pictures."

The guy brought the camera down. "Don't freak, brother. Just a couple of snapshots." He raised the camera quickly and took a shot of Daniel.

Daniel's ire knifed up into his throat. He took two long steps and grabbed the strap of the camera, yanking it from the man's hands. Without thinking he swung it against the ground, shattering the lens and sending pieces scattering across the dirt floor. The guy knelt and scooped up the wrecked camera. He said, "What is wrong with you?"

"Leave now." Daniel pointed through the open front doorway at their car, and saw that the other woman was leaning against it, smoking. Foley was nowhere in sight. He picked up a two-foot length of rebar from near the wall and carried it toward the man, who still stood motionless inside the barn. "I mean it," Daniel said.

The man held up a hand, saying, "Whoa man," and scrambled toward the car. Greta had already gone out to her friend. Daniel saw Foley step out of the bunkhouse.

"What's going on?" Foley said, heading toward his friends.

"What were you doing in there?"

"Nothing. Just looking for a bathroom."

Daniel pointed his weapon at the car. "Leave right now."

"You got us wrong, buddy. We're friends."

"I'll start with the car," Daniel said, raising the rebar and taking a step toward the Mustang.

Foley walked to the car without a word and started it. They all climbed in, and as they spun in a U-turn Greta waved and smiled brightly again at Daniel. He couldn't decide whether she was mocking him or still flirting.

The second visit came seven months later, amid the escalation of tourists that followed the story in *LA Weekly*. Daniel and Ben weren't exactly inundated, but once the story came out they began to get two or three a week. Foley had found Daniel's expired driver's license in his search of the bunkhouse and learned his full name, and the film in the camera had survived, so there were pictures of the tree, and one of Daniel. Cam said he had waited so long because he didn't want to disrespect Daniel's solitude. He arrived on a motorcycle and came straight to the door of the bunkhouse, where Daniel was lying on his cot reading. Daniel had heard the engine but had not bothered to look, resolved to staying out of sight. But then the knock on the door, which was unusual since most who knocked went automatically to the trailer, which was clearly inhabited. When he opened the door and saw his friend there, Daniel's soul twisted. He hadn't known he was lonely, but in the moment of its relief his loneliness revealed itself.

Cam laughed as they embraced.

Daniel laughed with him and invited him in. They sat at either end of the cot, which was the only furnishing in the room. The frame of the second cot had been incorporated into the tree.

"When someone told me about the *LA Weekly* story on you I was so happy. So relieved to hear news of you. I figured if you wanted visitors you'd have been in touch, so I didn't come right away. But I couldn't stop thinking about it. I hope you don't mind."

"I'm glad," Daniel said. "It's been too long, and I'm sorry for that. When I got out I needed some kind of absolute space. I ended up here."

Cam had showed up to visit him in jail at the very start, when Daniel was awaiting trial. It was unexpected, but Daniel had been glad of the company then. Somehow Cam's presence, and their strange fledgling friendship, required nothing concrete from him, and that was essential during that time. His parents, and the few other old friends who came to him, all hungered for explanation. How had the Daniel they knew become a drug dealer with a deceased girlfriend? Who was this girlfriend most had never met? Her gigantic significance to him escaped them, and he couldn't bear to try and communicate it. Their bewilderment, and the onus on him to mitigate it, oppressed him. Cam had met Daniel and Rachel together, and so somehow understood him in that terrible time better than his family. To him their love was a foregone conclusion, and with him there was depth without any obtrusive history. He had continued to visit all through the trial, and every few months afterward, at the prison. He'd been Daniel's only visitor in prison after he had barred his parents. He had brought Daniel books and cigarettes, and their wide-ranging conversations in that gray cinder-block room with its small high windows and bolted-down chairs had been a surreal respite from Daniel's pervasive gloom. He'd often woken on the days following Cam's visits uncertain as to whether Cam had actually been there or he'd dreamed it. Sometimes he did dream it.

"I thought I'd hear from you when you got out," Cam said. "You know I drove up there, just to make sure they had actually let you out when you said they would."

"I spun off the planet for a while. It didn't feel like a decision. I just walked into the desert without a destination. I needed to leave everything behind. It's starting to feel like there might be a way back, though. I don't know."

Cam nodded, smiling. The two friends sat and talked for a long time. Cam had moved back to Los Angeles, where he was from, and was now promoting concerts. He was about to buy a music venue.

"Did you sell the ranch?"

"No, I still own it. Win lives there with a few of the others, but it's different now. Smaller, mellower. He's growing lots of vegetables and selling them, and he insists on paying me rent. He's taken up surfing, and he and Sarah have a little daughter. Then there's this business with Hugo and his group. I still can't believe it. I guess you've seen it in the news."

"Who's Hugo?"

"He stayed at the ranch for a while. Did you see them when you were there? They lived in tents down the hill, dressed all in white. Hugo was the leader."

"Oh right, I saw them. I asked Win about them. What happened?"

"They all killed themselves last week. Mass suicide. Down near LA, in Moorpark. Ten people."

"God, that's awful, I'm sorry."

"It's not like they were a real part of the scene. They left the ranch in late sixty-nine. I had no idea the group was even still together." Cam shook his head and looked out the small dusty window above the cot. "But a few of them were friends of mine before they joined Hugo. And I used to have conversations with him, sort of philosophical jousting sessions. I found him interesting. But once they started keeping to themselves people didn't really want them around anymore. Win and I sat him down and told him they had to rejoin the larger community if they wanted to stay, and they disappeared two days later. Fucking insanity. It's been in all the papers for a week."

"I don't get the news out here."

"Maybe you're lucky. Nothing's what it used to be, but then again, why would anything ever be what it used to be?"

"Infinite sentient flux," Daniel said, which was a term Cam had coined in his personal philosophy, one of their topics during those prison visits.

"Yes!" Cam laughed without sacrificing gravity. "All part of the ISF." He paused. "Think you'll come back to the world eventually?"

"I don't think much at all these days. I've been living with no future out here."

Cam's eyes engaged him. "That's a gift, I imagine."

Daniel nodded, and marveled at the unaccountable appearance of a friend like this one. When they had finished catching up, Daniel took him out to the barn and showed him the tree.

Some months after Cam's visit, Daniel finished building a small branch and could find no perfect place on the tree to attach it. This was a first. Each morning he would search for the right spot, beginning by staring up at the trunk, which was taller now with two more of the light poles cut in half and the thin ends welded together forming the tree's top, extending twenty feet above the barn's missing roof. Then he would get into his harness and climb around looking from different angles, before spending the rest of the day polishing, patching the bark, and grinding off small imperfections. The morning of the fourth day of this, Ben came into the barn as Daniel was getting his harness ready. The old man stood bowlegged in the wide doorway looking up in the last of the soft morning light. Soon the sun would appear over the mountains to the east, hardening everything.

"How's it coming?" Ben asked.

"Good," Daniel said. "I'm looking for where to attach that branch." He pointed at the curved branch lying along the inside wall. "It's been four days, and I can't seem to find the right spot."

Ben was quiet for a time, his hands pressed deep into his pockets, head tilted back. Without taking his eyes from the upper reaches of the tree, he said, "Maybe there ain't a spot."

"What do you mean?"

He continued staring upward, taking another long pause. "Could be it's finished."

Daniel dropped the loop of rope he was about to clip to the harness and walked over to stand next to his friend. He followed the old man's gaze up the trunk to the smallest twigs at the top, patterned against the pale sky.

2017

While Michael regaled the group, Roland leaned close to Celia and whispered to her, "Miles had a revelation, you know."

Celia nodded but didn't speak, focusing on Michael in hopes that Miles's shroom-kindled revelation might remain a mystery.

They were in the bar of the spa resort, and Roland and Michael were telling the clutch of gathered cast and crew the story of their weekend's vision quest. Michael was Roland's stunt double, and their similarity in size and shape created a mirroring effect as they passed the story back and forth, strangely taking turns standing up in front of the group as if it were a presentation. Their similarities ended at the neck. Roland's face was a glowering, guileful jewel. He swept the crowd with it like a spotlight operator, now and then aiming it directly at someone for added drama. It was a face that seemed to reveal itself anew each time one saw it, no matter how briefly one had looked away, and it was a lie, evincing a mystery entirely absent in Roland himself. Michael's face, in contrast, was a plainspoken autobiography. He was exactly the slightly sad erstwhile world-eater his leathery face and bright eyes suggested. He was a forty-year-old stuntman with a chiseled body and a life he loved despite having abandoned his movie-star ambitions. He was smart and friendly, and early in the shoot Celia had targeted him as a possible playmate before finding out he was happily married.

"He figured out the ending," Roland whispered.

"You know what it is?"

"No, he won't say. But he says that's all that's left. We're going to shoot it, and then we're all going home."

"Jesus. Really? That'll be a relief."

"Yeah, I guess," said Roland. "I was starting to like this weird scene, after all this time. I kind of wish we could stay a while longer."

"Careful what you wish for. Miles might rewrite the whole movie tonight and we'd be here till next year."

Roland laughed. Celia's phone buzzed.

It was a text from Leo, asking what she was doing.

In the bar at the spa, she answered. Bunch of people here. Miles is supposed to come talk to us but he's MIA. You back in Bisbee?

No, I'm here.

> You should come and save me
> from them.

They might figure us out if I
show up.

> Let them. I hear we're wrap-
> ping soon anyway.

There was a pause this time, the shivering ellipsis of his indecision pulsing there under her text. She waited, then clicked the screen off. After two minutes his answer appeared.

Not ready for that.

She typed back, My room. 5 mins.

"Who you talking to over there?" Roland asked. She had leaned back and angled her phone as best she could so he couldn't see.

"My kid," she said, before realizing that it was ten o'clock. "He's with his grandfather and he had a nightmare."

"You should go call him," said June, who was sitting on her other side in the oversized booth. Celia realized that in hiding the phone from Roland, she'd had it right under June's face. "He'll want to hear his mommy's voice." She smiled and looked through her dark bangs at Celia, reminding her suddenly of her childhood best friend, a girl named Billie. June Hense was playing one of the court ladies and was a good egg, Celia could tell, though they didn't know each other well. Was it possible she'd been filming with these people five months and knew them this little?

"You're right. I'm going to do that. Text me when Miles shows up." Celia nudged Roland and he stood to let her out.

She walked out into the vaulted beige-tiled lobby, with its scarlet-upholstered furniture and cast-iron chandeliers, and saw Lars, Miles's Austrian majordomo, sitting in an armchair with a briefcase in his lap. He nodded at Celia and gave her his sickly smile. Sicklier than usual, she thought, but it might have been the light. She raised a hand and turned away from him, going through a side door into the courtyard, which was a garden-and-pool area encircled by the patios of the guest rooms in the main building. Unsteady wind curled down over the tile roof and shook the bushes along the path. The night sky was bright with stars. She skirted the pool and exited the courtyard through a breezeway at the back. Behind the main building was a small sloping lawn at the bottom of which were two groups of freestanding bungalows clustered around two smaller swimming pools. She looked for Leo as she walked, but didn't see him or the car. She went into her bungalow, turned on the light, and sat down on the bed.

The walk under the familiar Arizona sky had made her think again of Billie, the friend June had reminded her of. Those grade-school and early teenage years in Phoenix had rubbed themselves into a sunny haze in her memory. Everything that happened before her mother's death had become vague, except for her times with Billie. Billie was the girl her mother had forbidden her to see. Even when she was twelve you didn't need to have heard the rumors to look at Billie and know she would have some kind of reputation. It was a look she cultivated. There had been an incident with a joint falling out of her pocket and that was all Celia's mother had needed. Then for two years Celia had been constantly obsessed with finding excuses to get away and secretly hang out with her. When she was with Billie, the other parts of her life with her mother fell away—the endless auditioning, the kids' catalogue shoots, flights back and forth to LA for TV ads and after-school specials. With Billie she hung out at 7-Eleven and smoked cigarettes, went to Starbucks or

Marshalls at the strip mall, or walked to whatever remote areas they could find just to kick pebbles and drink and talk about nothing. They caught rides with older boys to remoter places than they could walk to and made out with them. When Billie's mother was working they lounged at her house, eating Popsicles and sweating on the old gray sofa because the air conditioner didn't work. Billie lived with her mother in a Phoenix suburb called Surprise, and always said she was surprised to be living there. They had a tiny condo in a tiny development that brushed against open desert on its north side. Billie and Celia were both only-children of single mothers. Billie's mother was an alcoholic waitress at a chain restaurant, and Celia's mother, Diana, was a reformed-alcoholic would-be heiress with no fortune. The idle and unlucky generations that had preceded her had run through the money before much of it could trickle down to her, so she had been deprived of the wealth she'd been raised to expect. They lived in a small house which Diana owned outright, but there was not much else. Celia's career paid the bills, and Diana had visions of getting rich if she could just make a star of her pretty daughter. It worked in the end, but she didn't live to enjoy the money.

Billie's spell over Celia was powerful. She was very tall and wore black canvas high-top sneakers and jeans or cutoffs or tight striped leggings. Never skirts or dresses. Her awkward height and bony limbs removed her from the realm of acceptable grade-school beauty, but her face had a smudged loveliness, a flat symmetry. Her high ankle bones were prominent above the tops of the sneakers when she wore leggings, and Celia envied her black hair and her pale, pale complexion. She knew she wasn't gay, but sometimes Celia wanted to bend forward when they were sitting on the ground together and put her lips on those beautiful white ankle bones, to feel the hardness there. She remembered those nights with Billie as if they were razor-etched into her front brain: sucking mixed red and white wine, stolen from Billie's mom's kitchen, out of a plastic water bottle and kicking gravel at the faux-adobe sidewall of the 7-Eleven, which in the parking-lot fluorescence glowed like a giant stick of margarine under the bright-black desert sky. They would walk at sunset along the dry rutted drainage wash that ran along the back of

Billie's complex, waiting for the ghostly yells of coyotes and then imitating and encouraging them, every so often seeing one step gingerly from behind a sage bush to look at these strange coyote-sounding humans and then trot away into the dusk.

They would go with Jimmy and Charlie Harrigan to the arcade after getting high, and play wargames. Sometimes, when the boys had their father's car, they'd drive out into the desert and lie on the hood of the car drinking. Celia had given her virginity to Jimmy in the back seat of that old Ford when she was fourteen, while Billie was outside on a blanket with Charlie. Jimmy was seventeen and Charlie was twenty, and they were nothing special. Just two greasy boys with no mother who lived down the row from Billie. Celia, looking the way her mother insisted she always must, and being on TV sometimes, could have had her pick of the boys in school, but she liked being with Billie and whoever Billie chose. She gave in to Jimmy because she liked the idea that she and Billie were doing something almost together. But when she went to compare notes with Billie afterward, Billie seemed shocked to hear she'd gone all the way.

"You didn't?" Celia asked. She could feel her face growing hot, though she knew that Billie was not a virgin, had not been for almost a year. There had been a boy named Fausto who was her first.

"With Charlie Harrigan?" Billie said. "Hell no." And then, like a gift, she'd said, "Jimmy's the one I'd do if I was going to, anyway. Jimmy's the catch." Celia had never forgotten that gift, and her love for Billie.

Celia's mother had moved them to Los Angeles a year later when Celia had landed the role that first made her famous, playing Luna Francis on *Grandview High*. Their second month in LA, Diana Dressler's new car had been discovered embracing a tree only two blocks from their new house, where Celia had been sleeping. When she died, Diana had been drunk for the first time in twelve years.

Six months before getting the part in Miles Rossinger's film, just after getting clean for the second time, Celia had looked Billie up on Facebook and found her, Willa now, not Billie. She was still living in Phoenix. She had always said she would never have children or a husband, but now she had two of each: two young kids with the first husband, and a second husband who was captioned in one photo as "Stepdad of the year!" A regular guy in a baseball cap and goatee. Celia had thought fifty times of sending some kind of note, but had never done it. The happy-looking woman in the pictures was someone she didn't quite recognize, and the idea of muddying those adolescent memories with some awkward exchange held her back. Celia knew if she wasn't famous she would have done it, which made her sad because she understood it wasn't really the potential change in Billie that held her back, but the actual change in herself. She couldn't stand the possibility that if the reunion didn't take she might end up alienating her friend and making herself seem like a stuck-up celebrity. Every so often she scrolled through the pictures of Billie's life, which were open for public viewing, but she never went any further.

Her phone buzzed in her hand, a text from June: He's here.

There was a soft knock on the door, Leo's knock. Celia let him in.

"I left the car in the main lot so people wouldn't see it down here," he said.

"I've got to go back up to the bar. Miles just got there. He says he's going to announce something. I think it's that we're wrapping soon. They're waiting for me."

Leo looked stricken for a second but masked it quickly. "Okay, I can take off."

"No." She cupped the back of his neck and pulled his face to hers, kissing him. "Stay here, I'll be back."

When she got back to the bar the scene was less boisterous than it had been. Miles was not speaking to the group, but sitting quietly off to the side with Lars and, of all people, George Hughes. When he saw her, Miles stood. He patted George's shoulder as he walked away from the table. "Here she is," he said. "Have a seat, Celia, and I'll get down to it."

Celia took an open chair at a table near the group.

"Okay, so we're in the home stretch." Miles positioned himself by the sidewall where they all could look at him. "Everyone here has done incredible work. Really, it has been a great privilege to work with each and every one of you. I know that it's been challenging, and that we've flown by the seat of our pants a lot of the time, which has created a fair amount of chaos. But tomorrow, we're going to start shooting the new ending, which I wrote yesterday. There are some new cast members on their way here for it, and we should be able to bang it out in a week, two at most. Then"—he spread his arms magnanimously—"everyone can go home!"

There was a round of hoots and applause.

"But that," Miles said, holding up his palms, "is not my announcement." He waited for quiet. "The real announcement is this. I have re-envisioned the storyline here and come to a momentous decision. This film will be the first in an epic trilogy. The entire sweep of the project, in broad strokes, descended on me this weekend, and I have two note-books full of ideas and outlining for the subsequent films. I have spent the day today pitching the sequels to the studio, and everyone loves the idea . . . at least in principle." He lowered his chin and chuckled to himself, then continued, "I've also been lining up some additional cast for the new ending, and contacting reps for a number of you, the pri-mary cast, whom I know we'll really need. My sincere hope is that we will be able to get the whole company back for the other films, which would, I promise, make the shoots more organized and quicker, since we'll have our working relationships hammered out already. Also, be-fore we begin on the second film, I will be taking as long as it takes to finish, really finish, both scripts. No more overnight pages and im-promptu scenes."

A couple of ironic claps and nervous laughs.

"Well, not nearly as many, anyway," Miles said, and there was gen-eral laughter. "Final decisions can of course wait till we're done here and actually developing the next one. Lars has sent the new pages and call sheets to everyone's rooms, and they are arriving there as I speak. So take a look and we'll get back to work tomorrow!" He threw his arms up to indicate that his speech had come to a close, and everyone applauded. There was, Celia could hear, a tangible divide between the exuberant cheers of the Rossinger faithful and the measured clapping of the dubious, and she wondered which side she fell on.

"I'm going to bed," she said, but as she stood Miles took her arm and guided her to the far end of the bar.

"What do you think?" he asked.

"I think it's great," she said. "Congratulations on your revelation."

"I mean, do you think you're on board?"

"I thought we didn't need to decide now."

"We don't, but I was hoping to get a verbal from you, just to set my mind at ease. You're one I really can't replace. By the way, I had a talk with George, and he's in for number two. I know you guys get along. No more sex scenes with him, though, I promise. Lady Anna continues her reign as a ruthless warrior queen, and has a new lover who appears in this new ending."

"What about Roland?"

"Roland will find out when he reads the new pages that Varek does not survive. Lady Anna needs a lover worthy of her, and for all his brashness and nobility young Varek ain't it. She'll grieve him. His death will further harden her. Then we'll bring in someone new to melt her heart."

"I'm going to need to think, Miles. I have a child, you know. This has been a lot for him, me being away."

"We'll be shooting a lot of it on studio sets, I'm sure, so you'll be home more. There'll be some location work, of course, but we can try and stagger it. We'll make accommodations."

"Well, I won't lie. I'm flattered, and it would be very hard to see myself turning it down. My agent would draw and quarter me if I did. So you can put that in your hopper, okay? Yes, I do want to do it, but I will need to wait and figure things out before agreeing officially."

He smiled so wide and so silently that it began to make her uneasy. She smiled back, but his silence and awkward eye contact persisted. "Fantastic," he said finally, squeezing her shoulder. He spun and walked away.

CELIA CONVINCED LEO not to worry about spending the night. It was a movie set, she told him, and no one cared one way or another.

"The male actors are constantly fucking interns and prop girls, so why shouldn't I fuck my driver?" They were lying sideways across the giant bed's disarray. She was close against him and felt his laughter throb through her own body.

"Fair enough, I'll be your prop girl."

She slid her hand into his crotch. "You know the drill," she said, and they were off again.

Early the next morning, she had breakfast for two delivered to the bungalow. As they ate avocado toast and fruit salad, and Leo drank his coffee, Celia registered for the second time that her core fear, which plagued her most deeply in the morning, felt muted and distant. She'd grown so used to the fear and free-floating shame that invaded her in the raw unguarded hour after waking that she'd long since stopped questioning it. She'd learned the skill of rebuilding her defenses each day. The morning before, waking next to Leo at his hotel, she had been shocked to find herself calm. Not free altogether from any hint of it, but protected, as if in a sunny moated castle, insulated from danger. This morning she hadn't even noticed the relief at first, because, she realized, she'd expected it this time.

"I like waking up with you," she said.

He smiled. "Yeah, likewise."

They dressed together and drove to set. On the drive she reread the new script pages, which she had skimmed the night before. It was a very good ending. She could feel it. It excited her, and also it scared her because she feared not being able to do it justice. It did not rely on the death of Varek for its resonance, and it did not devolve into a bloodbath like the original ending. It brought both the character of Anna and the intrigues of her father-in-law's court to an inflection point where she, in her grief over Varek, finds herself on the very lip of suicide and is held back from it only by an opportunity to do damage to Kajika, who has killed Varek and become a dangerous enemy. She cannot pass up the chance to thwart him from achieving the power he craves. The desire for revenge saves her life, and then she finds herself in a position where it is clear the power will slide readily into her hands if she chooses to gather it. Celia recognized one of the new characters, Promus, as the future love interest Miles had referred to the night before. His appearance was made much of, and his role in the ending was major, even including a brilliant monologue in a scene with only she and him. She wondered who they'd get to play him.

When they pulled into the parking area, she saw right away who they'd gotten to play Promus. He was sitting with a small group under the awning they'd attached to the main building to create a shaded smoking area: Darren Styles. There wasn't another new role in this ending worthy of him showing up on short notice. It had to be him.

"Oh for fuck's sake," Celia said. She was riding in the front seat, and Leo pulled up behind a row of cars near the awning.

"What?" Leo asked, then said, "Oh," when he noticed Darren. Darren was not someone who went unnoticed. Even in a plain black T-shirt and battered jeans, with simple Ray-Bans on his face, he made an impression. People would have noticed him even if his features weren't burned into the prefrontal cortex of anyone who wasn't living off the grid.

"Fuck fuck fuck," she said.

"How long since you've seen him?"

"Five years, anyway."

"You going to be okay?"

"I'm fine," she said, perceiving and regretting the note of impatience in her voice. She didn't have the wherewithal in the moment to remedy it, so she climbed quickly out of the car and strode toward Darren, thinking, *Rip off the Band-Aid.* He saw her and stood from his chair, putting out his cigarette.

"Hey there!" she said, and hugged him.

"Hey Ceels." He embraced her full and long, arms encircling her like an old friend, and she felt an ominous twinge of the old energy that his proximity had always sparked in her, even after things went bad. A golden jolt; it harkened back to juvenile empty-headedness, and so was untroubled by present reality. When they met, he had been a lithe boy of twenty, and there had been a semblance in their statures, two young beanpoles. Now he had his movie-star body, like they all did, and she could feel the rigid contours of it against her chest, the shifting clouds of back muscle under her palms.

"Let me guess," she said, pulling away. "You're Promus."

"Yeah! It all happened quick, but I said, what the fuck. I've always wanted to work with Miles."

She shook her head and pulled out her cigarette pack, tapping it against her knuckle. Through her shock she was glad to see him, but she was also angry at Miles. "That unbelievable fuckface," she said. "He could at least have told me."

"What? He said he did!" He glanced over his shoulder, making sure Miles was not there. "I never would have done it if he hadn't told me you knew, and that you were fine with it."

Celia laughed, growing angrier. "I will be, don't worry. Once I get over the shock." She lit her cigarette and drew in a lungful of smoke, then turned sideways to exhale it. "It really is good to see you." The orange sun flared atop the mountain range to the east, and she took half a step toward it, away from Darren, and crossed her arms.

He said, "Yeah, same here."

She paused, and then laughed again. "That bastard. He sprung this on us."

On cue, Miles stepped out of the building and walked toward them. "Oh no!" he said, hurrying and waving a hand as he reached them. "Celia, you weren't supposed to find out like this. I had a whole speech planned for it, a moment."

"You told me she knew," Darren said, but his tone was bantering rather than blaming. He'd come under Miles's influence already, Celia could tell.

"I fibbed. I wanted to tell her only right before rolling, use her surprise in the moment when Promus appears, see if it generated anything. But," he threw his hands out wide, "the jig is up!"

Celia found it impossible in that moment to look at Miles. She was enraged, but her spontaneous gladness at seeing Darren was diluting her anger and she knew she wouldn't be able to maintain it if she engaged directly. She didn't want to let it go, to let Miles off the hook. She turned away from both of them, smoking intently.

Miles moved beside her, speaking softly near her ear. "Have I stepped in it deeply this time?"

"That scene's first up, right? Let's just shoot it, why don't we." She dropped her cigarette and crushed it under her sandal.

"You're okay?"

"Trust me, Miles, you don't want to have that conversation with me right now. Let's just do our jobs."

"Great," he said. "So . . . long term, you're good working with Darren?"

She mustered a withering look and turned it on him. "Darren isn't the problem." She was surprised when Miles nodded contritely and did not try to defend himself.

Quietly, after a pause, he asked, "How do you like the new pages? The ending?"

She snorted and shook her head. She didn't want to answer him, but she did. "They're fucking brilliant. Of course. You asshole."

He smiled at her, and she received it affectionately in spite of herself. She did like him, after all. Miles walked away. She looked at Darren, and then suddenly became aware of Leo, who was sitting in the car observing all this. She said, "I'm going to sit in my car and do a quick meditation, then I'll head in to wardrobe."

"This gonna be okay?" Darren asked.

Celia smiled at him. "I'm okay if you're okay."

"All right. See you in there." He went inside.

Celia climbed into the back seat of the car. "Everything okay?" Leo asked.

Celia nodded and took a breath. "Can you drive around the side and park? I want to meditate for a few minutes and the car is the best place."

"Sure." He pulled around the corner and stopped halfway down the long windowless sidewall. At the far end were the other chauffeured vehicles, two of the drivers leaning in the shade of the building talking.

"Well . . ." Leo was clearly at a bit of a loss.

"Can you give me a few minutes, Leo?" Celia asked. "I need to gather myself before shooting this goddamn scene."

"Yeah, sure." He twisted and looked over his shoulder at her, aiming for eye contact.

Celia looked out the window. "Thanks."

He got out and wandered down the wall. She saw him nod to the other drivers—one of them greeting him with a handshake—and round the corner to where the door to the crew lounge faced the back. She took a deep breath and closed her eyes. After a moment she took another deep breath. "Oh, for fuck's sake," she whispered on the exhale.

FOREST LIVED IN an ivy-covered house with superb views in Temescal Canyon. In the nine years his son had been living there Daniel had visited only four or five times, and never uninvited. There were two cars in the driveway when he pulled in. It was one of those hill-houses that at first seem to have the quaintness of a shack but on closer inspection reveal an underlying opulence, just as their bulk lies hidden down the hill below their airy top floors. Daniel knocked on the oak door, still mentally rearranging his old perception of Forest as a dilettante—sincere though he might be—lounging on his mother's money. Discovering this new respect for his son filled Daniel with a strange amalgam of emotion. He had never wanted to think of Forest the way he did. He had always tried not to, but felt that reality corralled him into it. Forest called himself a painter without ever seeming to produce any paintings, living high among the dissolute offspring of Hollywood players and dressing always impeccably. For Daniel, these skirmishes with his perception of Forest always led into a descending spiral of self-flagellation—for both his poor example (who was *he*, after all—ex-con, abnegated artist, living in a house gifted to him—to look down on his own son?) and poor parenting. Finding out he was wrong was at once exhilarating and shaming.

The door opened and the girl, Tamara, stood there. "Oh, hey," she said. "What's up, Forest's dad?"

"Nothing much is up," he said, smiling. "Call me Daniel. I found myself driving nearby and decided to see if he was home."

"He's home. Come on in."

Daniel followed her down the short hall into the spacious living room. Forest was standing at the open kitchen counter chopping a cucumber on a cutting board.

"Look who's here," Tamara said.

"Pop. This is an unexpected pleasure! What's going on?" He was in an expansive mode, king of the castle.

"Nothing, just wanted to stop in and say hi. I was driving nearby."

"Have a seat. I'll be done in a minute, and you can join us for late lunch."

"I just ate," Daniel said. "I'll only stay a minute." He walked into the living room, whose terrace jutted away from the hill on stilts, and sat at the far end of a white linen sofa. Tamara sat across from him in a leather chair.

"So, you visiting LA?" she asked.

"No, I live in Beverly Hills."

"You been away or something?"

"No."

"Oh." She hesitated. "Sorry, I just thought, since I hadn't met you. I mean, I've been living here a year and a half."

"You live here, with Forest? Well, he doesn't always keep me up to date on his private life."

"Pop," Forest said from the kitchen, "you might have the wrong idea. Tamara rents the apartment under my garage. She's Matty Jones's daughter."

"Oh! That's great," Daniel said, embarrassed.

"You thought we were involved? Oh my." She laughed. The act of laughing pulled her mouth wide, exposing big spotless teeth. A vestigial teenager's laugh. It seemed in that unguarded moment that her beauty rested, tantalizingly, on the brink of ugliness. "Not that Forest isn't a fine specimen. But he's practically my uncle."

"Well, I'm glad we've got it cleared up."

"Tamara is in school at UCLA," said Forest.

"That's where I went to school, nine hundred thousand years ago. Though I never finished. What are you studying?"

"Economics, mainly. And I'm dabbling in physics, too."

"She's an actual goddamn rocket scientist," Forest said. "If she uses her powers for evil, everybody better watch out."

When they were sitting at the small wooden dining table, Daniel accepted a plate of salad but declined the rice stir-fry.

"Pop," said Forest, "maybe you can help us out with an argument we were having. I'm under the impression that people Tamara's age tend not to distinguish between the serious and the frivolous—which often correspond loosely to the public and the private. They're hashtagging and Instagramming, and it's save the planet one second and look at my beautiful latte the next, and there's not much sense that the two things are different. Social media makes the private public, and it erodes and diminishes the public discourse, I think."

Daniel looked from Forest to Tamara. "And your response to this . . . ?"

She scoffed gently. "Bullshit, is what I say. For starters, public discourse didn't need my generation, or social media, to erode it—it's been eroding for decades, and you guys fucked it up as much as anyone. And on top of that, even if it's true about the mingling of the serious and the frivolous, so what? Maybe everything is serious, so we're just doing away with false distinctions. Certainly just because something is private doesn't make it frivolous. Maybe it's even the public realm that is trivial, in the end."

Forest said, "That's not a response, it's a checklist of possible responses, none given more weight than the rest. People are so used to seeing many sides that they mire in relativism and fail to reach conclusions. Or they jump to them through groupthink."

"You've become the thing you speak of," Tamara said.

"You're right! I'm doing it too! It's a fucking disease. Only in this flabby intellectual climate could someone like Trump get elected."

She barked a laugh. "You think it's *my* generation who elected this dude? Look at the numbers, man. It's your generation"—she looked over to Daniel—"and especially *yours,* who voted for him. Don't try and lay this at our fucking doorstep."

"What do you think, Pop?" Forest asked, turning to grin at Daniel.

"Honestly, she's making slightly more sense than you are. You're uncomfortable with the changes being wrought by technology, and that's understandable. I am too. But it's not up to us how those changes play out. It's up to her generation, and the ones coming after. They'll adapt, because people always do. It might take a while to find its level, though. Every new advance has been heralded as the end of civilization by those unused to it, and society has always absorbed the changes eventually."

"Thank you," Tamara said. "It's nice to talk to an older person whose mind is open." She was smiling jovially at Forest.

"That doesn't mean you're off the hook," Daniel said. "The opposite, actually. You guys are adapting to the most intense technological and cultural leaps in history, and it's not all pretty. How you handle it could have massive effects on the world of your children and grandchildren. There are some scary signs."

"Another reason I don't want offspring," she said. "Anyway, smartphones won't matter much if the planet is unlivable."

"Don't cop out on us," Daniel said. "Just because those who went before you fucked everything up so monumentally, that doesn't mean there's nothing you can do."

"Yes SIR!" she said, saluting. "Reporting for duty."

The three of them laughed.

"Glad we've cleared that up," Forest said. "So why are you really here?"

"I just decided to stop by."

He shook his head. "Gotta be some reason. Just tell me." Forest looked at Tamara with a tense smile, and she in turn smiled and shifted her eyes to Daniel, as if translating a complex idiom into simpler terms.

Daniel faced her as he addressed Forest. "Well. I found myself thinking about your paintings, is what it was. Realizing that they really spoke to me."

"How so?" Forest raised his eyebrows.

"I started making connections"—he was still looking at Tamara—"between the forms of your work and the way my mind functions, the way, I suppose, people's minds in general function. The way our psychic investment in the past, and maybe the future, imbues memory and projection with a kind of life, and they inhabit the world alongside us. Something like that."

There was a pause before Forest said, "Well, fuck. Why did I bother painting them when I could have just said that?"

Daniel dropped his gaze to the table. "I'm sorry. It's reductive, I guess."

"No, Pop. *I'm* sorry." The change in his tone was as genuine as it was sudden. "I'm an asshole, is all. I'm glad you like the work."

Daniel raised his eyes. "Can I ask you? Was there some inception point for these? Did they come from somewhere?"

"Yes, in fact. It started in a conversation I had with Tamara about her physics studies. She was trying to explain some of it to me. Quarks, atoms, strings. There's something Einstein called spooky action at a distance—that's a thing, you know. Entanglement is the official name for it, I think, but don't ask me to explain it."

"Don't ask anyone," Tamara said.

"So it got me thinking about this world of particles we can't see, doing essential work all around us, inside us. I didn't do research or anything, and I didn't try to paint the things she told me about. I just started imagining this alternate unseen reality behind the visible scrim—not just the physics, but human experience and unexpressed emotion and, yes, memory—and used that as a springboard. Maybe everything is particles. What if we could see them? So your thoughts fit right in there."

"That big one," Daniel said. "The photograph, it's the Malibu house, right?"

"Yes it is," Forest said.

"Who took the picture?"

"I did. I took all the pictures. But most of them are more recent. That's the earliest one. I took it with Mom's big Polaroid from the landing during a party. You were there, Pop."

"I remember you loved that camera."

"I was only maybe five. I still remember, probably because I've had the picture all this time. I woke up in the night and came out to watch the party from behind the railing. I remember a few people walking past me and smiling. I went into your bedroom and you were in there with Dennis Hopper. You remember this?"

"It's starting to ring a bell." Daniel remembered the party, the night doing lines with Dennis Hopper, but the detail of his son coming into the room triggered only a hazy image.

"You said I could take one picture if I went straight back to bed after. I went out on the landing and took it through the gaps in the railing posts. Then I brought the camera back and took the picture in and watched it develop in my room before going back to sleep. Kept it all this time. I had the picture digitized and converted to black and white, then reprinted. They did a cool process on it where they artificially boosted the resolution, sharpened it, so they could blow it up."

"Have you been making art this whole time? I mean, what I remember last is your grad school show, fifteen years ago."

Forest's face compressed slightly and he squinted. "Of course. I never stopped. Is that what you thought?"

"I didn't know. There was talk for a while after you graduated about you trying to get a gallery show, but then it stopped. Your mother stopped talking about your painting, and when I saw you, you never mentioned anything about it. I assumed you'd drifted away from it."

"How would you ever have known what I was up to, Pop? I almost never see you. And when I do you never ask."

Tamara stood up. "I'm going to get back to work," she said. "Good to see you, Daniel."

"Don't go," Forest said.

"I'm going," she said firmly. "I'll see you later."

She walked out the front door and father and son sat silent for a moment. Daniel nodded slowly. "I've stayed away too much, you're right. For a while I thought it was what you wanted. In fact, you actually said it was what you wanted. But I must have asked what you were up to when I did see you."

"You never said, 'What's going on with your artwork, Forest?' You were happy to leave that subject off the table."

"I didn't want to make you uncomfortable. I didn't want to pry or pressure you."

"Just because you're a hermit by nature doesn't mean all artists are, even your own son. And just because you quit making art even though yours was selling doesn't mean there aren't others who spend their lives persevering even if they sell nothing."

Daniel hung his head. "Maybe that's the difference. I was never an artist. Not really. I was just a lost young man who made one thing that suddenly everyone loved, and so for a while I convinced myself I was someone I wasn't, and made a bunch of stupid copies of the first thing."

Forest gave an exasperated laugh. "You spent years in the desert making a gigantic object of great beauty without ever knowing or caring if anyone would see it. If that's not an artist I don't know what is. Even those 'stupid copies' are fucking gorgeous. I've gone to see them, you know, Pop, the two that are left. I never told you, but I flew to Philadelphia and saw the one that's still up, and I tracked down the one in Illinois, but it was packed away in crates."

"I didn't know that," Daniel said. "I would have thought they'd scrapped it."

"When they took it down it was still worth something. Your little escapade made the ones left more valuable than they had any right to be, for a while. That senator branded you a terrorist and made the city take down your piece, but they weren't stupid. They weren't going to throw something like that into a junkyard. But then I guess people forgot. Time went by, and there it is, still crated up. You know who owns it now?"

"They sold it?"

"For a song. Two years ago."

Daniel waited.

Forest's face grew more serious, his eyebrows falling to rest and his gaze challenging Daniel's eyes. "Come on, Pop, take a guess."

"I don't know." Daniel tried to make his expression an olive branch. "I don't have a guess."

Forest smiled. "Me."

Daniel felt his breath catch. "God. What for?"

"Why do you think?" Forest stood abruptly and leaned forward on his hands.

"What are you going to do with it?"

"I don't know what I'm going to do with it!" He was yelling suddenly. He closed his mouth, sat back down, and took a moment to calm himself, looking out the bay window at the deck and the upper branches of trees down the hill. Then he spoke more evenly, "It wasn't about that. I just thought maybe it'd be nice if it was in the family, because otherwise they *would* have gotten around to scrapping it, eventually. It's at a storage facility in the Valley now, I haven't even opened the goddamn crates. I thought maybe you'd be pleasantly surprised."

Daniel looked down and studied the meandering grain of the wood under his hands. "You caught me unawares, Forest. I'm not reacting the way you want me to, I'm sorry."

"Tell me this, Pop. What would you do with it? If it was purely up to you and didn't matter to anyone else. Would you destroy it? After all this time, would that still be the goal? Because if it's important I can make that happen."

"It's not important. You should do anything you want with it. It belongs to you now. It seems fitting actually, now that I'm getting my head around it."

"What if I found a museum that wanted it? Would you be okay with me donating it? With it being on display somewhere?"

Daniel took a long breath, studying the passage of this thought through his mind. He marshaled equanimity. "I'm okay with anything you decide. I really am."

"No," Forest said. "I actually want you to weigh in. I was thinking that I might look around for somewhere that wanted it, but I wouldn't do it without your active blessing."

"You have it."

"So, you'd like that?"

"What do you want me to say?"

"Is that a real question? How about I treat it like one: Isn't it obvious? I want you to say, 'Forest, I'm moved by your respect for my work. I'd be happy, and gratified, if after all this time people still wanted to see it and thought it meant something. Thank you, son, for caring.'"

"Oh."

They sat silent for a few seconds, and then, like a stroke of divine intercession, they laughed. Forest's laugh was loud and spontaneous, and Daniel heard his own remorseful, relieved horselaugh spraying out of him like water from a thumbed hose. Relief was the gusher, remorse the thumb.

They went back, after a moment, to talking about Forest's paintings, and the conversation bore itself along more easily. Most of the show had sold at the opening, Forest told him, including the large one by the entrance.

"Congratulations," Daniel said. "Have you started working again yet?"

"No, not really. But I've got some ideas. I'm going to do something different, not using photographs this time."

"Watch out. They'll try and get you to do more of the same if it sells."

"Yeah, that's already happened, but Charles is a good man. He's open to new stuff. I'll come back to this technique again, I'm sure. I'm not done with it, but I've got to wait until it feels fresh again."

"Whatever you make, I'm looking forward to seeing it."

As he was leaving, standing near the open front door, Daniel said, "I do appreciate it, you know. You seeking out my work, your feelings about it."

Forest shook his head and smiled flatly. "Okay, but . . . ship sailed, for now, Pop."

Daniel nodded, thinking, *Fair enough,* and stepped out the door.

"Come by anytime, by the way. Just call first, maybe."

"I will. I'm going back down to look at your show again right now." He walked to his car. When he glanced back Forest had shut the door.

DANIEL PARKED IN front of the gallery and went in. He was staring at the smaller painting of the woman sitting on the bed when he felt his phone vibrating. He saw Rashid's name on the screen and answered.

"Mr. T. Hey. I'm here with Gerald."

"Is he okay?"

"Yeah, he's fine, but him and Mom had another fight, and he's refusing to go home. He walked to my place with a fucking suitcase." Rashid gave an exasperated sigh. "He can't really stay here, it's a studio and my girlfriend is between places and is staying here. I was wondering if I could bring him over to your place. Maybe you can talk him down."

"Yes, of course. I'm not there now, but I can be there in half an hour."

"Okay, thanks. We'll see you there."

As Daniel hung up he saw Charles Foreman approaching across the wide expanse of polished concrete. In the virtually empty space the paintings looked different, elemental in their solitude, and Foreman looked different as well, freed from the obligations of hosting a crowd.

His deep poise took on a more natural cast away from the clamor that had seemed to be its impetus.

"Daniel," he said as he neared. "It's good to see you again." They shook hands.

"Likewise," Daniel said. "Unfortunately I can't stay."

"I hope I didn't disturb your reverie."

"No. I just got an unexpected phone call, and I have to go meet someone."

"I'm sorry to hear it. I hope you'll feel free to come here anytime, and just wave me away if you want to be left alone. Think of me as a friendly gnat."

"Not at all. I liked our talk at the dinner. And I'm not someone who likes talking art, generally."

Foreman smiled. "If you call ahead, I could make sure I'm free to have a coffee with you."

"I'd like that, Charles. I'll do it. Right now I have to go."

"I'll look forward to it."

Daniel paused. "Let me ask you something. Did you have anything to do with Forest buying my Chicago tree, the one that's sitting in the warehouse?"

Foreman shook his head. "He told me about it, but my relationship with Forest began after he bought that piece."

"You think there's any value to it, and to the one in Philadelphia? I don't mean about money. I know you liked the original, but did you ever see any of the rest of them? The series?"

"I've seen the Philadelphia tree, twenty years ago when I was there once."

"Did you like it?"

Daniel saw him drop into thought, sifting his memory. "I liked it," he said. "It was quite beautiful, and a great boon to that city, such a gorgeous piece. People really associate the city with it, as a landmark, and of course it's the last one on display."

"But . . ."

Foreman nodded, hesitating. "But, it lacked some primordial quality the original had, an absolute . . ." He paused and let his eyes drift to the

ceiling, seeking the right word. "... *remoteness*. Something that emanated from far outside the humane realm of art as statement or art
as beauty-object, though it was, of course, beautiful all the same. Even
when it was planted next to the museum here, it carried with it that
quality of not being any kind of artifact. More like a discovery."

Daniel nodded.

"Of course I still admired the one in Philadelphia."

"Thanks for your candor."

Foreman chuckled, and there was intimacy in his eyes. "I'm incapable of anything else when dealing with someone I respect. May I ask
you ..."

Daniel waited, knowing.

"Why did you destroy *Thorn Tree*? It couldn't just have been your
antipathy for the buyer. That couldn't have been enough, on its own."

Daniel felt suddenly desolate, remembering the loss, but he smiled
because for the first time he could remember, this question did not
make him angry. When people asked why, it was almost always a question not about his reasons, but about his state of mind, the subtext being *What insanity possessed you?* Foreman asked with the curiosity of
someone who assumed there was a good reason.

Daniel said, "Charles, I've only ever told the whole story to one person, a long time ago, and he's surely no longer alive. If I ever get the urge
to tell it again, you'll be the one I come to."

"I'm honored, thank you."

"Now, I really do have to go. I'll come back another day." They shook
hands again, and Daniel walked out into a dusky sunset.

When he pulled into his driveway, Rashid's car was already there,
and parked behind it, halfway into his parking area from the main
drive, was Jack's BMW with its driver's door standing open. Rashid,
Gerald, and Jack were standing together in front of the house, talking.
Daniel sighed as he shut off his car and got out.

"Hey Rashid, hey Gerald," Daniel said as he walked up. "What's going on, Jack?"

"Hey Danny boy. I was on my way in and I saw these guys outside
your place. Just stopped to see what was up."

"Nothing's up, they're my friends. You can head on home."

"Okay, good. I saw your car wasn't here so I wanted to offer help, you know, in case there was anything they needed."

"It's under control, Jack. Thanks."

"You got it, buddy." Jack turned back to Rashid and Gerald. "You kids take care of yourselves now." Jack extended his hand to Gerald. "It's a pleasure to meet you." Gerald gave Jack his hand to shake but when Jack took it he just held it in both of his, leaning a little closer. He stared into Gerald's eyes. "You're a good kid," Jack said. "I can tell."

Gerald nodded but didn't speak, keeping his face hard, a new toughness there Daniel hadn't seen before. Jack got in his car and drove up the hill.

"Who's he?" Rashid asked.

"Neighbor. He lives in the main house now, with his daughter and grandson."

"At first I thought he was just being racist, seeing two Black kids in Beverly Hills. Maybe he was, I guess, but then he was so nice, asking us about ourselves and stuff."

"He's a little strange," Daniel said. He stepped over to Gerald to greet him. "Good to see you, Ger," he said, opening his arms. "Been too long." They hugged, and he felt Gerald transition suddenly from simple greeting-hug to fiercer embrace, and then he was crying into Daniel's sweater. "Hey hey," Daniel said, "it's okay, man. You're okay. . . ." He put a hand on the back of Gerald's head. After a second he said, "Let's go inside, okay?"

Gerald broke away from him and turned immediately, heading for the door, wiping his face with the cuff of his sweatshirt, and by the time they sat down in the living room he'd thrown in place a self-consciously amused expression, grinning at nothing in particular. "Still keeping the place clean, I see," he said, indicating the general clutter of the room.

They filled Daniel in on what was going on. Gerald's war with Tanya had come to a head, and he had told her—sworn to her—he wasn't going to live there anymore. She'd told him if he went to his father's place she would get the police involved and charge Raymond with child abuse. So he went to Rashid's.

"I'm sure you and her can work it out once you both calm down," Daniel said.

"No way," said Gerald. "She's gone, like, crazy or something. A switch flipped in her head and she won't listen to me. It's not like I really want to live with my dad. I just want to be able to see him. But she's made everything worse than it needs to be. Can I stay here for a while?" Gerald smiled imploringly.

Daniel took a breath, looking at the boy. He remembered Gerald, from when he'd first started seeing Tanya, as a skinny buck-toothed awkward eleven-year-old, laughing and horsing around at home and in the hallways at school. He was still skinny and a little awkward, and his smile rose still from that adolescent core, but at seventeen he had grown tall, and his muscles had begun to gain adult definition. He was handsome, though he didn't yet know it. He was on the cusp of manhood, and this trouble with his parents had knocked him closer to the line.

Daniel shook his head, returning Gerald's smile. "I strongly doubt your mother will go for that." He saw Gerald's expression skid toward affliction. "But if she says it's all right, then of course. I'd love to have you. Okay? Let's get her on the phone."

Daniel was shocked when Tanya immediately agreed.

"You want to take him for a while, be my guest," she said. "It'll be a relief to have him out of here. Just don't let me hear about him seeing Raymond. Not till I decide it's time."

They ordered pizza in and watched a movie, and when Rashid and Gerald stepped outside to have a cigarette, Daniel followed them.

"So much for not smoking around the youngsters," Daniel said to Rashid.

"I wouldn't normally, but Gerald said he needed one this afternoon and I gave it to him. He's a year older than I was when I started."

"Three years older than I was," said Daniel, "but that was back when cigarettes were good for you." The boys laughed.

Daniel watched Gerald blow a cloud of smoke toward the stars between the top of the plank fence and the long branches of the oak tree that shaded that side of his yard. "It's nice here," Gerald said. "I forgot how nice."

"It is, isn't it."

"You never told me how you got this place," said Gerald. "Obviously you don't make bank as a teacher, to buy a place like this."

Daniel laughed. "Hardly. You remember Cam, my friend who lived up the hill?"

"Yeah, of course."

"Did you know he died?"

Gerald nodded. "I remember. My mom told me."

"He owned this whole property, and he was letting me live here for free. When he died he split the property and left the guesthouse to me."

"Shit," Gerald said. "I'd like to have friends like that." He had his toughness back in place, but the smile that stretched across his lean face made him look like a much younger boy than he was. There was an innocence in him that had nothing to do with sexual or moral innocence. This new toughness was like a thin hard eggshell that served both to conceal and imply the yolk of childlike curiosity it contained. Daniel hoped he wouldn't let the shell grow too thick.

"I'm going to head home," Rashid said, standing up.

When Rashid had gone, Daniel went in to make up the guest bed for Gerald.

1980

The triangular concrete courtyard between the mall and the parking lot was empty save the steel tree and a few benches. The four-story glass walls that formed two of the triangle's sides met at an acute angle, giving the building the appearance of having pincers around the tree. It wasn't a bad effect, Daniel conceded privately. From the inside, the smoky steel tree graced those giant windows nicely. He'd spent the afternoon wandering in the mall, and then watching it from his car. When it closed, he'd moved to a chain restaurant across the highway, where he drank coffee and tried not to make an impression on the staff. From there, he had driven his van to the mouth of a wooded side street that faced the highway and the mall, and had continued watching through military binoculars until after midnight.

No one on the planet knew where he was or what had brought him there, and he experienced this fact as somehow revelatory. He haunted his own body, utterly present. He felt he'd been nothing but a dreaming observer to his own existence in the years since he'd finished the first tree, the only real tree, and left Ben's place. Before that, he could no longer remember with any confidence who he'd been. This, now, finally, was something new. The idea had risen slowly out of his bog of creeping desolation and drug abuse, and once it had taken shape had begun to shine like a grail in his mind. He guessed this was how revolutionaries were recruited: people broken down by the world, or by private mortification, suddenly offered gleaming purpose. He was vibrating, charged with determination. He knew it couldn't last, but didn't care.

The benign residential night cloaked him like a perfect disguise as he walked through it with his backpack. He was both visible and unremarkable, that safest of humans: a white man in suburban America. As he crossed the wide empty parking lot, he hid his face by keeping the visor of his cap pulled low and his chin down. All the way up to the tree he saw no one, though he could hear cars passing on the highway behind him. He placed the backpack snugly against the base of the polished steel trunk where it met the circle of gravel. With the exterior lit and the interior dark, the two glass-paned walls flanking the courtyard were virtually opaque to him, so he couldn't have known if anyone was watching from inside. Walking away toward the edge of the parking area, he expected the call of a security guard from behind at every moment, but it didn't come. He positioned himself behind the hedge that bordered the lot, still fifty yards from the highway underpass and his van. If he went much farther, the signal might not reach. He watched a while longer, to be sure no one was coming out to investigate, and then he pulled the battery-powered unit from his pocket and switched it on. First a green light, which turned red to indicate it had detected the receiver's fraternal signal. Daniel pressed the button, and the explosion was extremely loud across the acre of naked asphalt. Some of the panes on the glass walls shattered, and the tree itself seemed to hop upward before toppling away from the building, the trunk in three jagged pieces, the largest branch shearing off and clanking into the parking lot, slowly coming to rest.

No security activity of any kind followed the explosion. Alarms did not sound, guards did not rush out. The night's hush merely returned. Daniel heard a car pass northbound on the highway behind him, then another. It was as if the explosion had been a figment, but the tree lay there still, wrecked and scattered, as proof. He walked back to his van and drove away.

Ben hadn't needed him to explain his decision when Daniel had gone to him and asked if he still had a permit to buy explosives. He'd listened to the plan, looked closely, seen the resolve in Daniel's eyes, and just nodded. Daniel had not known how bad off Ben was, and was shocked when he saw his friend's wasted form lying on the hard little bed coupled to an oxygen tank. He was largely immobilized, only able on good days to use his walker to and from the bathroom. He had moved his ham radio onto a crate by his bed, and still communicated with the other astral travelers at night. The explosives permit could not be used by anyone but the holder, and Daniel told Ben he would find another way, but Ben insisted. Daniel took the oxygen tank out first, then carried Ben, light as balsa wood, to the van and placed him gingerly into the passenger seat. After they'd made the purchase, Daniel had spent six weeks in his old bunkhouse bed, caring for Ben. There came a time, near the end, when Ben could no longer speak above a bare whisper, and one night he asked Daniel to help him sign off for the last time. Daniel waited until the specified time, then powered up the radio and read what Ben had written into the microphone, and when he heard the replies start to crackle in he put the headphones on Ben's head. Ben closed his eyes and nodded now and then, and after a while fell asleep. After he died, Daniel drove back to LA and brought the explosives to a guy he knew who had been a munitions expert in Vietnam.

He understood that what he was doing was a kind of proxy suicide, and maybe that was the point. He also knew that it would not actually relieve his despair and self-loathing. But the world was vital for him again suddenly, especially after Fresno. The bright days on the highway vaulted longingly overhead, drawing him through their slow expanses with an intimacy born of purpose. And those purposeful nights on the road were somehow deeply American: trucks, billboards, fluorescent legends, town names floating by on green signs, the places themselves purely notional; all these human sundries scattered in heedless beauty under wakeful stars. For the rest of his life, when people spoke the word "American" as an adjective, he would think of those nights. He took his time, meandering but pausing nowhere for more than one sleep. He was in no hurry to reach his destination and end this vivid segment of his life.

After a week, Daniel quit meandering and headed for his destination, which was a suburb of Indianapolis, and his original tree. Two years earlier, he had spent almost a month on the estate of condiment magnate Driscoll Travis, installing *Thorn Tree* on a small knoll above the house.

When he arrived, he spent the afternoon driving around the perimeter of the estate, pinpointing the place on the south side where he would enter through the woods, and finding a spot near there where he could park his van unnoticed. Then he left the area and waited for dark. The two bombs he would use for this were ready, and were in separate backpacks in the rear of the van. He had dinner at a restaurant in a strip mall ten miles away, and found himself remembering his earlier trip to the estate.

The first surprise back then had been learning that the installation was going to be at Travis's home instead of the downtown square that had been the proposed location. When Daniel confronted Travis about it, he'd given him a story about city permits and red tape, and how this would only be temporary, just until the permits came through. Since that could take a year or more, he and his wife figured they might as well enjoy the piece themselves in the meantime. Daniel called his dealer and discovered that the contract specified his assistance with the installation, but not the location. No one had thought to get that in writing, since Travis had come in with an offer that included maps and drawings of the downtown location by a high-end landscape design firm. And the amount he was offering had been staggering.

So Daniel had gone ahead with the installation, and during that process the second surprise had been the deep, almost molecular loathing for Driscoll Travis that arose in him. The man had seemed gregarious and likeable while the deal was being hammered out, but something shifted once the sale was done and Daniel was there on his estate, now merely an employee doing a job. If it had just been entitled dismissiveness toward him, Daniel could have shrugged it off, but it was something else, a vague but unmistakable air of indiscriminate malice. Much of what Travis said at any given time seemed designed to subtly humiliate or wound those in his purview. This included the foreman and workers hired to carry out the job, and even his own caretaker, a man named Orval, who was a generation older than Travis and had worked for his father. Orval was so accustomed to being spoken down to by Travis that it seemed to have no effect on him. Once, a few minutes after Travis had visited the site and harangued Orval and Daniel about some nonexistent detail, Daniel asked Orval, "You been working for him your whole life?"

"Yessir," Orval said. "Him and his father."

"You don't ever get sick of that?"

Orval looked up at Daniel's sculpture, which still had a scaffold around it but was almost completely reassembled. He stood still for a long moment, and Daniel saw admiration in his face. Then he said, "His father was a decent man, a good employer, but not much of a father, I don't think." They left it there.

On the last day, when the scaffold had been removed and all the equipment loaded onto a giant truck, and only re-sodding the scarred earth around the base remained to be done, Travis came out from the house to have a closer look. He seemed calm, the flash of meanness absent from his expression. He put his hands on his hips and stared up at the tree. "Daniel," he said, "this is just about the most beautiful thing I've ever seen."

Daniel nodded and managed a grunt. By that time he'd mostly stopped speaking to Travis.

"From inside the house it looks unbelievable, like something God put here to remind us of something we've forgotten. That's how my wife put it, and I agree. Every time I look out the window it strikes me. Now people are going to enter our living room—admiring it as they always do, because it's a very impressive room—and when their eyes stray out the window their breath will catch. All that opulence is somehow thrown instantly into perspective."

Daniel was surprised by this disquisition. "I'm glad you like it," he said, and the platitude almost made him laugh.

"We do. We really do love it." Travis turned and faced Daniel. "We've been talking about it a lot, and we've decided to keep it."

"Keep it?"

"Yes. To tell you the truth, it's my wife who really refuses to part with it, but she's won me over. So, *Thorn Tree* has found its home," he announced, spreading his hands wide as if expecting a round of applause.

"That wasn't the agreement," Daniel said. "You said this was temporary. A public space was what we agreed on."

"Well, things change."

Daniel could feel his face tightening. "I'm not sure I'm okay with this."

"Well, I am sorry to hear that. I would love to have your blessing. I really would. I mean, look how perfect it is here." He looked at Daniel affably, his eyebrows raised.

"No," Daniel said. "You don't have my blessing."

The wormy meanness instantly resurfaced. "Luckily you being okay with it is not something I have to worry about. You've cashed your check, and this thing belongs to me now. I could destroy it if I wanted. I could melt it down and make forks and spoons out of it. I'm not asking your permission here, just letting you know my decision." He paused. "Orval will get you into town." He turned and walked back toward the house. "Nice work on the installation, by the way," he called over his shoulder.

It was after midnight when Daniel parked his van on a small unused dirt track in a patch of woods down the road from the back side of the Travis estate. He walked from there along the road, staying close to the woods, alert for any sign of approaching cars. There were houses spaced widely along the first section of his route, and lights on in a couple of them, glowing in earnest counterpoint to the windy night. The leaves were returning, and half-populated branches hissed above him as he walked. At this hour, the suburban woods reverted to a more primal disposition, and the character of the night deepened, overriding the place's residential tranquility. There was a sense of the preterhuman history in the earth that was obscured in daylight. This character of the night and the land would mostly go unnoticed by the people who lived in these houses. They could be counted on never to venture outside this late except in cars, and to keep their attention tightly blinkered as they moved from car to house after a dinner party or downtown concert. Their children maybe, old enough to drive but still just close enough to the source to be receptive, might feel the tug of the wind in the branches and look up as they closed the car door, might stand for a moment and feel it before going in to their TVs, or perhaps would even venture out on a weekend night with friends and pass a joint in a starlit clearing, their faces bright in this discovered primeval world. Later in life they would prize those memories but would attribute their magic to the bloom of youth and not to some perceptible character of the world they'd lost the will to see.

Daniel arrived at the place in the road where he'd decided to enter the estate, marked by a large fallen tree ten yards off the shoulder whose root structure had been pulled up into a giant earthen fan. He readjusted the straps on the heavy backpacks to distribute the weight evenly, and set off into the dark woods using a group of stars overhead to keep his sense of direction.

When he reached the end of the woods, he was at the base of the hill on which the house sat, and a giant sloping meadow lay above him. Some outdoor lights were on, and one downstairs interior light, but otherwise the place was dark. Staying just inside the tree line, he moved east until he had a direct path to the knoll where the tree stood without passing too close to the house. He had been worried that the sculpture might be lit by floodlights, but if they had been installed they were not turned on. He knew it was there but he couldn't see it yet.

As he climbed through the meadow, he began to make out over the first lip of the hill a wide white structure between him and the house. It looked surreal, as though a second house had been built on the lawn. When he topped the lip and moved closer he saw that it was a giant party tent, its white sidewalls rolled down and lined with small square windows. He walked along its back side, using it to shield him from the house, taking care not to trip over any ropes or stays. When he reached the far corner of the tent, he raised his eyes and could see his tree up the second hill above the house, its upper branches silhouetted against the night sky over the tree line beyond it.

Halfway up he found himself on a flagstone path leading from the house, which must have been installed after the tree. When he reached the top, he saw that the area around the base had been covered in flagstones as well, and landscaped with low hedges and a circle of stone benches. It occurred to him then that whatever damage he did could possibly be repaired, with Travis's resources. But it wouldn't matter.

Once he'd destroyed it, it would no longer be the same tree. Putting it back together would not recapture what he was setting free tonight.

He placed the two backpacks on either side of the wide steel trunk, then unzipped them and switched on the receivers inside. When he had them set, he sat down on one of the benches and stared up at the tree for a while. His years in the desert creating it seemed lost now, rubbed out by the unexamined decision to sell to the highest bidder. Daniel stood and walked over to it. He placed his cheek against the steel, just to see, and yes, it was still there. The life in it only made what he had to do more necessary. He wept silently. The other trees, the copies, he'd wanted to destroy because they had never been alive to begin with, and they had no place in the world, but this one was a prisoner here. Rachel was a prisoner here. He'd gone blind and abandoned her, and now these bombs were her only way out.

His cheek was still pressed against the cool trunk. "I'm sorry," he whispered.

"What are you doing?" a voice asked from behind him, and the sudden beam of a flashlight flicked around at his feet.

Daniel did not start or run. He turned toward the voice, which he recognized, and said, "Apologizing to my tree."

"Christ," said Orval, the light shining in Daniel's face now. There was a pause, and then he asked, "Apologizing for what?"

"For abandoning her here, for selling her."

Another briefer pause. "I thought you were some kids. We've had them up here using this as a place to drink and smoke at night. Had to wash off some graffiti once."

"I'm glad to hear that. She hasn't been neglected completely, then."

"Are you on something?"

"No."

"You having problems or something? Why are you here?"

"I'm going to blow her up. There are bombs in these bags." There was suddenly no space inside him for untruth.

Orval lowered the flashlight, and now Daniel could make out his face in the dark.

"I'm going to have to cast a vote against that plan of action," Orval said.

"This is very important to me. I won't even go into how your boss lied about where it would be located. I take responsibility for my decision, just as I'll take responsibility for this when I'm done."

"We heard about that one in Fresno getting blown up. That was you?"

"Yes."

"You can't just go around blowing stuff up, even if you're the one who made it."

"I know, which is why I'll go to prison when I'm done. I accept that, it's only right."

"So, you're asking me to let you do it?"

"I haven't asked you anything, but now that you mention it . . ."

Orval didn't speak.

"Does Travis know you're up here right now? Is he awake?"

"Mr. Travis isn't even home. He's in Florida. They get back this weekend. Their daughter's getting married."

"So you and your wife are the only ones here?"

"My wife passed last year."

"Oh god. Sorry. That's a terrible blow, I know."

"You lose a wife?" The question was a challenge.

"A girlfriend, when I was younger. She was why I made this tree. And then I lost sight of everything and sold her to a profound asshole, and I've hated myself for it ever since."

Orval nodded. "Listen," he said, "I can't let you blow up the tree. But I don't want to call the cops. Why don't you pick up your stuff and come down to my house, and we can have a drink."

Daniel unzipped the first pack. "Okay, I'm just going to shut off the detonators." He switched them off and then lifted the packs onto his shoulders again. Orval's presence seemed to take natural precedence over his own objective, and at least in the short term he was willing to follow the old man down the hill.

Orval lived in a small separate house hidden from the front driveway by a tall hedge, but with a view of the rest of the grounds behind it. When they'd covered half the empty expanse between the tree and his house, he said to Daniel, "On second thought, if you wouldn't mind, maybe leave those here."

"Understood," Daniel said, and gently put the two backpacks down in the grass.

They entered through the back door and went through the kitchen into the dining room. Daniel had been given lunch in Orval and Patty's dining room every day during the installation, and the place hadn't changed. The same russet-patterned ceramic tureen sat on a rectangular lace doily on the thick farm table. Even at a glance, Daniel understood that Patty still inhabited these rooms, that Orval was keeping himself company with her memory. Daniel followed Orval through the far door into the living room, and Orval poured them a drink from a small cabinet in the corner.

"How'd you notice me, anyway?" Daniel asked when he was seated on the sofa.

"I don't sleep much anymore. Sometimes I just sit on the porch at night in the dark and listen to the crickets. I was out there when you came up the hill. I saw you come out from behind the tent."

Daniel sipped his whiskey, but found he didn't want it and set it down. "I'm sorry again, about Patty."

Orval gave a small nod, putting his drink down without sipping it. "What have you been up to the past couple of years?"

Daniel laughed unthinkingly at the swerve into small talk, then felt bad for it. "Nothing," he said. "Less than nothing. I've been doing drugs at my wife's parties, running off for weekends with strange women, spending your boss's money, forgetting I have a five-year-old son. Just generally acting like an asshole."

"And you think this will redeem you?" Orval indicated the sculpture merely by inclining his head toward it.

"No, of course not." Daniel paused. "To tell you the truth, it's not how I'll feel afterward that I'm thinking of. When the thought came to me to do it, it just felt right. I knew right away I would, as soon as I thought of it. I was snorting and smoking and drinking myself into a useless puddle of goo, and suddenly I was galvanized. I figured that meant something."

"What about your son?"

Daniel nodded. "I have no good answer, except to say I hope he un-derstands someday. What would you rather have for a father, a puddle of goo messing up your life or someone new, someone with a future, who's done what he had to, even if he's in prison for a bit?"

"Are those the options?"

"It feels that way."

They fell silent for a minute. Both of them looked reflexively at their drinks on the table, but didn't reach for them.

Then Orval asked, "So, your tree was a tribute for someone you lost?"

"Sort of. More of a place to put my feelings about her, and maybe an escape from them too."

"Who was she?"

Daniel had never told the story of himself and Rachel to anyone. There were plenty who knew the bullet points, because the case had been in the news and had been dredged up now and then when his art had brought him attention, but he had never recounted it before, even to Amelia. He'd never even invoked Rachel's name in connection with *Thorn Tree*. But he told it now, all of it. He told Orval how they'd met, what she was like, how he'd agreed to take her along on the trip to do the acid deal, and how, while tripping, she'd fallen from a cliff at night as he sat staring out to sea from under a giant tree. The police had found the jar of LSD in his trunk and arrested him, and two months later, when the Manson murders turned acid-dropping hippies into blood-thirsty maniacs in the public eye, they had decided to prosecute him for killing Rachel, calling it a drug-fueled murder. There had been signs in the dirt, they said, signs of a scuffle at the spot she'd fallen from. He had been acquitted of the murder charge, but the judge had given him three-to-five for the drugs. He told Orval of his trek out into the desert, and his years at Ben's place in the Mojave, channeling his grief and guilt into the tree.

"By the time I was done, people had started to drive out to see it. Art people from LA started to come around. A friend of mine who had some money convinced me to let him move it into a museum in the city and rejoin society. I got caught up in the attention, and they talked me into making more trees, gave me money and assistants and paid me up front on commissions. I stopped at four—a *series* they called it. They look different but I call them copies. Then when the contract with the museum to keep the original on their grounds ran out, your boss showed up with his pile of money. By then I'd dissociated from what it was about almost completely, and just went along with whatever my dealer suggested. I was a little bit famous. I'd married Hollywood nobility. I was hanging out with movie stars." Daniel stopped. He could see that Orval was both calm and transfixed. "And so, here I am. Trying to set her free the only way I can think of."

"That's quite a story," Orval said. "I think we ought to get moving."

"I don't even know where to go from here."

"Well," Orval stood out of his chair, "if we're going to blow up that tree, we'd better do it before it gets light."

They followed the beam of Orval's flashlight back up the hill, retrieved the packs and placed them against the tree. Daniel took a breath before turning to Orval.

"You need a minute alone?" Orval asked.

"No. She's ready."

They walked down to the corner of the house, where they could shelter in case of far-flying debris. The ground itself shook when Daniel pressed the button, and the explosion knocked into them with shocking power, the two bombs somehow feeding each other and multiplying the force of the blast. Instinctively they both stepped behind the side of the house, but no debris came that far. When they walked back up, they saw that the tree was demolished completely. The only large pieces left were a few lengths from the longest branches, and the top section, which was lying mostly intact about forty yards away. The rest was pulverized into unrecognizable shards. It was clearly beyond repair, which made Daniel swell with relief.

"That was a lot louder than I expected," Orval said. "You better get moving in case anyone who heard it calls the police. You have a vehicle?"

"Yes, but it's on the other side of the property." Daniel pointed over to woods.

"Take my truck, the keys are in it. Leave it wherever you left your car."

"What about you?"

"I'll say you stole it. I'll say I took a sleeping pill and slept through it. I won't call anyone till midmorning if no one else calls it in. But you might not have that long."

Daniel shook Orval's hand, thanked him, and walked back down to where the gray pickup was parked by the house. As he descended the snaking black driveway he wept in hard, gasping sobs. He searched himself for signs of transfiguration. There was nothing so extreme, but he did feel something new. A small chink in a rear wall.

PART II

1968-1969

Johnny Knowles stood at the window. He pushed the canvas drape over far enough to expose a stripe of glass and see out into the driveway. In the blue predawn the narrow street lay empty. The streetlight at the end of the block still burned. Nicer Tucson streets had palm trees and cacti, green lawns; this one had only dented American cars and squares of khaki dust littered with sun-bleached plastic toys. It was cool out, but it wouldn't be for long when the sun rose. He walked over to his kitchenette and pulled a Coke from the fridge, popped it open, and flicked the tab across the counter. When the soda hit his throat, he sucked at it hard, thirstier than he'd realized, and finished it off in large gulps. He dropped the can in the garbage and lay down on the sofa, hoping sleep would creep in and grant him a couple of hours. He hadn't been sleeping much the past week, and it was starting to piss him off. Sure, he'd done a bad thing, but at some point you had to get over it, move on. You didn't do anyone any good stewing over it, feeling guilty.

Johnny knew he was a bad dude—he took pride in it—but he'd never thought of himself as a bad *person*. He was just bad enough to inspire a little fear, a little respect, in those who knew him. People were wary of him, but they didn't hate him. Before Rachel tried to leave him, he'd never done anything too terrible. Hurt some guys in fights, but most of them had it coming, and some of them had hurt him worse. Stole some cars, big deal. With the insurance money it was a victimless crime. Moved drugs of various kinds in small amounts. Just giving people what they wanted. So he had surprised himself with Rachel, how far he'd gone. He knew it had a lot to do with the fucked-up hold she had over him. She seemed so nice, so *good,* with her long clean hair, her school skirts, and that smile. And she *was* good, in most ways. She liked to have fun, sure, but wouldn't ever cross a real line against another person, even to get something she wanted. Johnny knew this, and it confused and inflamed him. But here was the thing: her personality, her youth, and her beauty combined with this tiny green animal spark in her whose refraction lit her eyes and every atom of her (he could never get quite close enough to it) and made him a little crazy. If he was honest, a lot crazy. And she knew it, didn't she? She knew she did something to him that he couldn't control, and she liked it. And if it was out of his control, and perpetuated by her, then was it really his fault? Which would make it . . . what? Her fault? He shook his head and took a breath, wishing he was dense enough to convince himself of that. It would have been nice to believe she had it coming. But she never had *that* coming. *Maybe,* he let himself think, *it was nobody's fault.* He gained a little traction with this thought. Maybe it was just how the crazy old human heart acted and there wasn't anything anyone could do about it.

He had fixated on her from the first time he'd seen her sitting with two friends in a booth at a pizza joint. The friend across from her was sexier, with her skirt hiked up and her blouse off the shoulder, but Johnny's eyes were drawn only to Rachel. She was his type, and he would have liked her just based on that, but it was more than that. She exposed some cellular barrenness in him just by glancing at him, and threatened with the thinness of her arm and the slight heft of her hip to alleviate it. When he saw her that first time he'd known she was a high school girl. That was all right, he loved high school girls—had ever since junior high, he liked to joke. And unlike back then, they were easy to talk to now, not so picky, especially if you got the right ones. But Rachel, she'd been tough from the drop. She had not made it easy for him. She wouldn't even tell him her name when he tried to talk to her, and she left with her friends soon after, but he kept coming back there at the same time, after school let out, and a few days later she was there again.

"I never got your name last time," Johnny said, standing by the same table, where she sat with the same two friends.

"That's right, you didn't," she said. The smile she shared with her friends dropped from her face when she looked at him.

"Well, how about giving it to me, so I'll know what to call you? My name's Johnny."

She looked across the table at the sexy friend, and Johnny could tell from the friend's smirk that the attitude among them toward him was not altogether negative. They were interested, even if she wouldn't let on.

"Her name is Rachel," the friend said.

"Hey!" Rachel's jaw dropped in faux shock.

"And I'm Morticia," the friend said.

"No you're not." Johnny laughed.

"I am! That's my name."

The other friend, who was sitting by the window next to Rachel, stifled a laugh and turned away.

"Nobody real was ever named Morticia," Johnny said. "Especially nobody from that school you guys go to."

"Well, now you've insulted me," the friend said, turning her sly smirk on him. She was very pleased with herself, and Johnny let his eyes drift away from her as if she hadn't spoken. He stared at Rachel.

"Listen, Rachel— Is that your real name?"

She looked up at him silently, and he could see that it was.

"Rachel, why don't you come on over to my table, just for five minutes, so we can talk without the aid of your interpreter. Your friends will be right here, keeping an eye on us. Nothing bad can happen. If you don't like me, I'll never bother you again. That's a promise."

She said, "Thanks for the invitation, but we're trying to study for a test here."

"Oh go on," Morticia said. "*Do* something for once. He's just a boy, he's not going to bite you."

Rachel looked to the other friend for support, but she just shrugged. Johnny knew that with the friends egging her on she'd do it. "Five minutes," he said. He gave her his best smile, the one that came from the place in him where he actually loved life. If he drew a bubble around that part of himself, shut out the rest, it became perfect and entirely real. The world was a goddamn playground, after all, a buffet of stuff to do that made you feel good. Look at these perfect girls with their brown legs and their lipstick and their brand-new tits hiding under those white uniform shirts. Look at all the cars to drive and drugs to smoke and snort. There were fifty kinds of cold beer in every corner store, and liquor bottles like gemstones lining every bar in town. It was America. If you didn't smile at all that, you were just an asshole. That was the place his smile came from.

"Five minutes," she said, "okay," and she smiled in return.

Something happened as they talked, something that moved his mind beyond the requisite information exchange, beyond his craving for the glow of her skin, beyond even the mysteries that lay south of the quivering hollow at the base of her throat as she spoke: Johnny Knowles started to open up. While he was pretending it wasn't about sex, and that getting to know her was what he wanted most in the world, while he was giving her tidbits of his own life and dredging up questions to ask about hers, like petting a skittish dog, he started to tell her things he hadn't planned on saying. Things that were risky, not seductive. Things that might make a person look down on him, except he knew somehow she wouldn't. He told her about the degenerative arc of his father's personality, how he had been fun and playful when Johnny was a boy, how they'd gone on fishing trips and to the rodeo, and how he had turned sour and quiet with constant drunkenness over the course of a few years, eventually exploding into violent rages that would have been unthinkable in that earlier incarnation.

"Oh gosh," Rachel said. "That sounds really tough."

"Ah, you know, it is what it is." He turned his face toward the declining sun coming through the window across the room, hoping it struck him in a way that made him look handsome.

"I never knew my father at all," she said. "It's sad, but I guess it could have been worse. Are your parents still together? Do you still see him?"

"No, he died a few years back."

"Oh, I'm sorry."

He knew he needed to spin it, salvage the conversation from this depressing place. "Thanks. What I do is, I just try and remember the good stuff. I believe that's who he really was, and the rest of it, his demons, were not the real him."

"Of course they weren't." She said it so solidly he almost believed her, though she had no fucking idea. "That's all you can do. You have to remember the good parts," she said.

He didn't tell her that his father had blown his own head off with a hunting rifle in their garage when Johnny was fourteen, more than a few years earlier. Thirteen years now. He didn't tell her about opening the door from the kitchen into the garage, the slump of the shoulders in that old lawn chair, the strangely misshapen head lolled back. He hadn't known at first what he was looking at. Asleep at some new project maybe. A shard of skull crunched under his sneaker, and he saw the gun on the floor then, registered the situation, his father's bare right foot still resting on the stock, one shoe and one sock laid neatly by the chair. All that was private.

As they spoke, he saw her eyes soften. Their steely rectitude turned velvet. The insecure girl trying to make an impression while holding him at bay disappeared, and was replaced by a young woman who seemed to be starting to like him. He was good at making girls want to fuck him, but he'd never felt as if any of them actually liked him. He'd never cared about that, and he had no idea what he'd done to accomplish it this time, he'd just stumbled onto it. But he didn't want to let it go. When she told him how her mother had raised her alone on a secretary's salary, and pushed her constantly, sometimes ruthlessly, to excel, so that she'd gotten a scholarship to this private school, he found himself smiling and congratulating her. When she told him that she and her mother did not get along, and that she'd begun to buck her mother's authority at every turn, he heard himself say, "It's all fine to want to make your own rules, but don't waste what you have at that school. Your mom's right about that."

"Don't worry," she said. "My grades are always good."

Johnny abandoned his original plan to try and convince her to leave there with him and come back to his place for a drink. He abandoned, for the moment, his lewd fantasies. When her friends were ready to go, he asked her for her phone number, and she gave it to him. "If my mom answers, tell her you're calling about my math study group."

"I could actually use some help with my algebra, so that works out," Johnny said.

Now here he was, half a year later, lying awake all night and expecting the cops to bang on his door any second—though that fear had started to abate. It had been four days since she'd gone home, and no one had shown up. Seemed like she might have decided to keep it to herself. Thing was, she still had her hooks in him. It wasn't just guilt and fear of the cops keeping him awake, it was being without her, knowing she'd never be back. His mind was a poisonous spiral, and every time he had finished cycling through the fear and guilt, he came around again to the plummeting emptiness of having lost Rachel for good. Half the time this left him simply desolate, which rekindled his guilt, and half the time it dragged him into a dark, hydraulic anger, which felt so much better.

The last two days he had started to park near her house just for the occasional glimpse of her, imagining he could talk to her for a second or two, maybe more, imagining the shift in her eyes when her love for him overcame his transgression. They could start over. *Let the healing begin,* a TV jingle echoed sneeringly in his mind. Fucking idiot. Those fantasies always evaporated in the flash-heat of images from the ordeal he had inflicted on her—her sapling wrists tied with an extension cord to the bedstead, the sweaty tangle of her hair after two days thrashing on the pillow. Worst of all, the glimpse of Jules's skinny bobbing ass through the open bedroom doorway as Johnny arrived home from the store the third day, and then the defeat in her eyes after Jules was gone, when she'd succumbed finally to hunger and allowed herself to be fed. When he reached this point in his circular thought-prison Johnny would retreat back into his anger, sometimes pressing his knuckles into a sharp table edge or chomping the inside of his cheek to generate a cauterizing wave of pain. After releasing her he had withdrawn all his money from the bank and packed a go-bag, in case the cops came after him, but when they didn't the idea of leaving had not faded, instead growing sharper. Today was the day.

He'd always suspected that California might be the place for him, anyway, and there was supposed to be some wild stuff going on in San Francisco. Jules had talked him into taking him along, even though at first Johnny could hardly stomach him after seeing his white ass bobbing through that doorway. In the end, he was Johnny's only friend,

and they'd known each other since the fifth grade. That had to be worth
something. Jules also had a guy who sometimes fronted him smack to
sell, and he said if they were leaving for good they could rip the guy
off. Johnny had some money saved up, but a stash to help fund the trip
wouldn't hurt, so they got a package fronted, saying they were going
to sell it to a buyer in Phoenix. The dealer was dangerous, but he was
strictly local Tucson, and they'd be long gone before he figured it out.
Johnny said nothing to his landlord, nothing to his boss at the land-
scaping company, nothing to his mother, just packed a few more things
into his ancient Chevy truck.

On their way out of town, he couldn't help going by Rachel's house
one more time, just for a look. He pulled up thirty yards down the
block, across the street, and stopped.

"What are we up to?" Jules asked.

"Nothing. Just taking a look for a minute here." Johnny stared ahead
at the small brown house.

"Tell me this ain't that girl's house."

"It is none of your concern whose house it is."

"That means it is," Jules said, smirking. Jules was his friend, but
Johnny hated his eyes sometimes. With most people, when they smiled
you could see it in their eyes, but with Jules it was only a change in the
shape of his mouth. It made you want to hit him.

"You looking to get popped?"

"She coming with us?"

"Last warning," Johnny said.

THE CHEVY ATE gas, and they wasted some of their cash on a motel
with a pool in Kingman, so when the truck blew its head gasket in a
little town called Atwater, California, they didn't have enough to fix it.
Their smack would do them no good in the sticks. The mechanic they
found offered to buy the truck for fifty bucks and a ride to the Modesto
bus station. Johnny talked him up to sixty. When they got to the bus station, there wasn't a San Fran bus until the next morning. Johnny hated
waiting overnight with that package of smack rolled up in a T-shirt

in the side pocket of Jules's pack, but they didn't have a choice. Jules slept slumped against his pack. Johnny stayed awake all night so they wouldn't be hassled for vagrancy. He didn't trust Jules to keep watch if he fell asleep.

He'd been feeling better ever since they'd crossed out of Arizona. It was an arbitrary border, he knew, but it was like a load lifted off him to be breathing different air than her. Even the tepid, bleach-tainted air of that bus station tasted like a fresh start. Rachel was just a girl, he told himself, just one more human in the big bad world, and he had no reason to stay hung up on her. California stars stretched overhead and the Pacific waited to the west. Pacific meant peaceful, and that's how he'd be. After all, she was free now, too, with him gone. Wasn't she? Worse things happened to people every day and they got over them. What he was doing now—getting away from her—was the best thing for both of them. With distance, he could feel himself peeling free from her oppressive magnetism, which had drawn from him such a bewildering explosion. He hadn't known himself capable of that, and the discovery had knocked him a little silly. Now he would escape from that knowledge and back into normal life. He would go back to being the old Johnny Knowles, bush-league Casanova and semi-bad dude.

A trio of bearded hippies trailed in around three in the morning and sat on a bench opposite them. Johnny was glad to see them, since they'd likely draw police attention before him and Jules. They sat close together in a jumble of fringes and dusty denim even though there was room to spread out. As Johnny eyed them, the tallest one said, "You guys heading to Frisco, brother?" His long, bare arms hung from a leather cowboy vest, and six or seven beaded necklaces were draped across his brown chest. Johnny shook his head and looked away, closing his eyes.

IN THEIR FIRST two months in San Francisco, they met everyone they would need to know. A riptide of the nation's rebellious youth was surging through the city. There were so many people coming and going through the scene that you had to find a few who were fixtures and latch on, otherwise you'd flounder. Lucky for them they found Chinese Bill.

Chinese Bill wasn't Chinese, but affected to wear a long, tightly braided ponytail, a wispy mustache and goatee, and a bamboo coolie hat. In no other way did he act or seem Chinese. Johnny had told some guys in a bar their second night in town that they were looking to unload some smack, and they said Chinese Bill was the man to talk to. They didn't know where he lived, but they named a bar called the Pearl Diver.

When Johnny and Jules walked in, he was sitting in the corner with a small hairy dude all in black. The coolie hat gave him away. This was not a hippie bar. It was not near the Haight, and the music was strictly old-school crooners. The four men at the bar looked like longshoremen. It was very dark, and the bartender did not hail Johnny and Jules as they approached from the doorway, instead turning away as if that barren establishment hadn't just gained two potential new customers. Johnny had been planning on ordering a drink before going to the corner table, but he veered off from the bar and headed over. Chinese Bill and his companion stood out almost comically in that dim straight-world dive, like two characters on a quest out of some book with gnomes wandered into a union dockworkers' haunt. When he stood by the table, Johnny said, "I'm going to take a wild guess and say you might be Chinese Bill."

"Bill. Just Bill," he said. "It's a means of differentiation, really."

"What?"

"Chinese Bill. It's what people call me to differentiate me from other Bills, or from some random Bill. It's not what I call myself." If he lost the hat and braid, and the clipped nasal style of speaking, he could have been a biker, with his ropy tattooed arms, his sleeveless T-shirt, and his wallet on a chain hooked to his jeans. The little guy with him was wearing some kind of robe or vestment, all black. He was much older, maybe fifty or sixty, with a wild gray beard, buggy eyes, and a bald head. He was, possibly, a psychotic retired jockey turned whiskey priest.

"Okay, Bill." Johnny lowered his voice to where it wouldn't be heard over Dean Martin in other quarters of the bar. "We were told you're the man to talk to about moving some junk."

"If you'd talked to anyone who actually knew me, like Percy here," he inclined his conical hat toward the small man, "they wouldn't have told you that. They would have told you that on the off-off chance I ever had something to sell, which I don't and never would, I would never sell it to someone not known to me. They would have told you that when people I don't know come in here looking for me without an introduction they walk out pretty quick, or are ejected if necessary."

"Well, nobody told us that," Johnny said. He bristled at the threat, sizing up the pair at the table for a fight. There wouldn't be much for him and Jules to worry about, a fact so obvious that it was clear Chinese Bill could count on backup. If it was the guys at the bar, there would be a problem. "We ain't here buying, anyway, we're selling weight. Just got in from out of state. But if the answer's no we'll just shake your hand and be on our way."

"Ah, traveling salesmen. That's different. Take a seat and tell me your story."

Johnny and Jules sat down and told him what they had. The price he offered was far lower than they had expected.

"Prices where you're from are probably a lot higher than they are here, boys. That's the best you're going to do. And if you try and move it yourselves in drabs on the Haight, you'll run afoul of certain elements with whom I have agreements. Me, I'm a free-marketeer, I wouldn't give a fuck, but not everyone shares my attitude."

Over the day he spent vetting their product and carrying out the deal, Chinese Bill took a liking to Johnny and brought him on as a mule. "You're a working man, I can tell," he said to Johnny. "Not some free spirit on a gap year. I don't like employing hippies. Too unreliable. Too visible. And it'll help if you start looking less like one. People round this town have issues with longhairs." He recognized Jules for a junkie, though, and told Johnny never to leave him alone with any of the packages, or it'd be on him. "Also," Chinese Bill said, "I already have a Johnny on the payroll, so how about we call you John?"

"Fuck no. I hate John. My papa used to call me Jack for a while when I was a kid."

"Let's go with that, then." Bill leaned over the table, extending his arm and two fingers, and touched Johnny once on each shoulder, knighting him. "Jack, it is."

So Johnny became Jack. It felt right, being renamed, reinforced his fresh start. He cut his hair short and started delivering for Chinese Bill, who sold anything anyone wanted, and whose clientele ranged from rock stars to society dabblers to corner dealers, on down to cadres of street hippies pooling their money. He was plugged in everywhere. Bill never let the money and drugs be in the same place at the same time. You had to trust him. First you paid Percy, who handled Bill's money from his own separate table at the Pearl Diver, then named a place and met his deliveryman there. For higher-end regular clients, Bill would send a guy to pick up the money and then another to drop off the drugs. Jack was low on the totem, so he always handled the product, which was riskier. He got a map and learned the city quickly. One minute he would be delivering to a bush in Golden Gate Park, and the next to a suite at the Palace Hotel.

Bill ran the business out of a second-floor apartment on Clement Street, slightly removed from all the action and nowhere near the Pearl Diver. The bar was where people went or called to set up buys. Certain things, like reefer, speed, and coke, reds and 'ludes, acid, he usually had on hand, but he also had a few other dealers he'd buy from at discounted prices when people wanted something else. So Jack would sometimes need to meet with one of these to buy the product, and then deliver it.

Jack loved his job, and his relationship with Chinese Bill quickly became a friendship. He would often start his afternoons having a beer and shooting the shit with Bill at the Pearl Diver. Jack made a point of strict professionalism in his work, and tried to charm all the customers, and pretty soon he was known and respected in most corners of the scene. Doors opened for him, to bars, clubs, music venues, and homes. People he didn't know nodded to him on the Haight as he walked past. Chicks could tell he was somebody. Sometimes customers invited him to hang out and party. He was high whenever he wanted to be, but he was mainly a drinking man. A little reefer here and there, maybe a blast of speed or coke to keep the juices flowing on a late night, but that was it. He didn't want anything to do with the crazy stuff, the acid and DMT and mushrooms and whatever else the freaks were into. Jack was a simple man. A Marlboro and a whiskey and a ball session now and then, that was all he needed. He had his head on straight, and this made him better at his job. After a while, Bill offered to make him a money man, picking up payments, but Jack declined. He liked being the guy everyone was waiting for. He liked showing up like a star, holding the goods.

He rented a room from some guys who had a crash pad right off of Haight, but used it only for sleeping. Jules stayed there too, on the couch or in Jack's room when it was empty, and no one seemed to care. They were all stoned every hour of every day, and at some point Jack realized that having him in their pad, with the access to reefer he had, was a coup for them. His buddy on their couch was a small price to pay for the weed discounts and other perks. Plus, they actually seemed to like Jules. They were so glazed over themselves that they didn't notice the congenital glaze Jules lived behind.

In September Jack met Gretchen, who made a perfect old lady for him. She wasn't sweet or very pretty but she was funny, and she depended on him for the drugs that made whatever pained her bearable. She was skinny and fair and black-haired, and had a flat face that was lit from within by jaded humor. He hadn't meant to have a real thing with her, but she stuck around, and he liked her. She made herself available to him when he wanted her, and made herself scarce when he needed his privacy or was off with another girl. After a couple of months, during which she meticulously avoided cramping his style while somehow maintaining her presence in his life, it seemed to make sense for them to get an apartment, somewhere not populated by herds of drifters and heads. Jules stayed on in Jack's old room, and by this time had found work on the cleaning crew at a music hall so he could pay his own rent.

Jack fell into a routine with Gretchen, hanging around with her from midmorning till lunchtime and then starting his workday in the afternoon. He'd usually get home from his rounds a bit before sunrise, and he'd wake her up, get her high, and they'd ball before he went to sleep. Along with booze and grass, Gretchen liked downs, any and all kinds, and Jack stashed them away for her. She liked smack too, but he wouldn't let her do it around him. He began to care about her, and he tried to keep her happy. Sometimes, when he went elsewhere at the end of the night to meet another girl, he would swing by the apartment on his way, just to drop off a few reds or 'ludes, telling her he had to keep working. She would always kiss his cheek and thank him, saying, "Okay, Daddy, don't work too hard," and in her eyes he saw her full acceptance of him. It had never occurred to him that anyone would offer him anything like that, and to his surprise Gretchen began to feel like family. He wasn't about to marry her, but the idea wasn't as ludicrous as it had always seemed. With someone like her, marriage might have a chance. Half a year went by like nothing, living with Gretchen.

JACK LEANED INTO a stiff wind coming down Turk Street. The sun was out, the wind suddenly warm from the east: strange May weather. He was on his way to pick up some cash from an apartment by Jefferson Square. They were regular customers, and he was looking forward to a beer with them to break up his afternoon. He'd become warier of the cops since his life had started smoothing out, and was doing more money pickups now. He had dropped off a package on the way, and was enjoying the carefree feeling of not holding anything illegal. Nearing the corner of Fillmore he approached a long brick building there, from which emanated a low steady hum that had the quality of ominous background music. The dusty red color of the old brick sponged the daylight into its dimmer glow, usurping the sunny afternoon as Jack came alongside it. The bricks themselves seemed somehow to be the source of the hum, whose tenor corresponded with and amplified some disquiet in him. A wild-haired silhouetted hippie rounded the corner of the building like the very thing prefigured by the ominous drone, and, seeing Jack, approached him. Jack shook his head preemptively and waved the back of his hand at the guy to ward off the inevitable panhandling pitch. But it turned out to be Jules. They hadn't seen each other in months. His kinked sandy hair had grown much longer, covering all but a center stripe of his face, and he looked more troll-like than ever.

"What's happening, son?" Jack said.

"Johnny K! What's up. All good here, my brother. You still working for Chinese Bill?"

"Yeah. Fucking cherry gig." At first Jack had assumed, from appearance and prior trajectory, a steady decline in Jules's situation and personality, a decline that would neither have surprised nor saddened him. But there was something different about Jules, a strange new spark in his hair-veiled eyes. Could just be he's on speed now instead of smack, Jack thought. "What's new with you? Still living with Stan and the boys?"

"Yeah man, still there. What's new is I kicked junk. Left that dark-o shit behind."

"Is that so?" Jack felt an itch behind his breastbone. He pulled his cigarettes from his jacket and set about lighting one. "What's your thing now?"

Jules pushed one side of his hair back and smiled. It was a real smile, its influence visible in his eyes. He was transformed. "My thing? My thing, Jack-o, is *the* thing. Vitamin L. My friends at work turned me on, and helped me kick junk a couple months ago. You like tripping?"

Jack shook his head. What was Jules doing with *friends*? "Not me," he said. "I don't ever mess with that stuff."

"You're shittin' me! You haven't even tried it? You got it in your pocket every fucking day I bet!"

"That psycho shit ain't my scene. I like my head wired right."

"Oh, Johnny, you got no idea. It ain't about rewiring, man. It's about leaving the wiring behind. You have got to try it!"

"I'm good," Jack said. He pulled on his cigarette and blew the smoke up over Jules's head.

"Lemme have a square," Jules said.

Jack gave him a cigarette and his Zippo. "I got to go, bud. Got a pickup to make."

"Okay Johnny, or Jack, sorry. But serious, brother. You gotta trip with me sometime. Try it one time and see, that's all. If you don't like it, it's over in a few hours."

"I'll think about it."

"I'll give you a shout when there's a good show at the Fillmore, we'll do it up right. Stuff is happening around here that ain't no joke. You gotta peek behind the curtain one time."

Jack had heard some of this kind of talk before, from other acid freaks. He gave Jules a sad look. "There ain't no curtain, son. There's just the world."

Jules's smile grew now, deepened, and made Jack very anxious. "I'm going to call you."

"You do that." He waved his cigarette and continued east.

The encounter with Jules was still replaying in his mind when he headed home after dropping off the money with Percy. For reasons he couldn't fully define, seeing Jules so altered irritated him. The more he thought about it the more bothered he became. His picture of Jules as a deteriorating person had been somehow important to him without him knowing it. Jules was supposed to spike himself into the gutter, then a coffin. He wasn't supposed to kick and make friends. The meeting threw Jack's whole mood. He just wanted to forget it and get his head back on straight. He picked up a 'lude for Gretchen and one for himself, and went back to their apartment. Walking down the brown-carpeted hallway to their place he heard voices that he assumed were from another apartment, but turned out to be coming from behind his own door. He stood listening for a second. There was a man's voice alternating with Gretchen's; he couldn't make out what was being said. Was she cheating? The idea shocked him, but it had its upside. There would be shouts, threats, tears, maybe even a fight. The prospect cheered him a bit. He opened the door.

Sure enough there was that guilty bug-eyed look on Gretchen's face as soon as he walked in. She looked like someone had poured ice water down her back. But the dude, who was standing at the corner of the sofa, was not right. Not right at all. He was a straight-world guy, a buzz cut in a brown blazer and beige slacks. Clean white T-shirt under the blazer, as if he had spilled coffee on his dress shirt and removed it. Was she turning tricks? It was the first explanation that came to Jack's mind.

"What the fuck," Jack said.

"This is the guy?" the man asked Gretchen after he'd looked Jack up and down.

Gretchen was standing near the man, looking at Jack. "Baby, hey. I thought you were working all day."

"Well, looks like I'm home," Jack said. He smiled. Whatever was going on was going to be juicy, and it was just what he needed. "Care to introduce me?"

"Yeah . . . um, yeah, this is Eddie." Jack did not move to shake the man's hand, but engaged him with a baleful look that established his dominion in that space. "And this," said Gretchen, "is Miranda." For the first time Jack noticed that there was a child between the man and the sofa, hiding behind his leg. She was four or five years old and was peeking at him when he looked, but quickly hid her face. Her long straight brown hair was smoothly brushed and she wore a light blue dress.

"Well, hello little lady. So these are friends of yours?" he asked Gretchen.

"Yeah. I was . . ." She hung her head. "You know, they just showed up. I wasn't expecting them. I thought I'd tell you later. . . ."

"Tell me what?"

Eddie, with his pudged sallow cheeks and his tiny dark eyes, said, "She's my wife. That's what."

"Well, shit," Jack said.

"I was going to tell you."

"So does that make you her mommy?" There was silence in the room. For some reason all three of them were looking at Jack—Gretchen and the little girl wide-eyed, and Eddie squinting—as if waiting for him to answer his own question. "And I guess you're here to try and take her back with you," he said to Eddie.

Eddie laughed loudly. The sound made Jack want to choke him.

"Take her back? Oh no," Eddie said. "We're way past that. You can have her, my friend, she's all yours. But just because she's become some kind of drug whore doesn't mean she's not a mother anymore. I got things of my own I want to do. I got a life to lead. I was just leaving, anyway, and I don't need to explain myself to you." He walked toward where Jack stood by the door. The girl clung to his leg and was dragged along. "Sweetie," Eddie said, peeling her little hand away, "you have to stay here now. You're going to stay with Mommy for a while."

The girl made a keening sound that loosely contained the word *no*, still clinging fiercely to his slacks. He pulled her arms apart and lifted her up, hugged her, and carried her to the sofa. He turned her sideways and laid her down on it, and when she curled into a ball he quickly walked to the door. As he passed Jack, he did a little sideways dance step, almost falling, flinching from a punch Jack hadn't thrown. Jack had not even twitched. Eddie's own cowardice made him angrier, and he shouted over his shoulder, "Hope you're happy with your whore," slamming the door behind him.

Jack stood looking at Gretchen. Her eyes were still wide. "Can he do that?" Jack asked.

She shrugged, and they both shifted their gazes to the child, who was curled up, her face hidden.

"I don't think he can do that," Jack said. But the difficulty of the situation was obvious to him even in those first moments. The child needed care, and you couldn't just go shove her through that prick's door again. His own decision would end up being whether to walk out on Gretchen or stay and figure it out. This realization made him livid. It was a bad deal either way, one which he'd had no hand in creating.

"You never said nothing about a kid."

"I know," she said. "I'm sorry. . . ." She seemed about to go on, but she looked at the small body on the sofa and stopped. Her gaze was frozen, and then something collapsed behind her eyes. "I haven't seen her in over a year. He wouldn't let me unless I came back." She sat down and put a hand on the child's shoulder. "Miranda," she said, "are you okay?" There was no answer, no sound or movement of any kind from the girl. "Hey," she said, and lifted the tiny body gently into her lap. "Do you remember me? Do you remember Mommy?"

Miranda nodded but kept her eyes closed and her face buried in her arms.

"It's okay, sweetie. You're okay. Are you hungry? Do you still like macaroni and cheese?"

The girl lifted her face up to Gretchen, opened her eyes, and began to cry. Gretchen looked at Jack. "Can we work things out later? Please baby?"

Jack took a tight-lipped breath. Then he nodded. "I'll go get some Kraft Dinners and milk," he said. "Maybe some ice cream too."

Half an hour later, they sat watching the girl eat. She still hadn't spoken, but had answered some questions by nodding or shaking her head. When she had finished her macaroni, Gretchen gave her a scoop of ice cream and she ate it slowly, her eyes calming a bit with the simple pleasure. "Are you in school yet?" Gretchen asked her. She shook her head. She was finished with her ice cream, but still gripped the spoon tightly in her small, sticky fist. Jack had lit a cigarette and was taking in this scene from his armchair in the living area. Miranda turned and engaged his eyes.

"What's your name?" she asked. They were the first words she'd spoken. Her voice was high and timid, trailing off softly, but her eyes were unwavering.

"My name is Jack."

"Is this your house?"

"Yeah," he said. "I guess it is. Your mommy and I live here together." The girl nodded.

Gretchen stood and picked up the empty bowl and pinched the end of the spoon in her fingers. Miranda looked at her and took a moment to release the spoon, which she'd been clutching unconsciously. Gretchen took them to the sink and began washing the dishes. The child looked again at Jack, and her gaze was deeply magnetic. He stood and walked to the table and sat next to her.

"Was your food good?"

"Yes," she said.

"The ice cream okay?"

She nodded. "I like strawberry better."

"Well, I'll remember that for next time." Looking at her, the smears of cheese sauce and ice cream on her cheeks, he somehow thought of Rachel. "You know you got nothing to worry about, right? You're going to be fine here, with us." He heard himself speaking and wanted to stop. The girl just gazed at him with her big resolute eyes. "I'm just saying," he said, "everything's going to be okay."

Miranda nodded. "Okay."

"You believe me?"

"Yes," she said, but it came out very quickly.

"Good. I'm going to have to get back to work now."

Gretchen turned around. "Can you stay with her for a minute while I take a shower? I really need one."

"Yeah," Jack said. "Just hurry."

When Gretchen left the room Jack turned back to Miranda. The girl was still staring at him. He'd been charmed at first by her bravery, but he was starting to feel uncomfortable. There was a combination of depth and openness to her stare that he was unaccustomed to. It perforated his defenses. He'd never spent any time with a child—at least not since he'd been one, and even then he'd been mostly alone. The little girl's eyes seemed to tunnel into him, and suddenly he found himself remembering flashes of what he'd done to Rachel, images he'd worked hard to sequester: the sweaty shock in her eyes when he'd first dragged her to the bed and bound her with the lamp cord, the greater shock when she realized he was going to keep her there, the deep red furrows on her tiny wrists from the plastic cord before he'd switched it for the suede belt from his jacket, the Cream of Wheat smearing onto her face as she spun her head and avoided the spoon the morning after that first night. He had grown more and more incensed with her the first day. He wasn't hurting her, just keeping her from leaving until he could convince her to stay. He tried to explain this to her, but she wouldn't acknowledge him. He had finally snapped with fury when he understood that what he was doing was unforgivable, that there was no going back. The source of all that fury remained obscure to him, but afterward, when it sporadically vacated him, what remained was only a dense and unwelcome shame. Rachel's face had been cold, almost as if dead, when he forced himself on her. Those flecks of dried Cream of Wheat still clung to her cheek, their exact shapes and configurations seared into his memory in vivid jolts. Then there was Jules's bobbing white ass through the doorway.

All this washed through in the space of a second, drawn from him by this child's steadfast gaze. "Hey," he said. "What are you doing?"

Her brow crinkled and she seemed about to get upset.

"Are you in my head?"

"I don't know," she said very quietly. Her mouth fell open.

When he was young he'd sometimes thought he could see the

thoughts in his mother's head, like movies projected into his own mind. "Can you see the things I'm thinking?"

She did not want to answer him; he could see that. "I don't know," she said. Her eyes had gone from steadfast to glossy with rising tears.

He said, "You need to sit here, at this table, in that chair, until your mommy comes out from her shower. You understand?"

She nodded.

"Don't move until you see her. You hear me?"

She nodded again. Jack got up and hurried out.

WHEN JULES TURNED his back, Jack plucked the tiny orange pill off his tongue and palmed it. It had stayed there only about fifteen seconds, but had already begun to soften and crumble. A second later, worried it could seep in through his skin, he dropped it to the sidewalk and wiped the crumbs on his jeans. He hadn't planned to spit it out, but something came over him once the thing was on his tongue, something that had as much to do with Jules's newly animated face and gnostic stare as it did with anything else. Whatever could produce this kind of alteration in Jules must be something to be reckoned with, and not something Jack wanted any part of.

They wove their way through the crowd in front of the Fillmore, and Jack occupied himself staring at navels and legs and cotton-brushed nipples. It was a good crowd, lots of chicks. Normally he wouldn't have wanted to see the Dead, though some of their music was pretty good. He had seen them once in the park, and had dug it up to a point, but got sick of wading through all the weird convolutions and hippie mysticism to get to the sharp riffs and funky blues he liked. He wouldn't have wasted his time with them again, but with Miranda settled in the apartment for a few weeks now, he had started finding excuses to be gone even when he wasn't working. The girl had shined on him from the start, and when he was there she never left him alone, always crawling on him, asking questions and wanting him to read to her. He couldn't say no to her, couldn't weather the disappointment in her furrowed little brow, and this inability confused him. He also couldn't fully shake the ridiculous idea that she somehow had access to the parts of his head he dreaded and evaded. Her presence rarely failed to make him feel rotten, no matter how nice he was to her. When he wasn't there he could put her out of his mind, so he stayed away as much as he could.

Jules's buddy let them in a side door, and they wandered the crowded lobby inside the venue, smoking and talking with people they knew. Jack saw Shawna, a chick he went home with from time to time, but she was with her old man and wouldn't even glance sideways at him, though she knew he was there. He left her alone. He was talking to the bass player of another rising local band, whose house he delivered grass to almost daily, when the refraction happened. It wasn't much, and it didn't last long, but for a moment he was standing beside himself watching the entire world, and every offhand movement of his fingers as he spoke was a planetary microcosm. And then it was gone. Not gone as in disappeared, but gone like the outdoors is gone when one steps into a windowless room.

Jules was standing next to him, and Jack asked him, "Has it been half an hour? It seems like we've been in this place for a year or two."

"Bud, it's been a lot longer than half an hour. You feeling it?"

"I'm feeling something."

"'Course you are." Jules smiled. His skin was mottled with blush-spots and his eyes were all pupil. A huge fuzzy droning exploded from inside the theater, deep and loud, and for a moment it seemed to Jack that the ominous hum he'd heard weeks earlier from that brick building on Turk Street had reasserted itself here and reached fearsome maturity.

"Oh, fuck," he said, not altogether sure what he was afraid of. The droning acquired rhythm and became a song.

"Yeaaahhh," said Jules. "Here we go, come on."

They went into the now-darkened main house and watched the band dredge up some pretty heavy shit. Jack didn't like it much, but at least it wasn't flimsy like a lot of the new stuff. The drug hooked the edges of his mind, making him alternately anxious and exhilarated, and then sometimes abated almost entirely, leaving him empty and clean. He was very glad he'd spit it out.

After a while, in the middle of the set, he wandered back out into the lobby and lit a cigarette, leaned against the wall. There were still quite a few people out there, taking advantage of the extra space to dance wildly, spinning, jumping, contorting, tracing dream-shapes with their hands. A long, terrible song ended, and the band began retuning their instruments. Jack found his thirst for cigarettes unquenchable and lit another one. He blew a cloud up toward the ceiling and watched Rachel float through the archway from the interior. She seemed a figment, and for a moment he didn't react at all, just watched. Her face was filled with contemplative light, and nudged the membrane separating his eyes from his mind. She was happy. For a minute she stopped and talked to a guy wearing only a blue blazer and gym shorts, and when he wandered into the theater she walked farther into the lobby. Someone offered her a cup and she smiled and drank from it. The relief Jack felt in that moment was oceanic. She was okay. It seemed as though he was being shown a projection of Rachel from some far-off place, seeing her healed and happy—and it was, pure and simple, a gift. After drinking from the cup, she turned and walked along the wall toward him. She was getting closer, but in his beatific state Jack knew he was imagining being there, was just an apparition invisible to her—knew it right up until the moment when her eyes fell on him. She was only ten feet away, and he saw all the peace in her disintegrate, replaced instantly by soul-terror. Desperation seized him.

"Rachel," he said, stepping closer to her, "hey. I can't believe it's you. What are you doing here?"

She was frozen, even as her eyes recoiled. "Nothing, just visiting."

"It's good to see you," Jack said, impaled. "I just want to say that. Baby, I'm just really glad to see you doing okay. That's all I want you to know."

"Okay, Johnny. Yes." Her head jerked to look over her shoulder. She seemed about to turn and run.

"How you feeling, Jack-o?" It was Jules, calling out as he approached from the other side. He hadn't recognized Rachel.

"Good, man. I'm all right."

"Going to introduce me?"

Jack felt his own mouth hanging open, and being wounded and tongue-tied made him suddenly angry. "This is Rachel."

"Very pleased, sweetheart," Jules said, extending his hand to her.

She reached robotically and shook it, saying, "Yeah, hi," and Jack saw Jules make the connection.

"Hey!" he said, grinning wide at her. "It's you!"

Her face clouded more deeply, and Jack was sure she was about to puke.

She said, "My friends are waiting," and went off through the arch into the theater. The band had started playing again, and it was as if when she flicked out of sight she had merged with the churning music itself.

"That was her!" Jules said. "The girl from Tucson!"

Jack didn't respond, couldn't. The awful moment when her eyes fell on him was lodged in his mind, fueling in him a dense and menacing current. It had the pitiless gravity of a wrecking ball.

Jules trailed after him as he followed her, and Jack turned on him. "Will you leave me the fuck alone for a minute?"

"Whoa. Happy to, brother." He went back out toward the bathrooms.

Jack wandered the crowd inside looking for her. The weight of the feeling in him wouldn't allow him to move away from her. He didn't want to surprise her and scare her again, so he searched the crowd at as great a distance as he could, moving in slowly from the doorway, looking for her faded red skirt and her white blouse. When he saw her, she was embracing a tall clean-cut boy—a long full-body hug that did not break for what seemed like a whole minute. Jack looked at the kid's face. He had a big sharp nose and serious eyes, dark hair. This was the smooth handsome face of the person whose embrace could calm her now, comfort her, as his never would. There was no mistaking the earnestness between them. The way the kid looked at her when he spoke, the easy way he touched her shoulder after the hug, as if it were part of his own body. After a minute the kid said something to a guy in a plain white T-shirt standing near them, whose face seemed familiar from somewhere Jack couldn't place, and then they walked toward the back. Jack stayed behind them until he saw them walk out into the street. He wanted to follow, but he resisted. Instead he wandered the crowd awhile and then went back into the lobby and found Jules talking to one of his coworkers.

"Hey brother," Jules said. "You okay?"

"Yeah, just fine." The music seemed to have stopped. "They done playing?"

"Naw, man. They won't be done for a while. Just a little break." Jules's eyes looked as though they might explode from his head. "Did you catch your girl?"

"Yeah, I did. But I think she left now."

"Left?" The possibility of this seemed to shock him. "Hey, she all right with you? After what all happened?"

"What are you talking about? She's fine with me. Only really bad thing that happened to her was you. What I did, I did out of love, she knows that."

"Shit. I hope she don't hate me. I was just having some fun. I was pretty fucked up. She seems like a good girl, though, like she can handle it, you know? And besides, it wasn't me who tied her up."

"Motherfucker," Jack said. He took the front of Jules's shirt in his fist and pushed his face in close. He spoke with all the venom in him, his voice a rasp, "I oughta cut your fucking throat for you. How'd you like that?"

Over Jules's shoulder, Jack saw the white-T-shirted guy stroll out of the interior, give a brief hug to the guy in the blue blazer, and then sit on the floor with a small group by the wall and light a cigarette. His face in the light became moonlike, not in paleness but with a kind of effulgence whose source was obscure. He radiated.

Jules said, "Aww shit, brother. Come on. We been through this, right?"

"Hey, just fucking with you, son. Calm down." He let Jules go and pushed out a laugh as though he'd been joking. He could tell Jules wasn't buying it. "Seriously, she's right as rain, like you say. I spoke to her again and she's basically over it. You know I think she kind of liked it, actually. I'm only guessing, but if we play our cards right, she might even want to do it again, with both of us I mean."

Jules's eyes widened. "For real?"

"Who knows? You know who that dude is?" Jack pointed. "The guy in the white T-shirt, sitting down?"

Jules looked over. "Yeah, man, that guy's got a ranch up north, bunch of heads live there. I ain't been up there but I hear it's a pretty boss scene. They always have acid."

"Can you introduce me?"

"Introduce you? I don't know any of them, I just see them around at shows."

"You know his name?"

"Yeah, I think it's Cam."

Jack walked over to the group on the floor. He stood by a minute while they spoke amongst themselves. Then, as the conversation continued, Cam looked up directly at Jack as if the whole world had disappeared and he was acknowledging the only other human left. "Hey there," he said.

"Hey brother," Jack said. "Your name's Cam, right?"

"Yes."

Jack squatted onto his heels. "I hear you have a real nice scene at your ranch, and I wondered if my friend and I might come check it out." He heard himself sounding like a freeloader and quickly added, "Not to stay or anything. We got places, we pay rent. I ain't no mooch. I'm just interested in checking out the scene."

Getting this close to him, Jack saw that the guy was his own age, pushing thirty, or maybe older. He was a man, not some kid like most of them. His brow gathered in friendly curiosity, and for a second Jack feared Cam would pierce his veneer and discern his motive somehow. But then he said, "Sure, man. We're having a party after the show, lots of people coming. Feel free. If you meet me out front after, I can give you a ride up."

"Far out. Thanks, my man. My name's Jack by the way."

Cam shook his hand. "Yeah, you're one of Chinese Bill's guys, aren't you?"

"I do some business for him, but I ain't his."

Cam smiled. "Of course not." He moved his face closer to Jack's and looked harder into his eyes. "You tripping? Usually I can tell."

"Yeah," Jack said. "But it don't affect me too much."

An easy, incredulous laugh rushed out from Cam's chest, and Jack couldn't help noticing the beauty of his mouth, the undulant lips tucking softly into a perfect crescent dimple. Jack stood, lungs burning from the unwelcome shock of seeing a man this way.

"See you after."

Cam nodded silently, still searching him with that curious look, and Jack turned quickly and walked away.

For the remainder of the show, he couldn't enjoy the music. Even when the band dropped into some mean-ass rock it just grated on him. He stayed in the lobby chain-smoking. The moment with Rachel reran itself ceaselessly in his mind: her placid expression collapsing when she saw him, the terror that replaced it, the petrifaction that seized her body. As the memory played and replayed, it acquired a force he was unequal to. He didn't understand why—he thought he had put her mostly out of his mind. He'd never expected to see her again, and now this was folding him up like a junked car in a crusher. The combination of shame and desire the sight of her triggered was shocking. Normally he would have found a bar and thrown down a few drinks, but with this sliver of LSD in his system he understood instinctively that booze would be ineffective. There had to be a way to climb out of the pit she'd knocked him into. The shame had to be treatable, even if the desire wasn't. By the time the show was over, he had wedded his future peace of mind to a narrative in which he would engineer his escape from shame. He would go out to this ranch; if she was there he would find a way to speak with her, and he would express his remorse. If she didn't forgive him that was okay, he knew he'd feel better for trying. Even partial relief would be worth it. And if she did forgive him . . . he didn't let himself go too deep into that fantasy, but it sure would solve a lot. You never knew. There was, after all, magic in the air.

THE TWIN RED circles of the old Ford's taillights were easy to keep in sight once they emerged from the city's south side, so Jack left them far ahead. He thought if he lost them he might even feel relieved. He had waited by the bonfire for Rachel, but she and her boy had stayed inside the house for a long time. He had kept an eye on their car as the night went on, and the longer they stayed hidden in the house the more anxious he became about missing her somehow. He had eventually taken a seat under the big leaning tree where he had a clear view of the front of the house and the cars, and had stayed there watching. Cam and his friend had come out early on and walked to the bonfire, where a makeshift band had started to play, and then some time later Cam had headed back to the house with another guy. Then Cam came back to the party, and a few minutes later, finally, Rachel and the boy had emerged, but instead of heading for the party they had put some things in the trunk of their car, climbed in, and the lights had flicked on. By the time Jack reached the pickup truck, the Ford had topped the rise and disappeared from view. The keys were sitting on the dash, and he started it up and turned it around. He looked toward the bonfire but didn't see anyone noticing or trying to stop him. At the end of the driveway he'd turned south and headed toward the city, and after a minute of gunning the engine the taillights came into view. He figured he'd follow them until he saw where they lived or were staying in the city, and then return the truck.

But now they were still heading south after passing through the city, and Jack was starting to wonder how far he'd follow. The narrative of redemption he'd envisioned was fading in his mind, as it became clear that apologizing was a poor reason for tailing someone hours down the coast. What he *was* doing, he couldn't have said, and after a while it didn't matter. He needed to follow her, that was all. They pulled into a gas station, and Jack was relieved to see his own tank was still half full. He cut the engine and the lights and waited on the shoulder. He turned on the radio and rolled the dial slowly until he heard Dusty Springfield. *The only boy who could ever reach me. . . .* Suddenly it seemed that everything—the night, the road, the wind, the radio—was speaking to him personally, trying to instruct him, and Jack wondered not quite idly whether the boy in the car with her might actually be a preacher's son. The word *only* soured in his gut. *Yes he was, yes he was. . . .* He saw the Ford appear, make a slow left turn under the station's fluorescent sign, and continue south. Half an hour later they pulled suddenly into an empty dirt turnout. Jack didn't have time to pull over inconspicuously so he drove on past. The road sloped downhill, and a minute later the

Ford was out of sight behind him. He found a wide spot in the shoulder and pulled over. He got out and started walking back up the hill, listening carefully for the sound of their engine. He was prepared, if he heard it, to dive into the underbrush. When he crested the hill, the Ford was still sitting parked in the turnout, and it was either empty or they'd lain down inside to sleep. He stopped, watching and listening, in case they were nearby and might see him. When he heard nothing, he walked slowly over to the car and peeked in. Empty. He looked around for signs of where they might have gone, but saw nothing. The far side of the road was a steep rock escarpment. Then he saw the gap in the shaded underbrush right in front of the car. He stepped closer and it resolved itself from the darkness into a trailhead. Jack followed the trail through thick, head-high bushes and taller trees until it broke into an open area, where the moon and stars coated the low scrub and grass brightly in silver. At first he didn't see them. He stared out toward the silhouette of a single gigantic tree that stood at the edge of the cliff. A small squirm of motion there caught his eye and then disappeared. He heard her voice carry across, muffled by the distance, and the soft sound of their joint laughter, and then he saw them, two tiny gray apparitions, just before they vanished under the tree's branches. He waited a moment and then walked, as carefully as he could, toward the tree. Each time he put a foot down, he did it slowly and deliberately, making sure there was nothing under it to crunch or crack. He knew if they stepped back out onto the trail now they would see him, and he started wondering what he'd do if that happened. He imagined himself falling to his knees and begging Rachel for forgiveness. He also imagined attacking her boyfriend, beating the piss out of him. These visions came and went in the rear theaters of his mind, like TVs running in empty bedrooms, but the front, where one foot got laid meticulously in front of the other, and where at a certain point he could hear their conversation and begin to make out the words, was a field of immaculate action, untainted by intent. He found a place in the shadow of a long extended branch, still outside the tree's spacious inner teepee, and listened. Their conversation meandered, as they discussed the experience they'd shared on acid that night. They had both been granted a sense of increase and infinity by the drug, and they wondered if it was genuine.

Some minutes later she told him she wanted to take a walk by herself. By this time Jack had stared so long into the darkness under the veil of branches that he'd found where they were, near the trunk on the far side, and could occasionally make out a flit of movement where a head became visible in turning. He couldn't tell whether the head was the boy's or hers; it was just a shadow in motion. Through the dead still night air, Jack could hear every word they said over the distant waves, until Rachel whispered something to the boy. The whisper's soft frication carried, but its words were lost. In the small opening he saw her stand up (it was her head he'd been watching). "I shall return." She paused, then spoke louder, "*And realize once more my thousand dreams. Wait for me, Daniel. Right here.*" These words seemed a declaration as if for the benefit of the night at large, and they gouged at the scabs on Jack's heart, finding the softer flesh beneath. He lay down, prone in the scrub, hoping she wouldn't see him when she emerged onto the trail, which was only a few feet to his right. But after a minute he realized the sound of her steps was getting farther away. She had gone out the north side of the tree and was moving along the cliff, away from him.

He stood again and stepped back onto the trail. If he rushed to catch up to her, the boy would surely hear him. He had to move as slowly and carefully as before. As he skirted the tree, he saw that the trail turned and continued off to the north. There it was flatter and dustier, and he was able to move a little faster. He didn't see Rachel ahead of him. The trail bent west and ran uphill onto a rocky bluff. Jack lifted his legs carefully as he climbed, the trail now dimmer in shadow since the low moon was on the far side of the bluff. His boots were good for traction on the rocks, and he enjoyed the ease and silence of his own movements. At the top there was a large boulder, and when he rounded it she was immediately in front of him. Five feet away. Jack froze. The sound of the waves was much louder here, since they were hanging out over the beach with cliffs falling away on three sides. She faced the ocean, her back to him and her hair moving gently, and after a moment he concluded that she hadn't heard him. He looked past her at what she was seeing: the vast blaze of stars around the lowering moon, the sea webbed and striped with light, the threshold of the continent stretching away north and south.

He prepared himself to drop to his knees when she turned, to show her the depth of his remorse, and the image of himself kneeling suddenly rankled him. What would it accomplish, really? He would feel no different unless by some outlandish miracle she took him back. But he had to do something, didn't he? He moved one foot forward in preparation to bend his knee, and it crunched on a small rock. The sound cracked in his ears.

"I hope you didn't follow me because you didn't trust me to come back," she said, not turning. "I hope it was out of love and not fear."

She stayed absolutely still, and so did he. She stared out to sea. She thought he was the boy, Daniel, of course. He noticed then a delicate inclining of her head toward her left shoulder, opening up the right side of her neck. An enticement. Jack knew it, and the boy would have known it too: her subtle way of inviting touch. A small step forward was all. He laid his hand softly across her nape, felt the curve of muscle there. She took one breath, a beautiful easy sigh, and then against his palm he felt the imminence of her turning. He imagined the ghastly moment when she would discover him there and not the boy, and became instantaneously unwilling to suffer that moment. He simply extended his arm roughly forward, pitching her over the edge. She fell in terrible silence, and whatever sound she made landing was erased by the rising rush of a wave, which receded slowly into near stillness, and then was followed by another.

When Jack arrived back at the ranch the sky was lightening. He shut off the engine as he piloted the old pickup down the dirt drive, letting gravity pull him close to the house and stopping off to the side. There were still people awake over by the dying bonfire, so when he got out he skirted the far side of the house to avoid being seen. He walked around and stopped behind the house, facing down the long grassy hill that flattened into thick forest at the bottom. He sat down against a wooden latticework that cordoned off a dirt-floored storage area under the back of the house. The sun's meniscus was cresting the eastern horizon. Everything was happening on its own, even things he was doing. He had put himself into a trance of necessity—survival mode—which gave him the benefit of a blinkered perspective, seeing only one essential action at a time, but he knew it wouldn't last, he could feel it eroding.

Along the edge of the woods at the bottom of the hill was a group of five tents, two of them flat walled and large enough to stand in, and three small pup tents. No one was outside the tents, no people at all in sight from where he sat. As the sun obtruded into the sky, its cruel light swelled but stubbornly refused to incinerate him. Jack wondered whether there might be a firearm somewhere at this ranch, and thought of his father. He understood a little better. Maybe if he could get himself a few hours of sleep he could put himself back together, then climb into a bottle for a while and wait it out. A wave of euphoric satisfaction swept through him, which had been happening intermittently, and he tried to find purchase in it, to stay with it somehow: He had merely done what men had been doing since the primeval birth of jealousy. *Just a spoon of love from my forty-five, save you from another man.* Howlin' Wolf was just singing about what thousands had wished they could do, and probably *had* done, before there were cops and laws and all the rest of the arbitrary bullshit. And it had felt good, hadn't it? That electric moment had been like no other in his life. How little it had taken! Just a small movement of one arm. Thinking about it he could bring back that exhilaration—but it faded a little every time. It would eventually fade away altogether, he knew. And what would be left?

The grass between his legs was matted and dry, and he ripped up tufts of it and sprinkled them thoughtfully into a small pile, his head hanging low and his purview contained within the canyon of his knees. He stripped a small twig of its bark and chewed on its tip. When he raised his head again to mark the progress of the sun, he saw a man standing outside one of the small tents. He was dressed in a thick white shirt and loose white pants, and he was staring directly at Jack. Jack found his own gaze trapped for a moment by this bearded specter. The man raised a hand in greeting and smiled. Jack gave him a small two-fingered gesture and tried to look away, but still somehow couldn't. The man beckoned him with a wave. Jack shook his head and began to stand, intending to go back around the house and out of view, but once he was on his feet he walked downhill, and the helping hand of gravity felt soothing.

"Good morning, friend," the man said when Jack stood before him.

"Hey," said Jack.

"Everything okay with you?"

"Yeah, I just been up all night."

"You have some trouble in you. It's good you're here."

Jack shook his head as if to clear away fog. "I'm coming off a bad trip kind of thing, you know. That's what it is. Any chance I could grab some shut-eye in your tent? Just a few hours and I'll be right."

"Yes, you can sleep in my tent. I'll help you." His face, behind the thick brown beard, was unlined, but he was at least forty. His bright blue eyes floated, cold and burning, under a receding hairline that had left the front half of his cranium egg-smooth. The back half sprouted a chaos of wiry brown tendrils still splayed from sleep.

He led Jack over to the small green tent and held the flap open. Jack was relieved to see there was no one else in it. A stack of blankets lay rumpled, and there was a pillow at the far end with a row of books near it. Jack crawled in.

"Mind taking off your boots?"

"Yeah, sorry," Jack said. He sat up, unlaced his boots, and kicked them off into the grass. He pushed himself back, reclining on the bedroll, and was surprised when the man entered the tiny tent and sat beside him.

"Don't be alarmed," the man said.

"I ain't alarmed. Just looking to sleep."

"You're not going to be able to sleep, not with your head the way it is right now."

Jack stared at him.

"I'm not making a pass at you," the man said, reaching out his hand and sliding it under the back of Jack's head.

"Glad to hear it."

"What's your name?"

"Jack."

"Jack, my name is Hugo. Close your eyes."

The red-black cavern of his own eyelids surrounded him, and Jack felt the truth of what Hugo had said. Sleep was a possibility as remote in that moment as levitation. He couldn't even keep his eyes closed for more than a second against the swelling dread in his chest. Hugo's face flicked back into view, hovering over him. Jack felt another hand now, on his chest. At some distance in his mind he experienced an instinct to lash out physically against this intimacy, but it drifted away.

"It's okay, close your eyes, feel my hands."

Jack closed his eyes, and the slurry of terror rose again, but he observed it from afar this time. "You're very tired," he heard Hugo say. "You need this."

It was hot when he woke, the bright green air in the little tent soggy and close. Jack was sweating, but his sleep had been deep and fully unmoored from the earth. He breathed a great sigh, feeling the revitalization that comes only rarely, from the best sleep. Only after a minute—as his mind retraced unhurriedly the steps that had preceded him waking in an unfamiliar tent in the middle of a June afternoon, skipping around from the show to the bonfire, Jules, the acid—did he remember. It was as if the trip south and the scene on that rocky bluff were a dream he'd had, early in his sleep maybe, buried way back behind a galaxy of forgotten subsequent dreams, and had returned to his memory only by chance. He'd been about to push aside the flap and crawl out to get some fresh air, but when he thought of Rachel he whirlpooled back into himself and lay still. After a few more minutes, it was the thought of alcohol that got him moving. He dragged his cumbersome skull toward the front of the tent and crawled out into the matted grass as if falling from a birth canal. His boots had been placed neatly by the corner of the tent, and Jack lay in the grass with his face near them, gasping at the cooler drier air.

"Welcome back, brother," a voice said. Jack looked up at a young man whose ugly, clean-shaven face was pitted and uniformly pink, as if it had been crafted from used bubble gum by an untrained sculptor. He was wearing a white shirt and white drawstring pants, as Hugo had been. "You want some water?"

"Got any whiskey?"

"No, man. We got nothing like that. That stuff will just mire you in ignorance."

"I'm countin' on it," Jack said. The kid walked away.

Jack was glad to be left alone, and he dropped his head back into the grass. He was preparing for the task of putting on his boots when the kid came back with a plastic jug and a white bowl with a spoon.

"Here you go, this is what you need."

Jack sat up and took the jug. He drank all the water in it, and the kid took it back and handed him the bowl and spoon. The bowl was filled with white mush. "What's this?" Jack asked, readying the spoon.

"Just Cream of Wheat. It's all we have right now. Hugo's gone with the others to get more supplies."

Jack ate it quickly. It was almost flavorless but he felt his body requiring it, sponging it up. He scraped the last of it and put the bowl beside him. He started putting on his boots.

"Thanks, son," he said. "Tell your friend I appreciate the use of his tent."

"Hugo said to ask you to stay."

"Can't. Got to go." He finished tying his laces and stood. "I got a job to get back to."

"A job so great you have to drink whiskey soon as you wake up?"

Jack looked at the guy. He had one of those faces you couldn't truly hate; it was too pitiful. Still. "Listen." He stepped closer to the younger man. "Don't think you know my business, motherfucker. I ain't in a mood. You get me?"

"Yeah, brother, I do." His eyes did not harden at Jack's challenge, but he also didn't look scared.

"Good. Whatever crazy shit you guys got going here, I ain't part of it. I got a world of trouble all my own."

The kid smiled. "We're all part of the same crazy shit, the same world of trouble. No way around that."

Jack was unexpectedly consoled by these words, and by the self-effacement in the kid's smile. He laughed as he walked away. "You got yourself a point there, I guess. I'll catch you on the flip side."

Climbing the grassy hill was a chore, and he took it slowly. He still wasn't sure whether anyone knew he'd borrowed the truck the night before. He had considered ditching it, but returning it seemed the best way to avoid detection or suspicion. If they knew he'd borrowed it, he had a story ready about needing to see his wife and stepdaughter in the city. He went around the house on the far side again, away from the site of the bonfire and the main community of tents and lean-tos. There were two old cars in front of the house, a Chevy and a Beetle, but the green truck was not there. A guy with very long hair was sitting on the wooden bench by the front door, smoking a cigarette.

"Oh, brother," Jack said, approaching him, "I could really use a smoke if you got one."

The guy dug in his pocket and pulled out a pouch of loose tobacco, holding it out to Jack. "There's papers in there."

Jack rolled a smoke slowly and silently, relishing the small task, and gave the pouch back. "Anyone heading into the city soon?" He lit the cigarette with his lighter.

The guy shrugged.

"I guess Cam's not around," Jack said.

"Cam's here. He's inside. I think so anyway."

"Oh. His truck's gone."

The guy shrugged again. "Someone else must be using it."

Jack sat on the end of the bench and settled into smoking. The day was warm and bright, cloudless, and the small shaded porch had attracted crickets that leapt back and forth from sun to shade. The hippie finished his cigarette and said, "Peace," before heading into the house. Jack didn't want to see Cam, so he stayed outside. He realized he also didn't want to see Jules, who might or might not still be around, over by the big tree. Jack sat still, trying to imagine himself a tiny cricket, chirping in the shade of an endless summer. After a while the green pickup topped the rise in the driveway and rolled down the hill. As it neared, Jack could see it was Hugo behind the wheel. There was a woman in the passenger seat, and two other white-clad men in the bed behind. They bounced up to the house and shut off the engine. The two men each unloaded a crate of food from the back. Hugo got out and walked over to the porch.

"Hello, Jack," he said. "Sleep well?"

"Yeah," Jack said. "Like someone knocked me out with a tire iron."

"That's good, I hope." Hugo smiled. "Will you come down and have lunch with us?"

"Thanks, but I have to get back in town. I have work."

"Surely you can miss one day. It's already half over."

"It's a night gig. And I already missed yesterday."

"You have a ride?"

"Not yet."

Hugo jerked his head back toward the truck. "I'll drive you."

"I'm sure someone will be going in soon enough," Jack said.

"Come on, I don't mind." He walked over and opened the driver's door. "I'll be back," he said to the woman, who merely nodded. The two men had already carried the crates of food around the side of the house.

Jack followed him and climbed into the passenger seat. They drove in silence back up the driveway and out onto the main road southbound.

"So, what's your deal?" Jack asked.

"My deal?"

"The bunch of you. All dressed in white and talking weird, living separate. What's your thing?"

"We don't have a thing; we just live according to the truth we've found."

"Which is what?"

"Nothing special." He turned his head and gave Jack a smile, and even with his half-bald head he looked like a child harboring a happy secret. "Just that life is unreal. It's nothing new, really. You know the song, merrily, merrily, merrily, merrily."

"That's it? Life's a dream?"

"Well, that's not *it*. We've gotten glimpses of what's beyond it, too. Where we could be headed if we play our cards right."

Jack snorted. "Yeah, I get it. Of course. Do right and you'll get to heaven. Do wrong and you'll end up in someone's version of hell. It's all the same shit in the end."

"No! It's not like that at all. There is no right, not really. There is no wrong, either. How can there be if none of this is real? Getting where you want to go when you leave this world isn't a reward, it's a science."

"So, like, what? There's no God? Just science?"

"You're not asking the right questions. But I'll answer. There probably is a God, or some creative entity, it just stands to reason, but whoever he she or it is, they don't care much what we do and what happens to us. We've been thrown into this quicksand illusion, and given precious little in the way of clues. So, ultimately, the place we want to end up is somewhere we can have more control, more knowledge, more happiness—not necessarily to hang out with God, or whoever. God's not interested in us anyway, God's too big to pay attention to us, I think."

Jack nodded. "Well, I ain't all that interested either."

"Fair enough."

They drove a while longer in silence. They entered the highway, and eventually the Golden Gate rose up in front of them.

"You did something to me, though," Jack said. "Before I slept. What did you do?"

"I just communicated with your original self. I let you know that whatever was troubling you is a figment of a dream, and you could relax and let your body recharge."

"A figment of a dream? You got no idea, son. This ain't no little breakup or legal hassle." Jack clamped his mouth shut.

"You're right, I have no idea, but that doesn't make me wrong. I mean it. Whatever it is, it's part of an illusion. Maybe your house burned down. Maybe your wife died. Whatever it is—and I don't mean any disrespect—but it doesn't *actually* matter. That can be the hardest thing of all to accept, but it's absolutely liberating, I promise."

"My *wife* died? The fuck are you talking about?"

"I'm just talking. Just giving examples."

"Well keep that shit to yourself. You can drop me off on Oak, by the end of the panhandle."

"Sure thing, Jack."

They went the rest of the drive without talking. By the time Jack was getting out he had calmed down a little. He reached across the seat to shake Hugo's hand. "Thanks for the ride, and the tent. Sorry for getting bent out of shape, I'm still loopy from last night."

Hugo shook his hand and made eye contact. "I know," he said. "Friend, you're welcome to come visit us anytime. Forgive me, but you're ready, I can see it. And whatever you have going on, whatever your trouble is, it'll evaporate in the light of the truth. It might seem big, but it can't be big if it isn't real." He regarded Jack with the elemental peace of a desert night sky, the sky of Jack's boyhood.

Jack said, "All right. Catch you on the flip side," and turned and strode off.

HE WENT STRAIGHT to work that afternoon without going home to change. The thought of seeing Gretchen and Miranda was insupportable. He took a shower at the stash house and borrowed a T-shirt from Percy. He threw himself into the job and worked all night, volunteering to be the last one sent home. He paced himself over the course of the night, tempering booze with speed, but he was properly drunk by sunrise. When he did get home, it was seven o'clock, and Gretchen was awake. She was at the kitchen table having her morning cigarette.

"Hey baby," she said. "Want me to make some eggs for you?"

"No. I ate," he said. "Kid still asleep?"

"Yeah."

"Don't she have school or anything?"

"She's not even in kindergarten till the fall. It's summer now anyway, no school."

Jack sat down and pulled a small handful of reds from his jacket pocket, letting them clatter onto the blue speckled tabletop. Next to them he placed an almost-empty pint bottle. He took two and swallowed them with the last of the whiskey. "The rest are for you," he said.

"Thanks, daddy, I'll save them."

"You ain't had none since I left two days ago."

"I know, but she'll be up soon, and I don't want to be out of it."

"You know," Jack said, "you ain't much fun since your kid's been here."

"Just because I don't want downs?"

"No, because you ain't fun. You used to be a funny gal. We used to laugh when I got home. We used to ball whenever we wanted. Now there ain't no laughing. And with her around we can't hardly ever ball because I'm gone while she's asleep."

"Jack, we can figure that out. We'll do it more, I promise. She loves you, you know."

Gretchen usually didn't use his name, he realized. She called him *baby* or *daddy,* and hearing his name from her irritated him.

"Well, I didn't ask for that. I didn't sign up to be a goddamn father."

She was silent, and he wished she'd say something to stop him from going on, but she didn't.

"How long you think she'll be with us?"

Gretchen hung her head. She spoke as if trying to remain silent even while speaking. "I don't know, baby. She's my daughter."

"I don't know either. I think it might be time for her to move back in with her papa."

She looked up at him with frightened eyes. "Jack, please. I can't do that. I can't."

He nodded and lit a cigarette, realizing that this was the answer he'd been hoping for. It calmed him. "I get it," he said. "I respect that. I guess maybe it's time for us to split up then, 'cause I ain't no family man." Jack looked at her and felt his heart shrivel. "I'll give you enough to get you set up somewhere, don't worry. I ain't going to put you in the street."

Three days later they were gone. She didn't fight him or beg, which angered him even though he wouldn't have changed his mind. He gave her a pretty nice chunk of change, more than most would have felt obliged to after eight months together, and this helped him feel a little less terrible. But being alone was almost as bad as being with people, and Jack made himself sick swinging between speed and reds, coke and 'ludes, washing everything down with a constant river of whiskey. Rachel's death was in the paper. They had arrested the boyfriend with a trunkful of liquid acid, and the stories implied he was suspected of killing her, or at least causing her death by filling her with drugs. Nothing about a third person at the scene, nothing about a green pickup truck. Being in the clear weighed on him as heavily as being implicated might have, though differently. He told himself he'd get past it the same way he had after what he'd done the first time. It would recede and he'd move on. He told this to himself every morning when he exhumed himself from unconsciousness, but every day it was necessary once again to hammer his brain into oblivion and stay in motion while doing it, like an inebriated shark. His father intruded more and more frequently into his thoughts, and so did Hugo, with his offer of transfiguration. After a month, it began to seem as if he must join one or the other of these figures, as if he was left with only those two possible alternatives to a miserable alcoholic death. He reasoned that he could always follow his father if all else failed, so it made sense to start with Hugo. On a clear July night much like the night of the Dead show, Jack took off from work and had an acquaintance drop him at the head of the ranch's driveway in exchange for half a lid of good weed.

As he walked down the driveway, the place seemed very quiet. There were some people sitting in the grass around a lantern over by the big leaning tree, and two silhouettes on the bench outside the front door of the house. The sun had been down for an hour, and Jack couldn't tell if he'd been noticed as he came down the hill. He veered off the driveway to skirt the house, watching the ember of a joint hover and flare between the silhouetted figures on the porch.

When he'd rounded the house, Jack could see a fire near the tents at the bottom, its light making the leaves of the forest wall slide and bob. The hill steepened in the middle and the ground was just blackness. He stumbled twice on the uneven footing, but didn't fall. In fact he felt very sturdy, moving toward the light. When the slope began to level off he slowed his pace. Seven people were sitting around the fire, all of them dressed in white, and they hadn't seen him yet. He decided to watch them for a moment, to try and suss out the scene a little. He stood still. The woman who had been in the truck with Hugo that other morning was sitting with her arm around a skinny little boy of five or six. She looked lovely in her young maternal radiance, her blond hair throwing off the firelight. She and the boy were on a large sawed-off section of tree trunk, and the rest were sitting on the ground. There was a larger, older woman facing toward Jack, and a couple of younger ones with their backs to him, and two young men. Jack recognized the pink-faced guy who had given him Cream of Wheat, but he didn't see Hugo among them. There did not seem to be any conversation going on. They were all just staring at the fire dreamily, and then with no precursor the older woman began to sing. Her voice was high and very beautiful, and the song was a strange, foreign-sounding melody whose words Jack couldn't make out because she was stretching them to such great lengths. Some of the notes seemed to fall in between the ones Jack was used to, which made him uneasy but also made the familiar notes heartbreakingly beautiful when they arrived. He would wait until she'd finished, he decided, and then approach the fire.

"Pretty, isn't it?"

Jack was so violently startled that he almost fell over. He wheeled left, his fists raised.

"Sorry." There was a chuckle. "I can't help myself sometimes." It was Hugo, standing six feet from him in the darkness. He was actually quite visible in his white clothing, and Jack couldn't figure how he'd missed seeing him.

"Holy fuck," Jack said. "You been watching me this whole time?"

"Yes. I saw you coming down the hill, and I walked out to meet you."

"Good way to get clipped, sneaking up on a guy in the dark."

"Come on. You wouldn't clip me, Jack. Would you?"

"I guess that depends."

"Well," Hugo said, walking over and placing a hand on Jack's shoulder. "I'm glad you came back. I had a feeling you would."

"Yeah," Jack said, unsure of how to proceed.

"You're still in a lot of pain, aren't you?"

Jack took a step back, relieving himself of Hugo's touch. "You know something about it?"

"I know you wouldn't be here if you weren't."

Jack found his speech center suddenly and completely vacant, so he just stood there. If he could have thought of anything back up the hill behind him that he wanted, besides another drink, he would have turned and walked away.

"It's not necessary for you to tell me about your trouble, but it might be a good place to start," Hugo said.

"I don't think I can do that."

"Let's go sit. We'll talk. Tell me what you want to, and not what you don't. It's not about what you tell me anyway. It's just creating a context for truth. We're conditioned here to need contexts." When Jack didn't respond, Hugo turned and walked toward the far side of the tents, away from the fire. Jack followed.

2017

Celia rode the wave of the work toward the promise of happiness. Maybe, she thought, the closest thing to real happiness is the promise of happiness. If happiness is positioned in the future, it can't be proven lacking, so why not feel good heading toward it? Plus, the work itself felt great. It wasn't happiness, quite, but exhilaration anyway. She'd tasted tiny morsels of this feeling when she was younger, doing *Grandview High,* when she knew she'd gotten a tough scene right. She remembered the famous earthquake episode, her character almost dying, finding out her friend had been killed. She'd felt so good after that, a little hint of this current feeling, though everything back then had happened behind a dark-tinted filter, clouded by her mother's death and by her secret relationship with Richard Slayton, her manager. She had moved into his apartment in the immediate wake of her mother's accident, and on her second night there he'd brought her into his bed. To the world, he was her proxy guardian, but behind closed doors they lived as a couple for years. The strangeness of it was less obvious to her then, though she understood it needed to be kept secret. She also kept her cavernous shame over it secret. Her aunt in Phoenix, who was ostensibly her primary guardian, mostly ignored her when Celia visited on breaks from shooting. After a year she stopped visiting, and no one cared.

But now. This was the thing itself, real artistic exhilaration, and to share it with a troupe as they worked together was even better. They had direction now, with the end in sight, and they had a shared faith in the destination, which made the final two weeks of shooting a blissful, exciting time, a time during which it seemed only natural that she should start sleeping with Darren again.

He visited her bungalow the first night and talked so lovingly about his wife, Georgia, and their newborn daughter that Celia could not see the harm in a little fling. He was tied up with his other life, deprived of sex by a nursing wife, and would never again be available to her. Whatever they did could not possibly have legs. She had Leo (if she really did) and he had Georgia, and they were just doing a little nostalgic thing. And, if she was honest, it felt good to get a taste of revenge, to do to Georgia a small fraction of what Georgia had done to her.

"Someone told me you had a thing going with your driver for a while," Darren said after the first time. "True or false?"

"True. And he's not just a driver, he's a musician. You should hear his stuff, it's amazing. And by the way it might still be going between me and him, so don't you breathe a goddamn word to anyone. I don't want him finding out about this."

"You think I do? I'm the one who really needs secrecy. I'm the married one. Imagine the shitstorm."

"You? You're the outlaw golden boy. The people want you—*need* you—out there making your own rules. Nobody will ever hold anything against you, baby, not for long."

"Georgia will, that's who."

"Well, she shouldn't be too surprised, should she?"

"No"—he eyed her to show he'd gotten her meaning—"because she will never find out, so there'll never be anything for her to be surprised about."

The freedom that came from knowing they could never be together created a magnificent bubble around their fucking, unleashing a kind of madness, an unruly abandon that drove them to unforeseen heights and uninvited depths. She told Leo she needed solitude at night to stay prepared for the work she was doing, and spent every night with Darren. On their drives to set in the mornings, and the returns in the evenings, she and Leo went back to a friendlier version of their old professional relationship. Celia hated it, but didn't give herself time to dwell on it. She sensed that Leo was half-relieved by her distancing herself from him, and she would have been more hurt by this if she hadn't been so busy. During the day she was immersed in the exhilaration of the work—feeling truly confident in her own abilities and part of a tribe of equals—and then at night consumed by the profligacy of forbidden sex with the man who had been her first love.

Even her morning fear was squeezed into a narrow sliver, easily ignored. It wasn't the dissipation she'd felt waking with Leo, but a suspension, a foregrounding of so much else that the fear had to wait its turn. It was patient, she knew. It would hold its place at her core.

The last morning at the spa, Celia woke with a start, sure there had been some movement, and a sound, by her bed. In the dim coppery glow, she stared hard at the space by the desk where the sound had seemed to originate. Finding nothing, she was skewered from brainstem to loins by a blade of animal panic: the unseen enemy. She rolled and looked instinctively to the other side of the bed, but knew she was alone. Darren had left the previous night for a commitment in New York. She dragged her viscid thoughts into fuller awareness, sat up, and put her feet on the floor.

The revelry at the spa the night before, following their last long day of shooting, had amounted to a wrap party, but Celia had retreated from it after socializing briefly. The bulk of the party had been up the hill in the courtyard of the main building, so the noise hadn't kept her awake, though she'd woken once in the night to voices and laughter by the bungalow pool outside her sitting area.

She drank the glass of water by her bed, used the bathroom, and then sent Leo a text. His reply followed almost immediately: he was on his way up from Bisbee. He would arrive earlier than necessary for the drive to the airport. She asked him to come straight to the room, and ordered breakfast for two.

While she waited, she thought about how she'd left things with Darren the day before. They had hit all the right notes of a happy, unattached goodbye. He was glad, he said, that they'd had this time to close out their relationship in a more positive way. She was glad, too, she said, that they could both live easier having placed the other in a loving context now, instead of surrounded by tumultuous memories. It was a good thing they'd done here, they said, something necessary for both of them, and now they could move on as friends. Or be friendly, anyway, from the distance of their separate lives. But lying underneath all that was the knowledge that they would be working together again. There would be two more films to make, and neither of them spoke about what might or might not happen in the future.

Leo arrived a few minutes after the breakfast, and he sat down to eat in the chair she'd pulled up for him.

"How does it feel?" he asked.

"What?"

"Being done. Did the ending go well?"

"It did. It feels great, actually. I think we made something really good, though you never can tell at this stage."

"That's got to be a good feeling. I'm sure the film is great."

"I do think so."

"Darren left?"

"Yeah. Yesterday."

He nodded, shoveling in a forkful of eggs. "Mmm-hmm." He swallowed. "How did it go, working with him? Seemed like things were good between you."

"Yes, things were good. We worked well, and it was good to see him. Enough time has passed now."

Leo smiled at her. It was an undefended smile. He was not hiding the fact that he had an idea what she and Darren had been doing, but neither was he trying to confront her and wield his injury against her. He was making an attempt at equanimity and acceptance. She saw the attempt, but she also saw jealousy marbling through it. Something shifted for Celia in that moment, like a slide changing in a projector, and she perceived Leo again, as before: a man who had really shared himself with her.

"I'm awful," she said. "Leo, I'm sorry."

"Don't be. I had a great time. I had no illusions." His words came out as if forced through too small an opening. He looked down and took another bite, closing the subject. The affair with Darren began suddenly to blanch in her mind, becoming grainy, and Celia felt a charged regret massing. Was this the source of the panic she'd woken to? Reluctantly she went back to eating.

Once they were on the highway, Celia asked if she could hear more of his music. She had still only heard the one song. He seemed to consider this at some length, watching the road, and then said, "Sure. I've got a couple of brand-new ones I recorded in my hotel last week." He cued them up on his phone as he drove. "You're the first person to hear these. They're definitely not finished yet." Celia nodded and stared ahead, the glaring desert sifting through her along with the music. She heard, in these raw song-nuggets, Leo's hidden heart. The first was remorsefully sweet, the second bitterly sad. When they were over, she knew not to offer an opinion, and he switched back to his old iPod. They didn't speak until they were approaching the outskirts of Phoenix.

She looked at him as he drove. "Let's find a place to stop and talk."

She wasn't sure he'd heard until a few minutes later when he pulled off the highway into a giant box-store parking lot and stopped at its barren outskirts. He shut off the engine and looked at Celia.

"I don't actually know what I want to say," she said.

"Me either."

"I'm an idiot. And an asshole."

"So am I. What does it matter?"

"It matters because I wish I wasn't. I wish I'd done differently."

"I know. But in the end . . ."

"In the end what?"

"There wasn't really another outcome, was there? If there's no future, then we were just digging a hole, and one of us needed to quit digging and jump out of it."

"There are better ways to stop digging," she said.

"I guess."

A small bird skimmed past the window behind Leo, and Celia followed it. She watched it land by some fast-food boxes discarded on the pavement and start pecking at crumbs. It was joined by two more. The three birds hopped, businesslike, around the white boxes, eating as if unaware of each other. She turned back and Leo's eyes had drifted away. He was looking glumly and distantly through the windshield.

"I really am sorry," she said.

He nodded slowly, but then a change entered his face, his mouth hardening. "Fuck that," he said. "If what happened was real, then don't be sorry." He looked at her, his eyes suddenly sharp. "Okay? I don't want you to feel sorry, and I won't, either. I'll feel ashamed for being un-faithful, I can't help that, but not sorry for what we did, because it was something real. I mean, wasn't it?"

"Yes. It wasn't supposed to be, but it turned out to be. It had a mind of its own." Without the air-conditioning the inside of the car was getting hot. Celia stared at her own damp palms in her lap and became aware, again, of the monolithic fear located behind her sternum. "I guess I got scared of it."

Leo nodded. A hermetic moment passed during which she was afraid he would speak, but he didn't. When the moment was gone and the traffic sounds from the avenue behind them filtered back in, he looked at his watch and said, "You're liable to miss your flight." He started the engine and pulled toward the exit, but stopped the car again before reaching it. He slid the transmission into park, and Celia was reminded of the way he'd slid it into reverse that first night they'd spent together, when she had asked him to take her to Los Angeles.

"There might be an issue with your tenses," he said.

"What?"

"You said *had*."

"I did?"

"*Had* a mind of its own."

An odd ecstasy burrowed up from her stomach. Her breath was charged and shallow. She hardly dared move, but she knew she couldn't leave the responsibility on him. She reached with her right hand, fac-ing him now, and turned the ignition key. The disappearance of the engine's idling left the space between them raw. He dropped his hands from the steering wheel. She let herself wait another moment before touching him.

ONCE SHE'D MISSED her flight she decided to drive back with Leo. She texted her father to let him know she'd be later, and he wrote back say-ing simply, No worries, all fine here. They made good time, and were approaching Palm Springs at sunset. The mountains behind the town reared up like a dark wave toward the orange sun.

She thought of Dean, and realized that he would be asleep by the time they arrived in LA. She said, "I know a nice little hotel in Palm Springs. We could stay the night and get back tomorrow."

Leo looked at her and nodded, crimping his mouth inscrutably. "Okay."

It was offseason and over a hundred degrees, and they seemed to be the only guests.

When they were in their room, Celia called her father's phone and had him put Dean on. Just hearing him say "Mommy" over the line, his voice bounced to her from space but still somehow bearing his essence, blew a cloud of warmth into her chest, making her at once happy and guilty. She was supposed to have been home already, tucking him in. She wished him sweet dreams, and in the end happiness won out over guilt because she could hear that Dean wasn't sad once they'd talked.

She sat next to Leo on the bed and began unbuttoning his shirt. Her phone buzzed on the nightstand and she leaned to glance at the screen. It was a text from Miles: Got a second to talk?

She stood, waving her phone. "It's the boss. He wants to talk to me."

Leo nodded and pulled out his own phone as she touched the call icon next to Miles's name. He picked up right away with a simple "Yes."

"Got your text," she said.

"Right, I wanted to give you a heads-up. I had a conversation today with Bucky Tripp, and your name came up. He's casting something, and I told him he'd be wise to get you involved. I sent him a few of your scenes, the bedroom scene with George, the death of Varek, and the throne room scene at the end. He's going to watch them, and if he's sold he might reach out to you. I gave him your number. Hope that's okay. I didn't want you to be blindsided by it."

Celia felt panic invade her, disarranging the exultant thoughts the name of the iconic director generated. Nothing could be bigger than getting a call from Sterling Tripp (Bucky to his friends), who famously didn't hold auditions for primary roles, but simply decided who he wanted and then told them where and when to show up. Agents were afterthoughts. At seventy-five, he still made fierce, hip films that took the award ceremonies by storm. She sat down in a chair by the window.

"Oh . . ." she said, "wow. I don't know what to say. Thank you, Miles."

"Don't thank me, it's my pleasure. Everything that's coming your way now, you deserve. But get ready, 'cause it's coming. Even if he doesn't call you for this, things are going to change for you. Keep your eye on the ball and swing for the fences, baby."

Celia said, "I will," but the rushing sound in her ears was making it hard to hear.

"I'll be in touch. We're jumping into editing this week."

"Okay."

Miles hung up and she sat holding her phone. Leo was still engrossed in his texting. Celia tried to feel the bright future Miles was talking about, but was instead flooded with radioactive dread, as her core fear liquefied and started to seep through its barrier walls. This was exactly what Miles's film was supposed to do for her, but she'd somehow never imagined it would actually happen.

Leo looked up at her. "Everything okay?"

"Yes, fine." She dropped her eyes to the black screen of her phone as if confirming something there, taking a second to gather herself. "Nothing important. What should we do for dinner?"

"Whatever you want."

"We could go out, or order room service. The food here is good."

"Let's stay in," Leo said, flopping heavily back on the bed, spreading his arms wide as he bounced. "I'm wiped."

Celia picked up the leather hotel binder from the desk and focused on paging deliberately through it looking for the menu. Her heart was a grenade with no pin, and she gripped it very tightly.

Jack descended the driveway in the BMW his daughter had bought him. On his way past the former guesthouse, he saw Daniel by his car unloading groceries. Daniel looked over his shoulder and Jack waved but kept going. He hadn't had a plan of any kind when he'd talked Celia into buying this house. He'd just been following an impulse to journey back in time, toward the source material of his life.

Daniel had been easy to find online, though his exact location had required a PI. And then the house being for sale had seemed like a meaningful coincidence. The house, incredibly, had been owned by Cam Cooper, who Jack remembered from his time at the ranch in Marin, back when he'd first come to know Hugo. Celia had been talking about moving anyway, since her former house was a rental and she wanted to own. She'd been fresh off her relapse, and it hadn't been hard to get her to put him in charge of the search, and then to convince her of the soundness of the investment due to a recent drop in the asking price. The place was bigger than she wanted, but it had a lot of charm, and once she'd seen it she gave in.

He wondered now what he'd been thinking, moving in here and trying to befriend Daniel—who would, if he found out the whole truth, probably want to kill him. Jack's feelings toward Daniel had evolved now from vestigial animosity into something almost fraternal. Daniel's life, like Jack's, had been irrevocably altered by his association with Rachel, and Jack couldn't help but feel a kinship over that, though he knew it could never be reciprocated.

Thinking of Rachel, he entered a familiar spiral. Was there no fucking end to it? He raged sometimes at the thought of how long her shadow over him had persisted. It made him hate her. There had been a chunk of time in the middle of his life when Jack had felt more at ease with himself, free and functional, swaddled in the detachment of Hugo's philosophy. Much of that period had been spent incarcerated. Prison had been strangely easy for him, aside from feeling abandoned when he heard about the group's exodus. He remembered reading the news stories in his cell two years into his bid, the mixture of pride and envious rage he had felt. None of them had even come to visit him, to tell him they were leaving. Ten dead in one house, one survivor, a twelve-year-old boy. It made all the papers. The Moorpark Death Cult, they'd dubbed it. And they'd made Hugo out to be like Manson or something, fucking joke that was. Hugo was a conduit, that was all. During his years in the group, Jack had become Hugo's most trusted man. If the robbery hadn't gone south, he would have been there, would have gone out with them. In prison, a place bound by such strict parameters, he had been able to maintain the remote perspective of the Knowledge, but once he was out, removed from both the cohesion of the group and the circumscription of confinement, a corrosion had begun. It had taken a few years to run its course, and he couldn't pinpoint a specific moment, but at some point he realized his mind no longer aligned with most of it. This left him vulnerable, again, to toxic remorse.

The beauty of Hugo's philosophy—the Knowledge—was that it offered the freedom of nihilism without the nihilism: there *was* a bigger picture, but instead of placing greater responsibility on people, that bigger picture relieved everyone of virtually all responsibility. The absconded creator, the inertia of false morality, the absoluteness of freedom and self-sovereignty and action. Existence was not a set of rules and constructs to be adhered to, but a conundrum to be deciphered. In the years after his release, Jack had been robbed of all that. It hadn't, of course, been hard to continue believing that nothing mattered—in fact he understood that this was most likely the case—but true nihilism, that inert and universal absence of meaning, was no comfort at all; it was just depressing. And more importantly, it left him puzzlingly unprotected from his own remorse. Believing there *was* a god who simply didn't care, and that existence was nothing more than a series of dreams that didn't end with death, had been a gift, and he pined after it.

He remembered the time in between Rachel's death and his joining Hugo at the ranch—those terrible few weeks during which alcohol and pills had been his only refuge. He felt he was actually worse off in the years after prison, because that pre-Hugo version of himself had been a natural brute, unreflective, and chemical oblivion was achievable on that dull foundation. But Hugo had taught him to think actively, to practice introspection and parse the obscurities of the self so that when the time came one could transform into a self-guided missile and reach the Destination. That was an engine that couldn't just be switched off when faith evaporated. So while he could still drink himself into stupors, those stupors were not as watertight as the ones he remembered from before. He pined after those as well.

And don't get him started on the time before he'd met Rachel. Pining for that made him hate her worse than anything else. After all, if she hadn't shown up in his life, he never would have killed her. He never would have met Hugo and gravitated to his philosophy, never been talked into robbing a bank and then spent fifteen years in prison. Rachel was the fulcrum on which his life had shifted. Sometimes, especially when he was half drunk—fully conscious but not in full control—his rage overtook him and he found himself reveling helplessly in the memory of that night. The moment was crystalline in his mind, its serrations sharp as ever, and when he went there he could still feel the skin of her nape on his palm, the sudden electrifying shove, his arm straightening almost involuntarily, like the unleashed string of a crossbow. He would find himself staring at the muscles above his right elbow as if at a co-conspirator. At those times, he was so angry at her for being the source of his pain that he was glad he'd done it.

He took some consolation in Celia, and even more in Dean. They gave him respite from the lowest of his troughs. If he'd never been to prison, he would not have ended up in Phoenix after getting out, would not have met Diana Dressler in that bar, talked his way into her bed, and eventually impregnated her. Those six weeks living and drinking with Diana would have been a blip in his past by now if not for the chance conception of a child. Diana hadn't wanted him around for the birth or anything else, and he'd been grateful for that at the time. She had wanted him gone, so he'd obliged and gone down to Tucson—his original destination when he'd left California—and moved back into his mother's tiny house, which became his a year later when she *traveled on*, as Hugo would have put it. Almost a decade had gone by before he got an urge to try and know his daughter. When he'd contacted Diana, she tried to keep him away, and for the most part it worked. He'd managed to engineer some visits when Celia was nine and ten, a few weekends that were amalgams of awkwardness, sadness, guilt, and frustration, dissolved in the toxic broth of his discomfort at the lack of alcohol in his body, one of Diana's prerequisites for visitation. He retreated again from Diana and Celia after that.

As he stopped the car in the mouth of the driveway, he returned to wondering why the hell he'd sought out Daniel. All the suppressed trouble of his life, which in his gloomy way he'd come to coexist with, had been stirred up since they'd moved in here. And to what end? He and Daniel were like oil and water—more like oil and vinegar, he thought, since though they didn't mix they still complemented each other somehow. He had discovered in himself a perverse desire for Daniel to like him, though he knew that was possible only under false pretenses. And now, without even giving himself away, Jack had alienated Daniel. In a misguided impulse to seek out his past he had trapped himself, living pressed up against the worst thing he'd ever done, and it had begun taking a toll on him that he hadn't anticipated.

But at least it had prompted him to dig out his copy of Hugo's book and reread it, after all this time. He'd been shocked at the undiminished vitality of his connection with it, and its eerie power—somehow also undiminished—to purge his remorse. Thinking of it now gave him a shiver of boyish excitement. He touched the frayed spine of the little white paperback wedged between his seat and the console. The first page was inscribed in ink that had faded from black to brown: *For Jack, carry the flame into the future with open eyes . . . —Hugo.* He'd watched Hugo write the inscription in the living room of the house in Moorpark when the box of books had first arrived from the printers. That sharp, steeply leaning cursive, the capital H five times the size of the rest of the name, the pen wielded by a large, gentle thin-fingered hand now long decayed and gone. But the end of the hand couldn't have been the end of the man. Especially not *that* man, who wore his body as lightly as a paper kimono. Maybe the hiatus from Hugo had been simply a misstep, Jack thought. A twenty-five-year misstep. Wouldn't that be something?

He pulled from its mental compartment the memory of his *anam-nesis*, as Hugo called it, the night when he'd gone from forming ideas and images in his head based on what Hugo told him, to knowing. It had been so potent, in its moment, that he'd considered it permanently unassailable. The entire world, including his own physical and psychic being, had shuddered, rung like a great fearsome gong, and the truth of Hugo's Knowledge had struck him with the kind of voltage gener-ally reserved for immediate mortal danger. It wasn't discovery; it was remembrance.

The two of them had taken acid—two drops of clear liquid apiece—on a cool fall night at the Marin ranch, only a week before the group left there and started drifting south. Jack was the last one. Every member of the group had already gone through this process one at a time, most before he had joined. Jules, who'd come on board a few weeks after Jack, had done it the night before. Even little Brandon, who was only seven, had taken the journey. Hugo had given him a single tiny drop from the tip of a hairpin. At the time, Jack had been shocked. He'd done a lot of things he wasn't proud of, but who gave acid to a little kid? Eventually it all became clear. There was no indiscriminate tripping among them, in fact none of them ever took acid again after their own individual journey with Hugo.

Jack and Hugo took their two drops sitting by the fire with the whole group, and Jack could feel the fused collective attention on him, that ring of wavering golden wide-open faces, flame-shifting eyes yanking at him expectantly, but before the drug came on Hugo led him into the dark woods. Jack followed, almost blindly at first, crashing through underbrush and sometimes losing sight of Hugo's white clothing up ahead, but after a few minutes his eyes adjusted and he could see well enough in the tree-shaded starlight. When the acid came on, his vision improved even more, at least until the enhancements began. Hugo must have known where he was going because they ended up at a small clear-ing just as the moon became visible, and he dropped the thick blanket he was carrying onto the ground and spread it out.

"The first part is fun," Hugo said. "Just feel the doors opening and let it happen. Do whatever you feel like doing. We'll know when we need to get down to serious business, but we have some time yet."

"Okay," Jack said, and the sound of his own voice, after hearing only breath raking through him for what seemed so long, resonated in his skeleton with new clarity, like some beautiful alien horn sounding in him. He morphed unexpectedly with it because the voice emanated from an entity larger than he'd realized he was. It was on this night that Jack had told Hugo about Rachel. Every detail of what happened he'd ended up revealing that night in the throes of the trip.

Initially, as the drug surged inside him, he'd felt strangely fine, drawn up to his feet by it and closer to the beckoning dark trees. He'd climbed one of them, his body a perfect steady instrument, wholly confident, then sat on a high branch and gazed first down into Hugo's colossal blue smile, and then up through leaf silhouettes at the star-strewn sky. He felt only eagerness for more expansion, for Hugo to lay the big Truth, the Knowledge, on him. The moon rose resplendent, like a divinity. But at some point later a sliver of confusion entered the evening, and it was then that Hugo, sensing it, asked what was troubling him.

"Nothing," Jack said. "I just can't get my eyes to work right." They were sitting on the blanket then, and he lay back and looked straight up at the sky, thinking this might clear his vision of the knot of accusing faces billowing from the air, from nowhere. Just get a clear line of sight, he thought, a clear path of mind.

"When you came to us you had some deep trouble, and I see it still with you every second. Whatever it is, bring it into your mind right now. Focus on it."

Jack flinched. The directive brought him a sharp pain in his frontal lobe that shot out through his eyes. "Bad idea," he heard himself say.

"Do it." Hugo's voice was not severe, but it left no leeway.

Jack heard himself groan, then bark once to banish what had been asked of him. Then he dropped in, as if into a pit. The feel of her skin on his right hand, the feel of the wind off the ocean, the crash of waves, the shove, the silence. Someone was writhing on a blanket somewhere, screaming, someone weaker and more stricken, someone he hated.

"Tell me something," Hugo said. "Anything. It doesn't have to be everything. Just tell me one thing."

He reentered himself smoothly, understanding that Hugo had facilitated this, and opened his eyes. Or they were already open. He said, "I loved her." He was gasping. "I swear."

"I believe you," Hugo said.

Jack almost got up and walked away. The impulse and the wherewithal came to him arm in arm, but then washed out into the surrounding trees. "I did something. Something I can't ever take back or make up for."

"Okay, good. That's tough. But we are going to walk through it and we are going to come out the other side, and you are never going to be bothered by it again. This is why we are here. You will have nothing less than complete freedom. Do you believe me?"

"No."

"That's fine. You only have to be willing to take the journey. Faith is not necessary. Are you willing?"

"Yes."

"All right. When you've gathered yourself, you're going to go back to the very beginning of the story, where this story starts for you, and you're going to run through it in your mind detail by detail, without skipping anything. If it helps to do it out loud, you can tell it to me. If you want to tell me only some parts, that's okay. Or you can tell me nothing. But you need to go through all of it, all the way to the end, so you can hold it whole in your mind. And then we will place it in perspective and it will cease to hold power, that is my promise. And once we get there you'll see it's just the jumping-off point. There's so much more that comes after. So, start at the beginning, wherever that might be, take it slow. We have farther to go than you can imagine."

Jack was still on his back. Hugo's eyes directly above him looked very large, and his head, too, looked huge, blotting the sky and the moon, taking up most of the clearing, shiny on top and shaggy around the sides into his thick beard. Jack focused on the eyes, the twin backlit orbs unblinking above him, blue teeth flickering when he spoke. Then

Hugo's head withdrew, ending the lunar eclipse, and Jack breathed a while before sitting up. He said to himself, *If it doesn't work I can always kill him, too.* His voice emerged, calm again, that otherworldly horn:

"I met her in a pizza joint in Tucson. . . ."

But telling the tale was not the key. And hearing Hugo tell him that the world was an illusory backwater and morality a false construct was not the key, either, though it was closer. Once he'd gotten it all out, Hugo told him to keep it whole in his mind, to imagine an invisible container holding the entire story, so that when he released it there would be nothing left behind. It was that moment of release that was the key. Hugo talked him through it, led him right up to the precipice of freedom, toes hanging over the brink, and then let him take the final step himself. Nothing in Jack's life had ever felt like that. He thought he might explode with euphoria, or float free into space. And Hugo was right: nothing false could produce a feeling like that.

Once he'd had a little time—laughing and whooping—to enjoy his new freedom, Hugo gave him the rest of the Knowledge, and not for a millisecond did Jack doubt any of it. His newly emancipated mind recognized the treasure of Knowledge, and though it was coming out of Hugo's mouth it was really being excavated from inside him. He was not learning, he was remembering. Everything that had gone before had been blanketed with ignorance, all of which had just slid off him in one great cosmic shrug.

As he drove toward Dean's school, Jack felt that luminous moment still alive in him, still electric despite having been so long neglected. None of it had abandoned him, he realized. It was all still there. He laughed aloud, then let out an unbridled whoop, cracking the car's hermetic quiet.

And now, in his rekindled interest, he'd found this subreddit about Hugo and the group run by a writer who seemed to know everything about them. It was a pretty barren thread aside from the writer's posts about his research, but there were a couple of commenters who somehow had a copy of Hugo's book, and talked like flame-carriers. Jack wondered if they might know others. When he had told the writer of his history with Hugo, the guy had flipped and asked to meet him. Jack had agreed, but insisted on including the commenters.

The trip to Dean's school went quickly, and he got there a few minutes early, pulling in behind the growing phalanx of luxury cars piloted by sleek young moms and live-in help. Some of them were gathered in twos and threes outside their cars exchanging small talk. Jack idly pictured joining them. Doubtless they'd have advice for him on how to improve his mottled skin and drop a few pounds. A cleanse maybe. He gave a caustic grunt. He had sunglasses on and angled his face nonchalantly while checking out the asses of the ones in yoga pants. He scrolled through his iTunes and punched up some Stones—"Live With Me," just to make them a little uncomfortable if they could hear the lyrics. There were two in particular that he studied when Jagger sang *Come on now, honey, we can build a home for three. . . .*

Just after three o'clock, the school doors opened and a slow trickle of children filed out after a teacher with a clipboard. Jack got out and waved when he saw Dean, and the teacher waved back. Dean walked over and climbed onto his booster in the back seat, where he knew he had to ride at least until they were out of range of the school. After that, Jack usually let him sit in front using only the lap belt, with the airbag turned off.

"Good day at school, bud?"

"Yeah," Dean said. "We made a video for YouTube about not using plastic bottles."

"Good for you. When can I see it?"

"Anytime. It's on YouTube."

"Already?"

"Yeah, Miss Parker put it up right after we made it. You signed a permission last weekend."

"Right. Very cool, bud. Well, no one is at the house right now, and I've got an errand to run. You mind coming with me?"

"No."

"Okay then, it's in Venice."

Jack pulled into a convenience store to get Dean a snack and move him into the front seat. Then he took surface streets over to Venice, following his phone's guidance to the address. It was a dark gray craftsman with two leafy trees in the high-fenced front yard.

"Whose house is this?" Dean asked as they were getting out.

"Just a guy who's interested in meeting me. He's writing a book about those people I told you about, that I used to be friends with, and he wants to get some information. There's going to be a couple of other people here too. People who are interested in the same stuff. You want to come in?"

Dean looked at him for a second, pondering. "Yeah, I want to come in."

"Put your phone down while you eat your breakfast," she said, facing the television news.

Chris didn't look up. "I'm figuring out meeting Hunter."

"She's coming to pick you up, same as every day. How complicated could it be?"

Chris clicked from the text thread he was on with this Jack person over to his thread with Hunter, typed *See you out front*, and put down the phone. He heavily peppered his scrambled eggs and shoveled in a few bites, pretending hunger he didn't have. He pushed his chair back and picked up his backpack. She looked up from the TV.

"Did you take your pill?"

"Yeah, I took it."

"You're sure it's helping?"

"Yeah, Mom," he said. "It's helping."

Her eyes drifted back into abstraction though tension still skewed her mouth. She dropped her gaze to the TV. "Now you can vote," she said. "You and your friends need to get together and vote this sucker out of office."

"We will, Mom."

"Have fun at school," she said, as if to the TV. Her face relaxed again in the familiar wash of upsetting news, the wrinkles smoothing but not disappearing. She was almost too old to be his real mother, that was clear to him now, but he hadn't registered it before finding out two years earlier, when his thirty-one-year-old sister had died of an overdose. His parents had decided that her funeral was a good time to tell him that she was in fact his mother, not his sister, that she'd been sixteen when Chris was born, and in trouble with drugs, so they had taken him in, and later adopted him. The names Mom and Dad were ingrained by then, of course, but he still couldn't decide what to do with the words "mother" and "father."

He reminded himself that none of it mattered and shook his head with relief as he shouldered his bag and opened the kitchen door onto the driveway. He stepped out and looked up at the blue morning, which as usual entered him through his first outdoor breath and instantly thickened to bitter sludge in his lungs. An unfamiliar bird flicked by and disappeared into the neighboring yard. Being outside had become even more oppressive for him since he'd begun taking the Paxil. The intrusive thoughts had not only multiplied, but now seemed to take up physical space in his skull, intensified by the swelling emptiness around him. He could feel them in their endless variety of shapes chafing and gouging his brain, sometimes sinking down through the middle like iron balls through a barrel of warm bacon fat, sometimes slicing through like splintered pool cues. These were the kinds of side effects that supposedly meant the drug wasn't working, the kinds he'd been told to report to his parents or to Doctor Harden, but if he did they would take him off it—and while the effects were tough, he now understood they were actually a truer perception of his situation than he'd had access to before. They allowed him to understand. He had developed an almost clinical interest in the venomous goop sloshing in his own skull and lungs, and this new drug was like putting it under a high-definition microscope. When it got out of hand he could control and endure the worst of it with the oxy and Klonopin he got from Hemholtz at school, but the thing that got him through better than all else was the knowledge that it was temporary. He would be healed and done with it, and he needed this terrible clarity to facilitate the process.

He walked out to the end of the driveway and looked down the street. Hunter wasn't there yet. He looked back at the little peach-colored house, sullen under the rigid-blue Van Nuys sky. His hatred of it had tempered recently, and now he sometimes even felt a budding nostalgia for the place where he'd spent his entire life. He was distantly fond of the weathered basketball hoop over the garage door that his dad had somehow imagined he would use. The crack in the front wall left of the living room window, which snaked up under the eaves and seemed to widen a bit every year, was no longer embarrassing or worrisome, but an old friend, as were the barren gray flower beds by the front step. These friends at least had never lied to him.

He unzipped the top of his backpack and reached in to make sure it was there—the worn white paperback. His fingers smoothed the cover, and he pulled it up far enough to see the title, all alone on the front, *The Anamnestic Journey*. The strange phrase in red ink had risen right off the faded cover when he'd first seen it, misting and then reconstituting sharply in the air between his face and his hand as he flipped through a box of books at a yard sale four houses down from his own. No author name, nothing else. He had opened it and read the first sentence. . . . *One million two hundred and twenty thousand years ago we forgot everything that mattered, and are now plagued exclusively and unceasingly by things that don't.* Something had slid sideways in him, disengaged for a brief instant from the dreary chaotic corridors of his thought factory. It was only a single second, but he knew the book was his. He'd pocketed it without paying and carried it hungrily home.

He heard the clean rising hum of the engine as it turned onto the block. He could see Hunter's head and shoulders in silhouette as she drove between the two rows of parked cars, and he could see the *Coexist* bumper sticker on the front left bumper. He found himself happy for a second, looking forward to the drive to school with her. That unfamiliar sensation caught him off guard, stirring fear up behind it. He strode to the curb, and when she pulled up he climbed in quickly. He restrained himself from commenting on how ridiculous her ripped stockings, sleeveless denim vest, and matted goth-black hair looked behind the wheel of her brand-new emerald Range Rover Evoque. Nothing was really incongruous in the end, anyway. Or maybe everything was.

"Hey," she said. She leaned over and kissed him with tongue, another thing whose appeal had diminished with the increase of Knowledge. Or it could have been the Paxil. "We'd better not hit much traffic, or we'll be late for history," she said, yanking the car into gear.

"Why do you care?"

"Because we've been late the last two Thursdays, and Miss Friedrich'll be pissed. It's always you and me, trailing in last while she's trying to talk."

Chris shook his head and snorted. "You still think history matters?"

"No, 'course not. It's just a pain if she reports us, is all."

"Don't get me caught up in your negative bullshit. The only thing that actually matters—you know this—is visceral experience, the more intense the better. I thought we'd learned by now. Studying history is like drowning in ignorance."

"God, I *said* it's not about fucking history! I just hope we avoid the hassle of being late, is all I meant."

Chris looked at her steadily for a moment as she drove. "Why are you still talking about this?"

He could see the frustration in her frown, but she shut up. For a while, he hadn't understood why almost everything she said had begun to grate on him, but then he realized that the more he transcended the ignorant muck of everyday life, the less tolerance he had for its concerns.

"After school we need to go to Venice to do something," he said.

"Do what?"

"We're going to meet some people. People who can maybe help us."

"My fucking mom is going to kill me, Chris. I'm supposed to go straight to therapy after school. She's on the warpath lately. I'll have to tell her it was your idea."

"No you won't, baby. She thinks I'm her dream come true, doesn't she? We don't want her changing her mind, then she might try and keep us apart. You don't want that, do you?"

"No."

"Okay, so if it comes up, you just tell her I tried to talk you out of it but you went anyway. Say it was another Craigslist audition, and I went along just to make sure you were safe."

Her face drew in on itself. "Why do I have to take all the shit?"

"It's just how it is. We all deal with what we deal with. You handle your mom's bullshit and make sure things run smoothly for us, that's your thing, along with the *exterior vision,* of course. And my thing is I tunnel into the fucked-up heart of reality so we can finally understand it. Want to trade places?"

"Maybe I do."

"Well, if we could, be-fucking-lieve me I would. You got any idea the places I go?" They were at a stoplight, and he pushed his face close to hers, irritation rising in him. "Any *fucking* clue? You think I *want* to be finding out the shit I'm finding out?"

"Don't you?"

"NO!" He surprised himself with the sheer volume of it, the sound coming alive in his throat. "IT'S FUCKING *KILLING* ME!" He watched specks of spit fly from his lips onto her cheek. "DON'T YOU *GET IT*?" *Visceral experience,* he thought. The release of rage felt good and then just as quickly it was gone, giving way again to the lifeless muck that surrounded him always. He pulled back and set his jaw, took a breath. Hunter's eyes were welling with tears. He said, "Ah, fuck, baby. Come on. I mean, it's not the Knowledge that's messing me up, it's the *learning process*. It's a fucking ordeal—but you know, the book said it was going to get harder and harder to connect with truth in this world, as ignorance gets thicker and heavier all around us. So that's what's happening. We're fighting through it. It's hard on both of us, but there's no other way." He stared, waiting for her to acknowledge him, but she didn't. The car was moving again, and she concentrated on the road, crying softly. He said, "Okay?"

Without looking at him she said, "Okay."

AFTER SCHOOL, CHRIS met Hunter in the parking lot and they drove to Venice. When they got to the address, Chris told her to wait in the car. It was a small gray house behind a head-high plank fence. The top halves of two trees in the front yard were visible from the street. He got out and went through the gate. A bird caught his eye, a small crow, skimming in over the fence to his right and landing in the nearer tree. Chris stopped and stared at it to see if it was one of his own. It would not be a surprise if one of his birds came to him now, here. When he was a child flocks of birds had followed and spoken to him. They had shared with him astonishing things, things he never fully understood. For a long time they had come to him both singly and in frenzied throngs, talking over each other, a cacophony of only intermittently decipherable prophecy and insight, their discourse directing the flow of his thoughts, illuminating, guiding. Now they were rarer, and came to him only alone, but he knew they were the same birds, or what was left of them after all this time.

He stared at this crow. He recognized it. But it did not speak. Its black beak remained perfectly frozen in space, and he saw that it was almost visibly bloating with the weight of what it had to impart to him. Something gigantic. He waited. The air became charged as the bird's stillness gathered portent. Then the front door opened and it sprung from the branch, clearing the fence with a sad flap of its wings and disappearing in silence.

The guy who stood there was short and bearded, with a loose Mexican pullover open at the neck. "Hey there, brother," he said. "I'm guessing you're Chris?"

"Yeah."

"Jack told me you'd be showing up. Nice to meet you off of the chat. You alone?"

"My girlfriend is in the car."

"Okay, well, come on in, I guess."

"Is Jack here?"

"No, not yet," he said. "He's probably on his way."

The guy seemed harmless enough, so Chris went back and told Hunter to come in.

"Your name's Bernie, right?" Chris asked when they were sitting in the sparse living room on a couch even older than the one at his own house. The furniture was ratty, but the house was nice, and the paint on the walls looked fresh.

"Yeah, right," Bernie said.

"And do you know this guy Jack in real life?"

"I don't. He contacted me through the chat originally. He told me his history with the Group, and insisted I invite you over too. That's all I really know. What's your connection to Jack?"

"No real connection. He hit me up online too."

Bernie nodded. "How did a youngster like you get interested in all this, anyway?"

"I found the book, Hugo's book, in a box of free books on the sidewalk, and it just . . ." Chris stopped himself as he felt his heart begin to gallop. He might need to be careful here, it was hard to tell. He took a breath. "And then, after I read it, I googled Hugo and everything I could find about the story of the Group."

"Wow. You know, there are maybe four known copies of that book left around, from what I can gather. I've had mine since 1997." Bernie's eyes lit up slyly. "And you found it on the sidewalk. What are the odds of that, my friend?"

"I don't know. I mean, someone was going to find it."

"Yeah, but you read it, and made a connection with it. Most would have tossed it. Maybe the book sought out a kindred spirit."

"I guess it did." Chris felt excitement and looked over at Hunter, but she was sitting sideways and staring blankly out the window into the front yard.

"So," Bernie said. "You found it, you read it. Then what?"

"Like I said, I googled the title and found out about Hugo and the Group. Found your Reddit."

Now Bernie's eyes—slippery dark eyes—locked onto Chris's. "What's your interest level here, kid? You a casual rubbernecker, a death tourist?"

Chris looked again at Hunter, and she was paying attention now. She smiled at him, which calmed him. "Me and Hunter took a trip," he said. "Like that chapter in the book. We went into nature and moved right into each other. We read those passages aloud, followed what the book said to do."

"And?" Bernie raised his eyebrows. "You catch any exterior vision?"

"I think so." Chris looked at Hunter.

She said, "Yes. I saw it."

Bernie nodded, turning to her. "Those just little cuts? Or did you really try and check out?" He was looking at her wrist, where scars were visible at the edge of her thick leather bracelet. "They look sincere."

Chris was about to step in to protect her, but she spoke up quickly, unfazed. "They're for real. Almost worked too. But it was a while ago. Two years. I'm in a different place now."

Bernie gave her a long look, then turned back to Chris. "You know, I have been trying to figure out if this guy Jack is legit. Do you know anything about him?"

"No, but he knows his stuff about Hugo. What did he tell you?"

"He was with the Group for years, supposedly. He says he would have gone out with them but he got put in prison before the . . . event. He might even know the secret part. The unwritten chapter."

"I know," Chris said. "Maybe he'll share it with us."

Chris's eyes drifted again to the tips of Hunter's knotty white scars. When he'd met her two years earlier, they'd still been dark and fierce, though the bandages had been removed. He'd been new in school, having scored perfectly on a standardized test and been invited to a scholarship spot at their private school in Brentwood. He hadn't had any real friends at Van Nuys High anyway, though he'd known some of those kids all his life, so he didn't really mind the switch. He remembered hoping that a smaller school might make it easier for him to meet people, a thought that now made him laugh. Hunter had showed up in one of his classes a month into the school year, having been institutionalized, and her shrouded existence combined with the stories circulating about her generated in Chris a fascination he couldn't shake. The tattoos on her broad pale shoulders cemented his fixation. There was a mysterious circular symbol on her left shoulder, with wavy tentacles flowing inward from the outer circle all fading out short of the center, where a golden bell hovered as if waiting to be rung. On the other shoulder there was a raven that Chris recognized immediately as one of his own birds. Hunter was a little heavy and her hair was chopped messily, her clothes almost exclusively black and ripped, all an effort to ensure her outcast status, even from cliques of other outcasts. No one really hung out with her, but no one bullied or bothered her, either, whispering always in semisecret the only piece of information about her that seemed to matter: she had tried to kill herself. There was a kind of celebrity in it. Chris's social isolation at that point was complete and beginning to seem permanent, but when he introduced himself to Hunter one day at lunch, she had smiled and seemed relieved for his company. She'd kept him at arm's length at first, allowing him to eat lunch with her and talk to her but remaining distant. Then, once she'd let him in, the pendulum had swung swiftly in the opposite direction: she became deeply attached and dependent, which, along with the sex, was new and intoxicating. Chris had never had sex before. He'd also never had power over another person before. It turned out he liked both.

When the old man, Jack, arrived, he had a little blond boy with him, and it was the boy Chris studied first, since his eyes always instinctively shied away from old people. The sight of them irritated him, and he always wondered why they weren't embarrassed to be seen, with their wrecked skin and their crumpled features. Any young person with skin like that would cover it in shame, but they seemed oblivious. He couldn't understand why they didn't at least wear long sleeves and high collars and hats—the ones who did made more sense to him. This old dude was in a plain gray T-shirt, jeans, and black Adidas runners, so Chris let his eyes linger on the boy at first: he was holding the old man's hand and had a face like a lemur—wide eyed and small mouthed with a molecular watchfulness. He looked around the room from object to object as if cataloguing them, shyly avoiding the people until he saw Hunter smiling at him, and he squinted curiously back at her. When Chris allowed his gaze to move up to Jack's face he knew right away, instinctively, that this was the genuine article. His usual disgust of the elderly was seared quickly away. This beat-up old dude, with his sagging whiskered jowls and psychotic gray hair, his eyes like sinking orange suns, burned with lifetimes of Knowledge. He was tall, and seemed both powerful and ravaged, as if only by some inner magic had he survived all that his vast and terrible life had thrown at him. Chris felt electrified in his presence.

"Ain't this a sorry-looking crew," Jack said when they'd all been introduced. No one knew how to respond. He wasn't wrong. He looked at the boy, and then at Bernie. "Is there a place he can hang out with his tablet?"

"Sure," Bernie said. "He can chill out in the bedroom if he wants. I'll show you."

"Come on, bud," said Jack, leading the child to the mouth of the hallway and through a doorway there. A minute later, Bernie and Jack returned. "So!" Jack said, lowering himself into a chair. "What are we all doing here? Right? That's the question?"

"Well," said Bernie, "you did contact us."

"That's right, I did. But you guys have been discussing Hugo, and

I wonder why. Something drew you, and I'm interested in what that might have been. Start with you, my man. I've read your blogs or whatever they are about all this. You told me some already, but start again at the beginning. Tell me what got you interested. Was it a long time ago?"

"Yeah, way back. I was in grad school at Reed College, getting a PhD. I started studying cults for my dissertation, and then looking more specifically at suicide cults. Then when I looked at the story of Hugo's Group, I realized that no one had really done a study of it. The internet was pretty new then, and using it I found a copy of Hugo's book, which had been mentioned in some of the news items, but no library or agency seemed to have it. I lucked into a guy who'd been interviewed locally about the event, who knew the Group and had spent a little time in the house. He had a copy of the book, and I bought it off him."

"Uh-huh." Jack nodded. "What was his name?"

"Dashman. Something Dashman. Jim, or Bill. Called himself Dash. Said he used to drive a tow truck."

Jack laughed softly. "I remember Dash. He was a funny dude. Hugo didn't really want him around. Said he couldn't get serious. I liked him though. How's he doing?"

"Well, he was fine twenty years ago. He was still living in Moorpark. Now? I have no idea."

"And so, did you write your study?"

"Not exactly. I worked for a bunch of years on the dissertation, which compared a few of the smaller suicide cults—the biggest being Heaven's Gate, which had just happened at the time. I spent a bunch of time looking into that, doing some freelance reporting while compiling research for the paper. But something happened, on top of the fact that I got overwhelmed and couldn't finish. The more I read Hugo's book, the more I saw the sense in it. It made *sense*! It wasn't like the crazy literature of these other groups. Everything about the philosophy made more and more sense to me, and so I delved as deeply into it as I could. I mean, if you subtracted the fact of the event itself, this would have been an entirely workable and appealing philosophy and worldview. I could never quite figure out why it turned out the way it did. I know there was another part to the book, that last chapter that's alluded to but was never printed or published that I know of. Maybe that explains it. But I don't know. I mean, why was it necessary to take it to that extreme, in the end?"

Chris nearly rose from his seat as he started to speak, though the question hadn't been addressed to him. "Because it has to be intentional! Isn't that obvious? The whole thing is based on taking action, living with absolute intention and free from false constructs and passivity. Obviously that applies to dying too—maybe more than anything else. It's the most important moment of our lives, the only true inevitability, and yet most people avoid even thinking about it. We treat it like it doesn't exist. If we surrender our lives to the random currents carrying the universe, we surrender all our power and live at the mercy of chaos. The same goes for our deaths, obviously. If we just wait for it and let it happen, how can we have any idea where we'll end up? You don't need to read the secret chapter to figure that out."

"Kid seems to understand it all pretty well," Jack said. He smiled, but his smile didn't contain the approval or implicit concordance that Chris had been hoping for. It was a resigned, unhappy smile. Jack looked again at Bernie. "Did you try and generate exterior vision?"

"Yes."

"And how'd that go?"

"I think I saw some things. But I was never absolutely certain."

"Who'd you do it with?"

"My girlfriend. But she was highly skeptical."

"Hunter saw it," Chris said, pointing at her. "We did it just like they said, and she saw it."

Jack looked at her, and she nodded. "I saw . . . something."

"Well, shit," he said, smiling.

"I have to ask," Bernie said. "Have you seen the unpublished chapter of the book? If I knew what was in it, I could really tie all the pieces together and finish my paper. Maybe even make a book out of it."

"Seen it?" Jack said. He leaned forward, staring at Bernie, but just before he spoke he faced Chris. "I have the goddamn thing memorized word for word. Word for fucking word. We all did."

Bernie raised his chin suddenly. "That's the gate," he said. There had been a sound outside. He stood and went to the door.

Hunter said, "Oh fuck!" She was looking out the front window, covering her mouth. She slid off the couch, kneeling on the floor in front of it, hiding from the window. She looked at Chris. "It's my mom!"

"What?"

Bernie was looking through the glass porthole on the door. "This is your mother? Who invited her?"

"No one," Chris said. "Okay, here's the story. You put an ad on Craigslist casting a small indie film, and that's why we're here, okay? Hunter wants a part in your movie. Let me handle her." He stood up and went over to the door. Bernie stood aside for him.

"How the fuck did she find us?" Hunter whispered.

"Obviously she tracked your phone," said Chris. There was a knock, and he opened the door. "Mrs. Treadwell," he said. "How did you find us?"

"Where's Hunter?"

"She's right here." Hunter had moved back up onto the couch, and grimaced in embarrassment as her mother entered.

"Why aren't you at therapy?"

"I tried to get her to change her mind," Chris said. "But she wouldn't listen. She found this audition online, and was going to come here with or without me. I figured I had to come along, to make sure she was safe. I mean, anyone can put an ad on Craigslist."

"Why didn't you call me, Chris?"

He hung his head, nodding. "I should have. I'm sorry."

"Hunter, let's go."

"No, Mom. I have my car."

Mrs. Treadwell turned her ire now on Bernie, who was standing off to the side. Her eyes fixed on him. "And what do you think you're doing, mister? Getting young girls in here to exploit them?"

"Lady," he said, "you have me all wrong. I'm just trying to make a little piece of art. I can't control who answers my ad."

"And what about you?" she asked Jack, who was lounging in an armchair. "What's your role here, sir?"

Jack grinned widely, deep wrinkles etching sunbursts around the cold challenge of his eyes. "Just enjoying the show, sister," he said. She tried to hold his gaze, Chris saw, but she couldn't, and turned back to Hunter.

"Hunter. Now." She reached an arm forward and beckoned her daughter.

"No, Mom. I'm not leaving my car here."

Bernie said, "I think you better go with your mother, kid. You're not getting the part anyway, sorry."

"Give me your keys," Chris said. "I'll bring your car to school tomorrow."

Hunter gave Chris a murderous look as she walked to him and handed him the car key. "I'll see you later," he told her. "It's okay."

Mother and daughter walked down the path to the gate only after Mrs. Treadwell had given Bernie another pointed look and said, "You're lucky I don't call the cops on you."

Bernie closed the door. "What the fuck was *that*?" he said. "I do not need that kind of shit in my house, man!"

"Calm down," Jack said.

"Calm down? That bitch might call the fucking cops."

"She won't call the cops," Chris said.

"And," said Jack, "you didn't do anything wrong. None of us did. So calm the fuck down." He looked at Chris. "You think she'll cause more trouble?"

"No. She just worries about Hunter. Long as Hunter's with her she'll be fine."

"That girl can't come back here," Bernie said.

"Thing is, we need her."

Bernie raised his eyebrows, looking at Jack. "Need her? What does that mean?"

"She's the only one who's had a clear exterior vision. Hugo always said women and kids were more likely to have it. We can't go anywhere without her."

"Where would we go?"

There was a long pause, as Jack stared at Bernie, and Bernie's gaze grew slowly heavier until he understood. Jack then laughed suddenly and forcefully, the sound like a jackhammer in the small room. "Oh, man! I got you there, huh? You thought I was getting heavy on you. Lighten up, son." He turned from Bernie to Chris. "And what about you, kid. What led you to Hugo?"

Chris told Jack the story he'd told Bernie before, in pretty much the same way. But this time his listener engaged his eyes, leaning forward with his elbows on his knees, and while he spoke Chris could feel the old man's firm influence coiling about his mind like a gentle python. Those burning eyes did not waver, and it felt good, as if it might be safe to relax a tiny bit. He didn't relax, but just the prospect of a space in which it might be possible was magnificent. He sensed a silent understanding forming between them.

When he was finished, Jack looked away for a moment, and the sudden disconnection jolted Chris. He turned his head and was almost surprised to find Bernie still sitting there, looking at him.

Jack said, "Listen fellas, I've got to get my grandson home. But I'd like to continue this when we have more time."

"Yes," Bernie said. "That secret chapter. I would love to hear it, maybe transcribe it."

"Listen, bud, don't you worry—I'll get you that chapter. I'll type it into an email and send it to you. Then you can finish your book or whatever. How about that?"

Bernie nodded, mustering a grin. "Could I interview you about all that, too? I'd love to get your story on video sometime."

"Sure, why not? Whatever you need." Jack stood up. "Don't have time right now, but we'll work it out." He went to the bedroom door and opened it. "Hey Deano. Time to go, okay?"

After a moment the boy appeared in the doorway holding his tablet.

"You need to pee before we get in the car?" Jack asked.

The boy seemed to consider this carefully, and then shook his head. "Nope," he said.

Jack said, "Okay, we're out of here, kids. I have your numbers. Catch you on the flip side."

Chris had an urge to call out, to try and stop them from leaving. Instead he followed them to the door saying, "I'll go too. Gotta get home."

Jack took the child's hand, draped his other arm around Chris's shoulder, and guided the two of them down the walk. "Don't worry, kid," Jack said softly to him when they were away from the door. "I'm going to call you." None of them glanced back at Bernie before passing through the gate to the street. Chris looked around for his bird, but it was gone.

HE FELT FREER and freer. The trend was suddenly encouraging. There seemed to be interior progress. The following day skated along at something approaching a normal pace, and the novelty of this gave Chris a strange feeling of lightness, like helium filling his throat. It didn't dissolve the dense dark sludge in his lungs, but did counterbalance it. He tried, again and again in quiet moments through the day, to identify the lightness, to define it or name it, but the proper language, the applicable thought patterns, eluded him. There was a word just beyond his reach.

When he didn't see Hunter at lunch, he knew her mother had kept her home. She'd probably booked her some kind of therapy or observation. Chris tried texting her—innocuously in case her mother had her phone—but didn't hear back. As he was finishing his plate of chicken salad, Emily Green came to his table and sat across from him. She was a skinny blond girl with big teeth who was in AP calc with him. She'd been friends with Hunter when they were little kids.

"Hey Chris," she said. "I got a DM from Hunter. She wants me to talk to you."

"Okay."

"She said her mom took her phone and laptop, so she can't text. She got to another computer and DM'd me since you're not on Instagram."

"Yeah. What did she say?"

"She wants you to keep her car. Her mom is going to try and get you to drop it off, but Hunter wants you to hold on to it. She told her mom that you guys had already agreed you could use it this weekend to visit your sick grandfather up north somewhere."

"Where is she?"

"I don't know. But she said she might not be able to hear from you for a few days or something. Is she okay?"

"Yeah," Chris said. "She's fine. She just got into trouble with her mom for skipping therapy. Thanks."

Emily walked away. Chris ignored the texts he received the rest of the day from Hunter's mom, even though she seemed to have accepted the story about him needing the car. She only asked that he bring it by when he returned on Sunday.

At the end of the day, he was supposed to go to intramural soccer practice, but he went so seldom that showing up there would only have confused the coach and the team. Seniors were given latitude, especially academically high-performing seniors in noncompetitive sports. He veered left around the side of the gym into the parking lot and got into Hunter's car. Usually the pleasure of driving it skated uselessly on the surface of his gloom, but today, as he swung a hard right out the school driveway, he felt it adding to the nameless lightness he was already feeling. He maneuvered a few turns till he was eastbound on Montana along the golf course. The smooth acceleration pressed him warmly into the leather seat, and the two rows of trees began to snap by—eucalyptus on the left shielding the country club, antenna-thin palms punctuating the low houses on the right. He cut down Bundy to Wilshire and put himself onto the 405 heading north in thickening traffic. When he looked up and saw the Getty Center on the hill above him, he felt suddenly drawn up to its height. There were in that moment two of him, as if he were floating sagely above the city at the same time as he crawled through it on the choked freeway below. He was twinned: the mired, muck-poisoned yet intrepid teenager—his everyday self—was still there, trembling nervously underneath this delicate new buoyancy. Suddenly the word came to him, the word that had been eluding him all day. Strange that it should be so simple—one syllable and a new galaxy. Hope.

When he got to his exit he did not get off the highway. The grim banality of his home would not coincide well with this moment. The traffic was loosening as he passed Victory Boulevard, an incitement to keep driving. About a minute later, he knew where he was going. The first part of the route was in fact etched in his mind, though he'd never traveled it before, had only studied it on the map. A few miles up, he swung onto 118 westbound, an electron pulled by a cathode. He sailed twenty more minutes down the Ronald Reagan Freeway until it bent south, and then exited onto Los Angeles Avenue in the town of Moorpark.

When he was off the freeway he swung into a McDonald's parking lot and put the address, which he knew by heart, into his phone. It was close by, in an old occluded neighborhood where the block-long streets had women's names. Chris pulled the Range Rover onto Ruth Avenue and parked along the curb near the corner. He got out and walked, knowing the address was at the other end of the block. He didn't mind subjecting himself to the open sky, maximizing his psychic rawness; sometimes it helped with clarity. The only encroachments on the endless flat-screen sky were two small palms on the left, halfway down the block, and a larger shaggy tree on the right, visible over the roofs from the next street over. The rest was just bushes and shrubs and a lonely uniformity of single-story houses. The neighborhood seemed to cower under the colossal blue, the sky itself blank save for three fading contrails which taken together formed a backward N, as if some exterior entity had written that letter on the surface of the atmosphere from the outside. He ran through possible N's: No, Never . . . Now?

The numbers on the mailboxes got smaller as he continued down the block, and he felt his excitement building as he came closer to the one he was looking for, which would be on the right with the other even numbers. When he got there, he faced it, and was struck with a peculiar combination of deflation and influx. The house was unexceptional, another crumbling coral ranch house under California blue, less well-kept than the houses on either side, no car in the driveway, but with healthy grass, potted plants in front of the paneled-glass outer door. The window frames and the garage door all looked warped and original, in need of paint, and the tiled driveway almost matched the color of the house. The thing that struck Chris, the source of the influx, was that he'd been born into a house almost exactly like it. *Look for the connections everywhere,* the book said, Hugo said. *Even when you don't see them, they're there, peeking from the tiniest places. The universe is a guidance system, designed and set in motion a trillion years ago to show us the way to go wherever we decide. These mechanisms are decrepit and elusive, sometimes dauntingly obscure and sometimes hiding in plain sight, but they still function in spite of disuse.* He searched for a detail that might connect the two houses, something to complete the circuit, maybe a corresponding crack in the front wall, but didn't find anything. Then his eyes fell on the ancient basketball hoop above the garage door. The paint on the metal backboard was streaked with flaking rust and the net was reduced to a few ragged strands of chain, while his own was made of fiberboard and string, but the brand logo in the upper right corner was the same: a single, red, fully spread wing. Birds, again. It had probably been there when the Group lived there. It looked as old as the house. The thought of some of those people possibly shooting hoops in this spot brought the reality home to him. Chris felt it sink in. Probably they'd never distracted themselves with so trivial a thing as basketball, but this was the *place*. It wasn't all just heady philosophy and psychedelic weirdness in a book, or old news stories archived on the internet; it was something that had happened, and this was where it had happened. There were people alive who remembered it, who had known the Group, lived with them. And the universe was revealing to him a connection between him and this place.

He stood and stared at the house for a long time, long enough for the galvanic linkage to begin to cool and reality to recongeal. The world was still the world, and he was still a kid named Chris. The red hem of his mom's skirt, lifted by her wrinkly hand to dab at his eyes as he lay with his head in her lap after being smacked hard by his dad, his brain still quivering from the flash of shock—the memory intruded on him in the usual way, a bubble risen from the sludge, arriving at the surface unbidden. Other familiar images crowded up behind his eyes, things that claimed space in his memory in spite of him:

The small blue star, above the picture of a split peach on the label of the canned peaches he loved as a child, which occupied a white circle amid four straight blue lines signifying its radiance—he used to stare fixedly, almost ritualistically, at the star as he ate his bowl of peaches and drank the clear syrup. Then he remembered the greasy, wiry gray fur of his parents' ancient terrier, Pepper, who had died when he was five, the only pet he'd ever known—Chris had hated the feel of Pepper's patchy fur and scaly skin, and the dog's perennial glandular stink, but his soggy brown eyes were persuasive and he would always flip to expose his belly and the ugly apple-sized goiter there immediately upon being touched. Petting him was repellent, but neglecting him felt cruel.

Chris brought his attention back to the moment. He felt the image of the house in front of him sinking—sadly, inevitably—into the quicksand of his memory along with everything else. He hadn't started any of this, and he wouldn't be the one to end it. He was, after all, just a *speck of cloistered consciousness in a vast delusion,* and if he wanted to get where he was going he would need to see things clearly. Hope was well and good—he couldn't see anything wrong with that—but delusion would have to go.

"You looking for something?" A woman's voice, from behind him.

Chris turned and beheld her with a shimmering ambivalence. She was over sixty, with straight brilliant white hair and skin whose ruddy flush was somehow undiminished under the creasing and sagging of age. Like Jack, she bypassed Chris's disgust of the elderly, but mainly because she was still beautiful. She wore tapered black sweatpants, a linen shirt, and Birkenstocks. No one had ever minded looking at her, and it showed in her bearing. She stood on the opposite curb, having probably emerged from the house across the street. Her interruption of his reverie contained some kind of challenge.

"What?" he said.

"I'm wondering if I can help you with something. I saw you standing here."

"No," he said. "I'm not doing anything."

"You know Barb and Jim?" She pointed past him at the house.

"No."

"Who are you looking for?"

"I'm not looking for anyone."

She crossed her arms. Her bright eyes had gravity, even from a distance. "It's the house, isn't it?"

He waited a moment, and then nodded.

"You're a little young, aren't you?"

"What do you mean? I'm eighteen."

"Right. You weren't even born till twenty years after. We used to get people once in a while, like you, but not for a long time now. Back when it was fresher there were quite a few. People were curious, I guess."

Chris stood silent for a moment mirroring her obscure challenge, waiting for her to turn and go back to her house, but she remained, her eyes unflinching. He found he didn't want to turn away himself, both because it would feel like a capitulation and because he liked looking at her. Why couldn't all old people look this way? "Did you know them?" he asked.

Her eyes narrowed and she squared her chin. After a second she said, "A couple of them. They were weird, but no one expected what happened. Most of them were kind of nice, actually."

"What about him? Did you know him?"

"He wasn't too talkative with me. He came and went, was out of town sometimes, I think, but didn't spend much time hanging out with outsiders. I don't think I ever exchanged a word with him beyond maybe a nod. What about you? You connected somehow? Related to one of them?"

"No," Chris said. "Just interested."

She shook her head. "You ought to get home, kid. There's nothing here to see, and there never was."

"I'm here," he said. He spread his arms in presentation. "You're here." He smiled now, felt it bursting forth miraculously. "We're not nothing, are we?" The unaccustomed muscles of his face were helplessly seized. He knew now, they'd need to do it here. "Are we?"

Her scrutiny of him faltered. She looked away, saying, "All right," as if to herself. She speared him with a last blue flick of her eyes before heading up the walk to her door. Chris turned and strode back down the block without even a final glance at the house, his tall shadow swaying out in front of him, swinging its arms.

"You need the car today?" Gerald was drinking a cup of coffee at the kitchen counter.

Daniel regarded him incredulously. "Yeah, I need my car today, Ger. It's LA, everyone needs their car every day."

"Okay." Gerald smiled. "Sue me for asking."

"We should leave for school in fifteen minutes." It was October, and Gerald had been staying with Daniel for a month. He put two slices of bread in the toaster. "You ought to eat something." He poured himself coffee.

Gerald shook his head. "Not hungry yet. I'll get a snack at school."

"Sure, starve yourself and then eat candy. Would your mom stand for that?"

"She lets me eat what I want."

Daniel shrugged and raised his hands. "I recuse myself. You're about to be an adult soon anyway. Technically."

"You wouldn't know it from the way people treat me."

"Hey, I give you a fair amount of autonomy. I didn't ask where you'd been when you got home last night, did I? Even though clearly you'd been drinking."

"I was out with some friends, that's all. I was safe, I took an Uber home."

"Like I said, I didn't ask. Long as it's not frequent and no one drives drunk. Long as you have things under control. I don't treat you like a child, do I?"

"It's not you, so much. It's just regular bullshit at school, with the counselors and teachers, and then there's my mom, always tripping about something. At least my dad trusts me to take care of myself, even if I do disgust him."

"You don't disgust your father; he's confused by you. It's ignorance, is all."

"Yeah, poor guy. He got so confused he smacked me."

Daniel hung his head. "I didn't say 'poor guy.'" His toast popped up.

"This is what I mean by being treated like a kid," Gerald said. "You don't need to baby me. I know the truth, and ignoring it or painting it a different color doesn't change it. My father is disgusted by who I am, and that's why he freaked the fuck out."

Daniel sat down with him at the counter to eat. "Fair enough," he said. "I hope things with him improve. I'm sure they will. Raymond does love you, and he'll come around, I think."

"I know that," Gerald said. "He just needs to get his head around it and change his thinking. But that won't happen in a vacuum. I need to be able to see him."

Tanya had insisted Raymond see a therapist about Gerald, and he'd agreed on the condition that Gerald not be told about it. "Your mom said Christmas, right? He will have done his time by then. So just hang in there."

Gerald nodded, finishing his coffee.

"So, you need a ride home after school today? I'm free later on."

"No. I'm going to my friend's, which is why I wanted the car. I can take the bus back if I don't get a ride."

After dropping him at school, Daniel drove to Tanya's place. The situation with Gerald had brought them back in closer touch, and they'd started furtively seeing each other again. There'd been no conversation about what it might mean, and she insisted they keep it secret from both her sons, especially Gerald. Most days Tanya's shift at the hospital didn't start until the afternoon, so Daniel would go over in the morning, once Gerald was at school.

She lived in a pleasant yellow apartment complex, not far from the airport, with a garden courtyard that was remarkably lush. Some of the residents, including Tanya, did extra work on it in their spare time. Daniel walked through the arch at the entrance and under a white trellis of vines that took him past the small swimming pool. He climbed the outer stairway of the two-story building at the back. Tanya's was the first door off the stairs, and she answered quickly when he knocked.

She smiled but turned without kissing him and walked toward the back of the apartment. She was wearing a loose white T-shirt and powder-blue pajama bottoms. "Want coffee?"

"I've had enough, thanks."

She sat at the small dining table in front of her cup and a recently finished plate of eggs. "How's the kid doing?"

"He's fine, mostly."

"So he wants to stay on indefinitely?"

"No. But, for the time being. If you're okay with it, obviously."

"It sure has been more peaceful around here. I guess it's up to you."

"I told him I wanted to have you over for dinner sometime, so you can see him. He seemed to like the idea."

"We better figure ourselves out before we start hanging out with Gerald."

"Also, I know he wants to spend Christmas with you."

She smiled. "It's very nice of you to have him."

"I really don't mind. I get lonely over there anyway, especially since I quit teaching. He keeps me occupied." Daniel smiled. "Don't freak out, but he came in a little drunk last night."

She shook her head and sighed. "You think that's a problem?"

"I don't think so. It was the only time. He's just cutting loose a little. He was with friends, and he took an Uber home. I gave him my account to use, sparingly."

She nodded, pausing. "You get lonely, huh?"

"Well, sure."

"That why you're here? 'Cause you're lonely?"

"I guess it's one reason. Not the only one." Daniel had known this conversation was coming. He felt ready for it. It needed to happen.

"Yeah, well . . ." She drained her coffee, swallowed, put the cup down, and engaged his eyes. "I get lonely too. As you can imagine. So it's nice, of course, to have someone coming around. And if that someone happens to be you, I told myself, then what's the harm?"

"Yeah, sure." Daniel felt he should maybe say more, but didn't.

"Except there is harm. It's not sustainable."

"What *is* sustainable, really."

She frowned. "Don't do that shit, Daniel."

"Don't do what?" he asked, though he knew.

"Get all pedantic and abstract. This is real."

"Sorry."

"I've been thinking," she said. "And I think we ought to nip this. It's a recipe for trouble. You mean a lot to Gerald, and we don't want our shit blowing up and hurting him again. I was going to give it a little more time before saying something, but here we are."

Daniel paused. He nodded. "If you think so." Which wasn't what he'd meant to say.

"Don't *you*?"

"I don't know." He turned his head and looked across the open kitchen counter to the window above the sink, through which he could see the white cylinder of an electrical transformer on a wooden pole and the sloped red-brown roof of the building across the street. He felt very calm, which struck him as unusual.

Tanya just stared at him. Her face was framed lopsidedly by her short gray-touched dreadlocks, and though he wasn't watching her, he knew how beautiful she looked in that moment and didn't return his eyes to her. He needed to keep his head clear.

"I'm sorry I never introduced you to Forest," he said. "I should have."

"Daniel . . ."

"I didn't want to involve you in my inadequacies as a parent. I thought you'd judge me, rightly of course. But I see now that you *were* involved whether I liked it or not, and all I did was compound my inadequacy as a parent with inadequacy as a partner by keeping you at a distance."

Tanya laughed suddenly. "You been going to therapy or something?"

"No." He looked at her, mystified by the humor in her face. Her laugh had surprised him.

"I'm sorry, I just can't help myself." Her face fell into seriousness. "What is it you think you're doing right now?"

"I'm just saying some things I wish I'd said before."

"Why bother?"

"Because we're here, talking. Because I care about you."

"And you think it's going to help me to have a conversation we should have had a couple of years ago?"

"I don't know. Maybe. It could help both of us."

She leaned in toward him, her expression softening, her eyes steady. "All this stuff is water under the bridge. I've left it in the past."

"But maybe we shouldn't have." Daniel took a slow breath. "I've been thinking a lot too. About us."

Tanya tucked her chin and glared sidelong at him. "Be careful, boy."

"I am being careful." This was a lie. He found himself standing squarely outside the lines he'd drawn around this talk, and suddenly the idea of stepping back inbounds depressed him. "Don't you think there's still something here?"

She looked away. "I don't know. I guess if there wasn't we could just fuck peacefully a couple times a week like we set out to do. Or maybe we wouldn't want to." She returned her gaze to him. "But none of our shit has gone anywhere. It's all still there, waiting for us. You know that, right?"

"I know it."

She slumped in her chair, shaking her head. "Just thinking about it is making me tired. It was fucking exhausting, Daniel, trying to engage directly with you. And truth be told, I don't believe you right now. I don't think this is coming from careful consideration. I think you came in here ready to break it off again, or at best oblivious, and then you got a pang of loneliness when faced with it and now you're saying some stuff off the top of your head that you don't even know if you mean. That's my honest assessment of this situation."

Daniel kept his features under control. She was right, of course. He said, "You don't think I mean what I say?"

She paused a moment. Her eyes gave no ground. "Okay then. I'm listening. What is it you're saying?"

"I'm saying," said Daniel, praying there was an honest other-end to this sentence, his heart soaring with fear, "that I think maybe we made a mistake. Or that I did. I'm saying that you're right that this is unsustainable. But there are two ways we could deal with that, not one. We could nip it, as you say. Or we could start reexamining what we have, think about trying again, maybe."

"And is that what you want?" she asked matter-of-factly.

Daniel fell silent, his mind a traitorous vacuum.

"I mean," she said, "you've been thinking about this so hard, ruminating so carefully, you must have an idea what you want. Don't hold out on me. Let's get it all out in the open."

"Yes," he said.

"Yes?"

"Yes, I want to try again. Or at least talk about what that might look like. Okay? Yes."

She was silent a long time, staring at him. Then her shoulders sagged. "How about you go home now? I need some time to think without you here, before we have this conversation."

"All right."

"But I want you to promise me two things."

"Okay."

"First, you say nothing to Gerald until I decide."

"Of course."

"And second, if, when you walk out the door, you realize I was right—if you were just trying to forestall your own loneliness, and you have second thoughts about what you're saying, I want you to send me a text and tell me. Just text me the word *sorry*, all by itself, and I'll know I can stop worrying about all this. I won't hold it against you. We can go back to being friends. But I need that promise."

Daniel opened his mouth to speak but she saw the intent in his eyes.

"No," she said. "Don't reassure me, don't explain. Just promise me."

He nodded. "I promise."

"Okay. We can talk later." The fierce look on her face was so beautiful—sharp mouth-corners pulled slightly down and eyes gone diamond-bright—that he almost tried to kiss her, but he thought better of it.

He said, "I'll see you," and walked out.

He let the cerebral escapism of Steely Dan carry him home in the car, pulling into his driveway twenty-five minutes later. He shut off the engine but did not get out. He sat with his hands on the wheel, breathing, thinking, and after a minute he picked his phone up off the cradle and opened the message app. Tanya's last text to him, from ninety minutes earlier, said, You want to come over? He had answered, On my way!

Daniel typed the word Sorry into the message box and stared at it, probing how it might feel to hit SEND, keeping his thumbs safely away from the screen. Tanya was a fifty-one-year-old woman who'd been through a lot. She didn't need him messing with her heart. And he was all the things she said he was: distant, self-involved, trapped in the past, lonely. Which was really why he needed her—not just to assuage his loneliness, but to force him to change, to participate more in the world. That was the obvious part. On the other hand, he couldn't think of any real reason why Tanya would need *him*. Except of course that she was lonely, too, and they had a good time together. It wasn't enough, not in the long term. If he stepped back into her life, he'd need to become worthy of her love, and the pathway to that was obscure to him.

Daniel thought then of all that he'd never shared with Tanya. She knew the structural elements of his story, but little of the substance. In talking to her about his past, he had framed the first half of his life as "the crazy years," and had created an artificial dividing line that made drug use the engine of his troubles, and quitting drugs the catalyst for his reform and mellowing. It was a simple equation, easy to pass off, with the benefit of having some truth in it. When he'd gotten out of prison the second time, he'd redescended quickly into dissolution and cocaine abuse, spending a few years flapping in the wind until the money he had left was gone. Then, after quitting cocaine with Cam's help, he'd begun building the life he now inhabited. But that story ignored the deeper factors that had driven him into problem drug use in the first place. Tanya knew about Rachel, and the accident, but in conversation he'd relegated his grief over her to the realm of ancient history—no need to dwell. Same with his brother. Same with his mother and father. He'd gotten so used to being alone, he realized, that he'd stayed that way even when Tanya had come along and thrown her heart open to him.

Loneliness came crashing in on him now, bitterly, stinging his eyes, and there was a second when he almost did it, his thumb sliding precariously close to the phone's screen and the SEND icon. He was startled by a knock on his window. He turned and saw Dean there, next to the car, smiling and waving. Standing a few yards off, closer to the main driveway, was Celia Dressler. Daniel deleted the text, opened his door, and stepped out.

"Hey there, buddy, what's going on?"

"Hi," Dean said. His face fell into a searching expression, looking at Daniel. "Are you okay?"

"Yeah, fine! How about you? How's school going?"

"Good."

"We saw you pull in from up the drive," Celia said, approaching, "and Dean wanted to say hi. He said he misses you."

Daniel smiled at Dean. "Well, it's good to see you, my friend. I miss you too. You guys want to come in for a minute?"

"We're on our way out," she said. "But maybe we could schedule a visit, so you and Dean can hang out."

"I'd like that. This weekend maybe? Saturday?"

"Yes. Sounds good."

Daniel squatted onto his heels and looked at Dean. "Want to come over Saturday? We can have another Nerf grudge match, maybe eat some pancakes. I happen to be one of the world's great pancake chefs."

Dean beamed in spite of a clear effort to remain stoic, child-joy seizing him. "Okay," he said, chewing unconsciously on two knuckles.

"Great." Daniel looked at Celia. "Come by anytime midmorning, and I'll lay in some pancake mix and syrup."

THEY ARRIVED AT eleven on Saturday morning. Gerald was in the living room playing a video game on his laptop, and when the doorbell rang he said, "I'll go play this in my room."

He was crossing the front vestibule when Daniel opened the door, and he waved quickly as he passed.

"Stop for one second and meet Celia and Dean," Daniel said.

Dean looked past Daniel and said, "Hi Gerald!"

"Hey there," Gerald said.

"You guys know each other?" Daniel asked.

Gerald had stopped, but he slouched impatiently toward the hallway as he spoke, "I was exploring around a couple days ago, met up with Dean and his granddad."

"When was this?"

"I don't know, a couple days ago. You weren't here."

Celia stepped forward and smiled. "I'm Celia, Gerald. Nice to meet you."

"Yeah, I know, hi," Gerald said.

"Gerald is staying in my guest room for a while," said Daniel.

"Great—you like it here?" Celia asked.

"Yeah. It's all right. I got to go do some homework." He went down the hall.

"I didn't know they assigned video gaming," Daniel called after him cheerfully. Gerald went into his room and closed the door.

"So," Daniel said as he led them to the kitchen, "I have one very important question for you, Dean."

"What?"

"Do you take your blueberries inside the pancakes, or on top?"

"I don't want blueberries."

"I'm going to pretend I didn't hear that, and you better pray the pancake gestapo were not listening in, because they will come for you."

"Pancake what?"

"They're like the secret pancake police. They crack down on pancake criminals wherever they find them, and not having blueberries with your pancakes when there are blueberries available is a very serious offense."

Dean laughed once as he went around the counter into the living room. "Very funny," he said.

Daniel looked at Celia, who was smiling. "Coffee?"

"I don't do caffeine. I'm good with some water."

"What about pancakes?"

She grinned. "Of course."

"Tell you what, Dean. I'll make a few with the berries, and some without, and you can try it both ways. If you really don't like it, I'll sneak them off your plate and we can just pretend you ate them." He poured Celia a glass of water.

Dean had picked up the Nerf basketball and was setting up for a shot from the far side of the coffee table. "Aiding and abetting," he said as he launched the ball. "Pancake police will get you too."

Daniel laughed.

Celia said, "Aiding and abetting? Where'd you learn that?"

Dean retrieved the ball. "Grampa Jack's TV shows."

Daniel poured pancake mix into a bowl after giving Celia her water, then broke an egg in. Suddenly Dean was standing under his mother's stool.

"Mom, can I go see what game Gerald is playing?"

"No, sweetie, leave Gerald alone."

"Please?"

"Honey, no. He doesn't want you in there."

Dean's face became monumentally indignant. "How do you know?"

"I can check if the game is something violent," Daniel said. "Gerald might not mind. He's a nice kid."

She looked at Dean. "I thought you came here to see Daniel."

"I did! Just until the pancakes are ready then I'll come out."

"Okay, Daniel can ask Gerald, but if he's busy you have to stay out here."

"Okay."

Daniel went down the hall and knocked on Gerald's door before opening it. "Hey man. Dean wants to come watch your game for a minute if you're not busy. Is the game you're playing appropriate for a kid?"

Gerald paused the game and looked up with knee-jerk annoyance at having been interrupted, but when he spoke his voice was jovial. "Yeah sure. It's just a maze adventure. Tell him to come on in."

"Thanks." He went to the living room and led Dean back down the hall. "Don't get too wrapped up, because you have to eat your pancakes when they're ready."

"Don't send the pancake police after me," Dean said, and he closed Gerald's door after him.

Back in the kitchen, Daniel continued making the batter and Celia sat across the counter drinking her water.

"Man," she said, "anytime there's the prospect of a screen to stare at. It's hard. Some of his classmates already have fucking iPhones. First graders! He's been starting to ask. It's crazy."

"I can only imagine. When I was a kid my parents wrung their hands about a few hours of TV a week."

"I was a child actor, so I passed TV off as research. It was perfect."

Daniel smiled. "So, your movie shoot is all over with?" he asked.

"Yup. Wrapped."

"How'd it go?"

"Great. It was long, but a good experience."

"You're happy with the movie."

"Well, I'm happy with the work I did. The rest of it I can't really control or predict at this stage. But in fact, yes. I think it's going to be something really good. I had that feeling all along. I think we all did."

"That's good. Miles Rossinger hasn't made any stinkers, as far as I know. So you're in good hands."

"True. I'm lucky to have gotten the part."

"Other projects coming up?"

"Nothing yet, though I've had some calls," she said. "I'm going to try and lie low for a little while. Spend more time with Dean."

"He's such a great kid."

She smiled broadly. "He is, isn't he? And he loves you. You've made a real impression on him."

"And he on me. You know he just showed up down here that first time, walked through the backyard gate and said hi like he'd known me all his life."

Celia laughed. "That's his style. Though as we said, he shouldn't be left to wander like that."

Daniel was whisking the batter. "How'd it go, by the way, with your father? Did you get someone in to help?"

"Yes, I got our nanny to come more often. But now I'm back, so it's not as much of an issue. I'll avoid leaving him with my father for too long in the future if I have to go away. Jack is fine with him day to day when I'm around, it's just when he's on his own for a while."

"Jack was upset with me for talking to you. He didn't take it well, initially."

"I didn't say anything about you to him. Nothing you said to me."

Daniel poured the first pancake into the pan. "I know," he said, "but I think he figured it out."

"You guys are still friendly, though, right?"

Daniel shrugged. "Not exactly. I was a little taken aback by his reaction, so I put some distance between us. Not a big deal. Not everyone is meant to be friends."

She nodded, about to question further, but then seemed to change her mind.

"So, you have any family, Daniel?"

"I have a son, lives here in LA. He's a painter."

"That's great. You two close?"

Daniel paused. "We're fine. Could be closer, but we're working things out. I had some lost years a while back, and he was collateral."

"I hope I'm not being nosy. I know about lost years, believe me. Thank god most of them were before Dean was born."

"You're not being nosy."

"So just your son? You an only child, like me?"

"Not an only child originally, growing up. My brother died in Vietnam, when I was eighteen."

"Oh, that's terrible. Sorry."

"Thanks. It was a long time ago."

"What was his name?"

"Gene. Eugene."

She nodded and gave him a sympathetic smile. Daniel held her eyes a moment. Her face was such a pleasure to look at.

"So," she said, "you live here alone. There's no girlfriend or boyfriend?"

"I have sort of a girlfriend. She's Gerald's mother actually. We broke up for a while, but we've started seeing each other again. It's possible we might be getting back together, which Gerald doesn't know yet. But we'll see." He flipped the pancake. "Kind of a complicated situation, currently in flux."

"Oh, you are talking my language!" She laughed. "Those are the only kinds of situations I seem able to get involved in. Unless you count one-nighters. I've got my own complicated situation fucking with my head, so I can sympathize."

Daniel transferred the pancake onto a cookie sheet he'd placed in the warm oven, dropped a pat of butter into the pan and poured another one. "Should we do it?" he asked.

"Do what?"

"Talk about our complicated situations? I mean, we've got distance from each other, and that can be good for perspective." He gave her a look that he hoped told her he was keeping it lighthearted.

"Don't tease me." Celia flashed him an open, playful smirk. "Because I can talk about my shit all day. One therapy session a week is so inadequate! And I'm not even fully honest with her, because I don't want to have to kill her and get a new therapist if I tell her too much."

Daniel laughed. He said, "Then there's me, who doesn't talk to a soul on this earth. Outside of sometimes Tanya herself."

"That's her name, Tanya? Okay, you go first. Tell me about her."

WHEN THEY'D LEFT, Gerald borrowed the car to visit a friend and Daniel parked himself on the patio, listening to Sonny Stitt. Instead of mulling his situation with Tanya, or Celia's affair with the married musician/driver that she'd told him about, he found himself thinking about Gene. It had been a long time since Daniel had said his name out loud, and it had a certain effect on him.

When Daniel thought of his brother, he often sifted through all his final memories of Gene, repolishing the details he could still muster. There was a clearing in the forest where they used to go when they were young, Daniel and Gene. They would bring knives and throw them at trees. They would sit on logs and devise story-games and fantasies, plan their world-beating futures: Gene was going to be a famous writer, and Daniel a movie star. The clearing was formed by three giant fallen trees that lay in a triangle, creating the impression of an empty theater. One of the fallen trees was, they decided, very bad luck. The lower part of its trunk, where it had broken off near the ground, was slimy and almost unnaturally black where the bark had peeled off, flaring sometimes with clouds of dark moss in the summer. The color of its trunk made it seem, especially in spring when the woods around it were greening lushly, as though it had absorbed whatever bad juju was out there and was storing it up. Gene said if you even touched it lightly you'd ruin your luck for a year. Maybe die. Both of them stayed away from the tree religiously, and though it started as a joke Daniel sometimes wondered if Gene, like himself, nursed a secret irrational fear that they were right. Sometimes if Daniel walked a little too close Gene would shove him toward it by surprise, sending Daniel's heart into spasms. Sometimes they grappled into a sumo match, sneakers digging into the brown leaf mulch, Gene laughing and Daniel howling with fear. Gene was two years older and much stronger, but he never pushed hard enough to actually force Daniel into the tree, always pulling up short, which only added weight to Daniel's fear of it.

As they got older and spent less time together, their visits to the clearing grew more infrequent. The summer before Daniel turned sixteen, Gene got a job at a gas station and auto shop, pumping gas and cleaning up and learning about cars, and Daniel barely saw him at all. Gene spent all his time with his friend Ed Neary, whose father owned and operated the station. Ed had his own car, and Gene began to evaporate from the day-to-day life of their family. That was the first summer in a decade that Daniel hadn't gone once to the clearing with Gene.

The following spring, at Gene's suggestion, they went to the clearing together for the first time in over a year, and Gene told Daniel of his enlistment. It was April. Gene had just turned eighteen.

"You really want to go over there?" Daniel asked him.

"Of course I don't, you idiot."

"Then why?"

"Lots of kids I know are getting drafted. Ed got drafted, you know that?"

"No." Ed had dropped out of high school the year before.

"If I sign up I can have more control over where I go, and maybe get put in with Ed."

"What about college? I thought that would get you out of it."

"I wouldn't be signing up if I wanted to get out of it." Gene's voice sounded irritated. He took a cigarette from his pack and lit it. "I can't just watch my guys go over there and trot off to college like nothing's happening. Plus, maybe we do need to stop the Russians. Maybe Mom and Dad are wrong and future generations will thank us." He offered Daniel a smoke.

Daniel shook his head. "I better not. I'm running the mile this year."

They were sitting on the biggest of the three tree trunks, in their old spot near the roots where a groove in the bark formed a kind of bench you had to climb up to. This tree had stayed hard and brown longer because the roots had pulled up with it when it fell, raising a huge thick fan of earth above it. There were still living branches along the top of the trunk, straining skyward and sprouting a few leaves every year. The blackened moldy bad-luck tree was off to their left, near the top of the one they sat on.

Daniel let his head fall back and breathed up at the flat white clouds. "Fuck, Gene," he said. "Don't fucking die, okay?"

"I'm not going to die."

"Let me have a cigarette."

Gene gave him one and Daniel lit it. They smoked quietly until they were done. Then they spent a half hour talking about other things. When they jumped down from the log, Daniel walked toward his friend Rory's house on the other side of the woods. Gene went along with him to where their paths diverged at the top of the big tree.

"See you," Daniel said, but from the corner of his eye he caught a subtle tensing of Gene's stride, and some internal radar went off. He'd been running track, and had played football in the fall, and his body was lean and quick. He sensed Gene's move before he made it and stutter-stepped backward, so that when Gene went to grapple with him he encountered empty air. Gene lurched forward one awkward step and then caught his toe on a stick and careened, bizarrely out of control—speeding up as his feet tried to run back under his falling body—headlong into the trunk of the bad-luck tree. He put his arm out to stop himself and it sunk shoulder-deep in the rotten black wood, which was hollow underneath. His face smacked into the slick outer layer of mold.

Daniel felt the space around them go cold. He had an urge somehow to turn away as Gene was extracting his left arm from the hole
in the rotten trunk, covered in dark wet shards. His face was smeared
with black slime, and mirrored the shock Daniel felt. They'd gone their
entire childhoods without touching that tree, watching it get older and
blacker and more decayed, and this superstition they hadn't meant to
take seriously had somehow assumed ominous authority just by their
long-standing observance of it. There was a sense, now, of catastrophe.

"Gene, I'm sorry," Daniel said.

Gene looked at him, eyes still bugged with adrenaline, wiping his
face with his right hand but only smearing the black gunk there closer
to his mouth. Then suddenly he laughed, loud and open-mouthed,
bending and putting his hands on his knees. "Nice move there, champ.
You finally got me."

"I didn't mean to . . ." Daniel was so relieved to see Gene laughing
that he laughed along with him, though mirthlessly.

"Go on to Rory's," Gene said, brushing debris off his bare arm nonchalantly now. "I'll see you later."

The last time he saw his brother, Gene was given a three-day leave
to visit before he shipped out, and on the last day their father took him
on the long drive back to the base, not returning until well after dinner.
Their mother had said her goodbye to him in private, and did not come
out to the driveway that morning, so it was the three Tunison men,
standing around awkwardly in the bright late-summer morning. Daniel
wanted to make the drive with them, but Gene didn't want him to, said
it was easier this way. They stood in the driveway in the heat, hugging
as their father loaded Gene's bag into the trunk. "Write to me, will you?"
Gene said, and Daniel agreed to.

He tried to remember whether he'd had a sense of impending doom,
but he couldn't. The moment had put him on anxious autopilot, and
when Gene had said, "I'll see you when I get back. It's not that long,"
Daniel had nodded and smiled and said, "Okay," as if his brother were
headed to college or summer camp and not a war zone. He remembered
smiling again and waving as the car pulled out, remembered the sight
of Gene's red ear and new buzz cut when he turned to face forward,

and then when the car rounded the wooded corner fifty yards away he walked back inside. The memory—which he'd revived and isolated and filed away after Gene died—stopped there. He didn't remember what he'd done after stepping into the house's cooler interior, that part was blank.

Daniel was almost forty years old before he was able to fully jettison the idea that he might have caused his brother's death by exposing him to bad luck right before he went off to war. He'd told the whole story to Cam during the first year he was living in the guesthouse, trying to reclaim his life, and Cam's deep-rooted sanity had absorbed the notion completely. He hadn't tried to talk Daniel out of it, but had simply listened to the story, pressing here and there for more detail. In the end he'd simply nodded and smiled sympathetically, and from then on Daniel's grief over Gene had been untainted by superstitious guilt. It simply couldn't survive Cam's humane scrutiny.

All Daniel's gone people. Gene, gone. Rachel, gone. Ben, gone. His parents, gone. All of them gone so long that their goneness presided over far more of his life now than their presence had had a chance to. And Cam now, too, gone only two years earlier.

Daniel remembered waking in the armchair in Cam's bedroom and feeling the difference in the ether immediately, as if Cam had waited until Daniel was asleep and then slipped out unobtrusively just as the sun was coming up. Earlier in the night there had been upheaval, a lot of noise: breathing, coughing, groaning, Cam's enfeebled body shaking and seizing in a blend of acute distress and profound narcotic torpor. Daniel had walked across the house and gotten the home aide, Carl, to come in, but he'd said there wasn't much else he could do, and that Cam couldn't be in too much discomfort with all the morphine he was on; it wouldn't be long now. Carl was a good man, and he and Daniel had become friendly over the four months he'd been working shifts there, bonding over a shared love of music.

When Carl had gone back to his room, Daniel had called Cam's daughter, who was at home in San Francisco, told her maybe it was time, and then continued just to sit with Cam. He had been sure the convulsions were the very throes of death, but after a little while Cam had fallen into stillness, and shallow, even breaths. Daniel kept getting up every few minutes to check for life and then sitting back down when he felt the tiny puff of air. Hours went by like that. Then Daniel drifted into sleep, and when he woke in that soft nacreous first light Cam was gone. There had been no need to check his breathing. He'd known instantly upon opening his eyes that he was alone. He stood by the bed and placed his hand on his friend's now-smooth brow. He spent a minute there and then stepped to the window and looked out, as if he might see Cam departing, but the pale morning revealed only the dark wall of rhododendron behind the back lawn. He went to the guest room, shook Carl awake, and said, "Elvis has left the building."

It was just after Cam died, at the very time when he should most have wanted not to be alone, that he'd split from Tanya. She'd told him things needed to change, and Daniel had said it wasn't the right time to change anything. He remembered her answer:

"I don't know if it's the right time, but I do know it's the only time." It was hard to remember now what it was he'd been refusing her.

After the breakup, Daniel forced himself to dwell in the region of relief that being newly single can offer. He skated around the loneliness, sorrow, and remorse, and focused on his newfound license to relax. Like a man who's been on his feet all day and has come upon a chair, Daniel tried simply to appreciate the chair for a while, without worrying about the fact that it was located in a small windowless room with blank walls and no sustenance. By the time the chair had lost its luster, Tanya seemed part of the past.

GRAMPA JACK TOOK him to another neighborhood, closer to the ocean. They pulled into the driveway of a small white house on a narrow street. Looking out his side window, Dean saw an orange cat walking along the high fence of the house next door. It froze suddenly and stared down into the yard, its tail swishing fast, then jumped down out of sight. Dean liked cats.

"You want to come in?" Grampa Jack asked him. "I won't be long."

Dean said, "I want to come in."

"Okay, come on. But you can't tell your mom where we were, okay?"

"Okay." This made Dean smile. He liked all these new secrets, and he was good at them.

They went to the door. Dean wanted to ask whose house it was, but thought it might be a bad question and make his grandfather angry. It was hard to tell what kind of questions he would get angry about. A man much younger than Grampa Jack answered the door and looked at them.

"Why you bringing a kid here?" he asked.

"He's my grandson. He doesn't want to wait in the car."

The man leaned down and stared into Dean's face. "Celia's kid, huh?" Looking at him made Dean think of the kitchen sink, because his eyes were like shreds of the old blue dish sponge, and his skin was shiny gray like the metal of the sink. "I know your mommy," the man said. "She's an old friend of mine. Will you tell her Anthony says hi?"

"Okay," Dean said.

Grampa Jack rubbed Dean's head. "Remember what I told you."

They went into the house. His living room was messy and smelled like cigarettes.

"How is Celia?" he asked, talking to Grampa Jack.

"She's fine."

"Still clean and serene?"

"Yeah, she's hanging in there, far as I know. She just got done shooting a movie with Miles Rossinger. She's the lead."

"I heard she was doing that. Good for her. Too bad we never see her anymore, but I get it. Have a seat." He dropped into a big chair and pointed at the sofa.

"You got what I asked for?"

"Yeah, I found it. Had to make a few calls. It wasn't easy. Don't know why regular Xanax isn't good enough for you." He pressed two of his fingers against one of his eyes and rubbed hard, like the eye was not an eye but a bug bite on his face. "Going to cost you."

"That's okay. Just lay it on me."

"*Lay it on me*?" He laughed. "Far out, daddy-o. Hep cat. Why don't you take a seat? I hate when people want to just grab their shit and leave. Like I'm some kind of concierge service."

"You ain't even that," Grampa Jack said. "You're a dealer, and there is nothing wrong with that. Own your shit, brother, that's all you can do. Don't be ashamed of your station. It doesn't need to define you."

"Ashamed of my *station*?"

"Calm down." Grampa Jack sat on the sofa and guided Dean to sit next to him. "It just so happens that we have some time to kill, so maybe we will hang out for a bit."

"Yeah, well, not too long. I got other people coming by." He reached down into a canvas satchel next to the chair and pulled out a large pill bottle. "So, these are not for Celia?"

"No, they're for me. I'm the one who has trouble sleeping. Celia sleeps like a champion."

"Well, these oughta more than do the trick, but be careful with 'em. My pharmacist guy wrote some instructions on a note in there. Said be sure and read them." The man tossed the bottle to Grampa Jack and it rattled when he caught it.

"What's the damage?"

"Let's say five hundred."

"Fucking thievery." Grampa Jack pulled money from his pocket and put some of it on the table. "You know, I was in your line of work, back in the sixties. In the Haight-Ashbury."

"You were an actor?"

"You're a riot," Grampa Jack said.

Dean stared at the money on the table. Both of the men were now pretending it wasn't there.

"We gotta go," said Grampa Jack.

"One second," Anthony said. "I have something I want you to give Celia for me."

"Celia doesn't even know I called you. I can't tell her I was here."

Anthony reached again into his satchel and pulled out a thick brown envelope. He extended it toward Grampa Jack.

"What is that? She doesn't want anything from you, man." Dean saw his grandfather darkening, getting angry. He could always tell.

"It's my screenplay. There's a great part for her in it."

Grampa Jack laughed loudly, and Dean relaxed a little, hoping the joke would change things. "Aw, man! You kill me."

"Come on, just tell her you ran into me at Whole Foods or something."

"She doesn't want your script, Tony. Don't embarrass yourself." Grampa Jack reached for Dean's hand. "Come on, buddy." They went to the front door.

"Asshole," Anthony said behind them, dropping the envelope onto the table.

When they were pulling out, Grampa Jack said, "We're going to stop by Chris's house in Van Nuys now. You remember Chris from last month?"

"Yes."

"Chris and Hunter are with us now. They're part of everything."

"Do they know, too? About all the secrets you told me?"

"Yeah, they do. Most of it, anyway. Except how big a job you have."

Dean was excited that Grampa Jack was giving him an important job to do, but he was also scared. He didn't know yet what his job actually was, except that it would help Grampa Jack get where he wanted to go. He knew he had to memorize a bunch of stuff, mostly pictures in his head, but some words too, which he was good at. But what if he forgot something? He wanted to tell Grampa Jack about being scared, but wasn't sure he should. As they pulled onto the highway, his nervousness made him remember again the dream from a few nights earlier, and how much it had scared him. He didn't think Grampa Jack would want to hear about the dream either. And he probably wouldn't understand, because the dream wouldn't even sound scary if Dean described it, except it was. In the dream, Dean was standing by the pool in his bathing suit, facing the water. He wasn't going to jump in, but his mom was yelling from somewhere very far away for him to put on his swim wings. He was about to yell to her that he wasn't going in, when he became aware that Grampa Jack was right behind him. He didn't see him, but he knew he was there. And this was the weird part. Knowing he was there, in the dream, made Dean feel a fear in his stomach that was like the sudden ringing of a gigantic bell. The fear-bell was so loud it froze him in place, so he couldn't even turn around to see, and then he woke up. Looking out the car window at the tops of houses and trees from the freeway, Dean was glad he was awake now, because in the real world he knew Grampa Jack would never hurt him.

Twenty minutes later they pulled into the driveway of a little pinkish house, and Chris answered the door. "Come on in, guys," he said, walking ahead of them into the living room.

"We don't have to worry about your parents getting home, do we?" Grampa Jack asked.

"My father had a conference in New York, and my mom went with him. They won't be back till Monday."

Dean looked around the living room. The couch was dark brown and the white walls had big paintings on them that were very colorful but weren't pictures of anything. Just swirls and lines. They should have been fun and pretty to look at but for some reason that Dean couldn't figure out, they weren't. They made him feel tired. He said, "I have to use the bathroom."

Chris pointed to the hallway. "It's the last door on the left." When Dean walked toward it he said, "You're not going with him?"

"He's old enough. He doesn't need help. Do you, Deano?"

"Nope," Dean said. The hallway was dark and had light brown carpet. There was a thin rug rolled into a tube lying along one wall. Dean passed a closed door. At the end he could see two more doors. The one on the left was closed, and the one on the right was open with white daylight slanting through it. When he got to the end of the hall, he put his hand on the knob of the bathroom door, but a small sound made him look into the room on the right. The girl, Hunter, was lying on a bed on her side, facing him. Her eyes were open, and after a second she smiled. It was a tiny quick smile that let Dean know she was very sad.

Dean said, "Hi."

"Where did you come from?"

"Nowhere."

"That's what I thought. Will you come in here?"

Dean stepped into the room but halted just inside the doorway. "Why are you sad?" he asked.

"Am I sad?"

Dean didn't answer because he understood she wasn't asking him. More like she was asking herself.

After a second, she said, "I'm not sure why, really. It's life, I think. Doesn't life make you sad?"

"No," Dean said.

She flashed her smile again, bigger, with a little breath of a laugh this time. "That's good. I'm glad it's not everyone." She had soft eyes and a black leather jacket on, even though she was in bed. She was big, and pretty, almost as pretty as his mom but in such a different way. Dean knew from TV that grown-ups fell in love with each other. He wondered what that would feel like.

"What's your name again?" she asked.

"Dean."

"Right. Mine is Hunter."

"I know." Dean stared at her quietly for a while. They said staring wasn't polite, but he could tell she didn't mind. She just stared back. Then he said, "Well, I have to go use the bathroom."

She said, "Will you come and give me one kiss first?"

Dean went over to the bed. She didn't move when he leaned forward and kissed her cheek. It was very soft.

She was staring now at the ceiling. "Thank you, Dean."

"Don't worry," Dean told her. "You're going to live a lot of lives, and this is only one of them. My grampa says that's called reincarnation."

"You are a real trip, aren't you, little boy?"

"No. I'm just the same as you," he said.

"Really? You think so?" She had turned her face toward him again, and her forehead was crinkled in a way he liked.

"We're just living different lives. I think I had a hard one before, too, like yours."

She nodded and seemed a little afraid.

When he came out of the bathroom, the door to the bedroom was closed. He went back up the hall into the living room, where there was music playing now.

"Your friend is sad," he told Chris.

"My friend?"

"Hunter."

"Oh her. She's fine. She's just lazy. Likes to lie around all day and let other people do all the work."

Dean wanted to tell him he was wrong. She wasn't fine. But he sat down on the sofa without speaking. A new song started and Grampa Jack said, "This is it." Dean recognized the singer's voice. It was one of Grampa Jack's favorite bands, the Doors, but it wasn't a song he'd heard before. It was a little scary, with a good slow beat, *Five to one, baby, one in five . . .*

"Hugo met Morrison once," Grampa Jack said. "He said the man was a deep power source, one of those rare ones living his first life here, and maybe his last, if he found a way out like he was trying to. He was fresh from higher places, not mired in petty thinking. He knew it, right? Only one exit. Hugo said this song was like pure truth-channeling. I mean, *No one here gets out alive,* and *Get together, one more time.* It was about *us,* before *us* even happened."

They listened to the rest of the song in silence. Dean wondered about the line, *Shadows of the evening crawl across the years. . . .* He liked *You walk across the floor with a flower in your hand. . . .*

When the song ended, Chris said, "Maybe your grandson wants to go in another room for a while."

"Dean is hip, man." Grampa Jack looked at him, and Dean tried to keep his face from smiling. "Isn't that right, buddy?"

"Yeah," Dean said.

"In fact, you might as well know, Dean's going to be our witness. For ideal conditions we need at least three travelers, plus a believing witness, so that's why he's here with us."

"He knows?" Chris seemed a little puzzled.

"He knows what he needs to know."

"Okay. What about that guy, Bernie?"

"Nah, not him. That guy's a hindrance in the making. He does not project the right vibe. He's all clogged."

"All right, I hear you. And I really do think it matters where we leave from. We should use the same spot."

"You know, kid, it won't hurt, will it? When you told me you'd been up there and seen it, it just felt right to me too. I think we should try."

Chris frowned. "We'll need to be careful, 'cause there's this nosy woman across the street. She figured me out. Said she remembered the whole thing—even knew some of the Group and all, from back then."

"What'd she look like?"

"I don't know, old. Long white hair. But I could tell she used to be good looking."

"I wonder if it's who I'm thinking of. I had a little thing with a girl across the street, tried to get her involved. Can't remember her name now."

"Huh."

Grampa Jack looked over at Dean and smiled. Dean was trying to pay attention and understand everything they were talking about, but it was confusing. Grampa Jack turned back to Chris and said, "Yeah, so we should scope it out. I'll do that. We got a month till the date, so there's time. I'll call you. Keep listening to that song, and the others I told you about. Keep reading the chapter over, until you've got it memorized for real."

Chris nodded very seriously. "I will."

"Don't lose the paper copy. It needs to be destroyed."

Dean followed Grampa Jack out to the car. He still didn't know exactly where they were talking about going, or why Grampa Jack wanted to go there so badly, except that it was a magical place. He wondered what it would be like when Grampa Jack went away. Dean knew that before he was born his mom had been alone, without Grampa Jack, but it was hard to imagine it. "Have you ever told Mom about reincarnation and all?" Dean asked when they were in the car.

"You mean what I believe in? No, buddy, I don't think I have."

"Why not?"

"Most people, they get set in their thinking by the time they're grown up, and you only scare them or make them angry if you give them something that doesn't square with their version of the world."

"But you were grown up when you met Hugo, weren't you?"

"Yeah, well, it was a different time. Hugo was special. He had a way of saying the truth that made people really see it. He was like, magic that way. If Hugo was here, maybe he could tell your mom everything and she'd get it. But coming from me . . . I don't know."

"Maybe I can tell her sometime. She listens to me."

"That's true. Maybe you can. But not anytime soon, okay? You can't tell her all the things I told you, and you can't tell her about going to Chris's house or any of this. Okay?"

"I know."

"Someday, when the time is right." Grampa Jack started the car, and they made two quick turns onto a winding street.

Dean said, "I told Chris's friend something just now. Hunter, the girl in the bedroom. She was feeling sad, and I told her that this was only one of the lives that she would live, so she wouldn't be sad forever."

Grampa Jack rubbed Dean's hair. "You're a good egg, Deano. I'm proud of you. You're pretty special, you know that? It's not every six-year-old who could understand this stuff."

"There's some things I still don't understand."

"I know. But you will. The main thing is you understand that when a person dies, it's not the end for them. They just travel on into a different body in a different place. So when I die I won't be gone, I'll be alive in another place. And if we do everything just right, just like Hugo said, I'll be in a very special, beautiful place that's hard to get to, where Hugo and the rest of my friends are." Grampa Jack paused. Dean couldn't help that he didn't want Grampa Jack to leave. He nodded and tried to smile even though it made him sad. The car was at a stoplight and Grampa

Jack looked over at him. "I will always love you no matter what. You know that. People think leaving this life is scary, but if you do it right it's not scary at all. It doesn't need to be. You understand, right?"

Dean nodded again. "Right."

"Let's get some food, what do you say?"

"At home?"

"No. Let's get pizza. There's a good place across the highway."

"But isn't Mom supposed to be home now?"

"No, Deano. She's got a bunch of meetings going on."

"Again?"

"Yeah, sorry, buddy. There's not much for us at home. We'll go get some pizza."

"Okay." Dean tried to push away missing his mom, because he knew Grampa Jack didn't like it. They went under the highway. He looked out his window the way he liked to, with his nose on the glass. There was a long wire fence going by. On the other side of it was a golf course, and he could see people driving their carts on the grass, a man swinging a glinting club. They turned left and there was a bushy brown hillside that gave way to more houses, then a busy intersection flashed by as they crossed an avenue. Tall palm trees bordered a supermarket parking lot, and Dean let his eyes drift up their lean, dizzying trunks to the swaying tops borne aloft like flags. He wondered whether trees got reincarnated.

CELIA FINISHED HER meditation and transferred the green silk pillow from her lap onto the sofa. Being back at home and spending more time with Dean had helped calm her, and she found herself able now to meditate for longer periods. Where before she had topped out on good days at three minutes, she now easily managed ten. It tempered her fractured perception, thawing and joining some of the rifts in her. It was even possible that her core fear, which remained in place deep in her chest, was showing signs of permeability when she tried to breathe into it as her therapist had recommended. It wasn't exactly disintegrating, but she was beginning to think it might not be as monolithic as it had once seemed.

She stood, walked to the rear window of her bedroom, and looked out at the back lawn. She stretched her arms over her head, and then wide out to the sides, opening her chest, another technique Nora had shown her for breaking down anxiety: take up space in the world. The sun had dimmed into low western clouds, darkening the lawn, but the sky overhead was still clear and blue, the contrast adding peace to the green expanse in front of her. It still amazed her that she owned it.

As she watched, a coyote stepped from the rhododendron into the purple dusk and trotted along the hedge toward the corner of the property, carrying something. There was a patch of woods there, and just before entering the trees the animal stopped, placed what it was carrying on the ground, and turned itself around all in one deft motion, its nose lifting and freezing. It seemed to be looking straight at her, and she wondered whether from that angle it could see her through the window. It took a moment before she understood that the streaked coloration of the fur down its jaw and throat was in fact a stain of blood. In that primeval light the redness seemed to mark it as an envoy from a savage time, a time before this city, before property and lawns. After staring another moment, it bent and gingerly picked up its cargo, a small dead gopher, and slid into the woods. Celia was stirred by the moment, remembering the coyotes of her childhood in Arizona, but then she thought of Dean. She'd heard possibly apocryphal stories of children being attacked by coyotes. She'd never given them any credence, but then it had never been her child in the equation.

She heard the front bell ring through the closed bedroom door. It would probably be Leo. She picked up her cardigan and went down the hall to where Jack was already answering the door.

"Howdy, son," Jack said to Leo, who shook his hand and waved past his shoulder at Celia when he saw her coming.

Celia kissed Leo's cheek. "I'm glad you're early. We can have a chance to talk before the others get here."

"Yeah," he said. "I figured we might want that."

Jack went back into the living room.

Celia had not seen Leo in two months, and looking at him a smile surged to her face. He'd lost weight. The impulse to wrap him in her arms was strong, but she set it aside. "Step into my office," she said lightly, leading the way to her bedroom. He followed her and closed the door behind them. She walked to the sofa and turned, without sitting. The giddiness she felt was almost unpleasant, being both irrepressible and dangerous. She had no business feeling this way, and she wished it gone.

"How've you been?" he asked.

"Just fine. Relaxing mostly, though my agent has me taking meetings. Says I need to strike while the iron's hot for me."

"I'm glad the iron's hot."

She paused, then smiled. "I was expecting a pun."

"A pun?"

"Something to do with being hot for me."

"Guess I missed an opportunity." He grinned, the lost weight elongating his dimples.

It was true Renata, her agent, had her taking meetings, but only provisionally because they were still hoping to hear from Sterling Tripp. Renata said reaching out to him was out of the question, but it was worth waiting awhile before committing to something else, which was fine with Celia because stasis somehow suited her right now. She found her brightening prospects, and the heightened attention from Renata and

the agency, nerve-wracking. Renata kept saying the next move was crucial, and had Celia meeting with emerging indie directors developing
mid-budget projects, a diametrical change from prior strategies. It was
vital, Renata said, that the next thing, whatever else it did, cemented the
impression that she'd become a serious actor making serious choices. If
she went straight to some big studio project and had a misstep, it would
be easy to lose this opportunity to be redefined. But if Sterling Tripp
came knocking . . . all bets would be off. "If he calls," Renata said, "your
brass ring just turned gold." Celia had still not told anyone other than
Renata about the call from Miles about Tripp, and as the weeks went by
it was starting to feel like it had been a silly fantasy. Celia was secretly
relieved. At least it had given her a chance to pause.

Celia sat on the sofa, and Leo sat at its other end, turning sideways
to face her. "How's Dean?" he asked.

"Dean's fine. He's liking first grade, as far as I can tell. I told him you
were coming tonight, and he's excited to see you, though it's our neighbor Daniel he's *really* crazy about."

"Well, he only met me the one time."

"How's your little guy?"

Leo smiled, but then hung his head and let the smile fall, speaking as
if to the floor, "Gus is fine. He's good."

Celia didn't answer, knowing he was about to begin.

He raised his face up. "I told her."

"What did you tell her?" The blood in her body was all drawing in
toward her center. She leaned forward.

"I told her what happened in Arizona. I didn't plan to. I was going
to come here tonight without saying anything to her, to see where your
head was at with the whole thing. But I just found myself saying it." He
stopped, his eyes slightly vacant. When she didn't respond, he continued, "I guess what happened was I decided to tell her regardless of me
and you, come what may."

"How'd she react?"

"She was calmer than I expected. She asked questions."

"Do you think maybe she knew? Sensed it?"

"I don't think so. I think she's just a very poised person, more so than I realized. She asked me where you and I stood, and I told her I'd let her know when I knew."

Celia nodded, letting this sink in. "Wow. Okay."

"I didn't do it to put you on the spot. This doesn't need to affect your thinking about me if you don't want it to. I just decided to tell her."

She squinted at him, trying for playfulness. "Oh, sure, this doesn't affect *me* at all."

He didn't receive it as playful. He looked stung. "I'm just saying."

"It's fine," she raised a palm, "you needed to tell her, that's your business. So, she didn't kick you out?"

The thought seemed to take him aback. "No. But who knows what she will have decided by the time I get home."

Celia looked into Leo's soft brown eyes and saw anguish there that wasn't hers to ease. "Oh, man. You're in for some trouble aren't you. I'm sorry. I hope it's not *all* my fault."

"None of this is on you, as far as I'm concerned. But . . ." He sat forward and placed his right hand over the right half of his face, leaning on the elbow and staring at her through his uncovered left eye, which produced a strange bifurcation. "Where *is* your head at? Are we still feasible?"

Celia took a breath. "I have an instinct to be rigorously honest, fifth-step style, so here goes. . . . First off: Who knows what's feasible? I don't have a clue. I'm blank. But what's worse, what's really bugging me, is that I feel uncontrollably happy right now, in the shallowest fucking way. I feel like a kid on Christmas, and it's really annoying. This is serious stuff, lives are being shredded, children are involved, and I wish I could think like an adult. I wish I could just figure out what's best, what I want, try to put those into alignment. But I'm an empty-headed kid right now. All I can think is how bad I want to jump your bones." She paused. He continued to stare. "We don't have time, by the way."

He pulled his hand away from his face and nodded earnestly, suppressing a grin. "Well, at least we're on the same page."

Celia laughed. "Couple of jerks, huh?"

"Yeah, I guess we are."

She slid across and kissed him hard, then stopped. "That okay?" she asked.

"Highly okay."

THEY ATE ON the patio, the six of them, a dinner of tacos delivered from a nearby restaurant. Celia and Leo sat facing the house, giving Daniel and Tanya the view of the pool and the side lawn, and Jack and Dean occupied one end of the table. There was a place set on the other end for Gerald, but he hadn't come.

"He waffled all week," Daniel said. "But when the time came of course he had something more important to do."

"Is it a date?" Celia asked.

"I don't think so. Nothing so pressing. His friends were going out, and he wanted to go."

"He's seventeen, he needs to be with his friends," she said. "It's only right."

Tanya said, "Can't get him to commit to anything."

"It's not like I tried that hard," said Daniel. "It doesn't seem right for me to act like a parent. And he and Tanya are taking a little break, right?" Daniel glanced at Tanya.

She nodded. "He's coming home before Christmas," she said.

"In the meantime, I pretty much let him do what he wants, within reason."

"So he doesn't have a boyfriend?" Jack asked.

Celia looked at him. "Why are you so sure he's gay?"

"Come on. It's pretty obvious." Jack turned to Daniel, raising his eyebrows. "I mean, he is, right?"

Daniel nodded, almost reluctantly, Celia thought. He said, "Yes, he is. No boyfriend, though. Not as far as I know. He's got a little crew of good friends at school, but most of them are straight, I think. It's a small school."

"Must be tough, in that neighborhood," Jack said.

Daniel said, "Everything's tougher there than it is here."

"I get that," Jack said. "I just meant they don't exactly celebrate that particular kind of diversity as much as we do in Beverly Hills."

"Jack," Celia admonished him.

"What? It's not like I'm wrong."

Celia found herself unable to look at Tanya to determine her reaction. Her eyes wouldn't go there, so she looked at Daniel as her closest proxy. He was turning his head sideways and taking a big bite of his taco, almost as if he were oblivious. But she knew he was simply electing to absent himself from the moment.

"I suppose you're not exactly wrong," Tanya said. "Some Black people, especially poor Black people, have a higher incidence of homophobia, mostly because they're measured only against the white liberals whose voting habits they tend to mirror. Gerald gets full support from me and his brother, and almost everyone close to him, but of course his neighborhood—my neighborhood—is undoubtedly a tougher place to be gay than Beverly Hills."

"See!" Jack said, looking at Celia. "*She* knows! That's all I'm talking about."

"I wonder, though," Tanya said. "Why are you so attached to being right on this? What's your investment in it?"

"My investment? I mean, everybody likes to be right, don't they?"

"Yes. But still. While it's true that there are cultural differences between Black people and white people, I'm always a little wary when I encounter a white person who's eager to point those differences out. Especially negative differences."

"Wary? You saying you think I'm racist?"

"I'm saying no such thing," Tanya said.

"Jack," said Celia, "let's drop this, okay?"

"I will if she will," her father said.

After a pause, Tanya turned her attention to Dean. "Dean, what grade are you in?"

"First grade," he said. Celia saw him squinch his face at Tanya, showing he'd been listening to everything. "Grampa Jack isn't a racist. We learned what that is at school because a kid said something bad. That's a bad person. Grampa Jack is a good person."

"I know he is," Tanya said. "I'm sorry, Dean."

"Thanks for sticking up for me, buddy," Jack said. "Tanya didn't mean anything, I know that. Me and her are cool."

Celia gazed at her son's face and felt that rare enlargement in her chest that did not threaten to plummet into panic. Leo's silent presence beside her also contributed cool solidity to a moment that would normally have activated her anxiety. Dean looked up at her and smiled, then looked back at Jack.

"I saw a wolf in the yard today," Dean said.

"There's no wolves around here," Jack said.

Celia said, "It was a coyote. I saw it too."

"Goddamn, a coyote?" Jack was incredulous.

"They're all over LA," Daniel said. "Cam told me in the seventies that he had a family of them living here. But I've been here a long time and I've never seen any on the property."

"This one had killed a gopher, carried it right along the hedge and into the woods. Maybe two hours ago," Celia said.

"Is a coyote like a wolf, Mom?" Dean asked.

"Yes, sort of, only smaller. Wolves can be dangerous, but coyotes don't really bother people. You know, where I grew up, in Phoenix, we had lots of coyotes, used to hear them calling to each other at night. They sound like ghosts."

"Oh, cool."

"To some Indian tribes, the coyote is a trickster god. He would sometimes help you, and sometimes trick you and steal from you."

Dean frowned for a moment, then said, "I don't believe that."

"It's just stories, honey. You don't need to believe it."

"God is too big to care about us. Nothing we do matters to God."

Celia found herself expelling a short laugh, mainly from surprise.

"Wow," Leo said. "That's quite a thought, Dean. You a philosopher?"

"Old Dean's always thinking about big stuff," Jack said. "Always trying to figure the world out, what makes sense and what doesn't. Deepest-thinking six-year-old you're likely to find. Isn't that right, bud?" He rubbed Dean's head roughly.

"I can see that. That's pretty impressive," said Leo. "What other big stuff do you think about, Dean?"

Dean seemed suddenly confused. He'd been smiling at Leo, but now he looked down into his lap. "I don't know."

Daniel said, "Just don't become too sure of what you believe or don't believe, buddy. The world will always surprise you, and it's good to be open to it."

"Great advice!" Jack said, slapping the table. "Listen to Daniel, Deano. He's been around the block a few times. He knows a few things."

"Can I say something?" Leo asked. "Dean, just because God is big doesn't mean he doesn't care about us. Like, you know, the leader of a country might have a lot on his mind, but he still cares about the citizens and how they're doing."

Dean nodded without looking up. Celia rubbed his shoulder and gave Leo a look.

"Yeah," said Jack. "Like Trump cares about all of us, right?"

Leo smiled. "Bad example, maybe. Think Obama, not Trump."

"So you a believer in a caring God?" Jack asked Leo.

"I don't pretend to know much, but I think a higher power of some kind has helped me now and then."

"Why you?"

"What do you mean?"

Jack leaned forward over his empty plate. "I mean, why have you been helped and not the orphan in Bangladesh who's starving and working in a sweatshop?"

"I don't know."

"The lord works in mysterious ways, huh?"

"I didn't say that. I just said I don't know."

"Dean," said Tanya, "will you draw me a picture of the coyote you saw? I'd really like that."

"Okay."

"Do you have drawing things around somewhere?"

"In my room," Dean said.

Celia patted his shoulder. "Why don't you go get your crayons and bring them to the living room, and you can draw a picture for Tanya. Then you can have ice cream with us."

"Okay!" Dean trotted off, and Celia was relieved to see a contented spring in his step.

She looked at her father. "You think all that might be a little heavy for him?"

"What do you mean? That kid has a deeper mind than any of us do. He can handle a little metaphysical talk."

"Where'd he get this idea that God doesn't care about people?"

Jack shook his head. "Who knows? Maybe he made it up. Kind of makes sense if you think about it, though."

"What do you think, Tanya? You're a mom. You think it's okay to expose him to big stuff like that?"

"I think it depends on the kid. I don't know your son, and I try never to second-guess another parent's decisions if they're made with love. Different kids respond differently to almost everything."

Celia looked at Daniel. "What do you think? You know Dean."

Daniel nodded. "Obviously it's a personal choice, but I guess I agree with Jack on this. I don't see any point in shielding Dean from the fact that adults disagree on the big questions and don't have all the answers. Dean is a solid person, even at his age. He can handle it."

A quiet fell over the table and the patio, and, it seemed to Celia for a moment, over the city itself. There was a faint understory of sound, as if the ocean might be audible from this distance, though she knew it was traffic. Jack reached into the salad bowl, picked out a thick slice of carrot with his fingers, and crunched it, breaking the hush.

"Who's ready for ice cream?" he said.

JACK SAT IN his car watching the twin palms across from the house shift in steady wind. He was waiting for the woman, Barb, to climb into her gold Toyota Camry. It was his third day watching Jim and Barb Collins, and the house in Moorpark where he'd lived with Hugo's group in the '70s, before the bank robbery. The week before, he'd twice followed Jim to his job at a small Nationwide Insurance office. The office was a glass storefront at a dying strip mall in Simi Valley, and from across the parking lot Jack had watched Jim sitting at his desk, fielding calls, staring into his computer monitor, and meeting clients. He spent the whole day there both times, and did not go home for lunch, though it wasn't a long drive. He went to the Subway three doors down from his office both days. He left work between 5:15 and 5:30, and went straight home.

Jack sat in his car halfway up the block, waiting. Jim's car had pulled out and rounded the corner twenty minutes earlier. Today it was Barb's turn. He found he liked doing all of this, and it occurred to him that he probably would have made a good private detective. "Maybe I missed my calling," he muttered to himself. His eyes flicked to some motion on the left side of the street, where the palms stood. Someone came out of the yellow house opposite the one he was watching, climbed into an old pickup and backed out of the driveway, heading toward him now. As the truck passed him he looked idly at the driver, a slight woman of about sixty with straight gray hair, great skin, pre-occupied expression. As if from nowhere, her name popped into his head: Julie. He had forgotten about Chris's mention of the nosy woman he'd thought might be her. For a while in 1973, just after they'd moved into the house, her lithe teenage presence had gripped his mind in pre- and post-sleep fog, had dragged him through hours of fantasizing and scheming. He had tried every trick in his book on her, but she had drifted nimbly in and out of their little scene without ever becoming attached to him or any of them. Even at her young age she had proved herself formidable. He never got her to fuck him despite a couple of stoned cuddle sessions, one of them involving a very memorable hand down her pants. He had made her come, and the sound of her small glottal cry was engraved on his mind still, after forty-odd years, since he'd made use of it during many a lonely night in prison. But then she'd buttoned her jeans and left, saying, "See you, Jack," so blithely. Not even a reciprocal hand job. Seeing her now was a shock. His ruminations on the past tended to be nebulous and hazy, but here she was, a breathing person, driving a pickup and still looking good. She did not glance at him on the way past, and he doubted she'd even noticed there was a person in the car. He waited for her to round the corner in his mirror and then started the engine and spun a U-turn. Following her was a useless deviation, but he didn't question it.

A mile away she pulled into a supermarket and parked. He waited until she was inside and then parked his car two spots away from hers and went in. She was there near the entrance, in the produce section with her back to the door, standing over tiered rows of mangoes, testing them with her fingers. Just to her right was a folding table of samples attended by a thickly powdered lady in a red hat and apron. The table was lined with tiny paper cups of gluten-free granola—a tough sell in this joint, Jack imagined. The woman, a lover of her work, was beaming crazily at him as he approached. "Care to try some, sir?" she crooned. "You'd never guess it was gluten free, I promise. It's so tasty!"

"Well, now, don't mind if I do," Jack said, pouring one of the miniature cups into his mouth. "You know what? You're absolutely right. This is very tasty. I have to ask, though, what really is gluten anyway? Why's it bad for you?" Julie was still testing the mangoes at the table, six feet away, and he spoke loud enough for her to hear.

"Well, it comes from wheat, and it's hard on your tummy, I've heard." The woman paused. "I don't have all the details."

"Who does? Am I right?" Jack glanced Julie's way, and when she turned her profile toward him, he spoke to her. "You know what gluten is? What's so bad about it?" He felt absolutely certain that she would never recognize him.

She smiled. "Beats me," she said, turning back to her mangoes.

He continued to speak in her direction. "I mean, people have been eating bread for thousands of years, right? Now suddenly it's bad for you?"

She turned again toward him, with a personable smile. "I read a thing that said it's not the wheat, for most people, it's the chemical pesticides they use on it, which is why the so-called gluten intolerance is so widespread."

"Well, that would make sense, at least." Jack almost made a blunt joke about young people today being overprotected, a default icebreaker between two oldsters, but he remembered that she liked hippie guys, talked about politics and holistic remedies. Her father had been a college professor and an activist. She'd probably raised a couple of coddled millennials herself along the way. "Corporate farming has gotten so out of hand," he said.

"This is also organic!" the sample lady chimed in helpfully, holding up a box of her product.

Julie took this opportunity to go back to her study of the mangoes, and Jack conceived a rage toward the sample lady. These rages always rose out of nothing, materializing from empty spaces inside him like steam suddenly fusing and compressing into a needle. When he was young he'd been in closer touch with his rage. It had been a functional part of his personality. As he'd aged, he thought he'd become softer and more easygoing, but it was as if the rageful part had endured, somehow sequestered, and left to itself had become sharper, more vicious, and more autonomous. He papered this one over with a big smile and said loudly, "You know what, you've sold me. I'm going to get a box. Tell me, do you think it's better with yogurt, or with milk?" From the corner of his eye he saw Julie pick a mango and move on.

The woman smiled back, but when she noticed the intensity of his glare, she stammered, "I . . . well, I don't know. Whatever you prefer, I mean . . . either one would be good."

Jack leaned forward dramatically, inspecting the boxes individually as if trying to select the best one, though they were all alike. After an uncomfortable, too-long silence he picked one up, raised his eyes again to hers, and spoke very quietly, almost under his breath, "Thank you so much. You have a *great* day."

Her confusion clouded now with fear as her larynx robotically crooned, "You too."

"I always do," he said, walking away with the box tucked under his arm. He went back to the entrance and took a red plastic basket from a tall stack of them. He gave the sample table a wide berth as he reentered the produce section, and clocked Julie turning the corner at the back of the store with her cart. He meandered through the store, putting random items in his basket and keeping track of her as he went. He contrived to arrive at the checkout when she did, choosing a lane at the far end from her. When the kid at the register was done with bagging his items and accepting his payment, Julie was still in mid checkout with her larger cart. Jack made a show of staring at his receipt and pointed to the granola, turning it toward the kid. "I thought this was supposed to be seven ninety-five," he said.

The kid, whose spiked-chain-link neck tattoos were rendered ludicrous by his red polyester smock with the name tag reading KENNY, looked dumbly at it. "It says eight ninety-five."

"I know, but the lady at that table specifically told me it was seven ninety-five."

"Want me to do a price check?" the kid asked, clearly hopeful that this drastic action would not be necessary.

"Yeah, I think we should, don't you?"

"Um. Yeah, okay." He picked up a handset by his register, pressed a button, and said, "Price check on seventeen."

The woman in the line behind Jack sighed audibly. Jack looked at her. He was enjoying himself. "I mean," he said to the woman, "when someone tells you a price, clearly states it, and then they charge a dollar more, that ain't right, is it? That's just deceptive. We can't just let them do that. They're probably counting on it. Think of all the extra dollars they make in a year on a thing like that."

She crinkled her brow and nodded in grudging acquiescence. Then Jack saw Julie push her cart away from the register and toward the exit.

"Never mind," he said to the kid. "I don't have time." He dropped the receipt in the grocery bag and carried it toward the door.

She was loading her groceries into the bed of the pickup as he walked to his car carrying his lone bag. As he passed her, he said, "That granola lady lied to me, you know. Chiseled me for an extra dollar."

She glanced at him and smiled as if to commiserate, but did not speak.

"I feel like I know you," he said. "You seem familiar."

She had just placed the last bag into the truck, and she turned to face him. "I don't know," she said. "Do you live around here?"

"No, I'm just visiting someone. I live down in Beverly Hills."

She gave his face a silent appraisal. "I don't ever get down that way."

"Hm. Maybe when we were younger," Jack said. "Or maybe you just remind me of someone I can't place."

"I've lived here all my life. Though I did some traveling in my youth, spent some time in India."

"India? Wow, what were you doing there?"

"Studying yoga." She pulled her keys from her jacket pocket. "I should get these things home. Nice meeting you."

"But we haven't really met." Jack's instinct for seduction kicked in automatically as she began backing away. He could tell she was not entirely put off by him. Somewhere behind the standoffishness there was a door slightly ajar. He found himself channeling Daniel as he spoke. "My name's Daniel Tunison, I'm a retired English teacher, and current caregiver for my young grandson. I wish I'd taken up yoga back in the day, I'm sure my body would be in much better shape. Though I stay pretty healthy." He put out his hand and said, "Just to make it official."

She shook his hand. "I'm Julie Singer."

"I'm spending some time around here lately, so maybe I'll see you again. I have a friend who's sick and I'm taking shifts with him. That's what I'm doing here," he indicated the store by cocking his head, "getting him some stuff for the house."

"That's nice of you. Sorry about your friend. I hope it's not serious." She was straining visibly toward the door of her truck, but the bonds of social convention were strong, and Jack decided to intensify them.

"I'm afraid it is. He hasn't got much time."

"Oh no."

"Yeah, well, what can you do at our age. Mine and his, I mean, not yours, of course."

She laughed softly. "I guess we're all headed there one way or another."

"Very true. Very wise," Jack said. "Listen, would you like to get a coffee or something sometime? Just to get me a break from that house?"

"Oh. Thank you, Daniel, but I'm not really . . . available."

"Married, I get it. I didn't even mean anything like that, just a talk or whatever, but no worries, you have a great day, Julie."

"I really do appreciate it." She put out her hand again, and Jack shook it with a soft touch, smiling into her eyes as he imagined Daniel might, with kindly nonchalance. Her brow gathered for a moment. "You do actually look familiar, somehow," she said.

"I know! You see what I mean."

"Maybe from when we were young?" She was still holding on to his hand and staring fixedly. Then after a moment she let go and shrugged as if releasing the whole idea. "Probably we crossed paths somewhere in the mists of history."

"I like that," Jack said. "The mists of history. I shudder to think what you must have looked like back then." He laughed. "I mean, you're knocking it out of the park at, what are you, fifty?"

Now she laughed. "I'm sixty-one."

"Oh, well okay. I guess that means a slightly better chance we knew each other when we were young. I thought I was twenty-five years older than you but it's only fifteen or so." Jack wanted to try again for her number, but his instinct, which was still pretty sharp, told him to walk away. "Catch you on the flip side," he said, stepping backward toward his car.

She flashed her teeth and said, "All right," turning and getting into her truck.

Jack spent a moment fumbling with his keys, and then put the grocery bag in the trunk slowly, giving her time to pull out before he got in the car. At this point he had probably missed Barb, and he couldn't go straight back to that block of Ruth Avenue anyway, in case Julie spotted him there.

As he opened the driver's door of his car, he paused a moment, looking away from the store across the parking lot. The sun was bright overhead, and some of the small trees scattered through the lot had shaded off to red for fall. Cars nosed here and there through the cool glare, finding spots or heading for the exits, and people wandered to and from the stores, which were laid out in a standard L-shaped strip mall. It was nothing, a stock snapshot of American suburbia, but it was beautiful, and filled Jack quite suddenly with sadness. A breeze pressed his face and the bigger trees at his back shushed. Out of the derelict chaos of the unimaginably large universe, where the number of galaxies was greater than the number of stars in their own galaxy, people had fashioned, against all conceivable prospect, these quadrants of order. They were tiny, irrelevant, but they were also beautiful.

Bunch of sappy bullshit, but it was natural, Jack guessed. Everyone felt sad leaving their home, and this Earth, whatever else it was, had been his home for seventy-seven years. Maybe a lot longer. The chief problem with this world, it occurred to him now, might only be that you couldn't stay. You spent your whole life trying to find a tolerable situation, but even if you found it you had to give it up.

He envisioned, for the first time, the world completely devoid of himself. The barrenness of the thought opened a cavity in him. But then, also in that imagined future, the Earth retreated from him, shrinking to a drifting dust mote. After all, it wasn't him that would be gone, it was the world. Suddenly he thought of Daniel, their shared history, and snapped back into the moment: the breeze, the supermarket parking lot, Moorpark, Earth, the ponderous sadness still in him. His connection with Daniel, which he'd become somehow morbidly attached to, was now the impending loss his mind settled on—not his daughter, not his grandson. Daniel was different because their connection would be erased completely and instantly when Jack was gone. He was the only one cognizant of it. It didn't matter, of course, couldn't possibly matter. But it mattered to him.

CHRIS HADN'T SEEN a bird all day. As soon as he realized it, he understood it was significant, though he didn't know exactly how. He'd stayed home from school, trying to clear his head and prepare. No one really cared whether he went to school, but he'd used his mom's email account to write himself a note. Hunter, though, was under a lot of scrutiny, so she'd gone. She'd figured out that her mother had a tracking option on her car as well as her phone, so she would need to leave them both behind when she left school the next day. Jack was going to pick her up during second period. Chris wouldn't see her until she and Jack and Dean arrived at the Moorpark house, where he would be waiting to let them in. Jack was going to drive Chris up there tonight.

An hour earlier, Chris had stepped outside and walked around the neighborhood, both reveling and cringing at the feverish energy the exposure produced in him. He had stopped taking the Paxil a week earlier, but his mind had grown only a touch calmer. It wasn't until he got back from his walk and was sitting at the kitchen table eating a microwaved Hot Pocket that he realized he'd seen no birds at all. None the entire day. As he pondered what the absence of birds might mean, he began, involuntarily, to entertain some troubling doubts. He'd always trusted his birds, under and through and beyond everything else. They were a part of his life that could not be discredited. So, what if they were staying away because they knew he was heading astray? What if this whole journey was delusional and they were trying to tell him? He thought of the crow outside Bernie's house the day he met Jack, its gravid silence. It was also possible that he'd just been so preoccupied on his walk that he hadn't noticed the birds, though this was unlikely. To test this possibility, he decided when he'd finished eating to go outside again. He stood breathing in the kitchen before opening the door, trying to plumb the significance of every eventuality. If there weren't any birds, did that mean his fears were true? If there were, did that mean they were wrong? His mother would be home soon, and her presence would drive him back to the privacy of his room. He decided not to weigh himself down with pre-conclusions, to put them aside and go out.

One step down into the vacuum of space and sky, the fickle air, flat black asphalt under his white Vans, maddening void above, two steps forward forcing himself to keep breathing, and then he just stood in the quiet early dusk. Zero. No bird sounds, no car sounds, no human sounds, no movement. He scanned the sky, the bushes along the driveway. Nothing. His heart sank, but he decided to walk around again, continue the test, and to heed the result this time.

He became suddenly afraid. Fear was on him like a starved bear, crushing, gripping, and clawing. He wasn't sure he could even move his legs. Everything was at stake, and he was defenseless. But he was also resolute. He steeled himself and lifted his right foot, took the first step down the drive, when around the corner of the hedge, as if triggered by his resolve, came two buzzing projectiles rocketing directly at his face as if fired from a gun—his head snapping back in shock—veering around him at the last second. At first he thought they were dragonflies, but that didn't seem right. Tiny drones? Spinning his head, he watched them drop over the corner of the house and out of sight. But then one of them appeared again suddenly, with an almost invisible flutter, at the top of the wooden gate, just popped up and perched there, and he saw that it was a small green hummingbird. It turned sideways with a little hop and showed him its profile like something brand new, paradigmatic. An emblem of newness itself. The world of hope reopened to Chris. The bird produced a single high-pitched *chip* with a snap of its own head, confirming his impression beyond doubt, and all his savage fear dissipated. An unfamiliar bird was speaking to him, something that had not happened in years. There was nothing to fear because he was going to where he wanted to be. He looked toward a sound and from the corner saw his mother's car approaching. When he turned back the hummingbird was gone. Buoyant now, he hurried inside.

AT 4:00 A.M. Jack dropped him on Dorothy Avenue, a block over, and he went through an open side gate into a yard and then used the corner of the back fence to pull himself up and drop into the abutting backyard belonging to the house on Ruth Avenue. At that hour there was absolute quiet in the neighborhood, and every sound he'd made getting over the fence had seemed gigantic. Even his breath felt too loud. A film of silver moonlight clung to the house and lawn, and he could almost feel it draped and gleaming on his head and clothing. Chris looked around the small yard, heart hammering, and crawled into the space between their shed and back fence. There was just enough room for him to sit down sideways, arms around his knees. He froze, listening for any indication that he'd been noticed, but heard only a distant whine, maybe a garbage truck. When all had been quiet for a few minutes, he relaxed a little and let his head fall back. The moon was hidden from this vantage, but there were a few stars in the stripe of sky formed by the top of the fence and the roof of the shed, and their containment there gave Chris a proprietary feeling—these were his stars. At first he counted three, but after a moment he noticed a fourth, dimmer and farther north, just above the top of the fence. He imagined its dimness meant it was farther away. What if that was it? The place whose name had no linguistic corollary? The solar system where Hugo had gone. It was an idle thought, but as he stared at it the idea took hold. He tried to pick up a vibration from it, and at first its wavering light gave nothing away. Then it did. Truth popped through the skin of perception and spread like squid ink in his chest, pressurizing him, and he knew. He was looking right at it.

For the next few hours, he sat amazed inside his own charged awareness, and it didn't matter when the star dropped below the top of the fence. Normally, physical motion was a necessity for him when he was outdoors, the movement serving to smooth him and keep him present in his body. Sitting still outside for any length of time should have been torture for him, but with the Destination in sight he found he could let go and allow himself to experience the convolutions and obscurities of Truth and illusion—interwoven so closely, sometimes seamlessly. The riptide-power of the world against his leaky boundaries didn't threaten him as it usually did.

He flowed eventually from his body into the world, swirling up toward the vacuum of space, his body and skull inundated in his absence with a flood of the chaos that was the world's native element. The longer he sat still, the more irretrievably his human self was mingled with that flood, but he understood that now the world could not subsume him in its madness as he'd always feared it would, and that even if it seemed about to for a moment, he could ride it through. Soon enough he would jettison illusion. He was only being educated more thoroughly for departure. He eddied at the edge of the atmosphere, only distantly affected by the violent incursions into his body and mind far below, tracking the slow progress of the stars that huddled around him now, close enough almost to touch, orienting himself toward the one, farther off. A mockingbird chattered somewhere, bringing a smile, and that simple elongating of facial muscles brought him back into himself. He started over. Until it grew light there was nothing to do but wait, and expand.

When he heard the first car start, he looked at the clock on his phone, and it was 8:31. Just like Jack had said. But when 9:00 came he still hadn't heard the second car leave. He gave it a few extra minutes and then decided to peek out around the other side of the shed where he might be able to glimpse the driveway. He crawled along the narrow space, pushing his backpack ahead of him. When he got to the far side, he moved the pack behind him and pushed his head slowly around the end. The shed was in the yard's corner, and the side fence left a space slightly wider than the one he had just navigated, leading out toward the front. He squeezed himself around the corner and along the second alley to the front of the shed. From there he could see the gate to the driveway, but he was also visible to anyone who might be looking out the back windows of the house. He pulled back far enough to be hidden again. He hadn't been able to tell if there was a car on the other side of the gate. The gaps between the slats were not wide enough.

Chris sat on his heels and breathed. There was plenty of time left before Jack and Hunter were supposed to show up, but he'd had enough of being trapped outside. He was ready to have a roof over his head. Just as he was about to crawl out and creep up to the fence, he heard a car door shut, and then the motor start. He moved forward far enough to see the gate, and caught flits of movement through the slats as the car backed quickly out of the driveway. Barb was going to be late for work.

Following Jack's instructions, he waited exactly fifteen minutes, in case she'd forgotten something and had to come back. Then he pulled Jack's makeshift device out and spread crazy glue on the soft plastic pad attached to the end of a heavy screwdriver. He shouldered the backpack and stood up before stepping out into the lawn. Walk upright, Jack had told him, act like you belong in case anyone sees you from farther away. He went to the back door, placed the pad against the pane closest to the handle, and gave it two seconds to seal before putting the end of the screwdriver against the glass and pounding the handle. It broke on the second blow without much noise. The glass all stuck to the pad like it was supposed to, and he pushed it through as Jack had shown him, then reached in and unlocked the door.

When he was inside with the door shut, he had a wave of fear that someone was still in the house. He froze and listened, but heard nothing. He knew he needed to move beyond fear, beyond even the possibility of it. Fear of any kind could undermine and sabotage the departure. He forced himself to keep moving, checking all the rooms one by one until he knew he was alone. Then he went into the room that was set up as an office, closed the door, and sat down on the floor to wait. He texted Jack, I'm in, and Jack sent him back a simple ok.

Time ran aground now on the silt-bar of his mind, and Chris tried to stop his eyes from flicking repeatedly to the clock that sat on a shelf across the room. Eventually he stood and turned it around, but this was almost worse because then he compulsively hit his phone's button to check the time. He knew he didn't need to do this. The phone was in his hand and would vibrate when Jack texted to let him know they were close by. He breathed, trying with each breath to release all his fear of the world's oppressive chaos. Hugo said people survived here mainly by entrenching themselves in rote thinking and action, which camouflaged the chaos and bolstered the illusion of belonging and comprehension— but Chris was cultivating the courage to remove that crutch from his life. It was a prerequisite for intentional departure, for controlling one's own destiny. Hugo had set the example. The more Chris released, the more relentlessly the chaos coursed through him. He did not balk, though. He was ready. In only a couple of hours, he would step finally into the freedom of self-definition. This fact held him beautifully trans-fixed, even amid the foul currents battering him. The world was trying to reassert its ownership over him, but he let it wash through him unob-structed rather than fight it. Some thoughts were tougher than others.

His dad had tried all his life to provoke in Chris collections of emo-tion that would make him more comprehensible. The silent treatments started when he was very young. During these, he would see his dad studying him carefully for signs of the sadness or anger that were the desired responses. When he decided it had gone on long enough, his fa-ther would often say, "Act normal and I'll treat you normal." Invariably, Chris felt only confusion. When he got old enough to start guessing at what was expected of him he would try to mime it, with mixed results. It turned out, in the end, to be fairly good practice for getting by in the world.

Now, sitting on the floor in the small office with his back to the outer wall so as not to be visible through the window, he looked at the bottle of pills Jack had given him, sitting between his legs. *Fifteen apiece will be more than enough,* Jack had said. Chris felt the coarse fibers of the brown carpet on his hands, the hardness of the floor under it, the co-lossal weight of the planet's atmosphere pressing down on him, and the muddled gush of memory.

He thought of the cabin in Wilsonia where, for a few years, they used to go for two weeks in the summer. It wasn't so much a town as a group of cabins on narrow dirt roads near a miniature diorama of a town. Chris's inability to make friends with other kids had been a great burden on his dad, who hated the idea that other dads would see he had a weird kid, so he would force Chris into laborious pantomimes of play, whipping a baseball at him in front of the cabin, reddening and growl-ing at each small athletic failure. When Chris would suggest they play a game inside, like chess or gin, both of which he liked and was good at, his dad would scoff and say, "You'll have time for that stuff when you're old and gray." He would pull Chris out the front door of the cabin and point down the road to where some kids were kicking a ball and say, "Go play with them, why don't you." If Chris refused he would stalk off and stop talking to him, sometimes recruiting his mom into the silent treatment, so Chris would head toward the kids, dragging his sneakers in the dirt, looking over his shoulder every few steps to see if his dad was still watching. Chris would stand at the edge of the group staring at them until his dad got bored and went inside, then he would head into the woods and walk up and down a fallen tree he'd found, listening to the homilies of his birds, then jump to the ground and rip up moss looking for bugs.

When they'd told him, after his sister's funeral, that they were in fact his grandparents, Chris remembered his dad saying, "We never found out who the father was. She might not have even known, herself. God knows what kinds of people she was sleeping with to get drugs." And there was no mistaking the hint of relish at finally being able to verbalize his genetic disavowal of this strange boy.

These inert memories were swirled through with brutal living hallucinations; movies of violent deaths inflicted on his dad paraded before him like a presentation made by some phantom hit man to advertise his services. Bullets and chain saws and wood chippers and car compactors did their work in full color. Chris watched these with a certain pleasure, though he did not wish his dad dead anymore, but then released even that pleasure and was carried on by the current. There were other intrusions, some impenetrable and some shameful, but nothing could stop him now. He needed only release them one by one, let them drift on out behind him. And between them, here and there, there began to be glimpses of translucent golden skyscrapers, emerald oceans, multicolored suns. The Destination. The place he'd seen from the yard a few hours earlier.

He set his will to establishing a conduit between his position and that place, when all at once he came to understand that the conduit had always been there, glimmering within him. *He* was the conduit. Hugo had been a conduit, and so was Chris. He'd always known it, hadn't he? The chaos gathered desperate intensity as it lost power over him. But he believed now, and was comforted. Nothing could hold him away from the place he sought. He was in the Flow.

He didn't recognize at first what the small buzz in his hand had been. It seemed to take fifteen or twenty seconds to travel up his arm, across the bridge of his shoulder to the brain stem, and through the blinding gusher of intrusion to a place where it could be interpreted as an incoming text message. He opened his eyes and looked down at the screen. At first it was as if his eyeballs were vibrating, blurring the letters, but he tightened them down after a moment and could read.

> Kid, something's wrong. Your girl said she's not going to go today. She stopped answering my texts. I'm here at the school waiting for her. Will you try her? See what's up?

It took a gigantic feat of concentration to focus on the ridiculous little device in his hand, to give it the subservience it required from him, and a force of physical will to bear down and make his thumbs turn the symbols on the keyboard into language. Hunter, what's going on? Jack is there to pick you up. I'm here waiting. Everything is set!

Right away: Chris, I'm sorry. No.

> What do you mean?

I'm not going.

> Hunter, this is just fear.

Turning my phone off now. You should just get out of there.

After that his texts stopped being delivered. He tried calling but it went to voice mail.

She say anything? Jack texted.

> She's not coming.

Can you change her mind?

> I tried, she turned her phone off.

A long minute went by.

I guess we postpone. I can
come pick you up.

> We can't. Today is the day.

There'll be other days. We need
her.

> We don't. I've seen it all today.
> The exterior vision and the
> Destination. With my own eyes.
> I can get us there. We don't
> even need a witness. I'm in the
> Flow. Hugo said it was possible.

Kid, the plan is off. I'm coming
to get you. That's final.

Chris stared at this last text for a moment, and then put his phone face down on the carpet. The idea of being reclaimed by chaos entered him like a spear. How could he be sure it wouldn't happen? The thought was terrifying, and fear was the thing that could throw him off course, the thing that must be given no quarter. He picked up the fat unlabeled pill bottle. He stared at his own thumb, its web of skin, the fingers—strangers to him now—stretched across the smooth arc of orange plastic. He focused through the plastic on the pale elliptical pills, like spaceships, and his fear slackened. He took the folded pages from his backpack and read the final chapter through one more time, then used his lighter to burn them in the tin wastebasket, making sure no word remained in the ash.

JACK SAT IN his car at the corner of Ruth Avenue, staring at the text thread on his phone.

Just walk out the front door like you own the place, he'd written last. I'm waiting around the east corner. That had been twenty minutes earlier. Chris had stopped answering well before that. Jack had originally told the school Dean wouldn't be in that day, but when Hunter hadn't showed he'd taken him there, claiming a schedule mix-up. Dean had seemed cheerful, undisturbed by the change.

Jack spent half an hour running through the various scenarios in his imagination. There was, unavoidably, one that loomed likelier than the rest. If it was true, there wasn't anything he could do. He tried to think whether there was a direct way to connect him and the kid? He'd been using a burner phone bought with cash and a dummy email address for this whole affair, so it would probably be tough to find him that way. He'd never told either of them his full name or where he lived, which didn't necessarily mean they couldn't find out. Did the girl know enough to connect the dots? He didn't think so. He continued waiting, just in case the kid had nodded out or something. He would need to be gone before Barb and Jim got home, but there was time before that.

He was parked close enough to the corner that he could look about halfway down the sidewalk of Ruth Avenue in the direction of the house. He kept hoping he'd see Chris's lanky frame walking up the block toward him. *Fucking kid. What was he thinking?* Jack found himself suddenly rigid and trembling, his right fist hurting from the pressure of squeezing the cheap burner phone with all his strength, breathing hard and emitting a deep growl that grew into a full-throated roar. If his muscles had been as powerful as his fury, the phone would have snapped and disintegrated. He tried to calm himself. Maybe he was wrong. Maybe the kid's phone was out of juice and he would turn up later. Maybe he'd walked west out of the house and was even now finding his own way home. Jack felt these flimsy thoughts glance inconsequentially off the looming truth, but he was able to slow his breathing. As the blood-rush in his ears subsided, he noticed a rumbling sound under it that was new. He spun his head and saw the grille of the pickup truck stopped just behind his driver's window. Julie appeared around the front and raised a hand when she saw him looking at her. She stopped a few feet away.

"Oh fuck," he muttered. He waited a moment, gathering himself, before he rolled the window down.

"Hi there," she said.

"Well, howdy," he said. "Good to see you again. You live around here?"

"Yes, just down the way."

"Wow, crazy. I just pulled over here to use my cell phone. It's so dangerous when you're driving."

"Listen," she said, "I don't know what's going on, but let's drop the bullshit. It's Jack, right? I remembered you before, right after we parted ways. It came to me when you said *catch you on the flip side*. You always used to say that."

Jack looked up at her. He felt himself smiling. "Wow. You got a better memory than most. I'd never have recognized you if I met you randomly."

"So it wasn't random. What is it, then?"

"Nothing! Just nostalgia, you know how it is. Revisiting the places of my youth. I was outside the house that day. I just came to lay eyes on it, I'm not sure why. And I saw you leave your house. I thought I remembered you, and I wanted to see if I was right, and . . ." Jack tried to give her a disarming grin. "I didn't plan on it. Just, you know, spur of the moment, I followed you to the supermarket. I know that sounds bad. But I'm not stalking you or anything."

"But you're here now."

Jack leaned back in his seat and faced forward. He took a breath. "Okay, you got me. I guess I am stalking you a little bit." He grinned and gave a short laugh, trying to make it a joke, or a compliment. "Not then I wasn't. But maybe now. I just kept thinking about you after seeing you that day. You know how crazy I was about you back then. You broke my heart by rejecting me. I thought maybe with all this time gone past we might revisit, you might change your mind about me. Give me a chance. It's stupid, I know." He'd said all of this while staring forward through the windshield, and now he looked back up at her. "I can't help it, I'm a romantic."

Her expression did not shift. "And the kid? What about him?"

"What kid?"

"Come on. This weird kid appears staring at the house, knowing the history, after all these years. And a week or so later there *you* are. Out of nowhere. Don't tell me it's not connected somehow."

"I don't know any kid," Jack said, channeling his most sincere impression of Daniel. "Seriously. Whoever he is, it has nothing to do with me."

She gave him a long look before saying, "Okay then. Well, it's best if you maybe just shove off. I have no interest in reconnecting with you."

Jack nodded. This was in fact the response he needed, since further connection with Julie could only complicate what might be coming, but he found himself stung. "Okay. I will respect that, I promise. But just hear me out quickly, will you? You destroyed me back in the day. You have no idea. I couldn't get you off my mind, couldn't sleep thinking about you. And when I saw you again the other week, the same thing happened." Jack wasn't sure why he was pressing the issue—it wasn't even true—but he forged ahead. "There was always something about you, for me. It's a rare thing, is all I'm saying, to be affected that way by someone forty years later. You might want to consider giving it a small chance."

"Back in the day? I was a child. You remember that?"

"Come on. You were eighteen going on thirty. You knew the power you had."

"I was sixteen. And you essentially raped me that one night."

"What? Are you crazy? I could never get you to give it up! I tried and tried and you always put me off. If I'd wanted to rape you . . ."

"I always said no, but that one night you ignored me and did what you did anyway. I know you remember."

Jack was getting genuinely upset. What was she talking about? "What are you talking about? I used my hand on you that night because you wanted it. Shit, you even *came*. I know you did. I thought if I showed you I knew what I was doing, you might give me a shot."

"I was a sixteen-year-old kid, and that was my first orgasm. I didn't know what I wanted. You forced yourself on me, and I went along with it because I was scared."

"Come on," Jack said. "No. Don't say that. You know that's not true. You hung out after that, even. You didn't stop coming over."

She glared at him. "I made sure never to be alone with you after that." She was about to say more but he saw her retreat from it behind her eyes. She looked away. "It doesn't matter," she said. "You believe what you want, whatever helps you sleep at night. But please, leave me alone. Will you do that?"

Jack sat silent for a moment. He was angry and he couldn't locate a release for it, which made him angrier. He clipped his fury off with a quick smile and said, "Of course I will. Sorry I bothered you."

She spun and walked around the front of her truck. She did not glance at him as she drove away, and Jack started his car and pulled a U-turn, heading toward the highway. He felt like kicking something or someone, an impulse he unleashed on the accelerator. Rage gripped him. He pictured ripping the steering wheel off its column and throwing it out the window, stomping the gas and letting the chips fall where they may. He found himself, as he sped onto the wide avenue, plotting imaginary paths for the careening rudderless car—through traffic and across medians, into buildings and oncoming vehicles. Some of those paths led to fiery death for him and others. He was forced to brake and loosen his rigid knuckles as he made the turn onto the highway ramp, and it occurred to him, as he began to calm, that he should destroy and dump the burner phone before he got home.

PART III

2017

Dean woke thinking about invisible buildings and a purple sky. Then other things he had to remember crowded his head too. He was good at remembering, but he was glad they had some extra time. He hadn't been ready on the day it was supposed to happen, even though Grampa Jack told him not to worry, that he was magic and whatever he did would be enough.

Every night before Dean fell asleep, Grampa Jack would recite to him from the secret part of the book, the part that wasn't written down, and Dean would try and remember. Grampa Jack had said, "See if you can think about it so much that it becomes automatic. So it'll be the first thing in your mind when you wake up." And now that was starting to happen. He looked at his Lego robot on the floor, and thought about how that used to be the first thing he thought of, almost the only thing he thought of, and even after he finished building it he loved looking at it and feeling proud, and deciding when and how he would play with it. Now it just looked like a piece of plastic on the floor, and he couldn't imagine why he'd ever thought it was so important.

Dean knew he was good at memorizing because he was way ahead of everyone with his lines for the school play. Miss Parker said she'd never seen someone memorize so quickly. *The way is paved in blue and orange, don't be snared by sensuous red.* Then more about colors. That was how the secret part started, though he didn't have to memorize all of it. The part he had to memorize ended with something about . . . *exit cleanly and the way will shine clearly*. . . . Something something . . . a bunch more stuff, descriptions of the never-dark sky with three multicolored suns, the invisible skyscrapers above a shining clean city, people who could fly through the air, and then, *So do not cling. Do not cling. Leave fear and doubt behind*. Repeat that three times and then start over. It was a lot, but Dean knew he could do it. Grampa Jack didn't seem worried and that gave him confidence.

Dean's eyes followed the bar of sunlight on the carpet toward the window—sunlight always moved in straight lines, even on Grampa Jack's new planet that would be true—leading his gaze to the plant on his sill, which Brenda had got for him. It was called a Hindu Rope, and had grown wildly under Dean's loving care, stretching along the sill and nudging the glass as if trying to find a way out. Its bunched green appendages looked almost frantic in the morning sun, and Dean saw with excitement that new, small flowers were blooming at some of the ends. He got up and went over to look at the flowers. The green leaves, which were like fins, had turned yellow near the budding light pink flowers. He knew that eventually these flowers would grow into round clusters and get even pinker. There was a picture that came with the plant. Dean had named the plant Angie, after a song Grampa Jack liked.

He heard the door to Grampa Jack's bedroom across the hall, and then the soft knock on his door before it opened.

"Hey buddy, good, you're up."

"I woke up thinking about the invisible buildings," Dean said, smiling.

"That's great, Deano. You're a natural, I always knew it. You might be one of the magic ones."

Dean thought about this. It was something Grampa Jack had said before, that he was somehow like Hugo and Jim Morrison. Hugo had been new to Earth, here only once to lead some special people back with him. And Jim Morrison had told people about the Crystal Ship, which Grampa Jack said was a metaphor. Dean said, "I don't think so."

"How come?"

"I just think I've been here before. Like you."

"Yeah, like most of us. Get on dressed now, and I'll meet you in the kitchen."

When Dean walked in, Mom was making oatmeal at the stove. The stove sat in the only shadowed part of the kitchen, and there were planks of bright sun arrowing in from the windows at an angle, igniting the pale wood of the breakfast table where Grampa Jack sat with his back to the light, drinking coffee. Mom heard Dean come in and turned slowly to her right, looking over her shoulder. Her face emerged from shadow as she turned, catching enough of the light to make the whole world shine right through into Dean's body. "Morning, nugget," she said.

Dean stood still and silent because to move or speak in the moment would have taken over some of the space inside him that his mother inhabited.

"Have a seat and I'll bring you your oatmeal. There's juice on the table." She turned back to the stove and stirred. Dean went over and sat across from Grampa Jack, who smiled at him. He gulped some orange juice, which Mom had strained the pulp out of for him. Sometimes Dean didn't like how things kept happening one after another, especially these things, good things; how they just wouldn't slow down and he couldn't think how to make sure they weren't lost—and then as he thought about that he would realize he'd just missed a part of what came next and he had to catch up. It was better if you didn't think, just enjoyed each thing for a second or however long; but when they were this good it was hard to let them go. This was why running and swimming and spinning around playing were so necessary. If you moved faster than things you could feel calmer about them. You could even get ahead of them for a second sometimes, and then stop and breathe and let them catch up.

Mom put his oatmeal down in front of him. It had a chopped banana and some pooled milk and a spoon of brown sugar on top. Dean liked to stir it all together himself, but not too much, only in the middle so it was sweeter there, and he picked up his spoon and started doing this. Mom sat down with her coffee and some oatmeal of her own, without the sugar and milk, just a banana. He liked eating with her there, looking at him.

"Should we order from Italo's for dinner tonight?" she asked.

"Yeah." Dean smiled. He liked their spaghetti.

"Spaghetti and meatballs for you? And chocolate cannoli?"

Dean nodded.

"A creature of habit," she said.

"We are all creatures of habit and must learn to transcend and jettison those habits," Dean recited.

"What?" Mom said.

"Visceral experience of the moment must become our only habit," Dean said. This wasn't even part of the section he had to memorize, but he just remembered it.

"What is this?" she asked. "What is that from?"

"It's from his lines in the school play," Grampa Jack said. "Right, Deano?" He looked at Dean with his forehead all crinkled and his coffee cup touching his lips, but not sipping.

"Those are lines from your first-grade school play?"

Dean looked into his oatmeal. He'd forgotten for a second that it was secret. "Yeah." He tried to raise his head to meet his mother's gaze, but his eyes were pushed away, and he looked out the window. "Miss Parker says I'm the best at memorizing."

"Well, good for you."

"What day is the play on, bud?" Grampa Jack asked.

Dean shrugged. He was nervous now, confused about what he was and wasn't allowed to say.

"It's on the last day before Christmas vacation, isn't it?"

"I think so," Dean said.

"Oh man. That's going to be fun!" Grampa Jack said. He was smiling, but Dean could tell he wasn't happy. Dean could always tell.

"Yeah, we're looking forward to it," Mom said. "Should I invite anyone else, Deanie?"

Dean shrugged again.

"What about Daniel? I bet he'd love to see you in a play."

Dean tried unsuccessfully not to smile. "Okay, sure."

"Good."

"I saw the coyote again last night," Dean said. He'd just remembered that he'd meant to tell his mother about this.

"You did? Where was it?"

"Over by the woods. I saw him out my window. You think he lives there? In the woods?"

"I think he might, but I don't know. Coyotes are shy, and they live underground a lot of times. They mostly come out at night. We could go out into the woods and see if we see any holes that could be coyote dens."

"Yes!"

"Is your schoolbag packed?" Grampa Jack asked. "We should leave soon."

Dean was almost finished with his oatmeal. Most of the sugar and all the bananas were gone from the middle of the bowl so he jumped up. "I'll go get it."

He ran down the hall toward his room, and Mom called, "No running after eating. It's bad for your digestion." He slowed down.

THE GOOGLE SEARCH turned up articles about his work as an artist, and about his trial and conviction for destroying his own sculptures. He had a Wikipedia page. It also brought up the name of the original famous sculpture, *Thorn Tree,* which he'd built at a salvage yard in the Mojave Desert. Celia did an image search for the sculpture, and there it was, standing next to the modern art museum, taller than the building itself. It was huge, with thick, meandering branches and bristling snakelike twigs. Most of the branches, while not attempting verisimilitude, were formed with inherently natural shapes and gnarled twists, but here and there some were deliberately hewn into shapes that could never have occurred in nature: curving double on themselves and then back again to form tight willowy S-shapes, or turning straight downward at acute angles for a foot or two before continuing up and outward, as if infused genetically with lightning. The ancillary photos showed the intricate abstract detail with which the leaves and bark were tattooed. Sometimes those engravings looked almost like images, though never quite possible to identify, and sometimes they looked like written language, with runes and letters like none she'd ever seen. Impenetrable images, sphinxlike writings, otherworldly shapes, all embedded in a strange whole that exuded a kind of primeval beauty partially—but only partially—derived from its massive size. The main core of its magnetism lay in some mysterious cohesion that, even in photographs, came through to Celia. God, and he'd blown it up.

She continued to scroll down, and came upon a black-and-white photograph of a bearded Daniel, shirtless, in a slice of sunlight inside the doorway of a barn, with the trunk of his tree in the background. Behind it she could see where some of the branches ran out through holes in the barn's walls. It was a different person, was all she could think—different even from the haunted but calm man pictured in the old museum write-ups. There was a feral desolation in his eyes, and his lean shoulders and arms looked wrought from taut bundled guitar strings. She clicked the link, which said it was from a story in *LA Weekly* in 1974, but the story was not archived, only a scanned image of the page with the photo on it.

"What are you doing?" Leo asked from across the room. He was regaining consciousness after a short nap.

"Nothing. I just googled Daniel."

"Find anything?" He rolled over and kicked the covers down, but didn't sit up.

"Yes. I found a lot. He was a famous artist for a little while in the seventies, after getting out of jail for drug trafficking. A sculptor. He married Amelia Stander, a big movie producer from an old Hollywood family, and their Malibu house was like a nexus of wild star-studded parties. Then he went to prison again, for blowing up his most famous piece with a bomb after selling it for a fortune."

Leo laughed. "Wow. The Most Interesting Man in the World! Can I have *that* life story?"

"There's always more to the story. He lost someone close to him, before all that happened."

"Which only makes him more interesting, of course." He paused. "I like him. He seems all right."

"Yeah, he does. Dean has a huge crush on him. I liked Tanya too."

"Tanya's awesome. Loved her. Wouldn't want to mess with her, though."

"Nope." Celia stood up and went to the bed. She sat next to him and then lay down behind him, rubbing his back through his T-shirt. Leo turned on his back and smiled at her.

"I've got Gus duty tonight."

"I know."

"I should take off."

"Don't let me stop you."

"She's got therapy, and then she's doing something with a friend."
Celia nodded.

"She wants me to see her therapist with her."

"Today?"

"No," he said. "Sometime soon."

"Sounds like probably a good idea."

He smiled again. "I knew you'd say that."

"Yeah, because it's true."

"Celia—"

She cut him off, "Don't come to me to try and work out your stuff with her."

"It's all I've got right now. That's the only stuff I have to bring up. Otherwise we're just fucking."

"Then fine, we can just fuck, for now. Anytime you want, within reason." She snapped the waistband of his boxers. When her eyes drifted up to him, he was looking at her. He was not in a playful mood. It hurt her sharply to see how tortured he was. Not for the innocent reason that she loved him and didn't want to see him in pain (that was there, off to the side), but because she could see that his love did not lie solely with her. Amid the upheaval he'd struck a vein of feeling for his wife that he had thought was depleted, and it was giving him second thoughts. She rolled away and stared out the French door to the lawn, thinking of the coyote she'd seen there a month earlier. She had not seen it again since, though Dean kept dusk vigils at his window and said he had.

"You *could* help me, you know," he said. "If you wanted to."

"But I'm not going to," she said, maybe a little too quickly. She was still facing away from him.

He left a long silence, and she worried he'd taken her more seriously than she'd intended. Or maybe that she'd *been* more serious than she'd thought she was. It was supposed to have been flippant, but had come out sounding angry. She spun back to face him, and he was staring blankly at the ceiling. He rolled his head toward her and said, "Let's not walk away on that note."

She nodded.

"How about we talk about your stuff. What's going on with you?"

"Besides drama with my married boyfriend? Well, I'm a little worried about Dean."

"How come?"

"It's probably nothing, but he's so serious lately."

"He's always seemed like kind of a naturally serious kid to me."

"He is, but he's been more so. I catch him brooding and he won't tell me what's on his mind. He doesn't seem happy very often. He's always talked freely to me but now he won't."

"You think something's wrong at school?"

"Possibly. He tells me school is fine. His teacher says she hasn't noticed anything strange. Jack thinks I'm imagining it. But Brenda agrees with me, she sees it, though Dean won't talk to her either."

Leo looked at her. She was afraid he was about to change the subject, but thankfully he didn't. "How worried are you?" he asked.

"It's not a big thing. Just something I've been noticing."

"Well, I guess kids go through stuff sometimes that they don't have words for. It'll probably pass."

"I hope so. I'm thinking about asking Daniel if he'll talk to him, try and see if there's anything going on. That's why I was googling him, actually." She grinned sheepishly. "Sort of background checking. Dean might open up to him."

"You think?"

"It's possible. Dean thinks of him as a friend, not an authority figure. I'm sure it's nothing major, like you say, but it might be worth a try."

"I guess it couldn't hurt." He glanced at the bedside clock and swung his feet to the floor. "If there's anything I can do . . ."

"Does Dean seem okay to you?"

Leo thought for a moment. "Yeah, he seems okay. But I'm not around. I don't spend much time with him."

She nodded, freeing him from the conversation. "Thanks."

He went to the armchair and pulled on his jeans, put his socks on, then came back and grabbed his sweatshirt from the bedpost. He sat and put his hand on her hip. "We okay?"

"We are okay."

He squeezed her softly. "Seems like there's something else."

"Of course there's something else, you idiot." Celia shook her head. She let him see into her eyes. "Just go home and see your child, will you? We're not solving anything right now."

When Leo had gone, she took a shower and went out by the pool, setting up in the shade of the awning with her laptop. She and Renata had tentatively settled on a new project for her. There had been some wrangling, because Renata had pushed her toward an indie passion project by an established director, but Celia had hit it off with a young filmmaker named Frances Oyemi, whose first film had done well in festivals and won some awards. In the end, Celia had won out and they'd agreed on Fran's film, in which she would have a big supporting role, almost a co-lead, as a white mother of two Black children, raising them in 1970s Harlem while struggling to be a writer. The film's true lead was the husband, a union worker turned activist, but the marriage was central to the story and it was a great part. She hadn't officially accepted the role yet, but was going to on Monday once she finished talking details with Renata.

She sent an email to Frances, asking her to lunch on Monday. As she put aside her computer and closed her eyes a moment, she heard music drifting up the hill. She couldn't make out the substance of it at first, but the tempo was very slow, the instruments trickling in around the bass and drums, then a high electric guitar whose clean-coarse tone was like a razor slicing paper, and after a minute a thin ghostly voice began singing. She listened hard but couldn't catch the words. She picked her phone up from the table with the thought of texting Daniel about Dean, but then put it in her pocket. She stood up and rounded the pool. As she descended the grassy hill the music clarified, but it was unfamiliar. Morose minor chords, slow to the point of plodding, a dirge, but charged with some manic alien energy, the lead guitar bursting now into aggrieved yowls. As she reached the gate to Daniel's yard, the guitar finished a quavering oration and the singer's voice began again, quietly, to sing about death.

She pulled the latch and went through into the yard. The sliding glass door was open, but she didn't see Daniel. The music was loud, and getting louder as the song escalated. Celia walked to the patio and onto the bricks, and then saw him emerge from his hallway into the living room. He saw her and she waved.

"Hey," he called, beckoning her in. "Hold on." He went to the stereo and paused the music.

"Hope you don't mind me stopping by. I probably should have called."

"No, it's fine. Come on in."

Celia stepped into the house and followed Daniel to the kitchen counter.

"Want something to drink?" he asked.

"No thanks. What was that music?"

"That was the Grateful Dead."

"Wow, intense. I guess I thought of them as happy-hippie music. But I wouldn't know."

"Well, they did a lot of stuff. I actually don't listen to them, like ever, so I'm no expert either. That was from a live album, from 1969, that I just downloaded. Someone told me a while back to check it out."

Celia leaned on one of the stools at the counter as Daniel cleared his lunch dishes—a plate and a large bowl and cutting board—into the sink. She said, "I have a small favor to ask."

"Sure."

"It's about Dean."

He rinsed his hands and stopped. He came around the counter into the living room, taking a chair and motioning her to the sofa. "Is he okay?"

"He's probably fine," she said, sitting down. She told him her worries about Dean, and he listened with a sharp attentiveness that she liked.

When she was finished, Daniel said, "I haven't seen him much for a while now, so I can't say whether I think anything is wrong."

"I was wondering if maybe you'd talk to him. Ask him what's going on. If there is something up, like a kid bullying him or whatever, he might tell you. We could set up a visit and do it without making a big deal of it. Get you guys alone together."

"Of course I'll help if I can. Have you asked Jack? They spend a lot of time together."

"I have, but he insists there's nothing wrong, that I'm imagining the shift in Dean's mood. I think maybe he doesn't notice because he's with him so much that the change doesn't register. The only person who's noticed the same thing is Brenda, the nanny, but she can't get Dean to tell her what's up either."

"Okay. When do you want to do this?"

"I was thinking it might be ideal if I'm not around at all. Tomorrow night I'm going to this endangered species gala, and Brenda will be at the house," she said. "Jack is away down the coast visiting some old friend of his. Maybe you could come up sometime before I leave, and then stay for dinner with Dean?"

"Sure, I'm free tomorrow."

"Thank you. I'll tell Brenda the plan. Can you come by around five thirty? My date and I will be leaving shortly after that."

"I'll be there. Who's your date? Not Leo?"

"No, I couldn't take him to something like this right now. My date's Rafe Diaz, you know, from *Grandview High*."

Daniel shook his head. "Sorry, not familiar."

Celia smiled. "Yeah, not your wheelhouse. He's an old friend I haven't seen in a while. Some fun arm candy."

When she'd passed through the gate and was climbing the hill, she heard the strange ponderous music start back up.

He'll come to your house, you know he don't stay long. . . .

CELIA HAD AVOIDED most of the public appearances her agency had thrown at her since the movie had wrapped, but evidently this event was something she had to do. She'd chosen this charity benefitting endangered species at her team's behest a while back. It was something she actually cared about that would also serve as good PR. Their gala was, for that reason, "unmissable," Renata had told her.

So she'd called up Rafe Diaz to be her date, and had gone in to be fitted for a Givenchy gown. Renata had complained that Rafe's current profile wasn't very high, and had offered to find someone splashier, but on this point Celia had put her foot down. Everyone loved Rafe and always had, she argued. Celia knew what Renata actually wanted: someone who might generate romantic speculation and get her more media space. Rafe was gay, and one of her oldest friends from *Grandview High* days. She'd seen little of him since she'd gotten clean, but they stayed in touch through social media and occasional texts, and she'd heard that he'd cleaned up as well some months earlier. In the end, Renata had given in, consoling herself with the fact that while he hadn't worked in a while, Rafe's Instagram following was huge.

Two days beforehand, there had been a call from the gala's celebrity wrangler with the information that Darren Styles and Georgia Winstead were going to be there. "We always like to make absolutely sure no one is blindsided, and find out if there are any possible issues," the woman had said.

"I appreciate the heads-up," Celia said, "but Darren and I are fine." She almost said they'd recently worked together, forgetting that Darren's appearance in the film was to remain a secret until the first round of audiences actually saw it in theaters. He was being kept out of all the press and pre-release hoopla, and would not appear in the opening credits.

"Well, that's a relief!" the woman said. "We usually would have made this call much earlier, but somehow this one slipped under our radar until this morning. I'll have to fire somebody, I suppose." She laughed as if this had been a joke.

Celia didn't ask who they'd called first, knowing the answer. The more important person would always be the first call, since if the first one had a serious issue they could then call the second with the expressed goal of convincing them not to come. Darren would already have been called, and had obviously said he didn't have an issue. "You might not want to put us at the same table," Celia said.

"Oh god! We wouldn't dream of it. We'll make sure your seats are far enough removed to mitigate any discomfort."

"Thanks, but it'll be fine."

Rafe came over in the afternoon so they could have some time to catch up and then ride over together. He carried his neatly bagged tux and a small shoulder bag from the car and Celia let him in. Two inches of thick black hair—his signature not-quite-pompadour—rose over his low forehead, and his immaculate troublemaker's smile awoke in her all the former selves who had loved him: the timid teenage orphan, the venomous secret sad-girl, the intrepid pre-addiction party animal chasing that one fabled all-nighter that would transfigure the world. Seeing him also brought an unexpected wave of relief and palpable warmth to her breast. In the year since she'd sobered back up and gone out to Arizona to shoot the film, she hadn't seen much of any of her friends. She and Rafe had fallen out of touch years earlier, but he was as close a friend as any she'd had after her mother died. She'd seen him once since her breakup with Darren, when she had talked briefly with him at a party she'd gone to during her relapse.

She put her arms around him. "Oh my god, Rafey, it's so good to see you," she said, her cheek resting against his chest.

He kissed the top of her head and embraced her.

"How've you been?" She stepped back.

"Me? I've been good, honey. Look at you." His smile and dark eyes held all their old kindness and love for her, and then performed a familiar quick-flip to sardonic hijinks. "You been keeping up your tally?"

Celia paused a moment and then remembered their old game of tallying sexual conquests. One didn't need to sleep with someone to chalk them up, just get them to the point where their willingness to do so was undeniable. "Oh god," she said, laughing. "No!"

"Well, I have, so you better start counting because I don't think you've got much of a shot against this champion." He put two fists in the air, head thrown back and eyes clenched to an imagined cheering crowd, and then laughed.

Celia took him out onto the pool deck. She'd put out some snacks on the table, and Dean and Brenda were there dipping chips in guacamole. Dean was wrapped in his purple pool towel.

"This is my old friend Rafe, Deanie."

Rafe crouched and smiled and said, "Hey there, big man!"

"Hi," Dean said flatly, not providing the reaction that Rafe's stance clearly sought.

"Great to meet you, Rafe," Brenda said.

Rafe spun immediately away from the table, ignoring both responses, and did a little dance step on the flagstones. "Oh, look at your pool! Why can't *I* have a pool like this?"

"Go for a swim if you want," Celia said.

Rafe was out of his T-shirt, sweats, and sandals, down to his underwear, almost instantly. He was still thin, but softer, not in the kind of shape he had been before. He dove into the pool and surfaced with a whoop. When he climbed out, he chased Celia down and hugged her soaking wet, laughing, and this got Dean laughing too.

"Can I go shower?" Rafe asked.

"Sure, I'll show you."

They picked up Rafe's bags from the living room, and Celia took him to her bedroom and left him to his ablutions. Brenda had brought Dean into the kitchen to give him a quesadilla.

"Where is Rafe from?" Dean asked Celia when she walked in.

"Well, he's from right here in LA, I think," she said.

"No, I mean, where do you know him from?"

"Oh, you remember how I told you my first big TV job was when I was on a show called *Grandview High*?"

"Yeah."

"Well, Rafe was on that show, too, played the most popular boy in school. We worked together for five years when we were just teenagers. And back then, he was like my best friend."

"Isn't he still?"

"Yes, of course. But grown-ups have different lives sometimes, and it's hard to see all your friends too often when you're doing different things. So it's been a while since Rafe and I have seen each other. But we still love each other, always will."

Dean nodded and kept eating, his attention drifting.

"Daniel is coming to visit a little later," Celia said.

Dean's expression shot through a fleeting prism of joy. "When?"

"In a couple of hours, before me and Rafe leave for this party."

Dean nodded and went back to his quesadilla, his affect flattening again. The quesadilla was big, and she ate one of the wedges. "So I'll be out tonight, but I'll be back later and I'll be here in the morning," she said.

"Okay."

"Brenda will be here too. Grampa Jack is still gone, visiting his friend."

"I know."

"Okay, just wanted to make sure you knew the plan." She picked up a napkin and tried to wipe some guacamole from the corner of his mouth, and he frowned and spun his head away. She said, "Okay then, you've got to use your own napkin."

He picked it up and wiped his mouth, smiling at her.

Her phone buzzed in her pocket, and she pulled it out and looked at an unfamiliar LA number. She vacillated for a second, and then answered it. "Hello."

"Hi. Is this Celia Dressler?"

She knew right away. That voice. Nasal and clipped, New York–inflected. The voice was indivisible from the man: the no-nonsense genius, Bronx-born-Jewish despite the waspy name, iconic interpreter of the American street.

"Yes," she said, faltering. "This is Celia."

"Oh great, I'm so glad to get you. This is Bucky Tripp. Is this a good time?"

"Of course," she said, standing and hurrying toward the door to the pool deck, the phone crushed against her ear.

"Good. I want to say first, I saw some of your work in Miles's movie, and it's just phenomenal. Really. Congratulations."

"Thank you," she said, cringing at the childish lilt in her own voice, and then found herself saying it again, in exactly the same intonation, when nothing else surfaced: "Thank you."

"I'm wondering if you and I might meet. I have a part in this new thing I'm casting that I think would be great for you. It's a really good part. A big part."

"Oh, wow. That's amazing." She winced again and silently cursed herself even as she spoke. She was outside now, by the pool, and without thinking she continued out onto the lawn, moving into open space.

"Any chance you could come to my office tomorrow?"

Renata had coached her on how to handle this call if it came, but Celia's mind couldn't track down most of what she'd said now. Don't mention agents, she remembered. "Sure I could do that."

"Great. Can we say three o'clock? If you text your address to this number I can messenger over the script. If you'd like to take a look."

"Yes, fine." She really was locking up now, her throat swelling. She tried to swallow.

"Okay, good. Looking forward to it."

"Me too, thank you," she managed, and hung up. Then for a second she worried she'd hung up before he was finished. She quickly typed in her address and sent the text, deciding not to embellish it with a note. She could be no-nonsense too. But she instantly second-guessed that decision as well. She walked back to the pool and sat on the edge of a lounger, leaning forward, her elbows on her knees. She laughed spontaneously in ecstatic disbelief. Then her gut churned and her chest compressed with a galactic terror that rendered her infinitesimally small. She looked at her phone's screen and started to pull up Renata's number, but the knot in her throat constricted and she put the phone down. She breathed with great effort, looking up at the motionless treetops, and was suddenly ecstatic again. Then she thought of Rafe. She had to tell someone first and start to get her head around this, and there he was, an old friend. She would go in and share her news.

Celia walked into her bedroom. Rafe was sitting shirtless on the far side of her bed, a towel tucked around his waist, his back to her, hunched slightly over. He straightened and turned, saying, "Oh, that shower was nice," and putting the framed photo he'd taken off her wall down next to him on the bed, three tiny white dunes still on its surface. He smiled at her, holding in his other hand the tightly rolled dollar bill.

Celia opened her mouth reflexively, but nothing emerged.

"You don't anymore, right?" he asked.

"No," she said, closing the door behind her. She walked to her closet and pulled out the gown bag, just to have something to do. She hung it on the door and unzipped the smooth white front. "I thought you'd gotten clean."

Rafe stood theatrically, dropping the dollar by the picture on the bed as if he'd forgotten it before his fingers even parted with it. "Oh, I did a spin-dry in the desert last spring. Which was great, don't get me wrong, but I just needed to rein it in a little. Get my wits about me. I don't really do blow anymore. It's such dour shit."

"Yeah, I can see that."

"Well, you can't really do molly at a gala. Or any other *actually* fun stuff."

"I get it. You only snort cocaine in the spirit of asceticism and discipline."

"*Ha!*" He pointed at her to acknowledge the barb. "Don't preach at me, girl. Not everyone has the same brainwashed idea of happy destiny." He dropped the towel in a heap and pulled his sweatpants back on, then went back to the bed for another line.

Celia's stomach slid sideways. "Will you take it easy tonight?"

"Like Sunday morning, honey, like fucking Lionel Richie." He put the picture flat on the bedside table. "I'll save these last two for before we leave and then I won't do any more at the party, how's that?"

She nodded, knowing what he'd said was untrue whether he currently meant it or not. Her call from Sterling Tripp hung in the air around her head, skewing her perception. "I'm going to take a swim myself, I think, before my hairdresser gets here and starts in on me."

Rafe looked in the mirror and pushed his wet hair back. "Can I get in on that action? Just a quick primp from her?"

"If you're very good, maybe."

Celia put on a bathing suit and went out to the pool, where Brenda had resumed her place at the table and Dean was on the grass brandishing a blue plastic light saber whose battery had died. She put her phone on the table and dove in across the deep end. The sleevelike embrace of the water rinsed her mind nicely for a moment, and she arched her back and angled her palms, bending up toward the surface. She went to the wall and then swam a lap to the shallow end, rested her arms on the tiled border. As soon as she stopped moving she was reinvaded, and she recognized another feeling now, an old companion. It wasn't a thought or desire or craving, or even a fear, nothing so direct and deflectable; it was the old ruthless alien signal, the buzzing in her cells throttled to a high whine as if she were an antenna. A swim wasn't going to help.

"Deanie, will you get me my phone off the table?"

He said, "You mean retrieve Obi-Wan's message from the Empire's flagship?"

"Yes, that's exactly what I mean. Without it the galaxy won't survive."

"Yes, Princess." He ran to the table, struck down two imaginary guards, then struck down Brenda, who looked up from her phone long enough to pretend to die. He grabbed Celia's phone. When he got to her, he presented it ceremoniously.

"Thank you, brave Jedi."

"I must go!" he yelled, and ran across the grass.

She texted Leo, Got a second?

She closed her eyes and breathed. She thought then of Frances Oyemi, and felt mortified. Their lunch would have to be canceled. Then came Leo's response: What's up?

> My date is currently blowing
> rails in my bedroom . . .

You ok?

> Sort of . . .

Give me a minute.

She turned the ringer on, got out of the pool, and dried off. It was cooling into evening, and she sat in the sun as she waited for Leo's call.

"I WANT TO take a rest before the rematch," Daniel said. "My arm is tired." He sat sideways on one of the pool loungers. They'd held a competition with Dean's foam archery set. Daniel glanced over at the target, which was on a tree near the pool with the three plastic arrows of Dean's winning round hanging limply from it. The rings of the target were fuzzy and the arrows had soft Velcro balls on the ends. The bow was air powered, and shooting it meant shoving a pump forward to launch the arrow. They flew surprisingly far. Dean dropped the bow and went and got his light saber from the table. He brought it over to where Daniel sat and held it high for a moment, staring past it at the sky. Then he lowered it and seemed to lose interest, dropping it by the chair next to Daniel's. He looked momentarily as though he was going to sit down, but remained standing, immobile, staring away from Daniel toward the tree where the target was.

"How are you liking school these days?" Daniel asked.

Dean shrugged. "It's good."

"You like your teachers?"

"I only have one. Miss Parker."

"You like her?"

"Yeah."

"And the kids in your class?"

"They're nice."

"Anybody you don't like? I remember when I was in school, there were a couple of kids who were so mean."

Dean seemed to consider this. He turned to face Daniel. "Not really. Peter stole half my brownie on Friday."

"Does he do that kind of stuff a lot?"

"No. He's my friend, actually. Sometimes he's annoying. But I like him."

Daniel nodded. He kicked his feet up onto the lounger and lay back. Dean sat in the chair next to him. Daniel gazed over the western treetops, where the sky was still dusty blue. Something occurred to him. "Hey Dean, remember when we all had dinner out here a little while ago?"

"Yeah."

"You said something that was kind of interesting. Got me thinking. You said that God was too big to care about us or anything we did. Do you remember that?"

"Yeah."

"You think it's true?"

A pause. "I don't know."

"How'd you think of that? I mean, did someone say it to you?"

A longer pause. "That's what Grampa Jack says."

"Oh, okay. Is there other stuff he says? Like about God or anything like that?"

The boy looked down and scraped his fingernail against the blue canvas of the chair by his thigh, making a rhythmic sound. Without looking up he said, "Not really."

"It's just that I'm interested in stuff like that, about the world and God and everything. I'm interested in finding out what people think."

Dean nodded. He looked at Daniel and smiled suddenly, a release of pressure, but he didn't speak.

"So, your Grampa Jack does believe in God?"

The boy's eyes grew distant. He leaned down and picked his light saber up off the ground, slow-motion swung it at imaginary targets. "Yeah, but he says it doesn't matter. God made us but never thinks about us. He's far away."

"Wow. That's kind of a sad thought, don't you think?"

"I don't know." He looked at Daniel. "Not really. Grampa Jack says that . . ." Now he fell silent.

"Says what?"

Dean stood up quickly, the tip of the light saber falling to rest on the ground. "Can we go around back and look for the coyote? He comes out this time of day. Sometimes I see him from the window."

"Sure, buddy."

Daniel followed Dean around to the rear of the house, where the wide lawn sloped toward a long hedge of rhododendron that marked the northern border of the property. Behind it was a wall, but the rho-dodendron had grown tall enough to obscure it.

"We have to be really quiet," Dean whispered, heading for a stone bench on a small unused patio. "We can't talk at all, otherwise we'll scare him away."

From the bench they could see the patch of woods at the northeast corner of the property. It covered about five thousand square feet, and had probably once been part of the acres of old woods across the road, which buffered a larger estate from the rest of the neighborhood. Dean pointed to the place where the trees and the hedge met, whispering, "He usually comes out right over there."

"Okay," Daniel whispered back.

"No more talking now."

They sat under the purpling sky and watched the tree line for a long time. Daniel resisted checking his phone. The only person he ever heard from was Tanya, anyway, and she was at work. The boy stayed abso-lutely still, and Daniel marveled at his patience. He wanted to ask more about Jack's metaphysics, whatever it was Dean had quit talking about, but he knew he had to wait. After a while, with the light failing and the constellations of leaves shifting more and more invisibly in the breeze, trees smudging into one another, Daniel slid into a shallow reverie. The thought of the coyote evaporated completely from his mind, so that for a second he was startled when the pale form drifted, wraith-like and silent, onto the black expanse of grass. Daniel put his hand on Dean's shoulder in case he had become distracted, but the boy was looking right at it.

She stopped. After a moment standing still, gazing across the lawn but not at them, she swung her head around and looked behind her, and as if by signal, two pups trotted out of the woods and joined her. The three of them loped along the hedge, the mother sniffing at its edges as she went, and when they reached the middle where there was a partially overgrown break in the rhododendron, they stopped again. She stared into the dark gap in the hedge, and the pups began quietly to romp be-hind her, knocking each other over. A small yip carried across the grass to where Daniel and Dean sat. The mother ran a tight circle around her pups, nosed them apart, and all three disappeared into the hedge. Daniel and Dean waited, stone-still, to see if they would reemerge, but they didn't. He remembered now that there was an old wrought-iron gate behind that gap, in the center of the wall, that faced out onto the street. They had probably slipped through it, heading to the larger woods across the road.

"Wow," Daniel whispered.

Dean looked up at him and beamed. "Puppies," he whispered.

"Have you seen them before?"

"No. I thought the coyote was a boy, but I guess it's their mom." He turned again and looked after them. "My mom said we could go to the woods one day and see if we can find the den. Can we go now?"

"It's getting pretty dark," Daniel said. "We'd better not. Besides, if you've seen the mother there a few times, they probably do live there. If we go and put our smell around the den, they might decide not to come back. Might be better to just watch for them in the evenings."

Dean stared into the darkness toward the almost-invisible cleft in the hedge where the coyotes had disappeared. "You're right," he said. "We should leave them alone." He paused a second. "She seems like she's a good mom, doesn't she?"

"Yes, she does." Daniel saw a way in. "You know, your mom is a good mom too. You're lucky to have such a good mom. When I was a kid, my mom didn't notice much that was good about me and my brother. She loved us, but she made us so stressed out because she needed us to be exactly the way she wanted all the time, and we never quite were. Your mom works a lot, like mine did, but she seems like she really cares how you're doing and lets you be you. She's in tune with you."

Dean said, "Yeah." He was still staring away, and it wasn't clear if he'd listened closely.

"Do you miss her when she goes away?"

"Yeah."

"But you've got your Grampa Jack too. He keeps you from getting lonely, or too sad."

"Uh-huh."

"He's good to you when your mom's not around, right?"

Dean looked at Daniel, and Daniel saw his expression drop into the moment like a tumbler in a lock falling into place. "Grampa Jack knows a lot of things."

"I'm sure he does. Like what?"

"Things he learned in a magical time when he was young."

"What kind of things?"

Dean looked away again, cocking his head toward the growing darkness. It was possible his young eyes could make out things there that Daniel's eyes were blind to.

"Dean? Are you afraid of something?"

The boy dropped his gaze to the flagstones at their feet. "I did have a scary dream a little while ago."

"What was scary about it?"

"I don't know why it was scary."

"Tell me about it."

"I was standing by the pool, and Mom was yelling from inside the house for me to put my wings on, but I didn't need them because I wasn't going to jump in. Grampa Jack was there too."

"What was he doing?"

"Nothing. I couldn't see him, but I knew he was right behind me, and I got really scared, and then I woke up."

"Were you scared he was going to push you in?"

Dean shook his head, but also shrugged. "Maybe I was scared of that. I don't know." He gasped suddenly and looked at Daniel. "I just remembered something else! You were in the dream, sort of, too."

"I was?"

"Well, that's what I was doing by the pool, listening to some music coming from your house. I was trying to hear it, because it was such pretty music."

"But you were scared?"

"I guess, but not at first. First I just heard the music." He pursed his lips. "Grampa Jack would never hurt me, though."

"Of course he wouldn't. But sometimes if we're scared in a dream, it means we're scared in real life, maybe of something different."

"I think it's time for bed," Dean said, with surprising finality.

Daniel nodded. "Okay, let's go inside." He stood up.

As they walked around the corner of the house, Dean said, "You had a brother?"

"Yes. Eugene."

"How did he die?"

"He died in the war in Vietnam. A long time ago, when I was just a teenager."

"Do you miss him?"

"Sure, I still miss him. I don't think about him as much as I used to, but when I do, I miss him. He was a good person. A good brother. Hey, Dean, how did you know he was dead?"

Dean stopped walking. They were in the grass ten yards from the pool deck. The lights in and around the pool were off, and only a faint haze of incandescence from inside the house shivered on the black surface of the water. He looked up at Daniel, his face serious.

"I just thought he was."

"Well, you were right." Daniel moved forward. Dean followed and took his hand.

"He probably got reincarnated, so don't worry."

Daniel took a breath, thinking of Gene. "Is that something your Grampa taught you about too?"

"Yes, but it's a secret, kind of. I can't tell you more, okay?"

"Okay."

"You're not mad, are you?"

"No, of course not. Definitely not."

"Good."

Inside, Daniel handed the boy off to Brenda, ruffled his hair and said good night. "Tell Celia I'll give her a call tomorrow," he said to Brenda. Dean, who had been starting to walk away toward his room, spun around and leapt across the distance between himself and Daniel, attaching himself to Daniel's side, hugging tight around his waist.

"Thanks, my friend," Daniel said, rubbing his back. "You have a good sleep."

Dean said, "Okay, my friend."

Daniel walked down the hill to his house, using his phone's flashlight to see his way through the gate in the back fence. He opened the sliding glass door, but found he didn't feel like being inside yet. He closed the screen against insects and sat in his Adirondack chair, resting his head back on the slats and looking up at the multiplying stars. The same November stars, it came to him now, that he'd stared up at from Venice Beach with Rachel almost fifty years earlier, a guitar sing-along and various rowdy conversations, along with the sounds of roller skates and bicycles, drifting to them from the boardwalk thirty yards away, cool sand cupping the back of his skull and Rachel's fingers tickling his palm. The song the people were singing, he remembered, was "Proud Mary." The moment rose undiminished from blurred obscurity, as if preserved in amber, though nothing on either side of it was clear enough to pin down, and rather than push it away, Daniel inhaled it, his lungs trembling. It was starting to get cold.

He MOVED THROUGH cool blue daybreak down the main driveway. The old iron gate at the bottom, with its thick rusted bars and arcing flourishes along the top, had stood open for as long as he'd lived there. It was woven through and held fast now by the morning glory vine that topped the wall against which it sat. He had a regular route. He would make a right at the street and then a pair of lefts and up the hill to Coldwater Canyon Park, around the small park, sit for a while there, and back the way he came. He sometimes thought about getting a dog to force himself to make these early morning walks more regular, but kept finding reasons to put off a trip to the shelter. As he rounded the corner onto the sidewalk, he noticed a girl across the street, directly opposite the mouth of the driveway. She was leaning on a green Range Rover and staring at her phone. She glanced up at Daniel and seemed to scrutinize him before looking back down at the screen. She had spiky black hair and broad shoulders, and was maybe eighteen. Daniel continued on his way, assuming she was waiting for someone.

He'd lived in California for fifty years and still, on this standard-issue morning with the sun's blue influence just beginning to steal westward over Los Angeles—over lawns, palms, and hedges, streets and freeways, over houses and condos and projects and mansions, over the makeshift tarp hovels that clustered along vacant lots and in the compressed corners underneath ramps and overpasses (always invisible from neighborhoods like the one he lived in), the sky bluing smoothly out toward the dark-breathing ocean, illuminating all that human endeavor and green effusion—still, he experienced the dumb awe of the transplanted East-Coaster. He had never completely lost that mythic sense of California.

It was early enough that there was no foot traffic and very little car traffic on the street. A Tesla whispered by going the same direction as him and turned south toward Sunset. Then there was quiet, no breeze disturbing the manicured trees, only scattered bird sounds and that yawning of time engendered by the early morning outdoors. His memory from the night before of being on the beach with Rachel licked like a flame at his mind. It felt good to move his body, to knock loose and integrate some of the regret that could infect his mornings. It was not clear to him whether these worms of regret were a common experience for people moving into old age, or a unique result of his own shortcomings. At their worst they felt elemental and untraceable, which marked them as possibly universal (or maybe clinical). But sometimes he had no trouble attaching them to the actions and inactions of his life. His absence from his mother's deathbed, from Rachel's fatal moment, from Forest's childhood, all bubbled up to take their turns chanting at him, sometimes merging in somber harmony. His failure with Tanya was a currently resurgent theme, drawn back out by their rekindling. It made him realize how afraid he was of her, of what she represented for him; after all, if they were truly rekindling then why rehash the past? Because, it had come to him, he might be about to repeat it. These regrets and fears flourished some mornings, crowding through his chest, but were usually safely back in their compartments by evening. Daniel picked up his pace, striding around another corner and pushing himself uphill until he felt his heart rate plateau and his breathing settle into a good strong rhythm.

When he got to the park, he sat on a bench. It was full light now, and there was a jogger circling the park's outer path, a man close to Daniel's age in a maroon tracksuit, running slowly and shadowboxing. As he came around the path in front of Daniel they made chance eye contact as he neared, his gray-whiskered face a mask of ferocity, and Daniel smiled at him. The smile seemed to offend the man, and his expression flashed from fierce to hostile. He hadn't known Daniel was there, had been surprised in a private moment, and sudden embarrassment had made him angry. He looked away, grunted, and punched his invisible foe with extra violence as he continued to circle. Daniel almost laughed, but underneath its absurdity the moment made him sad, and mirth curdled in his throat. *Why are people all such wrecks inside?* he wondered.

Where were the people who understood him? The ones who'd shared his early times had disappeared, died, or, like Amelia, seemed to have unbound themselves successfully from those times. How might one go about that? He was visited by a familiar sense of being marooned in a false future, one that had splintered off the night Rachel died, as if the intervening forty-eight years had been an extremely persistent delusion. It came to him, not for the first time, that he had perhaps cultivated, or at least nurtured, this sense, rather than passively being plagued by it. Usually he let himself off the hook, but now he pressed this thought. Because, in fact, real life had been happening all along, not requiring his permission or his confidence, hadn't it? And he'd been a participant in spite of his dislocated stance. Had he forgotten how to truly engage? Was it still possible? He sighed, whispered *"Fuck"* under his breath. He didn't want to chance the touchy jogger passing by a second time, so he stood and set off again. Instead of heading toward home, he walked uphill.

Above the park he walked along the green fencing of the Franklin Canyon Orange Grove, the street and the sidewalk empty of people. Approaching the place where Beverly Drive peeled away from the hilly grove on the right, he stopped. Without interrogating the impulse he sat down on the sidewalk with his back against the wire fence. He let his neck release the weight of his skull, raising his eyes, and felt as if he were drinking the sky, the moment, this city that was his home. He thought he would weep, but didn't start yet. Instead, he thought about Forest's paintings, which captured secret lives that transcended the livers, the high-drama alternate reality of amalgamated memory and imagination that moved through and around all of us. The true bifurcation of life. He tried to picture a photograph of himself in this moment and how Forest's vision would augment it. He saw himself wide-frame from above in black and white, arms on raised knees, face open to the sky and the hovering camera, the orange grove behind him occupying the upper three-quarters of the frame, with wavy beams of celestial color—the reified past—flowing across the grove, weaving among the trees and grasses, staying low to the ground over the hills, all swooping and converging toward where he sat against the fence and crashing into his back, muddying inside him with only stifled vestiges making it through, luminous droplets leaking from his eyes and mouth and chest.

He looked to his left at some motion there and saw the jogger coming up the hill, just running now and not boxing. He was only twenty yards away, and said, "Hey, you okay?"

Daniel nodded, trying to assume a more natural stance, as if sitting on the sidewalk were habitual for him. "I'm fine."

The man stopped. "You need a ride somewhere? My car's just up the block."

"No, really, I'm okay."

The man didn't resume his run. He looked closely at Daniel. "You sure, buddy? Let me give you a ride home. Sometimes we all overdo it."

Daniel felt himself getting irritated at the man's persistence but then looked into his eyes and saw only simple concern there, untainted by whatever had set him off before. "Thanks, man," Daniel said. "I just sat down for a second for no real reason. Having a moment, I guess. But not a medical one."

The man nodded. "Okay, sorry to bother you. See that last driveway before the corner?" He pointed. "I'm right there."

"Kind of you, thanks."

He went on, walking now, and Daniel watched him turn into his driveway and disappear.

Daniel drifted back to the vision of this moment as one of Forest's paintings, and now changed the color scheme, putting himself and the world in color and the beams behind him in black and white; was that the secret, like some new age maxim? Something clicked. All at once he saw the entire picture in full color, no grayscale, past, present, and future part of the same vivid landscape, and he thought of Tanya. He thought of Gerald and Rashid. He thought of Dean, and a stippling of favorite former students. Forest. Yes, and Rachel too. His eyes did mist up, but only for a few seconds because he suddenly knew he would not make the same mistakes again with Tanya. Knew he couldn't. It would be new territory, with new mistakes, which was all they could ask for. This knowledge pulled him to his feet, and with a big inhale he started down the hill.

Turning the corner onto his street, he saw the girl and the Range Rover still there across from his driveway. When he got close he waved to her.

She nodded at him.

"You waiting for someone?"

She put her phone in her jacket pocket and stood away from the car. "I know this is a weird question, and it's not what you think, but does Celia Dressler live here?"

Daniel stopped a few feet from the girl's car. "It's not up to me to tell anyone where anyone lives. You have some reason you're looking for her?" She was too young to be paparazzi.

"It's not her I'm looking for. She has a son named Dean, right? A young son." She reached through the open window of her car and pulled out a tabloid magazine folded open to a page in the middle. She pointed at a picture of Celia and Dean taken outside a supermarket. Dean was looking right at the camera, and Celia was in profile with her head tilted back. "This is her son, right?"

"I think it's best if you don't hang out on the street here, okay?"

"I met that boy, and he was with a man named Jack, who said he was his grandfather. That's the person I'm looking for. I'm not some crazy fan. I'm here because Jack was involved in my boyfriend's death, indirectly. And if I'm right, the boy, Dean, could be in danger. Do you know Jack? Is he her father?"

"In danger how?"

"That old man is . . . not in his right mind, I guess. He's involving the kid in something dangerous."

"Tell me what you mean."

"I don't think he wants to hurt him, but he's planning on using him in a way that might be really bad for him. It's hard to explain, but I'm being straight with you."

Daniel stood staring at her, taking in her strangely chopped hair, the tattoo just visible at one shoulder where her jacket hung loose, the magazine crumpled and dangling now at her side. Something told him she was on the level, but he forced himself not to trust it. There was really no telling.

"Come on up to my place and you can tell me what's going on."

JACK FELT THE relentless present as an oppression. It weighed almost palpably on the soft tissue of his brain in every waking moment— and sometimes in sleep—no matter how much he drank. So lately he'd mostly quit drinking. It wasn't remorse or disillusionment, both tiresome old friends by now, but a prison of deadness. Somehow the death of the kid, Chris, had depleted him—and he couldn't think why. It didn't need to be this way. Chris had merely thrown himself back into the soup of chaos, or possibly, unlikely as it was, gone on ahead to the Destination, a thought that left Jack helplessly gripped with jealousy. To be left behind a second time. But there was no reason Jack shouldn't be able to move on without him. One well-versed traveler with a witness and an unswerving consciousness could succeed. There were even those souls who could go it without a witness. *There are no rules,* Hugo had said, *only catalysts and obstacles, and before the resolute mind obstacles dissolve.* But in the wake of Chris's death the departure plan had been sapped of all its color, its life. Jack felt cornered now at the tail end of old age. It was like looking down from a diving board and finding the pool replaced by an abyss and then looking back and finding the board protruding from a smooth wall stretching upward out of sight. Nowhere to go, no purchase left but this tiny plank. So when he got to the bottom of the driveway and saw Hunter's green Range Rover with its *Coexist* bumper sticker parked across the street, he found himself struck not by fear but by a startling wave of relief. Something was going to happen, things were going to change, and it almost didn't matter what or how.

He looked over and Dean was calmly staring out his own window. Jack had arrived home from his trip south late the night before and taken over school bus duty from Brenda this morning. He yanked a right turn and sped to the next block.

"What's going on at school today?"

"Just regular stuff, I guess," Dean said, looking over at him. "We're working on our science projects, and we have play rehearsal in the afternoon."

"Sounds like fun. You looking forward to the play?"

Dean frowned, considering. "Not really. But it's sort of fun to practice, I guess."

"How would you like it if you and me took a trip together, maybe soon. Somewhere with a beach and fun stuff to do?"

"Parasailing?" Dean grinned. They had watched someone doing it off the beach the previous summer and Dean had become obsessed with the idea.

"Yeah, of course. We'll do that for sure. Only thing is, we might have to leave soon. You might miss the play."

Dean tilted his head. "Is Mom coming?"

"Of course, but she might have to come separately. She might need to meet us there a little later."

"Can't we just wait for Christmas break? And then I won't miss the play? Because I'm playing Jonas Quizzenberry Dreamcake and nobody else knows those lines."

"That is the silliest name for a character I ever heard."

Dean laughed. "I know. Miss Parker wrote it."

"Well, we might need to leave sooner, is all. It might be the only way. And I just wanted to see what you thought. You don't have to. You could stay behind and be in the play. But it's one or the other. Then you'd have to wait until next year, or the year after, to go parasailing."

"No! I want to go! Should I tell Miss Parker I can't be in the play?"

"No, bud. Don't say anything. We haven't decided for sure yet, and you can't say anything to anyone, including your Mom right now. It's supposed to be a surprise. If we go, I'll tell her where to meet us before we leave."

Dean half smiled. "Okay." Then his face fell. "Is this about the book, and the secret?"

Jack put his hand on Dean's shoulder, pulling away from a stoplight with his eyes on the road. "No, Deano, that's on hold for now. This is just a vacation."

"What about Hunter and Chris?"

Jack took a breath. This was the first time Dean had asked directly. "Well, they had some stuff to do, and we just put it on hold for a while. It's no big deal, really. They said to say hi to you."

Dean nodded and looked back out his window.

After dropping Dean at school, Jack wondered how long he had. If Hunter's car was there, she must have discovered who he was, but why just the car? Where had she gone? Had she walked onto the property? Was she asleep in the car? How long till the cops showed up? And if they did, what could they even do to him? He hadn't done anything that would be easy to charge him with. Maybe accessory to B and E if they could connect him to Chris's texts. But even if the cops couldn't arrest him, there was Celia . . . If she learned the whole story she might cut him off from Dean, an intolerable possibility. He decided to head home, pack a bag, and stow it in the car, just in case. He'd begun preparing for this already, which was the reason for his trip south that weekend. He'd converted as much money into cash as he could from the accounts he had access to. It was under his passenger seat along with his passport and Hugo's book, so he was ready to split quickly if necessary.

Hunter's car was gone from the street when he got back. He allowed himself to imagine the whole thing blowing over, just disappearing, but found he didn't even want it to. No. Going back to pretending nothing had happened was slow death. And he above all dreaded geriatric stagnation. Now, at least, something was going to happen. As he topped the hill into the house's parking area, he saw Celia's car to the right of the front door, and next to it, farther over by the hedge, was the green Range Rover. Without stopping, Jack swung a tight U-turn and headed back down the driveway, hoping the sound of his car hadn't been heard inside. Things were happening quickly. It was decision time.

Getting Dean from school was easy. No one from the house had called. The school dealt with Jack much of the time anyway, and had no reason to question when he told them there was a minor family emergency. Ten minutes after he pulled up, he and Dean were on the freeway heading south.

"You said you'd tell me once we were on the highway," Dean said.

"Okay, I'll tell you. We're going on the vacation I mentioned. How do you like that?"

Dean smiled, but his brow gathered. "I thought that wasn't for a while."

"I thought so, too, but this is how it worked out."

"So where are we going?"

"First we're going to a friend of mine's house, just for a day or so. And then we're going to go to the best beach you've ever seen!"

"Who's your friend?"

"Someone I knew a very long time ago. Remember I went away yesterday and the day before?"

"Yeah."

"Well, I was at his house. He lives down near San Diego, and he's helping plan this vacation. You'll like him."

As he'd done two days earlier, Jack put the Chula Vista address into his phone's map. The car's own guidance system was still disabled from the prior trip. When they got to the first address he would power off his phone, remove the battery, and follow written instructions (which he'd received on WhatsApp and then deleted after writing down) to a second destination a few miles away. Bill wasn't fucking around, and he would need to be reassured that Jack had followed all protocols when he showed up again unexpected.

It was a different house than the one he'd visited in 1993, four years after getting out of prison, the last time he'd seen old Chinese Bill. Halfway through his prison sentence he'd run into none other than Percy, Bill's miniature right-hand man. Percy had retired from the drug business, but was in on a very old attempted murder charge he'd acquired under a former name and had the bad luck to be reconnected with. Percy had died in the prison hospital a year after coming in, but he gave Jack a postal box number in San Diego where Bill might be reached under the name Charles Hodges. "Drop him a note, but not till after you get out. Tell him you saw me. If he wants to speak to you he'll write back," Percy had said. Bill had gone into hiding after becoming a fugitive when his operation got rolled up by the feds, but he'd stayed in the business, focusing on a smuggling scheme he'd put together—just transportation now, no distribution. Two years after moving back to Tucson, Jack had finally, in a fit of drunken loneliness, sent a letter to the PO box. Two months later a letter had arrived in return. After a couple of years trading occasional notes, Jack had gone once and visited. Bill had taken a risk, letting him come. He had no way of knowing for sure whether Jack might be locating him for the feds to escape some other rap, though the two-year period between the first letter and the visit helped ease his fears. Bill was lonely too. The smuggling operation mostly ran itself, and the people who worked for him now were not his friends. That former house had been big, with a pool overlooking San Diego from a hillside neighborhood. Jack had spent two days drinking and smoking and reminiscing with Bill, and then gone back to Tucson. They had talked about doing it again, but it never happened. There hadn't even been any letters after that.

When he had written to the same PO box this time, twenty-four years later, it had been nothing but a shot in the dark. Bill would be eighty years old now if he was still alive. Jack had been shocked to get a note back within a week, with an email address and instructions on how to create an anonymous account to write to it from. Eighty years old and still handling things this way. There was a reason Bill had always eluded the law. He was fully retired now, a true unicorn: a career drug dealer who'd never done time and had left the business in old age to live out his golden years in peace.

When they arrived at the dummy address, Jack had been ignoring repeated calls from Celia for an hour. He removed the phone's battery and felt safer. Jack glanced now and then at the turn-by-turn instructions as they continued. Once they were close, he remembered the house from the day before. It was a lot smaller than the house Jack had visited in '93, a nondescript little beige ranch house set slightly farther back from the street than those around it, but otherwise cookie-cutter, with small trimmed box hedges flanking the drive and a Honda SUV in the open garage. Jack pulled into the driveway and they got out and knocked on the door. A slight dark-haired woman answered.

"Oh, hi," Jack said. "I'm here for Bill."

"Who are you?" she asked, with a faint Mexican accent.

"I'm Jack. I was here yesterday. A friend."

She gave him a glazed look, but eventually nodded and stood aside, then led them into the living room.

Bill was on the couch with the TV on and a blanket around his shoulders, just another blissful senior citizen living it up with premium cable. He was not exactly spry, but was lucid and in good shape for a man his age. "Howdy, man," Jack said.

Bill stared at him a moment, his ferocity making the wispy white tendrils growing from his ears resemble smoke more than they already did. The braided hair and Chinese affectations were long gone. "What are you doing here, Jack?"

"Well, the timeline got moved up on me, nothing I could do."

Looking at Dean, Bill softened. "And who do we have here? The famous Dean?"

"In the flesh," Jack said.

"It's nice to meet you, Dean," Bill said.

Dean mumbled, "Nice to meet you too."

"You hungry?"

Dean stood silent, managing a shrug.

Bill said, "I bet you are after the drive. Esme, you mind taking Dean in the kitchen and giving him something to eat? I need to talk to Jack a second."

"Sure thing," she said. She gave Dean a smile and said, "Follow me," walking through an archway on the left.

"Go ahead," Jack said, patting Dean's back, and Dean silently followed.

When they were alone, Bill said, "You have nerve. I ought to throw you the fuck out."

"I had to think on the go, last-minute, like. I didn't even pack a bag. I might not have made it out with him if I'd emailed and waited for you to answer. I took all the precautions, and my phone is fully disabled, just like last time. Scout's honor."

Bill shook his head. "Motherfucker." But he was calming down.

"I know. Sorry. It's about the kid, you know. I couldn't let him get sucked back into all of that."

He sighed, resigning himself. "Well, you're here. I'm assuming that means what we talked about is something you want."

"Looks that way."

"Might take a couple of days to set it up."

"Any chance we could stay here?"

"I thought as much," Bill said. "Yeah." He shrugged off the blanket testily, as if he'd suddenly realized he was too hot. He looked back at the TV, which was playing a beach drama, bikinis and danger and wooden dialogue.

Jack sat down on a chair by the couch and watched with him.

"I watch this dreck because I feel like it gets certain synapses firing. I can't get a goddamn genuine rise anymore, but a little T and A gets the mental juices flowing, right? Keeps me alive, for whatever that's worth anymore."

"Is your maid cool?" Jack asked. "She's not going to ask a lot of questions and get nosy?"

Bill looked at him. "Esme isn't my maid, shithead. She's my wife."

"Oh fuck, sorry!" Jack laughed. "Good for you, Billy. What is she, fifty-something?"

"She'll be sixty next week."

"But where was she yesterday? You never mentioned her."

"When I have business at the house I send her away. You counted as business—I didn't know what you might be up to. But you're here now. It'll be fine."

"Can I ask you not to talk to Dean about his mom, and the whole situation? I don't want him upset. I told him we were just going on vacation."

"Okay, you got it."

Jack had told Bill that Dean's mother was an emotionally abusive bottoming addict, with a physically abusive pervert boyfriend, constantly putting the boy at risk. He'd said his own prison record would keep him from getting custody, even if he fought for it. It was life or death, he'd said, and he wouldn't let the system swallow Dean up. He'd asked about whether Bill could forge them new identities and a new start, but evidently that wasn't in his wheelhouse. He could, however, get them quietly into Mexico, where things like new starts were more easily accomplished.

"You guys are on the news," Bill said the next morning, when Jack came in from taking a shower. Dean was in the kitchen being given breakfast by Esme.

"What?"

Bill pointed at the screen, which was showing a clip of the president berating reporters. "A minute ago. They've released the hounds, my friend. You neglected to tell me your daughter is a fucking movie star. Look at the ticker at the bottom."

The scrolling text under the picture said, *Police are searching for the six-year-old son of actress Celia Dressler, taken from her Beverly Hills house yesterday by his grandfather and believed to be kidnapped.* Jack said, "What difference does it make?"

"Is that a joke? If she was some crackhead skell like you implied, the missing kid would be nothing but a piece of paper on a tall stack right now, if that. But it's fucking national news. CNN has choppers flying over her house. Once the media gets on a case, the cops run with it like angry dogs. You should have told me."

"Would you still have helped?"

"At least I would have had all the information. This has to be done with special care now, obviously. I already moved your car into the garage."

"Listen," Jack said. "I actually need to go back up to LA for something tonight. Can I leave Dean here till I get back?"

Bill muted the TV. "Are you out of your mind? No, the kidnapped kid cannot stay here making me and Esme accessories to a federal crime more so than we already are. And you really ought to not go anywhere. Whatever it is, it can't be that important."

"It's something I gotta do. I had to leave so suddenly yesterday."

"Well, if you go, the kid goes with you. Period. I probably should make you find some other way out. I don't need this. At my age, after everything, if I die in prison behind *this* bullshit . . ."

"I hate to do it, Bill, but I ain't gonna make things easy on you if you don't help me and I get caught. Us getting away is your best bet at this point."

"Don't threaten me, motherfucker. I have ways to hurt you that you can't even guess at. And I know people who'd do it just for the entertainment value."

"But you won't hurt the kid. I know you, Bill. He's what's important now. You and me, we're getting to where whatever happens to us don't matter much, but him. He needs me."

Bill stared at Jack and shook his head. "I'm going to get you out of here as quick as I can," he said. "Maybe even tonight, so whatever you're doing up in LA you better do quick and get back here."

"I have to wait till dark," Jack said. "And I'm going to need to use your car."

THE HOUSE WAS quieter now. Brenda, who had stayed another night, was still there. Celia had told her she could go home, but she wouldn't. She was in the kitchen with Daniel, making sandwiches. Hunter and her mother had stayed long enough the previous day for the police to get whatever information Hunter could offer. Initially, the response had been quick but perfunctory. The Beverly Hills police were used to responding promptly to calls from celebrities, and a patrol car had arrived within minutes, but it had taken some calls up the ladder from Renata to get them to do more than put out an Amber Alert. Once they'd contacted the detective handling the death of Hunter's boyfriend in Moorpark, and established that there was a connection between the two situations, they had begun acting in earnest. The press coverage, which had ramped up overnight, hadn't hurt either.

A plainclothes officer had come by that morning to give Celia an update, along with two others in uniform who searched again through Jack's room and belongings. The update had been useless, since there was no progress of any kind. He'd given her his card and said to call anytime. Now all the cops were gone again, which seemed strange. While they'd been there, thumping around with their heavy shoes, their notepads and utility belts, their level voices and the awkward formality they cliquishly dropped with each other, it had seemed to Celia that something was happening, that she was involved in an ongoing effort, but now she felt unforgivably idle. There had to be something she was neglecting, just sitting on the couch. Renata wanted her to go on CNN about the kidnapping, but Celia had said no, sensing Renata's hunger for publicity behind the suggestion.

When her phone rang in her hand she jumped, her heart careening into hope. It was Leo.

"What's going on?" he asked. "This stuff about Dean on the news."

"God, Leo, I really don't know. Jack took him and disappeared, and he's ditched all communication. He's involved in some weirdness I can't even get my head around, and now he's taken Dean. No one knows where."

"Can I do anything? You want me to come over?"

"Yes, please. I would have called but I've been dealing with the cops since yesterday."

"I'm on my way."

Celia hung up and took another cigarette from the pack Rafe had left. She usually never smoked in the house. The entire surreal thirty-six hours washed through her again, and she tried again, in vain, to make sense of it. She could not seem to separate what was happening from the night of the gala, when in the limo with Rafe she'd leaned down and taken a line. Her terror over Dean now seemed fused into a meaningful continuum with the memory of the bitter drip in her throat, with the shame and dread of relapse pressing on the back of her lungs. It was hard not to feel that, somehow, one had emerged from the other, a retribution. There had been too many people at the gala, including press, who might have seized on seeing her with a drink, so she'd refrained—heading to the bathroom a few times with Rafe's little kit in her clutch bag—until shortly before leaving, when she had Rafe get her a rum and Diet Coke in a soda glass from the bar. Then they hit the bar in the limo on the way home, and had more drinks and lines back at the house, sequestered in her bedroom. It had been almost three when she'd heard the front door and gone out to investigate. Jack had a small duffel slung from his shoulder in the foyer, and he looked sharp-eyed, fully alert.

"I thought you were gone till tomorrow," she said.

"Yeah, I decided to head back tonight. How was your party?"

"Fine," she said. "Tuxes, salmon, speeches." She tossed her hand. "You know."

He smiled. "I don't, but I get the idea."

"Nice trip?"

"Yeah."

"Who was this friend again?"

"Just a guy I knew, sort of worked for, back in the day."

"Fun to see him?"

"Sure. He's pretty fucking ancient now, older than me." He laughed. "Which is saying something. So he's limited in the fun department. But he's doing good."

"When's the last time you saw him?"

"Early nineties, maybe. So yeah, it's been a while." His eyes gathered focus, looking at her. "You okay? Something up?"

"I'm fine. My date is still here, so I better get back to him."

"Yeah, you better." He grinned like an idiot, gave a nod, and turned to go.

She didn't bother explaining that Rafe was gay. "Good night," she said, and he didn't answer. Celia had turned this exchange over and over, examining every angle, trying to extract any useful information. At the time she'd been primarily concerned with not giving away that she was high. Rafe had gone home at sunup, and Celia had moved all the evidence of their consumption into the closet before crashing. She'd still been in a twitchy coke-nap when Jack had left with Dean for school. Brenda had rousted her when Daniel showed up with Hunter.

She drew hard on her cigarette and blew smoke sideways, spun the tip on the rim of the cup she was using as an ashtray, sculpting a symmetrical ember. The brown envelope with Sterling Tripp's script in it sat unopened on the corner of the coffee table. The meeting at Tripp's office the day before had not happened. She had not called or written to cancel it, and hadn't heard from them either. To take any action that had to do with her career while Dean might be in danger felt like an invitation to disaster. In her conversations with Renata the day before, she had meant to tell her, had slid along the edge of it a number of times, but each time had pulled back as if from a sheer drop. She was glad she'd written to Frances Oyemi before the gala to cancel their lunch. She hoped (though she tried not to, since even hoping might be an unpardonable deviation from single-minded focus on Dean's safety) that someone in Tripp's circle had seen the news.

Celia dropped her cigarette into the coffee remnant and picked up from the table the business card of the detective. She dialed the cell number written in pen at the bottom. He picked up right away.

"Hi, Detective Wallace, this is Celia Dressler."

"Miss Dressler. I'm sorry I don't have any new leads or information to give you at present. Is there something else I can do for you?"

"What do you think about me going on CNN, about Dean? Being interviewed. Could it help or hurt in any way?"

"Well, in a case like this, where it's a family member being sought, we sometimes do encourage that. It might jog someone in the public who has information. And it could prompt your father, possibly, to surrender or bring in your son. It probably couldn't hurt, is my feeling."

"Then I'll do it. Thank you."

"We've got everyone looking," he said. "We're doing everything we can, I promise."

"Thank you." She hung up and called Renata, told her to set up the CNN interview for as soon as possible.

She went into the kitchen. Daniel and Brenda were at the island, preparing sandwiches and salad. "I'm going on CNN," Celia said. "Leo is picking me up. I can't just sit around here."

"Have a sandwich first," said Brenda.

They sat at the kitchen table and ate, and Celia experienced only the mechanics of it—hands gripping, arms hoisting, teeth biting, jaw working methodically. Taste was absent. Swallowing was somehow difficult. The first bite made her hungry, but by the third she felt full. She pushed her plate away.

"What do we know about Hunter's boyfriend, his death? Or this cult? Anything?" she asked.

Brenda pulled her laptop across and opened it. "Hold on."

Daniel said, "I remember the cult from the seventies. A group of them OD'd on sedatives together at a house in Moorpark, the same house where her boyfriend went and killed himself. I guess he'd become obsessed with them."

"I know what's on Google," Celia said. "You know anything else about them?"

"Well, here's what's really weird. I came into peripheral contact with them myself, in 1969. My friend Cam, the one who owned this house before you, had a ranch up in Marin where a bunch of hippies lived back then. This group, and their leader or guru or whatever, were living at the ranch for a bit. I remember seeing them, all dressed in white. They stayed separate from the rest of the people there. Cam wasn't part of the group, but he knew the leader. He reminded me of who they were when the mass suicide happened afterward, in '75 or so. The group had left Marin years earlier, and ended up down here. If Jack was one of them back then, I guess it's possible he knew Cam also. It seems too bizarrely coincidental that he'd end up living in the house of someone who was once loosely connected to the group."

"What do you think it means?" Celia asked.

Daniel's face emptied in thought. "I really don't know."

During the drive to the interview, Celia began filling Leo in on the details of what was happening, but found that the outlandish information, organized into coherent sentences and explanatory through-lines, opened a deep pit in her and made her darkly afraid, and she had to stop. She looked out the passenger window and considered smashing her forehead against it, just to create an alternate sensation. Then she had a revelation: she was located, she suddenly realized, down underneath her core fear, in a place she'd never imagined existed. The fear she felt for Dean was so deep, so consuming, that it dwarfed and neutralized the old monolith. She was more afraid than she'd ever been in her life, and it had nothing to do with the mysterious fear-core she'd always ascribed such weight to. A cruel lesson in perspective.

"This is all so surreal," Leo said when they were on the freeway, and for a moment Celia thought he was talking about Los Angeles itself, the residential hills east of the 405 fanged here and there with knifelike cypress trees in twos and threes, the harsh bleached presence of the sun smearing Rorschach-like across the windshield, unobstructed by its customary circular parameter and corresponding roughly with the bleeding terror in Celia's chest. Traffic was bringing them pitilessly to a halt.

"I'm still trying to get my head around it," Leo continued. "Jack was in this suicide cult in the seventies? Is that right?"

"I don't know," she said. "I guess so, or that's what he told Hunter anyway."

"Has he ever talked about it? Did you have any hints of anything like that from him?"

"No. Can we please . . . stop. I don't have my head around it, either, and I don't really have it in me to try and unpack it right now."

"Okay. Sorry."

Celia reached across and touched his shoulder. "You don't have to be sorry. You're here."

Leo put his hand on hers and said, "Dean is going to be okay."

Celia nodded, genuflecting mentally. "Thanks," she said. "How's it going at home with . . . everything?"

"Things with Darcy have calmed down some."

"And you?"

"I'm okay."

"I hear something in there."

"I'm fine," he said. "I'm here for *you* right now, better to focus on what's going on."

Celia pulled her hand back. "I wouldn't mind focusing on something else for a minute. Tell me what's up."

"It's fine. Nothing is up. I mean, something is up, but it can wait."

She raised her eyebrows. "Not anymore it can't," she said, with a chuckle that felt like a soft tap on a chisel inside her.

"All right. It's one reason this all feels so surreal right now. I was up most of the night, talking with Darcy, and then after only a couple of hours of sleep I wake up and Dean's on the news, kidnapped."

"So you guys talked. . . ."

"Yeah. We came to a decision, finally."

"That's good," Celia said. "You couldn't go on that way forever." The chisel was slotted again into its fissure, held ready at a precise angle. She was anxious, and also it mattered not at all. Just the idea of it mattering was like some far-off ironic burlesque.

He looked at her for a moment, then back at the road. They were edging forward in stop-and-go traffic. A white eighteen-wheeler in front of them had a thick yellow stripe and the back of the truck read simply *MAY*. "And?" she asked.

"Well . . . it's become complicated."

"It can't be that complicated. You came to a decision."

"We did, but I changed my mind."

"How's that?"

"We were going to give it a go," Leo said. "After endless talks we decided we owed it to Gus, and maybe to ourselves. It had nothing to do with figuring out what I actually wanted. It was just a kind of ethical calculus. But after I left there this morning, I changed my mind, unilaterally."

"Before you saw me, or after?"

He considered this. "Once I saw you, it solidified."

"And does Darcy know you changed your mind?"

"No."

"What about me? Do I get a say?"

"What? Of course, I just thought . . ."

She saw his features contort in confusion and fear. In spite of herself the alarm in his face made her feel good. "Don't worry," she said. "How I feel hasn't changed. I just wonder if you're thinking clearly. If you're going to regret everything once it's done. You need to figure out what's really right."

"This is right. It has to be. Less wrong, anyway. It can't be right to stick it out and deny something truer. But I better tell her soon—that's only right too."

Celia rolled down her window and lit a cigarette. "You better not be doing this because of the situation, because you see me in need."

"No. It's not that."

She shook her head, smoking hard, torn, slouching and putting a foot on the dash. "None of this matters right now, anyway."

"I know. With what's happening, it seems stupid. I'm sorry."

"Again with the sorry. Stop."

"Dean is the only thing that matters, is all I mean."

"Actually now's probably a good time because I really don't care. Which makes me clear-minded, in a way." She paused but he just held the wheel, staring ahead at the traffic. "At some point I'll get around to being happy, don't worry," Celia said. Leo nodded and glanced at her with a tiny smile. She did, guiltily, feel relief, looking at him. His face now, that was hers. His time now, that was hers, not stolen. His resolute guitarist hands, his breathing chest under an old white Bruce Springsteen T-shirt, his vigilance. His love now, that might be hers. Uneasily, it did feel right. She let herself realize that she'd wanted this very badly, though she'd been deftly evading that desire by expecting the worst. A terrible thought suddenly conjured itself. . . . If her life became conquered by grief, his decision might not stand the test. She might not want it to. She grimaced and shook her head hard to wipe it clean of this, flicking the cigarette out onto the highway.

She had been trying, before this conversation, to figure out the best way to tell him about her relapse, to come clean, but now she put that on hold. No reason to further muddy things. She understood also, in some airtight place inside, that not telling gave her freedom—the kind which would leave her unimpeded to roam the old shadow territory if things went bad. Preserving that freedom was a scrap of dark comfort. If he comes back safe, she thought, I'll never go there again. Never, never, God, *never, I swear*. She meant it. The other whisper, though, happened behind a soundproof wall, inaudible even to the utterer. *But if he doesn't . . .*

He parked on the north side of the property along the wall that backed the lawn. The car's dash clock said 3:08 a.m. With the engine switched off and his window down he could hear gusts in the needles of the evergreens overhead. He spun the key and rolled the window up, leaving it cracked an inch.

"I need you to stay here, lying down," he said to Dean. The boy had been asleep much of the ride, but had woken up a few minutes earlier and recognized the neighborhood.

"What are you doing?"

"Deano, I'll explain it all later, but it's very important. Don't get out of the car and don't let anyone see you. There's nothing to worry about, but you just need to do what I say. Promise?"

Dean nodded. He was such a good boy. "I promise," he said.

"Good. I'll be back soon, just wait for me."

Jack walked down the sidewalk to the old iron gate in the center of the long wall. There was a rusty tin sign by the gate that read PERIMETER ALARMED, which he supposed had once been true. He looked back at the car to see whether Dean was watching him or had lain down as he'd asked, but the windshield was opaque. He grabbed the gate with his right hand, wedged his foot into one of the gaps, and hoisted himself to where he could swing his other foot to the top of the wall. From there he quickly slid over and dropped down into the rhododendron on the other side. Not bad for an old man. He stepped partially through the gap in the hedge and looked across the lawn toward the house. Living room lights off, Celia's bedroom lights off, some dim light from the dining room onto the patio. No movement. As he went out onto the lawn and walked west along the hedge, away from the patch of woods at the northeast corner, he knew he might be visible from the house if someone was looking, and he experienced a pleasant insouciance—one he'd been cultivating all day and had begun to have success with on the drive up from San Diego. Whatever happened, happened. There really was no such thing as a bad outcome. Every branching possibility, played fully out, led to the same terminus anyway. The truth of this expanded brightly in him.

He skirted the western corner of the property, descending around the hill where the swimming pool sat, on down to the back of Daniel's house. Jack was pretty sure Daniel never locked his doors, but he didn't know what his sleep habits were. He had tried to get Bill to let him borrow his gun, but Bill had refused, immovable. He would need to manage this situation very carefully. At the back fence he put his face up against the slats and peeked through. The lights were off. He knew from experience that if he pulled down on the gate as he drew the latch chain, the latch would make less noise. He slipped through, let the gate rest softly behind him, and went across the grass to the brick patio. The sliding door was not only unlocked, but was open a couple of inches for air. The screen scraped when he pushed it back, but the glass door slid smoothly and quietly and Jack went into the house. His eyes were already well adjusted and he saw his way clearly through the living room, knowing that not hesitating was equally as important as being quiet. If Daniel woke, if he'd heard the scraping screen, it was better to catch him before he shook off the grogginess.

The bedroom door opened without a sound and Jack was able to slide through silently. He stood for a moment just inside the door. The room was thick with undisturbed sleep. He had one of the plastic zip ties in his hand, approaching the bed, when a new problem presented itself out of the gloom: there were two people in the bed. Since when did this old fuck have overnight company? Then he remembered Tanya. There wasn't time to consider all options, as a stirring began in the bed. Jack could make out that Daniel was the one nearest him, and he stepped up and cuffed his left hand to the bedpost quickly. He grabbed Daniel's phone from the nightstand and retreated with it halfway to the door.

Daniel shouted, "What the *fuck*?"

Tanya was awake saying, "What's the matter?" and for a moment she was dealing only with Daniel, not yet knowing they weren't alone.

"You both need to be quiet, right now," Jack said. Tanya screamed and convulsed visibly at the sound of his voice. "Don't move and stop making noise, both of you. I have a gun and I will use it if I need to.

Daniel, it's Jack. I'm not here to hurt anyone, but get her to shut up, please." Jack pointed the big, still-closed folding knife he'd brought as if it were a gun, hoping they couldn't see well enough to doubt him.

She'd quit screaming anyway. Daniel stopped struggling against the zip tie and seemed to be assessing the situation. His face was in shadow.

"Everybody be calm," Jack said. "This is only a conversation. Tanya, don't panic. Just stay still and stay quiet and you'll be safe."

"What are you doing here?" Daniel asked.

"I'm here to talk to you."

"Is Dean okay? Where is he?"

"Of course Dean is okay. You think I'd hurt him?"

"Well, people are pretty worried."

"Tanya," Jack said. "I need you to very slowly and carefully, with two fingers, pick up your phone and throw it over here. Do it now."

She didn't move.

"I mean it, honey. This ain't a request."

She threw her phone toward him, and he let it land on the carpet.

"Good," said Jack. He picked it up and pocketed it with Daniel's.

"What are you doing, Jack?" Daniel said. "Your daughter is beside herself. You've kidnapped her son."

"That's not why I'm here."

A pause. "Why are you here?"

"To apologize to you."

"What? Jack, seriously. I don't need any apologies. All you have to do is realize what's right, and get Dean back to his mother where he belongs. It doesn't even involve me."

"Man, you got no idea. Your whole life is my fault."

"Don't be ridiculous. All that matters is—"

"You are not listening to me, son. I need you, *right now,* to mother-fucking *listen*! I have some things to say that you need to hear. So kindly shut the fuck up."

This got through. Daniel swung his feet to the ground and sat up. Jack could see him straining his wrist quietly against the zip tie, but it looked solid and tight. "Okay, I'm listening."

Jack took a breath. How to begin? Might as well be with the proof.

"Let me see if I remember this right." He pitched his voice higher, speaking in a falsetto, *"I shall return. And realize once more my thousand dreams. Wait for me, Daniel. Right here."*

There was silence, during which Jack could almost feel the dark weight dawning in Daniel's chest. "What?" Daniel said.

"That's what she said to you, isn't it? Rachel. Word for fucking word. Before she walked away forever off that cliff. In sixty-nine."

Nothing now. He was legitimately silenced.

"Yes, Danny boy. That's right, I was there. I followed you away from the party at the ranch, down the coast to that cliff. I was there. I heard you talking under the tree, and then I followed her up that trail and it was me, buddy. It was me all along."

"Who the fuck *are* you?"

"I believed her, by the way, that she would come back. Which is why I first came to you. I thought if I stayed around you for a while . . . that she might have found a way back to you. But it certainly isn't Tanya here. She's about the right age, but she's her own ball of wax. Just as a matter of interest, what year were you born, Tanya?"

After a pause, she said, "1966."

"So that settles it. And that ex-wife of yours was also alive long before Rachel died. Looks like she didn't mean it after all, I guess. Or maybe she got lost along the way."

Daniel's face remained absolutely still, his eyes just cavities gaping at Jack from the grayscale gloom. Jack could see his fist clenching, and his wrist straining against the zip tie.

"Did she tell you about me?" Jack asked. "About Tucson, and me and her? I was called Johnny back then."

Daniel nodded, slowly. "Yes," he said. "She told me."

"So now you know. This is what I'm sorry for. All of this. Being sorry is fucking meaningless, of course, but I would go back and do everything different with her if I could. I never loved anyone like I loved her."

"Loved her?"

"Yeah. You and I have that in common."

"You're out of your mind, Jack. Is that something you have any awareness of?"

"Sometimes it's hard to tell crazy from visionary. You, Danny, you ought to know that. I think you walked that line for a while."

Tanya shifted and Daniel reached back and put his free hand on her arm to still her. "Let me get one thing straight," he said. "You're saying she didn't fall. You pushed her. You killed her. Is that right?"

Jack was distantly aware of the long intake of his own breath. Then the breath was exhaled and another drawn slowly in. Continuing. Like waves. In the world people imagined they lived in, this actually meant something. "Yeah, man." He was suddenly exhausted by the utterance, and irritated by the necessity of it. "That is what I'm saying. I didn't intend on doing it when I followed her. I wasn't looking to kill her, but that's what happened."

"Because you loved her. . . ."

"Why not? *Yeah,* because I loved her." Jack found himself waving his arms. "Not everyone's got the same kind of white-bread love, son. What do you think Howlin' Wolf meant when he sang *Just a spoon of love from my forty-five, save you from another man*? What about *Down by the river I shot my baby*? Or, *Hey Joe*?"

"Those are songs."

"Sure, songs about a natural impulse. I ain't saying it's a good impulse, but it's not like I invented it. They even got a name for it. Crime of passion, right?"

"I thought you came here to apologize."

"Not for that. I'm apologizing to you because I fucked up your life, and I like you."

"I guess I'm lucky you don't love me."

Jack smiled in spite of himself. "I'm just saying you're a good guy who didn't deserve it."

"And Rachel? Did she deserve it?"

"'Course she didn't." There was a chair next to him by the wall and Jack sat down, leaning forward on his knees. He just needed to take the weight off for a second, rest. His voice quieted, though his anger was rising. "Truth is, nobody deserves anything. I know that, brother. Listen, my apology doesn't mean squat, I get it, like I said. Nothing in this old shitty world means a goddamn thing in the end. It's all illusion, including made-up ideas of right and wrong, should and shouldn't. Apologizing changes nothing. And honestly, it isn't even the real reason I came, anyway."

"What is?"

"I needed to have this conversation with you. I don't even know why. Something about this connection between us, and me being the only one who knew what it consisted of. I couldn't leave without telling you to your face. I needed you to know. I couldn't take that information out of the world with me. Does that make sense?"

"No."

"Plus, maybe you got a right to know."

Daniel snorted bitterly. Jack went on.

"I'll admit my motives originally were selfish. I thought I might find her with you, might reunite with her, whatever that means. But motives are as meaningless as being sorry, in the end."

Daniel slid the zip tie up the bedpost to the bulb at the top and then back down. He increased his pull on it until Jack could see it cutting into his skin, but it was secure. "So," Daniel said, "you knew who I was when you moved in here, obviously."

"'Course I did. I tracked you down. I remember your friend Cam, too, from the ranch. It was really through him that I met Hugo and changed my life."

"Hugo. He was the leader of that cult?"

"Another friend long gone. Though I might know where to find him." Jack stood up. "It's been nice knowing you, Daniel. Sorry the situation meant we couldn't be friends. You're all right. By the way, I saw pictures of that tree you made. It was something. No shit, I ain't much for art, but that was something. You know, I might be the only person who knew exactly what it meant when I saw it. I knew right away. It meant you never really left that tree behind, you're still waiting there for her, just like she said to. It's how I knew you loved her the way I did."

Daniel's throat shifted in the dim light as he swallowed. Jack envisioned lying down in the bed alongside them both and falling asleep, just for a while.

"Why, Jack? If you loved her, why?"

For a moment Jack considered the possibility of never speaking again. The simplicity of it. He sat back down in the chair. "I got a *why* for you. Why did you blow up your tree? Don't get me wrong, I respect it. It's a rare thing, to be willing to do something like that. To destroy something you love, just to keep another person from having it."

"Oh god. You think it's the same?"

"I don't think it's *so* different."

"Let me ask you this. Why do you think I never need to talk about my sculpture, don't think about it much, while you're here almost fifty years later making a confession, seeking some kind of absolution?"

"Absolution? That ain't it. I told you that." Jack's teeth ached with the pressure of his jaw.

"But you're here, and you're telling me, because you couldn't live with yourself, trapped alone with it. Me, I did my time based on the financial value of the thing, which was only right since I'd taken money for it. But I don't regret it. My conscience is clear, at least about that. Is yours?"

"A false construct. I don't need a conscience."

"Too bad you have one then. And of course it's why you're here. You poor bastard," Daniel said. "Really, I mean it. You might have starved and beaten and neglected it, but your conscience is still there, chained to a wall in the back of your mind."

"Not for long." He hadn't meant to say it.

"Jack, listen, it's okay." Daniel's tone shifted abruptly, softened. "I forgive you, if that's what it takes to get Dean back. Just drop him off and go. I won't say anything about you coming here tonight, and I will absolve you of Rachel's death. Just bring him back and you and me are square, I promise."

Jack was angry at the condescension, but in the moment his fatigue was more powerful than his anger. He hung his head and stared between his knees at the floor. There was a faint shine from the glossy triple-stripe on his black-on-black running shoes. Those three stripes, just the visual suggestion of them in that darkened room, spoke the name in his mind automatically: *Adidas.* Brand names, logos: a bizarre notion in that moment that opened a sluice gate for the entire ridiculous world to gush into his undefended mind. Humans, their endless things and thoughts. Their blind, useless lives. Someone ought to burn it all down. If you nuked the world and killed everyone at once, where would people reincarnate? He laughed aloud at this, two sharp staccato barks, and looked back up at Daniel.

"I don't need your forgiveness. Don't make me say it again."

Then Tanya's voice, new and burning, almost visible on the gray air. He'd forgotten she was there. "Yes, but you do need your own."

Jack laughed again, but softly this time. "If that's true I'm fucked." The words dropped out and he felt strangely relieved. "You know," he said to Daniel, "a lot of men would sooner destroy a person than a thing that might outlast them and give them a taste of immortality. You were willing to dynamite your legacy. That's the part I respect most. It shows that on some level you're not snowed by the illusions force-fed to us from the second we're born."

"That sculpture was not Daniel's legacy," Tanya said.

"It *would* have been if he hadn't blown the fucking thing up."

"His legacy is the kids whose lives he's affected as a teacher and mentor, and that's a legacy that never dies because it continues in the legacies of each of them, on down to the people they affect. It lasts as long as people do."

Jack stood up. "Thanks for the pep talk," he said to Tanya. He stepped forward and checked Daniel's zip tie. Then he pulled another out, pocketed the knife in his jacket, and walked around the bed. "Take this and attach your wrist to the bedpost," he said. When she'd done it, he tested it, pulled it tighter. He stepped back again and patted his pants pocket for their phones. "Take care, you two. Danny boy, I hope you and Rachel do find each other again, if it's meant to be, in some other life, I really do. And that's progress for me. You know, I almost killed you, too, that night. I seriously thought about it." He stepped halfway into the hall.

"Jack, wait. There's more to say. Don't go."

"I got to. It's time to."

"Dean is just a kid. Leave him behind. He needs his mother. Don't commit another crime against a person you love."

Jack felt the calm now, enlarging in him. It had been there all along, of course. And it seemed suddenly, startlingly possible that Daniel did, after all, reciprocate his sense of kinship. "No such thing as crime, son," Jack said. "I'll catch you on the flip side."

"What's going on?" A voice from the hallway and Jack spun.

The kid was directly behind him, in a white tank top and gym shorts. "Nothing's going on," Jack said. How could he have forgotten?

"Go back to bed, Gerald," said Daniel.

"No, get in here." Jack grabbed him by the back of his neck and shoved him into the room. When the kid registered the bonds on Daniel's and Tanya's wrists, he turned and tried to run through Jack to the door. Jack wrestled with him, which was harder than it should have been given the kid's skinny frame. He had the innate potency of youth. Jack had initially grabbed him as if controlling him were almost a nonfactor, but found himself suddenly in a wild struggle. The boy spun once and hit Jack in the nose, stunning him. He was about to actually make it to the door, pulling free from Jack's grasp, and Jack kicked the back of his knee, sending him sprawling, then he dropped his weight on the kid's back and punched the base of his skull. From his jacket pocket, he pulled the folding knife. The kid was still squirming powerfully, dangerously, when the crack came from behind him. Something had happened back there, and Jack knew he needed to turn around right away, but if he did the kid would gain the advantage. He struck Gerald in the side of the head with the metal butt of the knife handle, felt the bone-resonance of the impact, and then a loud clang—a hallucinated metallic sound that couldn't have been produced by bone and skin—and a fusillade of yellow and red detonations, all of which were contained impossibly inside his own skull. He'd been hit from behind, and he rolled off Gerald onto his back.

His eyes slowly gelled their focus through the fireworks and he made out Daniel standing over him holding the broken bedpost like a baseball bat, his wrist still cuffed to it. "Don't get up," Daniel said, but Jack sat up anyway, and when Daniel swung the post at him again he absorbed the blow with his raised left arm, pushing through the flash of pain to grip Daniel's arm near the shoulder. He flipped open the knife with his thumb—a hard snap when it locked—and proved himself. He pulled Daniel in, embraced him, his left arm spraying electrifying pain all through him. Two old men shaky from their injuries: it was a fight that for a moment took on the ungainliness of wanton lovemaking as they rolled on the floor. Jack ended up on top, saying through gritted teeth, "You think I want your fucking *absolution*?" His head hurt densely and rage had invaded him like a drug-rush, like an orgasm, his pain-drenched arm driven down onto the windpipe of the man under him while his other hand gripped the knife, whose blade was entirely inside Daniel's body. "I just came here to talk, motherfucker. Now look at you."

When he finally did pull his arm away there was not an intake of breath, but an exhalation. Just one. The face of this man who was a kind of brother to him fell oddly slack, and the eyes closed themselves. Jack was grateful for that; he wouldn't have liked to be stared at. The distant sound he heard was the woman screaming directly into the thick blood rushing in his ears, and it helped him refocus and stand. Just as he'd done all those years ago he thought of the first thing that needed doing, the soothing event-chain of necessity, and he dragged Gerald to the bed using only his right arm. In the ten seconds it took to get the limp kid there, close enough to zip-tie his wrist to the bulbous wooden leg of the frame, he'd regained basic faculties and he said to Tanya, "I swear to god if you don't shut up I'll kill you."

She fell silent. Then, almost calmly, she said, "Is Gerald okay?"

Jack leaned over and felt Gerald's breath with his hand, touched the strong pulse in his throat with his fingers. "He's fine. He'll wake up soon."

"What about Daniel?"

Jack straightened up and smoothed his hair thoughtfully, trying to control his breathing.

"He needs an ambulance," she said.

"No, he doesn't." He went out and quickly down the hall, out the back door, and through the garden gate, beginning to exult now in motion and action. Knowledge was in him, and to hell with the rest. He was living his experience and that was all you could ever do in this world.

He knew it wouldn't be long before she found a way to cut the restraints. On the hill he threw the two phones on the ground and quickly wiped the blood from his right hand onto the grass. He set off along the edge of the property, running softly, his sneakers silent on the grass, and he found himself shocked to feel lighter than he had before. His anger was mysteriously gone, along with doubt, in the deep current of timeless Knowledge. He thought about how Daniel had taken the revelation in stride, concerned only with Dean's safety. This deepened Jack's feeling for him, which swelled now, as he ran, into something approaching love. *Godspeed,* he thought. Daniel was off on a new adventure now. That's all it was.

As he neared the gap in the center of the long rhododendron hedge, there was movement there. He froze, his heart thumping from exertion. He'd been discovered. He was being stared at. . . . In truth not *at,* but *through*—seen right through, not by a cop or Celia or even Dean, but by a light gray coyote standing directly in front of him, holding its ground. He'd stopped only ten yards from it, and it was facing him, unmoving now. It seemed to be challenging him, though that was crazy because coyotes didn't challenge people. He knew that. They ran from people, avoided them. But here it was, looking right into him as if it knew more than he did.

He stayed still, and for a second it felt not like a standoff, but like a rendezvous. "Hi," Jack said. The animal held him in its fixed, remote gaze. "You got something to say?" Jack asked. "I'm listening." It did not move. Jack took a step forward to see if he could back it up. Then he thought of Tanya getting to the landline. "Hah!" he yelled, waving his arms, and the coyote bared its teeth and produced a high-pitched growl, giving no ground. He stepped back and stared, stunned. Their eyes were locked, and Jack then said very softly, "Rachel?"

The two pups slunk tentatively from the gap in the hedge. She glanced at them before fixing Jack again with her eyes, teeth still showing. The pups made a hard left and ran all-out toward the patch of woods, and after a moment the mother, satisfied he was properly chastened, turned and loped after them, looking back a couple of times before disappearing into the woods.

Jack stepped through the gap and when he went to climb back over the wall he found his throbbing left arm useless, surely broken. He managed to pull himself to the top with one arm and a raised leg, and tumbled off the other side, almost crying out in pain when he landed. When he got to the car, Dean was sitting up in his seat, wide awake.

"Did you see the coyotes?" Dean asked. "They came across the road."

"Yeah, bud, I saw them. The mama growled at me, to protect her pups." He started the car and pulled away.

"She's a good mom. Me and Daniel saw them the other night, and we could tell. She's a very good mom."

"I'm sure she is. I could tell too." He was driving fast but not too fast down the side streets, making rapid-fire one-handed turns, taking the back way to the highway in Bill's Honda. In the end he'd have to take Sunset to get over to the 405, but he avoided it for as long as he could.

"Just like Mom is a good mom too. Right?"

"Yeah, 'course she is."

When they turned onto Sunset, it was dark and mostly free of other cars. Jack drove faster, hoping she hadn't gotten to a phone yet. The sight of the highway ahead came as a relief, and swinging onto the south-bound ramp felt like surfacing after holding his breath underwater.

"Where are we going?" Dean asked.

"Back to Bill's house."

"I mean, after that."

"We're going to a great hotel with beautiful beaches and pools and parasailing and lots of other fun stuff. Like I said."

After another long pause, filled only with the broken white lines swimming sinuously past in the headlights, and the serene highway-drone of the engine, Dean said, "I don't think I want to go anymore."

"Buddy, it's all set up."

"What about Mom?"

"She's going to meet us there later."

"I want to stay. With her." He was whining, which was rare for him. "I want to go home now. I'll go with Mom and we'll meet you there." He began crying.

"You're going to start with this *now*? Crying like a little girl? Come on, Deano. Don't get this way. It's gonna be fun."

Dean stopped speaking, and Jack kept driving. His left arm, which lay limp in his lap, had begun to tremble, graver pain emerging as if from behind clouds. He was angry again, rage skewering him from the depths, ambushing him as it always did. This time it dragged behind it a profound disappointment. Just minutes earlier he'd thought his anger somehow resolved, dissipated, but here it was, as ever, inviolate. He'd just needed Dean to stick with him. One person. Was a single person too much to ask? In the whole world, in a life as long as his? Could he not have one person who would love and stick by him? For a flash he thought of Gretchen. She might have. Jack said, "I need your help, Deano. Don't you want to help your grampa?"

The boy just stared into his lap. His hands were clasped and shoved between his legs, squeezed tight, and the sight of the wounded, downturned set of his lips cut suddenly through and softened Jack's anger.

"Come on, don't sulk, buddy. Don't give me the silent treatment."

Dean didn't look up. "I'm not," he said.

"Well, okay, good."

"You said I didn't have to go. You said I could stay behind if I wanted to."

"Yeah, but you decided to come, and now it's all set up. Bill went to a lot of trouble."

"I'm scared."

"Scared of what?"

Dean didn't speak for a moment. He was looking out his window at the highway's sound-wall blurring past. When he did speak, it was hard for Jack to hear him with his mouth almost touching the glass and his voice coming soft. "I had a scary dream. I was afraid of you. I was standing by the pool and you were behind me, and I thought you were going to do something bad."

"That doesn't sound so scary."

"In the dream it was."

"I'd never do anything bad to you, you know that."

"Lying is something bad. You lied to me."

"What do you mean?"

Dean leaned back in his seat and ran his hand across his lap belt.

He crossed his arms. "I know it's not a vacation. I heard you and Bill talking. The police are looking for us, and Mom is scared. She doesn't know where we are. So you lied."

He took a breath. "I was trying to keep you from being scared, is all."

"Is Mom really meeting us there?"

Jack shook his head slowly. "Okay. No, but I'll make sure you get back to her soon."

"Are Chris and Hunter meeting us there? Is this the new plan?"

"No, bud, they're not. They aren't part of the plan anymore. It's just you and me."

Suddenly the boy was crying loudly, kicking the dashboard, saying, *"No-no-no-no-no whydoyoualwaysdothis? Makemedothings! Iwannago-home gohome!"* It was a shock. Jack had not seen Dean have this kind of tantrum since he was preverbal. He usually got quiet when he was upset, and sometimes he shouted, but this was not his thing. He was shriek-ing. The frenzied noise fractured Jack's concentration, and he found it suddenly hard to control the car with his one good hand and the pain squeezing into his eyes. His heart was ready to scorn him and go its own fluttering way, and the schools of surging white lines threatened to break formation.

"HEY!" Jack yelled, loud enough that it silenced Dean abruptly. "Quit that! Right now! Stop being a goddamn baby!"

The silence that followed was enough to offer him a focal point. He saw his knuckles on the wheel, and from there he extrapolated the mov-ing road and the Los Angeles night and reentered himself, re-captained his body. But the silence was artificial. He looked over and saw that Dean's face was contorted and streaming gouts of mucus from every opening. He was crying so hard he seemed unable to speak anymore, and Jack found himself braking and easing down an exit ramp. His anger remained, but was gashed now down its center, laid open and impotent. He felt helpless in the face of his grandson's high emotion. His love for the boy was crippling, and he knew all at once he wouldn't give it up for anything. He would let it eat him alive if it meant to. The realization staggered him.

At the bottom of the ramp, as he looked left for traffic before making a right turn, there were ash-gray silhouettes of tents and lean-tos along the sidewalk under the freeway. A man about his own age with a dreaded gray beard, gray hoodie, and white sneakers sat in a webbed lawn chair outside his tent-flap at the near end of the row of dwellings, close enough to the edge that pallid streetlight fell on him unobstructed. A triangle of bright orange T-shirt at his neck flared like an ember. He stared right at Jack, ankle crossed over knee, arms placed regally on the chair's tin armrests, with that simple, universal human proprietary air, like a man taking in a tranquil night at his hunting cabin and spying some passing creature at the tree line. Jack felt love for him too. Like a gift. Even if nothing mattered, you could still love deluded people.

"I'm going to drop you off," he said, turning west and accelerating. "Okay? I can't take you home now, but I'll drop you and you'll go home to your mom in the morning. Is that okay?"

Dean looked at him, slicked with tears and snot. His eyes and knotted-up face bore torment and fear that seemed to transcend his tantrum and become an indictment of Jack, of everything he had done wrong to anyone in his life. It was as if the boy, in his heightened state, had divined all of it, the totality of Jack's sins. Jack remembered the little girl, Miranda, Gretchen's daughter, who had seemed at times to be privy to his shame-wracked memories. Maybe some children did have it in them. And they were such soft material, you couldn't fault them for being molded by the world's constructs. It was a long journey to wisdom and clarity, to discarding morality and its attendant shame. He himself was still, after all this time, limping through the final stages of that journey, and he couldn't help feeling the sting of Dean's indictment for a few seconds before letting it drift away behind. He hadn't had the time he'd needed with his grandson. He wished Dean would speak, but the boy turned away again, still crying, pressing his face to the glass and watching the dark storefronts spool along the boulevard.

1988

The path was wider, gravel-lined now, and the parking area had been expanded and paved. There was a wooden sign on steel posts that read HALEY CLIFFS STATE WILDLIFE AREA. Daniel walked down into the front rank of trees, sneakers crunching gravel, through a wooded, bird-reverberating hollow and out the other side into the meadow. The ocean could be heard immediately upon stepping into the open. Swales of tall grass clouded with purple and yellow flowers were draped out to the unseen cliff, the path arcing through them toward the giant tree, which stood alone, full and green against the blue horizon.

He followed the path out into the grass. His eyes, drawn by movement, found a darting blue dragonfly, which was joined by another, and the two wheeled north and sped away together across the meadow.

He raised his eyes and his gaze readjusted to the distance, falling again on the tree. It was both larger and less otherworldly than the projection in his memory. There were two people farther up the path, near the tree, standing and talking. Though there had been a few cars in the parking lot, in his preoccupation he'd envisioned having the area to himself. But of course there were others. On a beautiful Friday in July, he was surprised there weren't more. Only the pair up ahead were in sight.

The sound of the waves swelled as he moved closer to the cliff; what started as nebulous thunder acquired watery detail, rolling crashes punctuated by brief silences that grew even briefer when eventually the soft hiss of retreat became audible, tapering into firmer silence that lasted only a moment before the next crash. He got close enough to make out that the two people up ahead were a woman of around fifty and a boy in his late teens, possibly her son, before they turned and continued north along the cliff on the rougher hiking trail that became a meandering streak through shrubs and grasses into the distance.

Arriving, Daniel stood for a moment at the threshold of the branches and looked up. The wind was made louder here in contact with the tree. The gravel path went around the south side, and he followed it to where it ended at an overlook. There was a plaque on a post, but he didn't read it. Instead of standing at the overlook and staring out to sea, as the land-scape designer had intended, he turned and went in under the branches, and immediately the world of the tree took over. He was surprised—he'd thought his memory of it was hopelessly colored by LSD and shock and time, that he had probably falsely mythologized every aspect of it and it would be just a place, with soil and roots and air but not the indwell-ing spirit he'd imbued it with in his mind. But it was as it had been—the wind quieting and the light clarifying, damping the sun into deep greenness—inhabited by a sense of protection and safety unchanged by the years of foot traffic and human attention. The dirt was hard-packed between the roots where people had walked and sat. Daniel was grati-fied to see not a single piece of refuse, no carvings in the bark. He went to the shallow root-formed hollow in the trunk that faced the ocean, and sat down exactly where he'd sat nineteen years before, when Rachel had walked away forever.

While the tree might have retained its aura and character, it was a very different person doing the sitting and thinking now. Daniel had been re-leased from his second prison stint almost five years earlier, and the shift back to an earlier self or evolution into a new one that he'd hoped for had not materialized. He'd fallen again into dissolute circles on the west side of LA, and had spent those years taking a page from Neil Tallman's book—middle-manning packages for extra cash, cultivating younger friends and temporary girlfriends he never got close to. He had also put the finishing touches on his alienation from his ex-wife and son. This was accomplished simply by not staying in contact with them, though they lived only a few miles from the tiny Pacific Palisades apartment he rented, which he had vacated three months earlier to stay in Cam's guesthouse.

Cam had talked him into trying something different. Since moving over to Cam's, Daniel had quit cocaine and other powders. He hadn't had anything but the occasional beer or toke of grass, and at thirty-nine he was about to start taking classes to get a teaching certificate. Technically, the school Cam had founded, being private, could hire him without the certificate, but Cam needed to be able to make a case for him with the board, and Daniel needed to have some idea what he was doing. He'd dug himself into a pit of despondency in his solo life, and it had made him suggestible. Cam had reminded him that if he didn't like teaching, going back to being a drug dealer and couch pilot would always be easy. He had little to lose. Risking a third-strike conviction, on the other hand, was very high stakes.

This trip north was a summer jaunt. Cam had rented a house in Carmel for the weekend, and Win and Sarah had driven down from Marin. They had two children, and together they had turned Cam's old ranch into a thriving organic farm and center for local and national activism, with summer camps for at-risk youth. Cam had donated the property, and it was now a nonprofit called the Marin People's Center. When Cam suggested the trip, Daniel had immediately thought of visiting the tree, an idea that had been flickering in the caboose of his mind since before he got out of prison. It seemed like something that might be conducive to the kind of change he was working on. He'd taken Cam's car that morning and driven up the coast from the Carmel rental.

Sitting under the tree, his mind was ping-ponging haphazardly as usual. Normally he wouldn't even have noticed what had become his native mental state, but being in this place, with its harkening back, made him sharply aware of it. He could not seem to bring to the moment the solemnity or focus it called for. He remembered his quasi-spiritual communion with the tree that night in 1969, but couldn't rekindle any spark of it. None of his thoughts resonated, but merely glanced through his head and trailed off after generating arbitrary tangents. He thought of Rachel, but even that didn't conjure the appropriate gravity. His mind had been sanded thin by jaded dissociation and drugs. Maybe, he thought, if he walked up the trail and tried to find the place from which she fell. But then it struck him as ghoulish to try and gin up an emotional response by getting closer to her death. He knocked the back of his head against the trunk, once, twice, harder a third time, breathed deeply of the sea air, and felt, merely, vacant. He wished he had a joint.

Daniel let the blue stripe of view between the branches and the land out in front of him imprint itself on his eyes. The line between the two blues, ocean and sky, hovered just above the rocky lip of the cliff. After a couple of minutes, he rose and stepped out from the tree toward the water and stood next to the plaque briefly without reading it, still looking toward the horizon. Then he followed the path back inland. He looked for the mother and son across the meadow and up the trail, but they were gone.

When he pulled the car out onto the coast road and turned south, accelerating through the brown-green hills and brilliant summer haze, being in motion began to unknot his agitation. He wondered why he hadn't stayed longer. The whole morning became smooth and mirrored, and flashed in his mind like a distant memory at the moment of death. As he'd walked away from the tree, something had kept him from turning around to look once more at it standing against the sky. He'd been holding in his mind the view from underneath, that blue double-stripe of sky and sea—remembering how at night it had been a stripe of stars and black, then of pearl and gray as dawn broke—holding it firmly in his mind and not looking back.

2017

Dean listened to the clanking and scraping sounds from the kitchen. The man was in there, taking doughnuts out of the oven on their metal trays. It was still early, with real daylight being only a few minutes old. He stared out the window at the suddenly sunny alley on the side of the restaurant, which was like a small street where businesses kept their garbage containers and people drove through to the parking area in back. There was a thin tree with dusty green leaves to the right where it met the street. There was a black dumpster across the alley whose two-piece lid was partially open because of some boxes piled inside it, and Dean had watched a spotted ginger cat squeeze into it while the sky was still night blue. He was staring because he didn't want to miss seeing it come out. He was afraid someone would close the lid and trap the cat.

In front of him was an empty cup of hot chocolate and a plate of doughnut crumbs. The counter man had given him extra hot chocolate for free when he'd said he was waiting for his grandfather to come back. Grampa Jack had made him promise to wait until the clock on the wall said six thirty before giving the man his mother's phone number. "If he won't let you wait, just tell him you don't remember my number," he'd said. "If he calls the police, don't worry. Just wait till they get here and then tell them your name. Okay?" Once Dean had promised, Grampa Jack kissed him on the top of his head, picked up his coffee, and walked out the swinging glass door. His leaving was very sudden, and Dean hadn't been ready for it. The counter man had only asked him once if he was okay, fifteen minutes after Grampa Jack left, and then gave him the extra hot chocolate and ignored him. Now there were only twenty minutes left until six thirty.

He had meant not to sleep, but he'd fallen asleep anyway, with his head against the glass, though not for very long. When he woke up it was just getting light and his fear was gone. He hadn't known until it was gone how scared he'd been. But in the early light he felt right away that he would be okay. He believed Grampa Jack's promise that he'd be with his mom soon.

He heard voices, sharp tones, disembodied at first and then two people walked down the alley from the back, a man and a woman. The woman's hair was very messy, and she wore black jeans and a black sweatshirt, and the man was almost as skinny as she was, with a brown leather jacket and a lopsided face. They were having an argument, and they stopped right outside the window where Dean sat. He felt strange staring but he wanted to make sure he saw the cat when it came out of the dumpster. He tried not to listen to the words they were saying, so he wouldn't be spying. He could tell from the way they were sort of quiet that it wasn't a bad argument. The woman was doing most of the talking, saying she'd told him something so many times she was tired of having to say it. After a minute she looked over and noticed Dean, five feet from them behind the window, and she stopped talking and smiled. She waved, and Dean waved back. The man gave him a smile, too, pointed a finger at him playfully, and they continued out to the street, no longer arguing. Dean felt like he'd helped them.

The cat slid out through the opening into the sunlight, looked around to make sure it was alone, and then sat down on the closed half of the black plastic dumpster lid and seemed to relax. Dean decided it was a girl. She began licking her whiskers, which Dean knew meant she had found something to eat. Then she started cleaning her face in earnest, licking her white-gloved paws and wiping first one side and then the other with practiced swipes. Something about the cat's repetitive movements calmed Dean. He had never had a cat, and so had never seen one do this, but he could tell that it was something all cats did, and that sense of instinctive action made him smile, which he understood was similar, something people didn't need to learn. Even little babies smiled. Shuffling footsteps from the kitchen pierced the calm place inside him, and then, without knowing why, he was very sad for a moment as he glanced over his shoulder toward the counter to see if the man was coming through the door. He thought of seeing his mom soon, and then he thought of seeing Daniel also, when he got home, and he felt better. There was a clang and a grating sound, and the footsteps faded again deeper into the kitchen.

When he turned back to the window, the cat had stopped her cleaning and was staring at the alley, just like Dean was doing. She didn't look at him, but Dean knew she was aware of him, and this made him feel they were spending time together. The two of them, sitting watching the morning. Then, in that blanket of early sun, the cat lifted her chin and closed her eyes, as though she might be remembering something from a long time ago. Dean closed his eyes, seeing if maybe he could remember too.

ACKNOWLEDGMENTS

I first need to thank those who read this book in various stages, and whose thoughts were invaluable to me in shaping it: Gordon Haber, Elisabeth Robinson, Jennifer Silverman, Marc Wancer, and my brilliant, steadfast agent, Peter Steinberg. Giant thanks to George Witte, my editor, whose discernment, vision, and impeccable guiding hand have brought the book to its final form.

Thanks also to my friend David Wike for his insight on the world of a film set. Any errors in that area remain solely out of my stubbornness. Thanks to all my colleagues and students at the Pratt Institute Writing Department.

And endless gratitude to my wife, Jen. I could never have dreamt of such a friend and partner before you happened to me.